DEAD KILL

BOOK TWO

I0642901

THE RIDGE OF CHANGE

Thomas M. Malafarina

SUNBURY PRESS

Mechanicsburg, PA USA

Published by Sunbury Press, Inc.
105 South Market Street
Mechanicsburg, Pennsylvania 17055

www.sunburypress.com

For information about special discounts for bulk purchases, please contact Sunbury Press Orders Dept. at (855) 338-8359 or orders@sunburypress.com.

To request one of our authors for speaking engagements or book signings, please contact Sunbury Press Publicity Dept. at publicity@sunburypress.com.

ISBN: 978-1-62006-671-3 (Trade paperback)
ISBN: 978-1-62006-672-0 (Mobipocket)

Library of Congress Control Number: 2016940274

FIRST SUNBURY PRESS EDITION: May 2016

Product of the United States of America
0 1 1 2 3 5 8 13 21 34 55

Set in Bookman Old Style
Designed by Crystal Devine
Cover by Lawrence Knorr
Edited by Allyson Gard

Continue the Enlightenment!

For my amazing wife, JoAnne.
You are and always have been my
one true source of enduring love and
happiness for the past twenty-five years.
Our marriage makes anything possible.

CHAPTER 1

Jackson Ridge was terrified beyond all human understanding. He didn't dare let even so much as a single breath escape from his tightly pursed lips while the mangled reanimated remains of what was once the Yuengsville Chief of Police, Brent Holden slowly trudged across the dirt barn floor toward him. Jackson was bound tightly with heavy bull rope and was unable to move. As if that were not a futile enough situation, large spikes had been driven through his palms crucifying him to a thick, heavy wooden crossbeam in the horrifying barn turned death chamber. In the distance, not very far away he could hear the moans of the other undead creatures milling about in the unseen pit he knew was there. He could smell their foul reeking stench. He wondered if they could likewise smell the warmth of his own blood coursing through his veins. And might the vile beasts possibly find a way to escape from their own prison and come for him? But he knew by then it would be far too late for him anyway.

Only minutes earlier Jackson had watched as the dead police chief had transformed into a savage, flesh-craving zombie. The ungainly clumsy creature had stumbled to rise, placing its twisted hands on the side cross rails of the barn stalls, using them to help it stand upright. Then the living dead thing had looked directly at Jackson. Its eyes had no longer held the same look of hatred, which living Brent Holden's contemptuous eyes had once reserved for Jackson. Now they conveyed something that he realized was far, far worse. Now they held a look of insatiable hunger in those deathly filmy orbs. A single glance at those hideous undead hungry eyes was enough to cause all of the breath to leave Jackson's lungs in one unwelcome gasp of terrified exhalation.

Despite all of the experiences he had dealing with undead creatures, Jackson still found it hard to comprehend the idea that this disgustingly horrifying creature had only been dead for a few minutes. The wretched thing was every bit as hideous as any other such specimen Jackson had ever seen. Its head hung askew, at an impossible almost ninety-degree angle to the right because the neck muscles, which were required to provide the necessary support for its head, were no longer intact.

Just prior to his death, Chief Holden had killed the evil villain Deimos who had been responsible for Jackson's crucifixion. Initially Jackson had thought this was a good thing and that the Chief had come to rescue him as well as the young girl, Sarah Stanton, who Jackson had come to find. Then Holden had shocked Jackson by shooting and mortally wounding his own loyal and unsuspecting police sergeant, David Evans who had accompanied him into the barn. It was then Jackson understood that Holden had been the real villain; the true criminal mastermind Jackson had been seeking. Jackson realized that the dreaded Deimos had been nothing more than a figurehead, a puppet put in place by Holden to play the part of the criminal genius while Holden acted as puppet master pulling the strings unseen in the background.

Holden had shot Sergeant Evans right through the throat. Unfortunately, for Holden he had forgotten to finish the job by putting another bullet through Evan's skull. After a few moments, Evans died, turned and came back from the dead. While Holden was looking in the opposite direction, the now undead version of David Evans had attacked Brent Holden, tearing out his throat, and leaving him to bleed to death, crippled and deformed. During the struggle for his own survival, Holden had managed to get off one lucky final shot and had put one through Evan's brain before he, Holden, collapsed dead on the dirt floor of the barn.

Jackson wished David Evans would have only bitten just a little bit further into Holden's neck and maybe then, he would have severed the spinal cord and essentially decapitated the man. If so, Holden would have remained dead. Apparently, however a few of the nerves in Holden's mangled spine had remained intact, just enough to allow for his eventual imminent reanimation. As a result, the hideous creature was still able to stand albeit clumsily and

2

move about. It was now driven by the same insatiable desire all such beings had; the need to feed and Jackson was the only easily accessible food source in the barn. The young kidnap victim, thirteen-year-old Sarah was still huddled in the corner of her stall cage terrified and in shock but thankfully there was no way the Holden zombie could ever get at her.

The creature began shambling steadily toward Jackson. Under normal circumstances, the creature's ridiculous gait and cocked head might have appeared funny, but then again these circumstances were anything but normal. As the thing approached him, Jackson clearly saw the hideous exposed meat of its neck stump as well as its pinkish-white bone. A small cluster of what Jackson thought of as garbage flies, those horrible bluish-green creatures had already begun to swarm about the tattered meat and gore of Holden's exposed neck. Jackson assumed they must have already been in the barn because of the other undead creatures he could still hear nearby in the pit. The flies' shining metallic-looking bodies landed on the flesh just long enough to vomit up their stomach acid then sample the coagulating globs of blood. Jackson suspected others might be laying eggs. He had no idea why such revolting thoughts were entering his mind at such a crucial junction in his soon to be short life but he couldn't seem to stop them.

Then as the creature got closer, Jackson's wonderings got even more bizarre. He found himself questioning which particular part of his body the zombie would choose to eat first. Would it be his nose, his lips or maybe even his eyes? Or would the creature simply sink its fingers deep into the tender exposed flesh of Jackson's stomach and rip him open like an eager child tearing open a present on Christmas morning? Then it would pull out his hot steaming innards not unlike Jackson's mother used to do while preparing their Thanksgiving turkey. He had no idea why he was interspersing such thoughts of happy holiday memories with such an impossible situation but the ideas now seemed to be coming at such a rapid-fire rate that they were completely out of his control.

The creature was almost on Jackson now with its snapping jaws spewing blood-soaked spittle through the air stippling Jackson's face with gore. The undead beast was now just inches from his face. Ironically, Jackson suddenly realized with absolute certainty he had the answer to his earlier bizarre question. The wretched creature was going to take his face first. It raised both of its rapidly cooling hands grabbing either side of Jackson's face. Its mouth, a practically vertical slit due to the creature's broken neck, opened impossibly wide, prepared for taking its first bite. Jackson could smell the thing's rancid breath, already putrefying and rank with the stench of death.

CHAPTER 2

Jackson sat straight up in his bed, sweat beading over the entire surface of his body; his tee shirt soaked with perspiration. He could smell the combination of his sweat and his own fear as he did every night when he awoke in this manner. The room was pitch black save for the crimson glow from his bedside digital alarm clock showing the current time; 4:44 am. It had been another nightmare; and not just "A" nightmare, but "THE" nightmare. It was the same horrifying nightmare he had been experiencing every single night since returning home from his emergency surgery at the Hospital in the Fortified City Of Reading, Pennsylvania. Next to him his wife Andrea slept solidly apparently unaware of his internal torment. Jackson was glad to see she was still asleep. That was at least one small comfort in this terrible situation. When he had first returned home and began having the dreams, she often would wake up with him and do her best to offer him comfort. Jackson didn't want Andrea to have to suffer because of what he had done and what had happened as a result of his actions. His problems were the result of a decision he had made and as such, it was his responsibility to deal with the consequences, not Andrea's. The thought of her losing sleep because of his constant nightmares was something he simply couldn't handle.

Fortunately, over the many months since the nightmares began Andrea had grown accustom to his nocturnal awakenings and somehow had adapted to sleeping through most of them. Jackson pivoted in bed, placing his feet on the carpeted floor. Then he got up as quietly as possible and shuffled into the bathroom, closing the door silently behind him. He sat down on the toilet and stared at the scars in the palms of his hands as he did every morning. The flesh was healing nicely, but it seemed to be taking much longer than he had anticipated. The scars were still pink and a bit tender, but as he slowly opened and closed his hands, he was happy to see he had regained almost all of his motor control. The doctors told him he might never return to 100% of his former ability, but overall he felt 95% was not too shabby. He could still type and that was paramount to his profession as a freelance writer and investigative reporter.

He had also begun playing his guitar again. Jackson had ignored his beloved Martin for many years being busy dealing with the business of survival. Prior to the outbreak, he had played regularly in a local acoustic trio, but now he assumed his band mates were long gone, since he had not seen them in over ten years. After surviving his recent close brush with death, Jackson decided he and his guitar needed to become reunited. As it worked out, playing the instrument also proved to be an excellent form of physical therapy. He had a long way to go before he would reach his original level of expertise, but he was well on the way and was determined to eventually get there.

Jackson was also grateful for the hours of physical therapy he had received at the local hospital. Although the exercises were grueling and more often than not frustrating, he knew it was largely responsible for his rapid recovery and continuing advancements. He only wished his emotional healing was progressing at the same rate or even showed some minor signs of improvement. He was seeing a counselor regularly, several times a week, but in his opinion; those results were lagging far behind his physical recovery. After all, he was still having the horrifying nightmares.

His therapist, Dr. Arthur Wakemen had told him he was experiencing a type of PTSD or Post Traumatic Stress Disorder caused by the life-threatening ordeal Jackson had been forced to endure. It was very similar to what some soldiers experienced when returning from combat. Jackson couldn't help but find it ironic how for ten years he and every other survivor on the planet had lived through a zombie apocalypse and the almost complete annihilation of the human race. Yet throughout all of that horror, Jackson had never shown the slightest sign of any negative mental side effects whatsoever. But now for some reason, this one traumatic incident had given him emotional scars perhaps greater than the physical ones on his palms.

Dr. Wakeman had said that what Jackson had experienced in that barn of horrors was about as personal as you could possibly get. Back during the wars against the rising undead, he was just one of a group of survivors constantly fighting to bring humanity back from the brink of extinction. However, in the barn it was him alone against a horrible force for evil and he had been defenseless and had no choice but to await his own imminent grizzly death.

The doctor told Jackson it was important for him to try to remember every detail of his ordeal and to talk about it whenever possible until eventually his mind came to grips with the fact it was finally all over. He had to get his subconscious to realize he was safe now and there was little if anything he could have possibly done to prevent what had happened to him. But Jackson knew that was not necessarily the case. He had taken some risks in the name of saving a young kidnapped girl named Sarah Stanton. Maybe if he had just done things differently . . . yet he knew it was far too late for second-guessing. Besides, he was safe now, Sarah too was safe and the bad guys were all either dead or in prison.

Jackson had to learn to accept the fact that he had done the right thing, the only thing he could have possibly done. During his waking hours, Jackson felt as if he had been able to do just that. But, at night, in the uncontrollable unconscious world of his dreams, in that place where we are all just frightened, helpless little children, Jackson could do nothing to quell his horrifying thoughts. Maybe in time and with more therapy, he might just be able to; he honestly just didn't know.

He looked at the clock Andrea kept on the shelf in the bathroom and saw it was 5:15 am. He decided he might as well stay up, since he knew he wouldn't be getting back to sleep any time soon. He washed his face, brushed his teeth and then crept back out into the bedroom and turned off his alarm. He wondered why he even bothered to set an alarm, since he hadn't slept long enough to need one ever since returning home. Besides, he worked for himself now and had earned enough money from the book and movie rights to his horrifying story that he didn't even need to set an alarm. In fact, he didn't even need to wake up if he chose not to. However, he learned that old habits tended to die hard, and he also understood that routine was good for him. So, every evening Jackson set his alarm for six-thirty and every night the terrors woke him before it ever had a chance to go off.

Jackson Ridge was by profession a freelance writer working for various news outlets in and around Schuylkill County, Pennsylvania. He recalled how for many years his opportunities were limited to the immediate area but since his recent celebrity status, he was now in constant demand, not just locally, not just nationally but internationally as well. That is to say, at least in those areas of the world where there remained pockets of civilization which were still capable of communicating with other civilized areas. Jackson had yet to get used to his newfound fame even though it was six months since his ordeal had become the stuff of legend. His capture had occurred in October of 2053 and now it was July of 2054, yet he still had quite a few requests for paid interviews and guest appearances seeming to come from every corner of the civilized world.

His wife Andrea had previously been a registered nurse working in hospice care, but since his return, she had been representing Jackson professionally as his agent. In fact, he was now actually a corporation; Jackson Ridge, Inc. and Andrea negotiated all of his deals, coordinated his various assignments as well as his personal appearances.

Jackson sat in his living room glancing down occasionally at his scarred palms. And no matter what Dr. Wakeman said, despite his reliving his ordeal repeatedly for reporters, talk show hosts as well as in books, articles and screenplays, Jackson wondered why he hadn't yet been able to exorcise those demons from his dreams.

CHAPTER 3

Eleven years had passed since 2043 when the first recently deceased individuals somehow reanimated, rose up from their deathbeds and began feeding on the flesh of the living. When humanity discovered an infection was responsible for the reanimation of the corpses, the particular strain responsible became commonly known as Virus Z43 (The Zombie Virus of 2043).

A year or so after the initial identification of the virus, scientists discovered there was a time limitation for infection of just a few days before the initial outbreak. Someone had to have been infected with the Z43 virus prior to death in order to become reanimated. This substantially limited the number of undead creatures shambling about the world, but it did nothing to stop more of them from appearing as soon as any living member of the infected living population died.

There were various theories of the virus's origin, from a secret government biological weapon gone awry, to a meteor bringing the virus to earth, to Mother Nature herself creating the virus to control overpopulation. Whatever the origin, the virus arrived and immediately began wreaking havoc on the world's population.

In the present, scientists believed due to the Z43 virus's ability to spread so rapidly and completely, it actually resided inside the bodies of every single living human being on the planet where it remained dormant until just a few minutes after a person died. In its dormant stage, the virus was essentially harmless. However, once the body shut down completely, the heart stopped and the brain died, the virus became active and that particular body quickly became reanimated as a cannibalistic living dead creature.

In the spring of 2043 after the first of many creatures had begun rising from the dead, the Z43 Virus began spreading faster than anyone could have possibly imagined. By the end of 2043, things didn't seem at all promising for humanity. This was especially true for many third world countries, which simply didn't stand a chance. In places having no sound infrastructure, unstable governments, poor healthcare, unsanitary living conditions and no understanding of how to dispose of their growing numbers of dead, the living populations of such countries ceased to exist.

In what most people thought of as the more technologically advanced nations many electric grids failed as did dams, utilities, phone systems both landlines as well as mobile Communication Unit based systems also known as CU based systems, and even nuclear power plants. Civilization began breaking down in a matter of just a few weeks. In areas beyond the reach of surviving governments and law enforcement, robbery, murder, rape and mayhem were a typical way of life with neighbors killing neighbors as the world burned to the ground. The world was rapidly becoming an insane Darwinian nightmare of animal-like savage survival of the fittest.

Other diseases previously considered benign began to flourish and spread as fast, if not faster than the Z43 virus itself, killing millions. People whom a few years earlier would have been considered perfectly healthy now died from things as simple as the common cold, sinus infections, strep throat or bronchitis; the sorts of things, which a simple antibiotic would have cured. Then, of course, those dead would return as flesh eating monsters. By 2044, more than 60% of the world's human population had been wiped out, and it looked as if there might be little hope left for what few remained. It looked all but certain that mankind was doomed. But then the tide suddenly began to turn.

Survivors started grouping together into small cadres resembling tribes or clans. Then instead of running from the zombies they found ways to destroy them. As it turned out, terminating the brain or severing the brain stem from the spinal cord as depicted in many of history's zombie movies actually did work to destroy the things. After that, their remains could be safely handled and disposed of through cremation.

Fortunately, all of the undead were slow, clumsy creatures and unless they were able to overpower humans by sheer force of numbers they could easily be taken down.

The people of the tribes learned to fight and defend themselves. They stopped killing each other. They learned to rely on their fellow man for their own survival. They also discovered that by eliminating the creatures' food supply, that being living humans, the undead would gradually begin to degrade. These creatures would eventually fall prey to their own natural enemies such as flies, maggots, vultures and other scavengers who prefer carrion to living creatures. It was not uncommon to see zombies clumsily stumbling about as various limbs simply dropped from their decomposing bodies. Turkey buzzards, crows, rats and other such scavengers could often be seen tearing apart any of the creatures which had become unable to defend themselves while whatever remained of their dismembered corpses twitched on the ground. The wretched things would growl in confusion until eventually their carcasses were picked clean and destroyed.

These various bands of survivors found abandoned towns and cities they could make safe and began forming small communities and creating their own new mini-governments. People in these safe zones were able to pool their resources and talents to defend themselves against the horrid creatures. Fences and walls sprang up around some small towns and cities. These perimeters were defended round the clock, and the zombies were soon destroyed by the hundreds of thousands. Where possible, these perimeters were expanded, increasing the amount of land survivors would have available and decreasing the feeding zones for the shambling dead. Soon the mini governments joined forces and new national governments were restored to power.

In places where there were such governments had arisen, bounties were placed on the undead, which immediately resulted in an army of thousands of hunters all eager to earn a very profitable living by destroying the zombies. There were also squads formed whose sole purpose was carting away the decomposing remains to landfills where they were placed on burn piles and set ablaze. During these early transitional years, most communities had funeral pyres burning round the clock.

II

Although it had only taken a matter of weeks for civilization to crumble, it was apparent to everyone that the rebuilding process would take much, much longer. Yet after just ten years of dealing with the plague, humanity had finally begun to consider themselves victorious. Things were in no way as they had been before the apocalypse and might not ever be the same again, but humanity had made great strides and was continuing to do so daily.

The United States, with its strong military presence and over-abundantly armed citizenry, was the quickest of all countries to respond to the threat. Considering that on average the general population of one single state in the United States had more guns per capita in the private sector than the entire armies of many smaller foreign countries, it was no surprise that the US had won the war against the dead much faster than most other countries had. It was a hunter's paradise to have every day declared open season. Plus having a bounty placed on the creatures made the call to arms even more irresistible.

Eventually, most of the surviving US cities and towns, now known as safe zones, had electricity, clean water and food, and even internet service as well as Communications Unit network service. With the exception of the walls, fences and crematoriums, things were starting to return to a state resembling normalcy; although normalcy was a relative term. The newly formed US national government had put a number of new laws into place to protect its citizens and deal with the Z43 plague. Some people felt these laws infringed on their personal freedoms. And if one were to be honest, many of them did. These regulations greatly changed the way most professionals in any fields involving contact with dead or dying did their jobs. There was much to learn and many new stringent guidelines to follow. It also seemed the more the government learned about dealing with these creatures, the more new laws arose.

The world learned to accept the fact that the horrible flesh eating undead creatures were still a real threat and they would always be as long as people died and their bodies were not properly disposed of. The monsters remained every bit as deadly to any living human as they had been since the start of the plague, but thanks to the various stopgap measures which had been put into place, there were now a lot fewer of the beasts remaining. There were also a lot more safe zones and by 2050 or so, the creatures had become relegated to being considered more of a nuisance than a serious threat.

The new unified national government of the United States had devised an official procedure, DK5479-45, which dealt with the eradication of the undead. What the letters "DK" actually stood for, no one seemed to know; likely some bureaucrat's initials or something. Regardless, the population took those two initials DK and began commonly referring to the program by the nickname "Dead Kill." That name was actually coined by some quick witted journalist who jokingly suggested that might be what the "DK" stood for. What started as an off-the-cuff remark, ended up sticking and soon "Dead Kill" became the accepted term nationwide. The purpose of the DK5479-45 procedure was to provide a method of monetarily rewarding citizens who destroyed the undead.

Every US citizen was required to apply for a personalized digital code, which identified him or her by what was once called a social security number. It was now known as a citizen number and in the event of a confirmed Dead Kill, that person could use his or her number to report a Dead Kill then automatically receive a $100 credit in the bank account of their choice for each confirmed kill.

In addition, because of a certain segment of society, which consisted of its less than desirable citizens, the government found it necessary to write, implement and enforce many new strict and sometime radical laws against the use of the living dead in the areas of entertainment, gambling and other games of sport or chance. Unfortunately, as with all catastrophic events, there was always a seedy, unseemly and depraved segment of society that chose to prey on the misfortune of others. These merchants of all things illegal had devised various games of chance involving misuse of the undead.

As it turned out, another even more revolting form of debauchery also sprang up among the sick and depraved. It was known as Z-Porn and was a previously unimaginable problem for a struggling society to have to deal with. As the name implied, this type of perversion depicted living humans engaged in sexual acts with the undead. Z-Porn was immediately declared illegal, immoral, reprehensible, and as such was unequivocally outlawed. Punishment for the purveyors of such filth was death, no prison time just real and final death. This was primarily because that particular industry tended to attract the worst of the worst society had to offer; murders, rapists, pedophiles, kidnappers, sex slavers and the like. Yet despite the government's best efforts to destroy this foul and depraved element of a newly rebuilding society, the unspeakable trade still existed among the degenerates.

This was especially true in the wild and savage unprotected areas between the fortified cities known as the outlands. In these places, not only did zombies still roam about unchecked but so did a breed of often murderous outlaws who chose to live outside of what they considered the stifling rules of the civilized world. These outlanders thrived during the early days of the apocalypse, and many people claim these individuals had lost touch with what it meant to be human, or at least a civilized human.

These people still longed for complete freedom in the form of lawless anarchy. And part of that lawlessness was what they felt was their right to do whatever they chose to do, without consequence. The only place they could find to behave in such an unchecked manner was in the outlands. There they could murder, assault, rape or whatever they chose to do. It was true survival of the fittest in the outlands. Once humanity began to make its comeback, the reprehensible merchants, catering to this most debased level of society, began to rapidly surface.

The outlands were a place no civilized person belonged. It was often difficult to tell the filthy savages from the undead and often even from some of the wild animals. Because of this lack of distinction, rumors began to spread among the civilized world; alleged sightings of strange mutated creatures. These unconfirmed reports spoke of creatures, no longer human, yet not undead zombies either. These alleged creatures were thought of as mutants and became the stuff of legend and folklore. In essence, they became the "Big Foot" of the mid twenty-first century. No one had proven they existed but a large number of people, especially those who had witnessed sightings knew them to truly exist, despite denials from the government and the National Center For Disease and Virus Control, the NCDVC.

CHAPTER 4

Sean Patel, assistant medical examiner for Schuylkill County Pennsylvania looked at the latest encrypted email document he had received from the NCDVC. It concerned the most recent findings about the Z43 Virus. The news he read had been really quite troubling. The report discussed a phenomenon, which seemed to be occurring in the media more and more each day. At first, it started as a few stories told by a handful of adventurous types who occasionally spent time in the outlands. Then there had been a few reports from crew members working on the city expansion crews. The NCDVC had done some clandestine preliminary investigations but had managed to quell these early alleged sightings. During the past several months however, the numbers of rumors spreading throughout the fortified towns and cities seemed to be growing dramatically. As a result, the NCDVC had stepped up their own investigation to try to get a handle on what was actually happening with the virus before these rumors began to get out of control. If they were able to provide definitive proof the rumors were unsubstantiated nonsense, perhaps they could prevent the further spread of these stories.

Sean recalled a time when only the occasional supposed sighting had been reported and that had usually been by a less than reliable source. But lately, it seemed more and more people, even those with spotless reputations had claimed to have seen what could only be described as strange mutations. Some alleged sightings spoke of giant flesh-eating beasts, which were not zombies but were so far removed from what most people considered human beings that the only descriptive term which came to mind was mutants.

The NCDVC had not and might never publicly admit to the existence of mutants or even that there was a possibility that the virus itself was mutating. But after reading the report, Sean learned it most definitely was. The document went into detailed descriptions of minor changes occurring at cellular level in blood and tissue samples taken from certain corpses.

The government did admit however that they had managed to acquire these corpses from medical examiners across the country who had noticed that some of the Dead Kills they examined were much larger than the average human. Although the report had not stated that the particular corpse in question were those of suspected mutants, Sean got the strange feeling that might indeed be what the report was eluding to.

For a moment, Sean recalled the enormous Dead Kill his friend Jackson Ridge had taken down the previous October on his way from The Ashton Cooperative to The Yuengsville Free Zone to start working on the assignment which would not only almost kill him but would bring him world fame. That creature was large enough to have qualified for this study, but at the time Sean was unaware of the study. In addition, he had just assumed the Dead Kill was a large undead human. Most of its face and skull had been unrecognizable due to the caliber of Jackson's gun. Now Sean wondered for a moment if that creature had actually been one of the mutations the rumors and reports spoke about. Then he put the idea out of his mind, thinking it was ridiculous.

Sean realized the authorities could easily find themselves with a dilemma. If these larger than normal bodies had been undead creatures then they would be considered legal and justifiable Dead Kills. However, if they were the legendary mutated humans and were not yet dead at the time of their destruction then how could they be considered legal Dead Kills? But what would they be considered? Murder victims? However, if they were no longer considered humans, could their deaths be considered murders or would they be thought of as some new form of Dead Kill? Another problem was the fact that the authorities would only acknowledge that these creatures, which were destroyed, were only zombies, as Sean had thought, since they had many of the same physical traits as the undead. However, it was remotely possible that the creatures were not actually undead beings but had only been mistaken as such and at the time they were destroyed.

17

Sean knew back in the days before the plague, such an issue would keep teams of lawyers, judges and legislators busy for years. However, such luxuries were no longer available. At some point soon the powers that be would have to decide what the legal ramifications might be. But since the governmental agencies weren't even acknowledging the existence of mutations, how could they possibly create and enforce any such new laws.

Since the report did at least admit that the Z43 virus was in fact mutating, the extent of the theoretical abnormalities were for the moment completely unpredictable as were the results of such alleged mutations. The government learned from reports in the media that these mutations seemed to be happening only in certain segments of society, so far only among those savage people living in the wilds of the outlands. The problem was because the outlands were lawless and untamed, the NCDVC wouldn't be able to pinpoint what it might be about these particular individuals, which had allowed the virus to mutate so quickly and cause such dramatic physical abnormalities. Again, this was all theoretical speculation since the party line at the NCDVC was that mutants didn't exist at all.

The accounts often spoke of enormous Neanderthal-like giants, but these weren't the only forms of mutations being reported either. Multi-limbed human/animal hybrids and creatures that seemed more reptilian than human were also being sighted. One unfortunate thing all of these alleged mutations seemed to have in common was the same desire for consuming raw human flesh as the undead zombies did. All of the eyewitness reports said this fact was true regardless of what form these strange transmutations assumed.

Sean wondered if this fact, assuming it were true, might make the legal dilemma he was imagining a bit easier to resolve. Living or undead, if the creatures did exist and were proven to kill and eat living humans then all humans could consider themselves potential victims and, as such, would have the right to defend themselves against attacks from these creatures.

"What was it that made them all want to consume human flesh?" Sean wondered as he continued to read the report. Although he thought the idea of the virus creating huge mutated humans might be far-fetched, he decided to allow his imagination to run wild for a few minutes to see if he could come up with some scenarios as to what these creatures might be like. What would attract them to consume human flesh?

Could it be the warmth given off by the living human body? Was it perhaps the blood, which coursed through the veins of all living humans? Or might it perhaps be something much more complex than that? Maybe it was some primal recessive gene, which normally remained inactive and the virus somehow managed to switch on. Could it possibly be that an ancient gene left over from our primitive selves many millions of years ago? He didn't know if such a thing could be, but somehow this seemed like the start of an idea that felt very plausible to Sean. He realized that maybe he was heading down the right track with this particular train of thought.

This was nevertheless a bit odd and new for Sean as he was attempting to logically reason a concept he didn't believe was real. So he began to think the process through starting with his knowledge of the Z43 virus and then speculated further.

He understood the virus remained dormant until the host died, and then it became activated. Whenever a person died, his heart and brain functions stopped and blood likewise ceased flowing to all of the vital organs. The Z43 virus must have some feature, which allows it to multiply at an incredibly rapid rate. It must also have some sort of mechanism, which enables it to propel itself throughout the body in just a few minutes.

Sean reasoned that perhaps the virus used some form of natural propulsion to move throughout the unmoving blood that is still present and coagulating in the blood stream. Then maybe the virus is programmed to look for anything it might find which will help its dead host reanimate and therefore keep it alive. Obviously, this is because if the virus were to continue to survive and multiply, it would require that its hosts survive in some form as well. Sean then began to speculate that perhaps the virus might crawl into the musculature of the corpse and then into what remained of the dying brain. The virus somehow must communicate with its millions of replicants within the host and commands these replicants to move throughout the muscles and in turn have some unknown ability to operate the corpse. That would explain why the creatures all are so awkward and clumsy when they walk.

There must be some sort of disconnect in the primitive communication between the various viral elements. This likely is what resulted in the spastic movements. Then, somewhere back in the most primitive recesses of the brain the virus must come into contact with some ancient gene; perhaps the one that tells the physical body it needs food to survive. The virus may take control and convince the body that it's starving. And being animal in nature the reanimated corpse automatically goes for the warm, blood-filled flesh of the living. It has no desire to feast on others of its kind because they have no warm blood actively pumping through their veins.

This all seemed to make sense to Sean. It might even help to explain the concept of possible mutations. The virus in its original form allowed only dead bodies to reanimate. Sean thought again of how mankind had so successfully driven back the hordes of undead by destroying them by the millions.

He wondered what if somehow the virus sensed its hosts were being depleted, its numbers dwindling and understood instinctively that it was in danger of extinction. It would have only one alternative for survival and that would be to find some way to evolve, to convert into another form, one capable of activating while the host was still living.

Sean supposed the virus might have mutated in a different direction and spread to animals, but so far there was no sign of that occurring; not even unsubstantiated reports. So if there was any credence to the stories, the virus apparently had chosen to remain in its human hosts, but to change.

He realized even though these thoughts were all nothing more than his own half-baked ideas with no actual scientific proof on which to base his makeshift theory, it seemed to feel right to Sean. As a medical professional, he knew viruses often mutated as their environment demanded.

He thought it rather ironic how mankind had honestly believed themselves to be victorious over the Z43 virus. In reality, if what he was hypothesizing was correct then humanity hadn't destroyed the virus, only the majority of its undead hosts? Sean marveled at how, once again, man's conceit had blinded him to the truth, and mankind had ignored that one very important fact. Viral mutation is a simple fact of science and nature Apparently, the Z43 virus was no exception. With the destruction of most of the undead and the government-enforced controls over the dying along with the proper disposal of the dead, most people tended to forget about the Z43 virus itself; or at least they managed to put it out of their minds.

People had begun to think of the zombies as being the real threat rather than the virus. This was logical and to be expected since the walking dead were everywhere and were killing and eating humans by the millions. However, in reality it was the Z43 virus, which was the actual culprit, silently creating an army of the undead. A dead body was just that, a corpse, nothing more. It was the virus that was actually responsible for reanimating the dead. Perhaps this blatant ignorance was mankind's involuntary and natural way of dealing with the knowledge that every living person still carried the virus inside them and some day when they died, they too would return as a walking cannibalistic corpse.

Sean hypothesized further that, since the virus had become the forgotten villain, it was also likely most people never even considered the idea that the virus might at some point in time begin to change, mutate and evolve. But that's exactly what the Z43 virus was doing. The report Sean had just read, as much as said that. Although the NCDVC would never admit to the existence of actual mutated humans, the number of reported incidents of mutant sightings among the living population seemed to be increasing.

Sean suddenly got a strange sensation or perhaps understanding that things might be starting to spiral out of control. Even though these emails were encrypted and top secret, if the NCDVC was willing to admit to its own scientists about the existence mutations at the viral level, although not the physically anomalous creatures, things were likely much worse than the NCDVC was letting on. Sean found himself torn between what he knew was the right thing to do for the public, and the information he had sworn to keep privileged as a government employee with classified status. He sensed he was at the forefront of something major. Sean knew he was standing on the ridge of change in regards to the dreaded Z43 virus.

He truly believed after everything society had been through over the past ten years the public had a right to know what was going on. Yet he realized he couldn't be the source to break such news. He understood if he did so, not only would his career be over, but he would likely end up in prison if he were to be caught violating his sworn oath of confidentiality. Yet he also understood somehow, he had to find a way to put this important information into the hands of the public.

He knew the most direct route to disseminating the information would be through the press. What better way to do that than with the assistance of his best friend, Jackson Ridge? Jackson was not only an investigative journalist but now had achieved world renown. Hearing news of the viral mutations from Jackson Ridge would guarantee the government would have no choice but to acknowledge the discovery and share the information with the people.

Sean wasn't concerned yet about the idea of actual mutated humans existing. They might or they might not, it didn't matter to him. He was currently concerned with the virus itself; any physical mutations were a secondary effect of the virus. Besides, until a parade of them marched down the center of Time Square in the reconstructed New York City, his bosses at the NCDVC would never admit their existence anyway. Whatever the truth might be, Jackson would be the man to sort everything out and get to the truth.

He knew that if he spoke to Jackson directly, Jackson would have to write the story and someone surely would figure out that it had been Sean who provided the information. Even if no one could actually prove he had spoken to Jackson, simply the fact that they were close friends would be enough to cast suspicion on Sean. Maybe such suspicion alone might not be sufficient to get him prison time, but it likely would get him fired from his current post and banned from any other government related positions. Sean was going to need to have some heavy-duty plausible deniability. He had to figure out some other way to get the information into Jackson's hands while not leaving any connection between the leak and him. At the very least he had to get Jackson interested enough to start his own investigation. He needed to funnel the information through another party, someone he knew but would not be directly tied to him.

"Andrea," Sean thought. She might be the answer. Since she had once been in the medical field and had been a hospice nurse, chances were pretty good that she might have heard about or maybe even seen things, which she couldn't quite explain. Maybe she already had some questions of her own. He knew Andrea had taken a leave of absence from nursing to take care of Jackson during his recovery. She had also become Jackson's business agent and was largely responsible for the book and movie deals he had gotten, as well as organizing all of his promotional events. Andrea had been out of the profession for over eight months now, and he wasn't sure when or if she'd ever return to nursing. But he assumed she must still have some curiosity regarding her former vocation.

Then Sean thought about Jyleen Wilson. She was a young African-American nurse's aide he had dated a few times several months earlier. He recalled how she said she had assisted Andrea on several occasions. He had told her he knew Andrea and that Jackson was his best friend since childhood. Sean had been trying to find some time to ask Jyleen out again. However, not only was his own schedule extremely hectic, but he knew Jyleen worked full time and also went to school at night trying to complete her nursing degree. They had spoken via email and CUs a few times as well; however, not nearly as much as he would have liked to and most definitely not for the last month or so. They both had an understanding that they were dating, but it hardly seemed that way of late. But regardless of their scheduling conflicts, Sean suddenly realized this might be as good a time as any to find a way ask her out again.

Maybe Sean could discreetly pass along a small amount of the information on to Jyleen through some subtle suggestions and innuendoes without actually giving any incriminating statements, which might be traced back to him. Then he could possibly ask her a few questions as to whether she and Andrea were still in contact. If the two still talked, maybe Jyleen would naturally relay the information to Andrea who in turn might pass it on to Jackson. Although it seemed like a hopeful stretch at best, Sean thought it might actually work. But he knew he'd have to be very careful in not only what he told her but he had to make sure there would be no possible way it could be traced back to him. He thought about it for a while longer then picked up his Communications Unit, found Jyleen's number and pressed the connect button. Even if his idea didn't work and he might have to come up with some alternate plan, at least he'd get to have a nice date with a girl he had been eager to ask out again for a long time.

CHAPTER 5

Jackson sat in front of his computer in his spacious home office as the sun slowly began to rise over the eastern mountains. He was doing a video chat interview for an adventure magazine in England, and Jackson was quite happy this interview had originated in the United Kingdom. Prior to the outbreak, he had known some reporters from the UK. During the on-air discussion, Jackson actually felt as if he had been the one doing the interviewing. He was so eager to learn everything he could about how England was progressing. He was thrilled to hear that, like the United States, the UK was now finally making its way back from the brink of extinction.

Jackson had heard numerous stories of just how bad things had gotten in the UK after the Z43 Virus had begun to run rampant there. From what he had been able to determine, the "Plague of Rotters" as it was sometimes referred to in the UK had all but decimated the population of Great Britain. Unlike the citizens of the United States, those in the United Kingdom didn't have easy access to firearms. This meant the exponentially growing hordes of undead had to be battled with knives, hammers, clubs, gardening implements and the proverbial sharp stick.

Although this was not an impossible task, it did involve far too frequent close proximity combat. As such, the odds of surviving such an altercation were far less, especially when compared to someone in the U.S. who could lean out of a second-story window and pick off the creatures roaming through the streets like fish in a barrel. As a result, it took much longer for the British to recover, and as of the spring of 2054, they were still lagging far behind advances made by the Americans. But at least they were faring better than the third-world countries had been. In those regions, the population had become about ninety-nine percent undead. And in many advanced countries, which happen to have the misfortune to share boarders with such downtrodden regions, the survivors had been forced to build great defensible walls to keep out the lurching zombie hordes. Twenty four hours a day, seven days a week these borders were manned by soldiers as well as civilians armed with high powered gasoline shooting hoses and flame throwers.

The masses of undead relentlessly attempted to scale the barriers often by crawling over the remains of those zombies involved in earlier attempts to get in. Since their numbers were far too great to consider destroying them with mere bullets, the survivors of the neighboring countries learned to burn them by the millions. The other good thing about this technique was it tended to turn the remains into ashes which took up much less space and were often blown away by strong winds and prevented other zombies from using piles of rotting corpses effectively to climb to the tops of the walls. As a result, this technique, which eventually became known a "toasting" likewise became the accepted method of high-volume zombie eradication. No one had any idea when these infested zones might be reclaimed by the living, but Jackson suspected it would be many years in the future.

Jackson signed off from the interview, disconnected then sat back with a sigh. He stretched out his sore hand muscles as he did every day by opening and closing his fingers repeatedly. Typing did a great job of exercising some of his muscles and tendons but unfortunately not all of them. Guitar playing added to his in-home therapy. He no longer had to go through the rigors of intense hospital-based physical therapy, but he did find he needed to continue to exercise his hands on a regular basis. Jackson wondered if he was going to have to continue this routine for the rest of his life; possibly so. But then again, it seemed like a small price to pay all things considered.

As he sat, Jackson recounted the events that had led him to where he now was. The previous October, he had been scheduled to start a new temporary assignment with *The Schuylkill Daily News*. He had worked numerous assignments there on previous occasions and had built both a good working relationship as well as a friendship with the newspaper's editor, Big Bill McCleary.

The morning Jackson reported for work, McCleary had asked him not to do his typical fill-in writer type of work but to take on a very special assignment as a favor to both him as well as the Mayor of The Yuengsville Free Zone. Up until that day, Jackson had never met the Mayor, so the idea of doing a special assignment for him was complementary as it was appealing. When he asked McCleary about the nature of the assignment, he learned the Mayor's niece, Sarah Stanton, had been kidnapped the previous evening from the city of Yuengsville while walking home from the library. Sarah was a very attractive thirteen-year-old girl. Based on a video retrieved from a recently reactivated traffic camera. police suspected it might have been the work of people tied to a criminal mastermind going by the name of Deimos.

Deimos was suspected of running one of the largest illegal empires in the outlands, catering to the twisted desires of the degenerates who populated those as of yet still uncivilized areas of the state. In the outlands very little law and order remained, although every year the fortified towns and cities reclaimed more of these wild areas. Deimos' activities included trafficking in drugs, prostitution, sex slavery, child pornography and even the dreaded practice known as Z Porn.

Jackson had questioned why the Mayor was asking for a journalist such as himself to take on a job which he felt would be much better handled by the police. McCleary told him the Mayor wanted to find someone who might be able to get close to Deimos' operation without raising suspicion. Jackson had been recommended as someone who could blend in and go unnoticed. His involvement in the operation was to be strictly fact finding and information gathering. The plan was once Jackson learned of Sarah's location he was to contact the police. That was to be the extent of his involvement. In addition, he would be under constant long-distance surveillance by police to help assure his safety.

Although he had been at first very reluctant to accept such an assignment, Jackson knew he couldn't just sit idly by but had to do something to help save young Sarah Stanton. He knew he would have to get Andrea to agree with him in order for him to take this assignment and that she would be even more reluctant to do so than he had been. But he also understood, if it was his own daughter, Kyla who was in trouble, he would want everyone who could help doing something to save her.

The reluctance on the part of both Jackson and Andrea came from an incident, which had occurred on an assignment several years earlier, somewhere around the fifth or sixth year of the zombie plague. He had agreed to go undercover in order to try to identify leaders of a local drug and prostitution ring operating within the city of Yuengsville. He had been successful but had almost been killed when his cover had been blown. And what was even worse than the physical danger he had placed upon himself was the emotional toll the assignment had taken on Jackson and Andrea's marriage.

In order to infiltrate the group he had to assume the guise of a sleazy small time middle-man dealer of drugs to gain the confidence of the criminals and had managed to do so very convincingly; perhaps too convincingly. Because on those occasions when he was able to return home to Andrea, he found it extremely difficult to jump out of character and completely drop the roll. As a result, he was often as sullen and aloof as the criminal he had pretended to be. After a time, it began to take a severe toll on their relationship.

Once the assignment was over, he and Andrea had to work very hard to help them both get their relationship back to normal. Her becoming pregnant and giving birth to Kyla did a great deal to help them rebuild their marriage. As a result, there was little wonder why they were both so reluctant to have Jackson start up another investigation that would take him again into that same terrible world. One thing about this new assignment, which had the potential to make it especially dangerous was that it might bring him in close proximity of the dreaded criminal Deimos himself. However, after much soul searching, Jackson had agreed to take the assignment, knowing he had no choice but to help find the missing girl.

Very quickly, his investigation had led him to the fortified city of Reading, Pennsylvania. To his surprise,

Jackson unfortunately wound up in the hands of the dreaded psychopath Deimos himself. Jackson had been kept in a barn, crucified to a heavy wooden crossbeam with large spikes driven through his palms. He was also bound tightly with bull rope and unable to move.

These were the same scenes, which haunted Jackson's sleep night after terrifying night. He replayed his near death encounter countless times, always awakening in a cold, cold sweat just seconds before the undead creature of his nightmares was about to devour him alive. In the beginning he woke up screaming his lungs out, but now he just awoke horrified. He wondered if maybe he was slowly getting better after all.

There was something about the actual experience and about the dream, which seemed to somehow be related. The scene which played out over and over was the final portion of his ordeal; the thing he believed he had imagined. At least he had managed to convince himself it as all just a figment of his imagination. It was that vision he had just seconds before everything went black.

Jackson had originally awakened after his rescue to discover he was in a hospital and his ordeal was miraculously over. He also realized he must have been hallucinating in the last few seconds, just before his blackout. He saw the former Yuengsville Police Chief transformed into flesh-eating zombie shot only seconds before the man's reanimated corpse was about to devour Jackson's face. This portion of the memory he knew had been true, in fact it had been part of the police report. But the part which remained a mystery, and likely was a hallucination, was what Jackson imagined he had seen a few seconds later. Jackson would have sworn on a stack of bibles that it had been his best friend Sean Patel, the Schuylkill County Assistant Coroner who had actually been the person to shoot the zombie Brent Holden and save him. But he later learned that had been impossible. Sean told him he had been in Schuylkill County in his office at the time Jackson had been saved and not in Berks County. Still the image Jackson had believed he had seen was so realistic it still made him wonder.

Maybe that was it. Maybe it was his not knowing who had actually come to his rescue which connected the reality of what had actually happened and what was causing him to have the nightmares. Perhaps if he could find out whom his savior had been the dreams would end.

CHAPTER 6

"Kyla? Kyla? Where are you?" Andrea cried out into the empty blackness she saw spread out before her. She was frantically looking for her five-year-old daughter, but the child was nowhere in sight. Where had she gone? Kyla knew not to venture far from her, even in the safety of their fortified town. She understood how important it was that she remained close by. Kyla had been standing by her side just a moment earlier then had suddenly seemed to vanish. Andrea's heart pounded with fright in her chest and her eyes began to rim with the tears. She was trying desperately not to panic although fighting the urge to do so was becoming almost impossible.

Andrea was standing alone at the intersection of Ninth and Centre Streets in the middle of the Ashton Cooperative. It was late at night, and it was dark, so very dark. A thick heavy fog had rolled in seeming to have simultaneously come from all directions. Within seconds, it had completely enveloped the town, dimming what little illumination was available from a small assortment of streetlights. Ashton, like most surviving towns, operated primarily during the day using as little electricity as possible during the late night hours. Andrea stood under the traffic light in the center of the two intersecting streets turning slowly in a circle repeatedly calling Kyla's name. She couldn't even recall why in the world she had come out there with her young daughter at such an ungodly hour of the night.

None of this made any sense to Andrea. How could Kyla have been standing next to her holding her hand one minute then be gone the next? And why wasn't she responding to Andrea's cries? Then thankfully, she heard a child's tiny voice, Kyla's voice calling from out of the foggy darkness. "Mommy? Mommy?" Andrea's heart felt as if it would leap into her throat with joy.

She raced in the direction of the voice completely oblivious of the sinister blackness and swirling fog, which surrounded her. After she had run about a block up the slope of Centre Street, she saw Kyla standing stock still in the middle of the roadway staring out at something. It was then that Andrea began to hear the sound of deep guttural growling. She instantly recognized it was not one single voice but the voices of many, dozens, perhaps hundreds.

When she finally reached her daughter, she bent down and scooped the child up in her arms holding her tightly. Kyla continued to stare out into the fog. Then she slowly raised her arm and pointed crying, "Mommy, Mommy. It's them. Those bad things. They're out there, Mommy."

Andrea heard the growling intensify accompanied by the shuffling of what sounded like hundreds of feet dragging along the street and coming ever closer. She slowly began to back up holding Kyla ever tighter. Then she heard similar sounds coming from behind her. She turned slightly and could see awkward, shadowed convulsive movement in the darkness behind her. In her mind, she heard a chorus of moans all sounding as if they were shouting, "The child. Give us the child." But she knew this was not even remotely possible. The undead walking corpses couldn't speak and most certainly couldn't communicate with the living. She had often wondered if these unholy creatures could communicate with each other through some type of telepathy. She seriously doubted that was possible. Then again, there was a time when the concept of reanimated cannibalistic corpses would have been considered just as impossible.

She realized if there were as many of the shambling creatures surrounding her as she thought there might be then she and Kyla would likely die within the next few minutes. She would never give up her precious baby to these horrible undead beasts; certainly not without a fight. But she had nothing with which to defend herself. Her husband, Jackson, was always bugging her to carry a gun even inside the safety of the walled towns, but she would have no part of it. Now she desperately wished she had that gun, even if it only had a few bullets, she would at least have one for Kyla and one for herself. As much as she would dread taking such a drastic action, murder/suicide was preferable to being eating alive by a hoard of zombies.

Looking out into the dark foggy streets, she could see dozens of pairs of shuffling feet coming ever closer. Some of the feet wore filthy ragged remnants of shoes, others didn't. Some of the feet barely resembled human feet any longer, as they were not much more than tattered remains with scarcely enough flesh left to cover the exposed bones. Andrea could hear the creatures' foot bones scraping on the blacktop like the click, click, clicking of a dog's toenails on ceramic tile.

She held Kyla close to her now smelling the scent of the little girls shampoo and feeling the softness of her tender cheek pressed tightly against hers. "I promise you, Kyla. I'll never let them get you." Andrea thought.

Then something unimaginable began to happen to Andrea. She suddenly started experiencing a series of strange sensations, the likes of which she had never felt before. She sensed the heat of Kyla's body and oddly, she would have sworn she could actually hear the child's tiny heart beating loudly in her ears, obviously frantic with fear. The rhythmic thumping seemed louder than Andrea had ever heard it before. It was as if she had placed a stethoscope against Kyla's chest then magnified the steady beating through a set of high-end stereo speakers.

And then Andrea suddenly realized for some unexplainable reason, she was no longer afraid at all. She should have been terrified by the fact that an unstoppable army of undead creatures was about to fall upon she and her precious daughter, tearing them to shreds. Then another bizarre feeling began to engulf her; a feeling of extreme and uncontrollable hunger. She suddenly realized with horror why it really was that she didn't want to let the others in that undead salivating mob of maggot-ridden zombies get Kyla. Andrea suddenly understood that she wanted the girl for herself. She realized she wanted nothing better than to bend down right at that moment and take a bite out of her little girl's face. She wanted to feel the child's warm blood flow into her own cold body. She was suddenly having fantasies about clawing into her baby's stomach and pulling out her steaming innards, devouring them as the child screamed in agony.

What the hell was wrong with her, she thought. This was not how she ever would have thought about her precious little golden-haired daughter. Only some sick, depraved homicidal lunatic Braino-addicted junkie could possibly have such thoughts. Or perhaps . . . perhaps a reanimated corpse might, as well.

Just then, Kyla leaned away from Andrea, perhaps sensing the strange change in the way her mother held her and looking back at Andrea the child let out an ear-piercing cry of anguished terror. "No! Mommy! No!"

Andrea looked down at the hands holding her child and saw they had drastically changed in appearance. Her hands had become grey, withered and covered with festering soars. In places, the flesh had rotted away leaving patches of bone visible. Flies buzzed around in front of her face and then she saw worms slithering about just below the surface of what little skin remained on her decomposing arms. She had changed. She was no longer Andrea. She was one of THEM now.

Her former desire to protect her only child had gone by the wayside. Now all she could think about was keeping the crowds of undead townspeople from getting her daughter . . . no, not her daughter . . . her prize . . . her meal. Yes, this child appeared absolutely scrumptious and no one would get to devour her but Andrea. It was a mother's right.

Andrea slowly lowered her head attempting to wrap her withered lips around the child's ear. If she could just reach it she would tear it free from the girl's small skull and swallow it whole enjoying every second of her feast of tender, warm flesh.

Kyla was repeatedly shouting her name as she pushed uselessly against Andrea's upper arm, "Mommy! Mommy! Mommy!"

CHAPTER 7

"Mommy! Mommy! Mommy! Get up Mommy!" Kyla called to Andrea as she pushed against her sleeping mother's arm.

Andrea opened her eyes wide with a start, momentarily causing Kyla to step back a bit and look at her strangely. The look in her mother's eyes had not only been surprising but frightening as well. Then Andrea realized she was in her own bed and was waking from some sort of horrible nightmare which thankfully was already starting to fade into oblivion as such dreams often do.

Kyla came closer once again having seen a now familiar look return to her mother's face and said, "Mommy. It's time to wake up. Daddy's up already." This came as no surprise to Andrea since Jackson was always the first one awake in the Ridge household. Andrea wondered if Jackson had once again experienced his horrible nightmare. Then she realized of course he had. He always did. But the previous evening had been quite different for her as well; she had experienced her own nightmare. Although she couldn't recall the details of the dream and was glad she couldn't, Andrea still felt the remnants of an uneasy feeling creeping around inside her like some multi-legged insect skittering about just below the surface of her flesh. She experienced an involuntary shudder.

She turned and looked over at the digital clock on her nightstand. It read 8:08 AM. As the fog in her mind began to slowly clear she thought, "8:08 AM here . . . that means its 1:08 PM in England." Jackson's interview had been scheduled for 7:00 AM Eastern Standard Time, and she had slept through it.

Andrea threw both of her legs out of the bed and hurried stumbling out into the upstairs hall and grasping the wall for support she shouted, "Jackson? Jackson? Did you remember your seven o'clock interview this morning? Ah man! I'm so sorry, babe. I overslept." She would feel absolutely horrible if Jackson had missed it. He tended to be occasionally absentminded and forgetting the interview was very possible. That particular UK interviewer had been bugging her for weeks trying to get some time with Jackson. And she had finally set everything up just the previous week.

"Morning, sweetie!" Jackson called up cheerfully from the bottom of the stairs. There wasn't a trace of concern in his voice. He was a natural morning person and seemed to welcome everyday as if it was his last. This was true long before his ordeal eight months earlier, and it was still true even in spite of his nightly terrors. He was just one of those people who loved mornings. "Yeah. Don't worry, honey. I remembered. And, boy oh boy, do I have some cool things to tell you about how the UK is progressing. I think I must have asked the interviewer more questions than he ever got around to asking me."

Andrea lifted her palm almost painfully in a stop gesture. Jackson's brain was firing full bore on all eight cylinders, and she could barely get her eyes to focus yet. She pleaded, "Wait . . . please . . . just . . . let me wake up . . . and get my shower first, babe . . . then maybe . . . after a cup of coffee . . . you can tell me all about it. Ok?"

Jackson stopped talking immediately remembering how his wife was definitely not a morning person, and as such had a strict regimen she needed to complete every morning before she could consider herself able to communicate with anyone with any level of civility. He pulled back his enthusiasm, understanding just how much morning people like himself drove non-morning people absolutely crazy. But despite her lack of morning luster, Andrea did still usually manage to wake up relatively early each morning; not by choice, but by necessity and with the reluctant use of an alarm clock. Regardless, it was always better for all concerned to keep their distance from her until she finished her morning routine. Jackson understood that failure to comply might result in a fate worse than death.

The only exception to that particular rule was her precious little Kyla. No matter how sleepy, sick or grumpy Andrea might happen to be, whenever Kyla woke her up Andrea always managed to rise to the occasion and find time for her little girl. Sadly for Andrea it seemed that Kyla was afflicted with the same morning person illness as her father. That was how Andrea thought of it, an affliction; a sickness. It had to be. What normal person could wake up with the energy and positive attitude of her poor mentally stricken husband and daughter? But she loved them both despite their obvious shared disorder.

Jackson calmly said, "Sure thing, sweetie. We'll talk to you when you come down later." Then he called to his daughter, "Kyla, honey. Come on down with Daddy while Mommy gets ready."

"Do I have to?" Kyla pleaded.

Andrea patted her daughter's head tenderly and said, "It's ok, Kyla. Why don't you go down with Daddy until Mommy is ready? Then I'll come down, and we'll have the whole day together. Ok?" It was a Saturday, Andrea recalled, and that was why there had been no alarm to awaken her. The UK interview had been special and regardless she had not thought to set and alarm.

Kyla reluctantly headed down the stairs grumbling all the way, "Ok, Mommy . . . but . . . but Daddy's boring . . . he's not fun like you."

Andrea shot Jackson a knowing look and an understanding sympathetic smile. The truth was her husband really was a boring, plain and ordinary sort of character most of the time. He had his moments, but thank goodness they were few and far between. Because whenever Jackson did find himself involved in a particularly interesting story, he was often thrust into situations that were anything but mundane. She often thought of the adage, "Bad things sometimes happen to good people." Whenever she applied it to Jackson, she modified the adage to say, "Exciting, dangerous things sometimes happen to boring people."

Jackson recognized many years earlier that some people tended to think of him as having a boring personality and despite her young age, Kyla apparently understood that as well. Being called boring, even by his own little girl, was not offensive to Jackson in the slightest. He often referred to his blatantly ordinary persona as his journalistic super power. It helped him to blend in with the crowd in almost any situation, to slip into a group of strangers in a bar or restaurant and go completely unnoticed. He could discretely gather his information and be gone with no one being the wiser. Boring? Maybe, but if that were the case then he liked to think of himself as "Captain Boring, Gatherer of Vital Information."

Even with that being said, his last adventure ended up being anything but boring had thrust him into the realm of international fame. Now he felt more like a superhero whose secret identity had unfortunately been discovered. He hadn't gone on any assignments since his ordeal and suspected the days of his being just another anonymous face in the crowd might be gone forever. He continued to write and always would but until all of this publicity died out and maybe not even after that, Jackson realized his days of going unnoticed were over. He supposed that boring or not his so-called superpowers had been greatly diminished.

"Well, Kyla," Jackson explained, "like it or not, until your exciting mommy gets finished with her incredibly interesting shower, you're stuck with your boring old Daddy for a while."

Kyla walked past Jackson, and as she did, he believed he noticed a bit of a heavier than necessary tread to her walk. It was almost a stomp. He turned and followed the girl reprimanding, "That better not be your feet I'm hearing stomping, young lady. Or else you might be spending the rest of the day sitting in your room in time out. Do you understand me?"

Kyla's walk became instantly quieter knowing she had crossed a line, which had the potential of getting her in trouble. Then she turned and ran to Jackson using the same charm her mother had apparently passed on to her through her genes. She hugged his legs and apologized, "I'm so sorry, Daddy. I love you, and you're not boring at all. I mean it."

Jackson let out a deep sigh knowing this precious little thing had him wrapped around her finger, just like his wife did. He laughed to himself. Kyla walked into the kitchen ahead of Jackson apparently ready for her breakfast. Jackson poured her a bowl of crispy cereal with milk and sugar. Although he knew Kyla loved her morning cereal, he felt a pang of sorrow over the fact that the Ashton Cooperative general store only carried five or six varieties of cereal, at least for now.

He could still recall at time prior to the outbreak when every large grocery store had a cereal aisle with rows and rows of shelves filled with literally a hundred or more different varieties of cereal. He wondered if or when those days would ever return. He hoped it would be soon. More than almost anything else, Jackson wanted his little girl to grow up in a world exactly like the one he had known. It might not have been a perfect world, but it was still a far better place than the world of 2054.

CHAPTER 8

One of the things Jackson missed more than anything about the time before the outbreak was Katie. No, Katie wasn't a long lost love or a dead relative. In fact, Katie wasn't even human and at present was safely tucked away in a box up in his attic where she had remained for the past decade and would likely remain for many years to come. Katie was Jackson's pet name for his KTD-35 unit (Knowledge Transfer Device, circa 2035). There was a time when Jackson wouldn't have been able to imagine not having Katie at this beck and call, yet here he was now more than a decade after the KTD network had crashed.

Knowledge Transfer Devices had begun to appear back as early as the second decade of the twenty-first century. By 2030 they were as common place in homes as personal computers had been at the start of the century. And unlike these other devices, KTDs could be completely personalized to the point of having something which actually simulated a human personality. They worked in conjunction with computers, television, radio, internet, printers and basically any household electronic device to make the lives of humans much easier.

The most common and affordable KTDs were human-like in appearance, with what appeared to be the top half of a human body consisting of torso, head and two nonfunctional arms used primarily for unit stabilization. The arms were bent at the elbow and extended out with the palms downward and flat against the top of the surface upon which it rested. The head was generally human shaped and smooth in the case of these more economical models with a flat oval monitor for a face.

Some of the higher end units owned by the wealthiest members of society could be made with latex molded animatronic faces to resemble whomever the person chose them to. The animatronics feature allowed the faces to produce an eerie collection of expressions while speaking. These units had a display screen inserted in the torso rather than in the face. Jackson always felt even if he could afford such a unit he'd never want one. Any such accurate representation of humanity in an inanimate object always bothered him for some reason.

Even with his precious Katie, he had chosen to leave the face blank, only to be used as a display screen. There had been software readily available which would have allowed him to have the facial monitor display any male or female face he wanted. But again, Jackson felt that was too creepy. Although he did give his unit a female voice and personality, its physical appearance was androgynous as was the case with all of the affordable KTDs.

What he missed most about Katie was her ability to be linked not only to the KTD network but to the World Wide Web in general. As an investigative journalist with deadlines and a tight schedule, not having to spend time searching the internet for information was a Godsend. His KTD unit sat in the corner of his office on a table and all he had to do was verbalize his request and in seconds he would have the answer. It was similar to the Siri feature on the old Apple iPhones but much more sophisticated. For example, while writing an article he could ask, "Katie, what year was the first lunar landing?" and seconds later she would reply, "Thanks for asking Jackson. Apollo 11 was the American spaceflight, which allowed the first humans to set foot on the Moon. Neil Armstrong and Buzz Aldrin landed on the surface of the moon July 20, 1969, at 20:18 Coordinate Universal Time or UTC. Six hours later, astronaut Neal Armstrong became the first person to step onto the lunar surface on July 21 at 02:56 Coordinated Universal Time or UTC."

This was also true for his personal information as well as his daily schedule. He could start his morning by asking Katie what was on his agenda for the day and she would not only provide him with a list of what he had to do, but if he wanted she could simultaneously print out a schedule for him. If he was heading out for an assignment and forget to check the weather Katie would say something like, "Jackson. Before you leave I would recommend you take your jacket and umbrella as there is a 95% chance of precipitation today."

Katie kept in constant contact with the millions of other KTDs on the vast network which meant any time he wanted to send a personal message to anyone who was tied to his unit he could simply say something like, "Katie. Could you please wish a happy birthday to my cousin Louis in Kansas City?" To which Katie might reply, "Wishes have been sent to Louis Ridge as you requested. Did you recall it was your Aunt Selma and Uncle Frank's wedding anniversary today as well? Shall I send them a note of congratulations?"

As far as Jackson was concerned, back then he couldn't imagine living a day without Katie, thinking he might not remember how to function without her assistance. She made his life so much easier, especially since he tended to be absent minded from time to time when he was busy. He had owned his KTD before he met and married Andrea, and Jackson often thought at time Andrea might actually have been a bit jealous of how much he depended on Katie. Before he met Andrea, Jackson's KTD unit had been programmed to speak to him in a much more sultry and sensuous tone. Once he met Andrea, he wisely reprogrammed the unit to have much more business-like vocal inflections. Still, Andrea often seemed troubled by their close "relationship," which Jackson couldn't understand. He guessed it must be a female thing.

But then again, Andrea had her own KTD unit, which she had named Thor. Thor, of course, had a male personality, but Jackson never felt personally threatened by her KTD the way she seemed to feel about his. Now in hindsight Jackson began to wonder if maybe Andrea had been right to feel a bit jealous, especially since here it was almost eleven years after the KTD network crashed for good, and he was still thinking about Katie.

And chances were very realistic that it might be another decade or two before any attempt could be made to rejuvenate the units. Bringing back the electric grid and the internet had been difficult, but enough people were still alive who understood the technology since it was so many generations old. But a lot fewer people understood KTD technology, and apparently most of them were dead. Also with all available humans dealing with the day-to-day business of survival and rebuilding society, there was little time for redeveloping such a technology of convenience. Jackson often wondered what Katie would think if she suddenly was reawakened after being asleep for two or three decades to discover how he and the world had changed.

But then Jackson's fantasy began to fade away as he recalled a world where things like Katie would be given any priority might be a very long time coming. Perhaps Kyla's children or grandchildren would be the generation that would finally have the opportunity to live in a world that in any way was similar to that world he and Andrea had known. Although things were getting a little bit better every day, the world still had a very long way to go. And it seemed as though it was always the little things like the limited selection of cereal in stores that served as painful reminders of just how much more the world needed to heal. Jackson let out a sigh of resignation.

After about fifteen minutes or so had passed, Kyla was finished her breakfast and moved into the family room where she was watching one of her videos. A few minutes later Andrea finally made her appearance in the kitchen. Jackson could see she was feeling much better than she had been when she had first awoken and that was certainly a good thing. He walked over, gave her a good morning kiss then turned to go and pour her a cup of coffee. As he walked, he started to tell her of his conversation with the reporter from the UK, but he noticed she wasn't responding in the typical way she usually would have.

He looked up from pouring Andrea's coffee and saw she was stopped dead in her tracks in the middle of the room staring out the large kitchen window; the one overlooking the neighbor's back yard. The people who lived next door were David and Marge Kinkaid, an elderly couple in their late seventies or early eighties.

Jackson could tell by the look on Andrea's face something was very wrong. She seemed both horrified and revolted at the same time. He had seen that look far too many times during the past decade from Andrea as well as many other survivors. She turned slightly and looked directly at Jackson without saying a word. She gave a slight cock of her head to indicate he should look out the kitchen window.

Behind her she heard Kyla call out, "Mommy. Mommy. Come in her and watch my movie with me."

"I'll . . . I'll be . . . right there, sweetie." Andrea called back to her daughter, trying desperately to sound like everything was fine.

Andrea nodded at Jackson sending a silent message to indicate she was going in to keep Kyla busy while he took care of whatever it was she had just seen outside their window. Even before he turned to look out, Jackson had a horrible sinking feeling in the pit of his stomach. He didn't know exactly what he might find when he looked out the window but he had a pretty good idea it was not going to be very pleasant. Jackson slowly turned and glanced over into the Kinkaid's back yard, and his mouth dropped open in shock. Time seemed to come to a screeching halt as he stared out the window at the horror unfolding just thirty feet away on his neighbor's back patio.

CHAPTER 9

Jackson stared in shocked astonishment as old Mr. Kinkaid, or more accurately the undead creature who had once been old Mr. Kinkaid, was on his knees on the stone patio of his home feasting upon the shredded and bloodied remains of his wife, Mrs. Kinkaid. Jackson instantly saw every detail of what was happening and had a good idea of why.

Apparently, Mr. Kinkaid must have passed away during the night or perhaps early that same morning. Then once he had turned, he had most likely attacked his wife. Mrs. Kinkaid must have tried to escape fleeing the house out into the back yard where she probably had tripped and fallen. That would have been just the advantage the creature would have needed to overpower the frail old woman. And now the thing he had become was kneeling over her feasting on her innards. Jackson could see that although she appeared dead, Mrs. Kinkaid had not turned yet. Perhaps she had slipped into a coma state just before final death occurred.

The old woman was wearing a thin translucent nightgown, which the undead Mr. Kinkaid had managed to easily tear to ribbons. She now lay on her back, her aged shredded breasts dangling in bacon-like strips by her sides while her mouth hung agape. Her filmy sightless eyes seemed to stare skyward as if looking yet seeing nothing. Old Mr. Kinkaid was facing in the direction of Jackson's house, his gnarled fingers glistening crimson, coated in his wife's blood. Laced between his fingers like fleshy playthings were his wife's intestines, at least those intestines, which were not already dangling from his mindlessly chomping mouth.

A pool of liquid, a mixture of dark red, yellow and brown colors from blood, bile and stomach contents spread across the stone block patio, forming ruby rivulets in the sand-packed joints between the blocks. The thick murky red liquid crept as if in slow motion along the top of the sand being absorbed along the way until there was not enough blood to flow any further. Jackson noticed how small swarms of early morning back yard insects had already begun to lite not only on the congealing blood pools but on the Kinkaids' flesh as well.

Jackson turned back toward the family room to see Andrea looking out at him and nodding acknowledgement of what he knew he must do next. Although he understood it was his civic duty and legal responsibility, it still bothered him. For more than ten years he had been dealing with these sorts of unpleasant matters and sometimes he simply felt sick and tired of it all. And to make matters worse, he knew and liked the Kinkaids. They had been good neighbors and more than that; they had been good friends. He returned Andrea's nod and turned to go out into the yard and over to the Kinkaids' to deal with the problem at hand.

He walked toward the back door and as he passed the hall coat closet he reached up onto the highest shelf and retrieved a long thin metal case, which protected a Samurai-styled Katana blade, something left over from his teenage years when he had studied martial arts for a brief period of time. He had also collected a number of bow-staffs, nunchakus and swords as well. However, all that still remained of that bygone era was this single blade. It also happened to be his favorite relic. Jackson would be the first to admit he was no Karate expert. In fact, he had forgotten most of that early training although he may have accidently used a few of the moves on the undead during the zombie wars from 2043-2047. If he were to be honest with himself, most of the time he simply stumbled about punching, kicking, swinging whatever he could find at the creatures, just like everyone else did who was attempting to survive. At least he still had his sword and that was quite a lethal weapon indeed, which would serve him very well on this terrible morning.

Jackson took a deep breath, steeling himself for what he was about to do; what he must do. He quietly opened the back screen door, pulling the kitchen door behind him and locking it as well. If anything bad, as in fatal were to happen to him within the next few minutes, he didn't want to leave a clear opening for the zombie to enter his home. He also didn't want to risk Kyla hearing the sounds that would follow shortly. There might be few or no noticeable sounds at all or there might be some God-awful howling. He never knew. No one ever knew for certain. He trusted Andrea to keep Kyla occupied until his task was complete.

He walked quietly across his patio; practically tiptoeing then stepped down onto the grass between his property and the Kinkaids'. He silently made his way onto his neighbor's patio, all the while raising the blade above his head and off to the right, gripping it tightly with both hands. The thing, which had been David Kinkaid, was so busy enjoying his morning feast he didn't even hear Jackson's approach.

Jackson gripped the blade raising it still higher and then said calmly, "David? Hey, David . . . its Jackson. Do you hear me, David?"

After a bit, the Kinkaid thing lifted its head and looked at first uninterestingly at Jackson. Blood trickled down the corners of its mouth and was smeared around his aged face like a crimson five o'clock shadow. Chunks of his wife's flesh hung from several of its teeth. Jackson knew the old timer wore dentures, and they apparently were in good working order and serving him as well in death as they had in life.

As the undead creature raised its head still higher, likely preparing to issue one of its horrible growls, Jackson brought down the blade in a wide sweeping circular motion, its shiny surface no more than a blur in the morning light. As it completed its arc with a silent swishing sound it came in contact with Kinkaid's stretched neck and severed its head from its body within a split second. The cut was amazingly clean and complete. Jackson saw the head separate, spin several times in the air then fall to the patio with a sickening thudding sound. Thank goodness it didn't roll. Jackson didn't know if he could have handled that so early in the morning. The spinning through the air was bad enough. A moment later that thudding sound was followed by the squishing plop of Kinkaid's headless body falling down over his wife's disemboweled corpse.

It was then that Jackson heard a shuffling sound followed by a slightly higher-pitched growl. Mrs. Kinkaid, or at least what remained of her, had been transformed into yet another undead creature, which Jackson knew he would have to deal with. The thing was now up on its elbows trying to pull itself free from the weight of the fallen corpse of Mr. Kinkaid. Jackson heard a sickening tearing sound as the horrid creature pulled its remaining torso away from the rest of its ravaged body. It was one of the most revolting sights Jackson had ever seen, which was saying a lot all things considered. Below its now tattered torso, its spinal column extended out like some sort of horrific yellow and crimson tail. Jackson could hear the bone scraping along the brick of the patio. It was a sound he knew he would never be able to forget no matter how much longer he might happen to live.

The creature looked hungrily at Jackson growling with the same unintelligible guttural moan all of these creatures seemed to make as it began to inch its way slowly toward him. Behind the corpse, dragging along entangled in the remnants of its spine were several pink and crimson intestines, which made horrible ruby snail trails on the patio resembling a cluster of crawling snakes. Jackson chose not to waste another second.

Bringing down the sword for the second time that morning, Jackson sunk the razor-sharp blade deep enough into the thing's skull to practically cleaving its head in two. The creature fell forward to the ground with the blade still buried inside its head having stopped just an inch above the old woman's mouth. Jackson stared at the carnage before him panting with exertion and stress from the horrifying act. He looked down at his injured hands and slowly opened and closed them multiple times to assure they had not been damaged further during the altercation. This was the first time he had exerted such force with his formerly wounded hands and was pleased to see they seemed to be still functioning properly. Obviously, the physical therapy and exercises had served him well.

Then taking a moment to further regain his composure and to prepare himself for the next step, Jackson placed one foot on the top of the severed right side of creature's forehead and wrenched the blade free from the gory, pulpy mess that had once been its skull. The force of his foot during this action caused the thing's head to split completely down the middle and the right half of its face fell off to the ground while the left remained precariously attached to its neck. Jackson flicked the sword through the air, snapping his wrist and causing most off the bloody debris to fall to the ground. Then he stuck the blade upright into the grass next to the patio.

He next walked around to the side of his house where his car sat in the driveway. He opened the front door, reached in the glove box and withdrew two bright orange flags, which were attached to metal rods resembling small car aerials with springs near the bottom. At the base of the rod, just below the large spring-like mechanism was a sharp metal spike.

Jackson took one of the two rods in his right hand gripping it tightly. He walked over to the old man's headless corpse, which lay on its stomach and was still clad in a yellowed wife-beater tee shirt splattered with his wife's blood. He brought the rod down hard and sank it deep into the corpse's stump of a neck. Next, he repeated the process with the remains of Mrs. Kinkaid by sinking the point deep into the exposed, severed and halved brain. It made a sloshing sound so sickening, Jackson thought he might vomit. He hated to do this to such nice people and former friends, but the law was the law. And celebrity or not, he was required to follow the laws of the land. He took out his Communications Unit and using its built-in high-resolution camera snapped two pictures of the devastated corpses being sure that both of the flags and their identifying bar codes were visible in the shot.

Jackson dialed a pre-programmed number in his CU and when the automated answering system prompted him, he said, "This is Jackson Ridge, citizen number 132-78-5498. I'd like to report a Dead Kill . . . actually two Dead Kills." He gave out the rest of the pertinent information such as his address and the address where the two corpses could be located. Within the hour, a truck from the Ashton Cooperative Dead Kill Removal Squad would arrive to haul the two corpses away. They'd be properly identified and held over for arrangements to be made by their next of kin. Most times the purpose of the identification process was to try to find out the identity of Dead Kills whose origin could not be readily determined. This was a long and arduous task which often resulted in less than desirable results. In the case where the Dead Kills were known, the process went much quicker. Jackson knew the Kinkaids had a son currently living in the city of Yuengsville twenty miles away, and as such he had provided that information in his message as well.

Jackson thought of how fortunate the couple was to have relatives nearby to claim and properly deal with their cremation. Burials were no longer regularly practiced although were permitted in certain areas after satisfying a number of stringent regulations and of course paying a very steep burial tax. Needless to say only those with the financial wherewithal to pay such a tax could choose to see their loved ones buried. As a result, most people opted for cremation.

Over the past decade, so many millions had gone missing and were presumed either dead or undead. And most of them would never be positively identified. These unfortunates would simply be listed as missing, leaving surviving family members to never have proper closure, but to imagine their loved ones either as one of the shambling undead or a victim of the hideous creatures. Some preferred to imaging their relatives as having survived somewhere out in the world and held onto the futile hope they would meet again someday.

But as the world returned closer to its original civilized state and fewer of the original lingering dead remained, people understood it was as likely as not that their long-lost loved ones would remain as such. If they had died or been killed at the start of the outbreak a decade earlier, it was almost a given that they had been slaughtered along with the millions of other undead during the zombie wars. As such their unidentified remains would have been cast upon the mountainous burn piles never to be seen again.

Jackson looked down and saw that his hands were now trembling, likely from the fading adrenaline rush he had just experienced. His stomach was sick over what he had just done as well. He didn't even care that his and Andrea's bank account would be credited two hundred dollars, one for each Dead Kill. All he had done was what he was legally required to do. The money was actually starting to seem insulting to him. However, he didn't have time to fret over such things now, he had to get back in the house and let Andrea know he was alright.

He walked back over to his own yard, pulling the Katana blade out of the ground as he passed and noticed an old tee shirt in a bucket near the garden hose. He remembered using it as a rag a few days earlier to dry off his patio furniture following a recent rain. Jackson bent down, picked up the rag finding it was still quite damp. Then he used it to wipe the remaining blood stains and bits of flesh from the blade. When the sword was completely clean, he tossed the rag into a covered trashcan. There was something so final about this simple act that it allowed him to somehow come to terms with what had just happened. The nausea and some of the guilt began to pass, and Jackson was beginning to feel like himself once again. He knew both sensations well; the feeling of anger, fear and disgust followed by the return to something resembling normalcy. It was the way of the world in 2054, and Jackson knew it was the way things would likely be for a very long time to come.

CHAPTER 10

Jackson walked slowly in through his back door, which slammed shut behind him with a loud bang. It was likely not actually louder than normal but with his nerves on edge it probably only seemed that way. He opened the hall closet door once again, returned his katana blade to its sheath and placed it high up on the top shelf of the closet. Way up there, it would be safely out the reach of his young daughter. He stood for a moment contemplating before closing the door, his head down, staring at the floor as it shook slowly side to side perhaps in denial of all that he knew to be true. He was both disgusted and frustrated not only with the issue he had just been forced to resolve but with everything; perhaps even with himself. At times like this, he was reluctantly reminded of just how bad things still were, even in the so-called civilized towns and cities. He often found himself questioning the decision he and Andrea had made five years earlier when they had learned she was pregnant with Kyla.

At that time, they both believed they had understood the difficulties they would encounter if they chose not to terminate the pregnancy; or at least they thought they knew what they were doing. The idea of raising a child in a world overrun with living dead creatures, in a world not even remotely similar to the world in which they had been fortunate enough to live had been beyond his comprehension. Yes, it was true during the time before the outbreak, people may have lived with the constant threat of nuclear war, terrorism, global climate changes and an ever-rising crime rate, but even at its worse that world was nothing like the past decade had been in this horrifying new world. This world was one of constant struggle to survive and to try to rebuild it into something at least vaguely resembling the world of their past. To say it was not the best environment to consider raising a child was a magnificent understatement.

However, the government had been encouraging young couples to have children for the previous six years, stressing the importance of rebuilding the population. The newly instituted laws required that once the decision to acknowledge and not terminate their pregnancy was made, the future parents had to attend special mandatory post-Z43 parenting classes. Jackson and Andrea had gone through special instruction provided by government-trained representatives. These instructors, known as "Parental Helpers" constantly assured the couples that their children would be perfectly fine in the new world, that they were the future of humanity and that things were getting better every day.

These instructors had noticeably neglected to discuss such topics as the incredibly high infant mortality rate, which would accompany these new waves of births. Jackson and Andrea had known several couples whose babies did not survive long after birth due to the poor medical conditions, which existed back at that time. In fact, even one of the mothers in their class had died during childbirth. This was another topic, which the government instructors had conveniently not managed to mention during their classes. They were strictly focused on repopulation.

The helper said the post-Z43 world was the only world any of these children would ever know. They would never long for things to be as they had been before the apocalypse the way their parents often did. The new world would be their world and as such, they and likewise their descendants would adapt and make it their own. The instructors warned that as parents, they might at times feel guilty because things would be so different for their children. They said this was a natural feeling and one they should expect. But they continuously assured the parents there was no need to feel guilty whatsoever. This disaster was not of their making, and it was the responsibility of all healthy citizens to begin repopulating the world as soon as possible. They also encouraged couples to have as many children as they could. Andrea had some complications after Kyla's birth and unfortunately was unable to have any other children. Since single children households was a rarity now, people often looked upon the Ridges as something of an oddity.

Jackson often questioned silently to himself if he and Andrea had made the right decision in having Kyla. He, of course, wasn't sorry they had their wonderful daughter, and he felt blessed that Andrea had survived the birth as well, but he believed the decision to have her might have been based more on satisfying his and Andrea's desire to have a child; and as such, little thought had been given to any needs Kyla might someday have. His knowing these guilty feelings were supposedly normal did little to help make the feelings acceptable.

He assumed this was the type of guilt the Parent Helpers had been talking about, and he also supposed that same bit of guilt had been haunting parents since the dawn of time. He well understood the concerns parents always experienced about what sort of world they might be bringing their babies into. But then again, never before in history had the world been such a troubled and dangerous place.

As he entered the kitchen, he saw Andrea sitting on the sofa in the family room with Kyla, still watching her video. Andrea looked up toward the kitchen, and their eyes met. Jackson suspected she had been making many such glances toward the back door since he had gone out. He gave a weary half smile and nodded his head, acknowledging he had been successful in completing his dismal deed. She returned a sympathetic but sad smile of understanding.

Jackson took a deep breath and assumed a more jovial attitude than he actually felt and walked into the family room.

"And how are my two favorite girls doing? He said pretending it was just another ordinary day.

Kyla glanced over and replied, "We're fine, Daddy. Just watching TV."

Andrea added,, "Yep . . . yep . . . just watching TV here . . . so, honey . . . is everything . . . um . . . in order?"

Jackson hesitated then said, "Ah . . . yep. Everything is in order . . . In fact . . . I was just thinking, maybe we should all go out for a nice walk. It sure is a beautiful morning out there. Maybe we could . . . you know . . . head over to the park; the one a few blocks away over by the school." His look enforced for Andrea that the Dead Kill retrieval squad would be arriving within the hour to pick up the bodies, and it might be better if Kyla was elsewhere when that occurred.

Andrea agreed, "Yes, I think that's a great idea." Then she suddenly stopped speaking and looked down, staring at Jackson's pants. She said with all the calm she could muster, "Um . . . yes . . . honey . . . that's a great idea . . . but maybe you . . . should get changed first."

Jackson looked downward and noticed a few splotches of crimson on his jeans as well as several tiny chunks of flesh and brain matter. He was grateful Kyla had been so engrossed in her video that she hadn't noticed.

"Ah . . . yeah . . . good idea. I'll be down in a minute." Jackson replied.

Then he went up to their bedroom to go find something clean to wear for their stroll. He put his clothing in a plastic bag knowing he likely would never wear that outfit again, and it would end up in the dumpster. As he changed, he couldn't help but feel absolutely terrible once again not only about what he had just been forced to do, but about what a horrible world he and Andrea had brought their precious daughter into.

CHAPTER 11

"I'm so glad you could join me for lunch today, Jyleen," Sean Patel said to the young attractive nurse's aide, "I've been meaning to call you for some time, but my schedule has been insane . . . um . . . just as I'm sure yours has been equally busy."

"That's for sure!" Jyleen exclaimed. "It's been unbelievable lately. As I told you I've been going to school part time at night working toward getting my registered nurses license."

Sean said awkwardly, "Yes . . . I remember. That must be quite a challenge for you, I'm certain . . . I mean working as many hours as you do and then still trying to fit in school and studying."

She smiled a weary smile and agreed, "Yes, it certainly is. Sean? Are you ok?" She suddenly seemed concerned about how Sean was acting, "You seem a bit . . . I don't know . . . a bit preoccupied or something. I can't remember you ever being uncomfortable around me before."

Sean hesitated for a moment then said, "Yes . . . yes, I suppose . . . maybe I am feeling a bit off my game."

She looked at him seriously then asked, "What do you mean, Sean? You have no reason to ever feel uncomfortable around me. I'd think we were beyond that by now."

His true discomfort came from trying to figure out how he would pass on his information. But he wisely decided to seize the opportunity to offer an alternative reason. "Well," he said, "the truth is . . . I felt really bad about not calling you sooner. I guess I was worried . . . you know . . . that you might be a bit angry with me because I took so long."

"No need to worry about that at all, Sean. I know how busy you are and as I said . . . I'm just as busy. So don't sweat it. We're cool, ok?"

"Ok. We are most definitely cool. So your school . . . tell me all about it. How it is going?"

"It's going great. In fact, what I wanted to tell you is that even though I'm still a few months away from officially becoming a register nurse, I've been promoted to a leadership position at the hospice group."

"Wow, Jyleen! That's terrific. Congratulations. Tell me more about it."

"Thanks. You see, we're really shorthanded when it comes to RNs. That was true even before Andrea Ridge left to manage her husband's career. We were already running very lean even back then. But when she quit it really kicked us in the butt. So the powers that be promoted me to a head nurse position on my shift, and way ahead of time."

"That's great!" Sean said, "These are still troubled times, and it's good to see that management has learned they have to be flexible. I don't know if I ever told you this or not, but that's actually how I ended up as Assistant Medical Examiner, even though I still haven't finished medical school yet. In fact, I'm not sure when or if I'll ever have a chance to go back to school now with the way things are in the world." Then he decided to take advantage of Jyleen's mention of Andrea and asked, "Didn't you work often with Andrea before she left?"

Jyleen said, "No, not all that often. Let's say not as often as I would have liked to. We always got along great. I think we made a great team."

"That's both good to hear and sort of sad at the same time, since she's gone. I suppose you never have the opportunity to . . . you know . . . see her socially?"

"No, not really," Jyleen said with noticeable disappointment. "Actually I always wished we could have gotten together sometime on a personal level, you know outside of work rather than over some old coot who was about to die and who we had to take care of . . . if you know what I mean."

As cruel as that sounded, Sean understood where Jyleen was coming from. He knew the requirements hospice nurses were forced to go through when someone was close to death. They had to make the family leave their loved one's bedside while they strapped the unconscious person down securely. Then they had to put on a strange contraption called the cranial helmet which was to be used after the person died and turned into one of the undead. The device shot long needles into the creature's brain, which not only pierced and destroyed the reanimated brain, but also filled it with a special poison to make sure the job had been completed. Then they had to pack away their tools of destruction and return the body to as close to normal as possible for the sake of the family. This was often an emotionally strenuous activity and to no one's surprise the burnout rate among these types of nurses was extremely high.

"Yeah, I do know exactly what you mean."

Jyleen criticized herself, "What am I doing complaining about my work to you? You have to deal with these dead heads up close and personal on a daily basis and not fresh and clean either like mine. You get them after they've had a long time out there in the world to rot and stink. That has to really suck big time."

Sean seemed to think about that for a beat then said, "Well, most of the time it's not too bad . . . you know . . . just a job. I suppose I've gotten used to it. And whenever I do get the opportunity to identify one of them who shows up on the missing list, it gives me a lot of satisfaction. Even though delivering such information to their living relatives is not very pleasant, there is something positive about finally giving them closure. But to be honest, most of the time the work is pretty mundane and generally uneventful. Every so often I get a . . . well, let's just say an interesting Dead Kill; one which is a bit different from most of the others. That makes things so much more . . . I don't know . . . I hate to say it . . . but the word fun comes to mind."

This seemed to spark Jyleen's attention. She asked, "What do you mean by different Sean? Different how?"

"Well . . . I don't know exactly." Sean said feigning misunderstanding while all the time he was deliberately beginning to plant the seed of interest in Jyleen's mind, "I mean, by the time I get these creatures on my table, they're often in pretty bad shape. They come in various stages of decomposition and often their heads are all but obliterated. I'm sorry, Jyleen. This really isn't very good lunch conversation, I'm afraid. Maybe we should change the subject."

"No, Sean. Not at all. It's just fine with me. This is all so fascinating for me. Although I get to experience some fairly

58

nasty things in my line of work as I'm sure you realized, at least my dead heads are all not as bad as yours." Then she let go with a bit of uncomfortable laughter, "But you were saying something about sometime the Dead Kills you get are different. What exactly did you mean by different?"

Sean hesitated deliberately, knowing he had her complete attention now. "Well . . . if you really want to know, I suppose since we're both professionals . . . I wouldn't be talking out of school if I mentioned a little of what I've seen."

"No. No, it wouldn't. Just one pro to another."

Sean said, "Well . . . there've been . . . a few Dead Kills that were . . . I don't know . . . let's just say a bit different looking than what most people would consider . . . you know . . . normal. That is to say if anything about these horrible undead freaks can be considered in any way normal. Maybe typical would be a better word. There have been a few Dead Kills that were much larger . . . you know . . . taller and broader across the shoulders . . . than most normal folks are."

Jyleen asked, "Taller? You mean like six-seven or six-ten? Like a basketball player or something? Or do you mean a lot bigger, like a giant?"

Sean knew what she was asking and he began to carefully feed her only the information she wanted to hear, "Well . . . yes . . . I suppose some could have been considered giants. I had one fellow a few months ago that was over seven feet tall with broad shoulders and a chest like a tree trunk. He barely fit onto one of my storage shelves. In fact, it was Jackson Ridge who was the one responsible for that particular Dead Kill. I don't suppose you ever had the opportunity to meet Jackson, Jyleen, have you? He's a very nice fellow and has been my best friend since childhood. I'm sure I must have mentioned this before."

"Yes, I do recall you telling me about Jackson but no, I've never met him. All of this is very interesting. Please tell me more about this giant Dead Kill Jackson shot."

Now pretending to be disinterested, as if what he was about to say was irrelevant, Sean said, "There's not very much to tell. It was big, huge actually. Its head was large like a block of cement, and the thing had a brow that protruded like . . . well . . . sort of like a caveman's. Its body showed signs of decay, of course, since it had been undead for quite some time yet it was rippling with muscles. That's about all . . . I suppose. Why are you so interested? I mean it's just another dead head."

"Maybe not."

Sean gave her a perplexed look and asked, "What do you mean by maybe not, Jy?"

"Well . . . I've heard things, Sean," Jyleen said hesitantly. "Things from people I've met while carrying out my hospice responsibilities. I've heard rumors from regular people, stories which being a man of science you might not want to even give consideration."

"Things?" Sean asked, pretending as if he didn't know exactly what she was about to say, "What sort of things are you talking about?"

Jyleen hesitated once again then let out a sigh and said, "I've heard stories, rumors about . . . now don't you dare laugh at me, Sean Patel, because this is very serious. People have told me stories about mutations among both the undead as well as living humans."

Sean did his best to project a look of astonishment coupled with disappointment and a bit of sarcasm, "Jyleen, seriously? You don't expect me to honestly give any credence to such nonsense do you?"

Jyleen looked sternly at Sean and said insistently, "Look, Sean. I've been told about these mutants from upstanding citizens. I've heard stories of strange and horrible changes, which seem to be occurring more to people living in the outlands. I've heard what you might call urban legends as well about sightings of giants very much like the one you've just described. And if you've actually seen and worked on one of these creatures then the rumors must be true."

"Whoa . . . wait just a minute here, Jy." Sean warned trying to act as if the entire idea was ridiculous, "I never said that the Dead Kill Jackson shot was some sort of mutant. Why would you think such a thing? I'm telling you those stories about mutants have to be nothing more than rumors and old wives' tales."

Jyleen looked at him seriously and asked, "Are they? Are they really? Think about it, Sean. You have more medical training than I do. Don't you see how obvious it is? Viruses mutate; they change. They do it all the time. So why would the Z43 virus be any different? And when you think about it, this virus is unlike any other virus we've ever encountered before in history. Even after all these years, we still know so very little about it. We don't even know its origin."

Although Jyleen was unaware of it, she was now heading right down the path of logic Sean wanted her to follow all along, and she was now coming to the exact conclusions he wanted her to deduce. Now he had to find a way to both distance himself from this whole idea and convince Jyleen to get Andrea involved.

Looking even more doubtful he said, "I don't know, Jyleen. I mean, what you said about viruses is true enough and especially what you've said about out lack of understanding when it comes to Z43. But what you're suggesting is a viral mutation so terrible, so drastic that it can actually cause the host's body to change, to deform to enlarge significantly. That whole idea is a bit out there, don't you think?"

"Out there? Seriously?" Jyleen exclaimed. "You mean to tell me that on one hand you can accept that this virus is capable of reanimating dead bodies and turning them into flesh-eating savages, while on the other hand you have trouble accepting it might also cause physical mutations in living humans?"

Sean pretended to think a bit about what Jyleen had said and did his best to appear surprised by her logic. "Well . . . well . . . when you put it that way . . . maybe it could make some sense." Then he decided to point her in the right direction, "It's too bad you and Andrea aren't working together any more. I'll be she'd have some ideas to add to your theories."

"Hey . . . wait a minute," Jyleen said. "Jackson is a good friend of yours, why don't you talk to Jackson about this?"

"Jyleen. Think about what you're suggesting," Sean said. "First of all this is your theory, not mine. Secondly, there's nothing out there in the form of definitive scientific proof of mutations whatsoever. Is there? Keep in mind, I work as the Schuylkill County Assistant Medical Examiner. My boss is the coroner and Chief Medical Examiner. If word got out that I was part of some group of people spreading rumors about humans mutating into monsters; I wouldn't have a job for very long, now would I? And no offense, but I'm not saying I even buy into all of this mutation stuff anyway. I mean if you want to discuss this with Andrea or some of your other friends that's fine, and that would be your business. And if she chooses to get Jackson involved that would be her choice as well. But you have to understand something, regardless of what I do or don't believe, I simply can't be part of such a thing if I want to keep my job."

She looked at him and a look of suspicion seemed to cross her face. She said, "You know what I think, Sean? I think you know something you're not telling me. I think you know more about this whole mutation thing than you're letting on. Is that true, Sean?"

"Nonsense!" Sean insisted. "I know nothing about any such matters. If you recall, it was you who brought up the subject of mutants. I didn't."

She hesitated for a moment realizing he was probably right, "Still . . . I still feel like you know something, which you either won't or can't share with anyone, including your friends Andrea and Jackson. And I think you want me to say something to her so she says something to him. Since he is an investigative reporter his curiosity will get the better of him, and he won't be able to resist investigating these so-called rumors. When he does, he'll probably find out the truth and you'll have . . . what do they call it? Oh, yes . . . plausible deniability."

Sean said nothing for a moment then said, "Wow, Jyleen. I didn't realize you had such a vivid imagination. I had no idea. Now I suppose it'll be just one more of the many things I like about you. But I assure you, I know nothing about any mutations. In fact, I have a much better idea. Why don't we forget about all of this mutant talk and concentrate on ordering our lunch and enjoying our time together. What do you say?"

Jyleen agreed saying, "I'll be more than happy to have you buy me lunch, Sean. And just for the record, I do plan on speaking to Andrea about this, sometime very soon. If she ignores it so be it, but if I can convince her to get Jackson involved, and he discovers something you're going to owe me another lunch. Deal?"

Sean let out a chuckle and said, "Deal." He figured he just made a win/win deal. Now he might get to have Jackson involved in investigating, and he would definitely have another excuse to have lunch again with Jyleen. Then he added, "And if the whole thing fizzles, you can buy me lunch."

CHAPTER 12

The lone figure walked silently through the underbrush doing his best not to make even the slightest of sounds. He knew better. He knew about them, about their kind. He had learned all he could about them. Unfortunately, he didn't know everything he needed to know, and that concerned him greatly. Yet at the same time, this particular element of uncertainty added a degree of additional excitement to his hunt. He was, however very much aware of what he had learned about their keenly enhanced senses. Some of his associates had told him these creatures could see in the darkest of nights, smell even the faintest of scents and hear almost every sound no matter how distracted they might be.

That was why he had been so very careful to approach from downwind. He was the hunter, and there was no way he intended to become the hunted. He knew he couldn't entirely mask his scent, his human smell. He could only hope the wind wouldn't shift. For if it did, his chances of walking out of the woods alive would be virtually non-existent. He still couldn't believe the government remained in denial of the creatures' existence. He suspected if there had been a way to downplay the existence of zombies the government would still be doing so. In fact, in the beginning the government actually did try to pass off the initial undead as being nothing more than Braino junkies, until things got too far out of control.

But then again maybe the government felt they were just keeping things from the public for their own good. That's what governments tried to do in the time before the Z43 outbreak so why would things be any different now? Politicians were, are and probably always will be politicians.

As he crept closer to the clearing, Death Bringer Jones, as he liked to be called, could hear the grunting and chewing sounds the horrid creature made as it feasted on whatever or whomever it was currently devouring. Now that he was close enough to see the victim through a break in the underbrush, he noted it appeared to be a dismembered and disemboweled human corpse beneath the gory pile of bloody entrails steaming in the cold evening air. It must have been a recent kill, a fresh one. And from all indications, it seemed to be a young victim as well, perhaps a male in his early twenties; the naked chest was flat and almost hairless.

Jones suddenly realized the reason he had been able to make it this close to the beast was because the mutated thing was likely so preoccupied with its meal it had quite probably let its guard down somewhat. Despite what he had been told, it appeared these creatures could be distracted, if only for a short time. Otherwise, he was certain the horrid thing would have sensed his approach. That's just how these creatures were; they seldom missed such things. Perhaps this time he had just gotten lucky.

The beast, this horrible deformed freak of nature was huge, even sitting in its squatted position. Its large block-like head covered in long, greasy matted hair, sat practically down on top of its shoulders; its massive, muscular neck barely discernable. The thing had a protruding fur-covered Neanderthal brow under which two beady black eyes darted constantly back and forth, scanning the area and always alert for potential trouble.

Those predatory animal-like eyes were sunken deep in their dark-rimmed sockets, which were bordered by high, strong ruddy cheekbones. Its nose was a huge flat thing reminiscent of a boxer's nose and had large flaring nostrils, which seemed to be constantly sniffing the air. A matted mass of facial hair surrounded its blood-covered dried and cracked lips. It did little to hide the creature's hideous mouthful of shark-like teeth. These fangs were perfect tools for ripping and tearing living flesh. Jones realized the stories he had heard about these mutations didn't do justice in describing just how utterly horrifying the beasts were.

Just then, the creature opened its huge tooth-filled maw and let go with a sickening liquid-sounding belch of pure pleasure, which echoed throughout the clearing. Even at a distance of more than ten feet, Jones could smell the vile combination of foul animal breath, stomach contents and rancid stink of blood drifting toward him. For a moment, he worried that he might not be able to hold back the impulse he suddenly felt, as his stomach did flip flops putting him on the verge of vomiting. But he closed his eyes, gritted his teeth and willed his insides to remain steady because he knew the sounds of his retching would surely give his position away. Luckily, once the vile stench had passed by him, Jones took a few shallow silent breaths, and he was again miraculously able to regain his control.

Jones decided he had better get down to business and do it quickly. He bent down on one knee, took careful aim with his high-powered rifle getting the center of the mutant's massive block-like head directly in his sights. He knew the importance of this first shot; the kill shot. It had to be right on. Because if it wasn't an instant kill, the thing might have enough life remaining in it to rip him to shreds before it finally did get around to dying. He had heard stories of such things happening to other would-be hunters perhaps less skilled than he was. At least he hoped that was the case. He let out his breath silently.

As Jones began to apply pressure cautiously to the trigger, he heard a noise in the distance. The giant mutated creature apparently heard the sound as well because its huge head snapped surprisingly fast in the direction of the far side of the clearing. What Jones had heard was a deep guttural growl coming from somewhere out in the darkness. It was the sound he knew very well of course, the sounds those other creatures made, the undead ones.

And if Jones was right about what he suspected was coming, he knew it would be best for him to wait for a few minutes and see how things played out. Then just as this realization hit him, Jones saw two of the wretched living dead creatures lumbering clumsily out of the woods into the clearing, arms outstretched; grunting, growling and moaning. They were heading straight toward the mutant creature and unknowingly to their own destruction. It appeared the virus's ability to reanimate these corpses did little to bring back that part of being human which told them when they were about to do something really stupid or fatal, which these two most certainly were about to do.

Recognizing the approaching threat, the huge creature rose up from its crouched position. effortlessly using the strength of its two massive muscular legs, which looked to Jones to be as big around as two tree trunks. Now the creature stood to its full height of close to eight feet of pure rippling leathery muscle. Jones ducked down in the underbrush not wanting either the mutant or the two undead devils to see him.

The mindless zombies paid no heed to the gargantuan-sized creature and continued shambling toward it. Then Jones realized they were not interested in the beast at all but in the same fresh pile of steaming flesh the creature was eating. Jones had heard rumors that sometimes these mutated mountains of muscle could walk freely among the undead without fear of attack. He believed it might possibly have something to do with the scent the huge creatures gave off; some built-in aroma, which fooled the zombies into believing they and the mutants were the same. This scent, if it did exist, apparently must be only active while the giants were alive. In fact, on more than one occasion Jones had heard stories about clusters of the undead feasting on the corpses of these freakish monsters. That was how he had developed his theory in the first place.

Nevertheless, two things immediately became very clear to Death Bringer Jones. The first was that the two zombies wanted to claim the pile of human remains for themselves. The second was that there was no way the massive beast was going to allow them to have it. Jones braced himself for the imminent confrontation which he knew was about to take place.

As the first zombie approached the steaming flesh pile and bent to feast, the giant reached out one of its enormous clawed hands grabbing onto the top of the unsuspecting undead creature's head. The mutant squeezed tightly, and Jones could hear crunching as the zombie's skull collapsed in on itself, sending shards of bone fragments deep into the undead thing's moldering decomposing brain. The corpse dropped to the ground in a heap, its head now nothing more than squashed pulp like that of an orange trampled under the foot of an elephant.

The second creature showed absolutely no sign of even noticing the destruction of its counterpart. Jones thought, "These things really were driven by an insatiable need to eat." So without hesitation, it too reached for the tasty morsels of blood dripping intestines. The massive beast raised one of its muscular arms with its talon-like claws extended. With one incredible swipe, the creature separated the zombie's head from its shoulders and sent it flying over top of Jones's hiding place where it smashed against the side of a large tree. Jutting out from the tree, were a series of sharp, broken branches. One of those remnants pierced the back of the decapitated skull and shot out through the head's left eye socket. At the very tip of the pointy branch, which was slick with rotting gray matter, a single filmed eye dangled from slimy filaments. As Death Bringer Jones looked up at the horrific sight, a single drop of bloody vitreous fluid dripped down from the suspended eyeball and landed right in the middle of his forehead. Once again, Jones was sure he was going to vomit but from behind him, he heard the second zombie drop with a thud to the soft forest floor, reminding him of his own predicament and forcing him once again to remain in control.

The behemoth dropped back to its squatting position and continued to dine on its feast, as if the minor interruption had never occurred. For a few tremulous minutes, Jones's hands shook not only from what he had just witnessed but also from his effort to remain quiet and his desperate attempt not to puke his guts out. Although he had often imagined taking down one of these heretofore-mythical creatures for some time, now that he had seen exactly what they were capable of, he worried he might not actually have what it took to kill one of these monsters.

Then he gave himself a mental pep talk, "You are Death Bringer Jones. You are the one and the only. You are legendary. You are a man without fear. You are killer of the undead, soon to be slayer of mutants and bringer of death to all creatures who dare to threaten him." After a few minutes of hiding and listening to the mutant slurping up the remainder of its kill while trying to build us his own confidence, Jones believed he was finally ready to do what he had come here to do. He once again took his position, aimed his rifle right between the beast's eyes then holding his breath he squeezed the trigger, and the gun sounded with a deafening roar.

The thing's skull exploded out in all directions in a shower of brains, bone and gore, annihilating most is the creature's head leaving only the lower half of its jaw and a fragment of its chin. As Jones stared at the sight in amazement, the dead thing's jaw seemed to momentarily move side to side just before the horrible headless corpse slowly tipped forward, falling into the bloody remains of its victims.

The sight was more than he could take. Jones took one last look around the clearing to make sure he was alone and then bent over with his hands on his trembling knees and began vomiting with more force than he would have believed possible. After a few moments which felt like a lifetime to Jones, his spasms subsided and he was once again able to stand up straight. Thank God that was over, he thought.

Then he stood tall and took a deep, much needed breath. He had done it! He had slayed one of the biggest and deadliest of the mutant breed. He lifted his arms high, gun in hand in a celebratory gesture. He was the one, the only Death Bringer Jones. But before he had time to truly appreciate his victory he felt a sharp stabbing pain in his lower back which shot right through to his stomach. He instinctively looked down and saw a huge clawed hand exploding out from his body with his intestines entangled in its hairy leathery fingers.

Death Bringer Jones had celebrated too soon. Death Bringer Jones had let his guard down. Death Bringer Jones had forgotten that he had not known everything about his prey. Death Bringer Jones had not considered that the creature he killed might have a mate or that this mate would be the bringer of his own death in this dark and lonely woods on this cold, cold night.

CHAPTER 13

Delbert awoke screaming at the top of his lungs. It had happened again, that damnable dream. This was beginning to get ridiculous. Why in the hell was he having the same dream over and over every night? A dream about something he had never done. It almost seemed like a premonition. Maybe because the dream was about something he was seriously considering. He really was still thinking about doing it wasn't he? Yes, he supposed he was but maybe the horrible dream was an omen, a way for his subconscious to tell him to leave well enough alone. The past was gone. Why was he insisting on trying to resurrect it?

For a time in his dream, he had once again been the Death Bringer and just when things were at their pinnacle, everything suddenly went wrong. It always did in this horrible nightmare. And the sad fact was it was not just in his dreams where things didn't work out for him, but unfortunately in his miserable life as well.

Once again, he was back to being simple old Delbert Bertram Jones; a nobody, just one more survivor in a post-apocalyptic world trying to get by. Before the Z43 plague struck, he had been a nothing and for a while, he had a gotten a good taste of what it was like to be someone special. Now all of that was gone.

In the before time, as many people called it, Delbert had been a customer service associate for one of the many big box department stores which existed back in those days. His job was painfully dull and often frustrating. Delbert often said that all anyone needed to be considered part of the general public was a pulse; no brains, just a pulse. He swore many of his most aggravating customers fit that description perfectly. He also often joked about how the undead zombies walking the planet had better functioning brains than many of his former customers.

Delbert had worked the graveyard shift at his store, which was open twenty-four-seven. Those few people who did come in to disturb his relatively quiet evenings were usually people of the night; folks Delbert thought of as the freakiest of the freaky. But on quieter nights Delbert spent most of his time sitting at the customer service desk reading his sword and sorcery comics and graphic novels while imagining himself as some larger than life blade-brandishing hero. This was despite the fact that he was about five feet ten inches tall and weighed only about one hundred and thirty pounds soaking wet. Having virtually no upper body muscle didn't help matters either. He had tried lifting weights and eating fattening foods in a feeble attempt to build body mass but no matter what he tried, he remained slight and thin.

Then without warning, in 2043 the so-named Z43 virus hit, the long-prophesied zombie apocalypse had arrived, and to his utter amazement Delbert not only survived but somehow he had managed to flourish in the new world of undead monsters as a zombie slayer. These undead creatures were fortunately incredibly slow, hopelessly clumsy, and Delbert quickly learned that you didn't need super strength to defeat them; you just had to be fast and a little bit skillful. He soon discovered he had a natural talent for and was quite good at killing the living dead, not only with pistols and rifles, but with swords, knives and virtually anything he could get his hands on. Apparently all the time he spent as a young boy playing video games benefited him as well in terms of skill and eye-hand coordination.

When the government implemented the DK5479-38 proclamation, unofficially known as Dead Kill, and placed a $100 bounty on the head of every wandering zombie, Delbert believed he had found his true calling. Within a few short years, he had managed to earn a great deal of money eradicating the wretched creatures. In the process, he managed to mature physically and build the muscles and body mass he had been striving for and lacking for so long. It was as if he had evolved into someone at least slightly similar to the very sword swinging super heroes he had read and fantasized about.

Delbert decided to play the role for all it was worth and as such dropped his first and second name Delbert

Bertram and for a while, he simply went by D. B. Jones. But that too only lasted for a short time. One day, someone from the Dead Kill retrieval squad who had been seeing D. B.'s identifying bar code more often than most others asked him what the D. B. stood for. He didn't want to say Delbert Bertram because in his mind it sounded completely lame. In addition, he was no longer the same man he had been. Then after only a brief moment of hesitation D. B. recalled the nickname given to him by a young woman he had rescued from a would-be rapist back on the first night of the plague and he stammered, "Um . . . Death . . . Death Bringer. Yeah . . . that's me . . . I'm Death Bringer Jones."

From that day on Delbert Bertram Jones was gone and Death Bringer Jones was born, or perhaps reborn would be a better description. Of course, with a new moniker like Death Bringer and a history of hundreds if not thousands of Dead Kills, it didn't take long for his reputation to grow. Truth be told; he did a lot of self-promotion as well. He had even devised a sort of Death Bringer costume. He wore a pair of black leather pants, snakeskin pointy-toed boots a dark black silk shirt under a black leather vest. He had all sorts of hiding places in his outfit for knives, guns, bullets and anything, which would help him take down the undead.

For a while he even wore a bandoleer of bullets, which crisscrossed his chest. Then he realized the danger of wearing his ammunition where it might accidently be struck and explode. As a result, he traded in the bandoleer for a black leather and Kevlar vest.

He even added a leather cowboy-style hat with a brown hatband and a silver buckle of a grinning skull with ruby eyes positioned directly front and center. His belt had a similar style buckle, and he had hand tooled the name Death Bringer on both sides of the belt for all to see and to know him well. Soon the children from many of the local protected towns began to think of him as a mysterious hero. His reputation grew to the point of being the stuff of legend.

A group of local artists and writers involved with a fledgling publishing business decided to take advantage of the local children's tales of Jones' exploits and created a pulp graphic comic magazine series called "The Tales of Death Bringer Jones." In it Jones was portrayed as a larger-than-life character with bulging muscles much greater than any he could have ever imagined. The cartoon character slaughtered zombies with much greater ease and in greater numbers than the real-life Jones ever did. He had finally become the legendary persona he had always dreamed of becoming. That is to say at least for a time.

After a few years as the number of undead began to dwindle, first to a controllable population, and then to a point where they barely even mattered, Death Bringer and other zombie hunters like him began to fade into obscurity. It had been a good run while it lasted but all too soon, it was over. Delbert didn't know which he missed more, the income from his many Dead Kills or the hero worship of the children of the towns he helped to rid of the damnable pests.

For a while, he took a job working as a spotter and hunter for the Fortified City of Reading as part of their Systematic Expansion (SE) Squad. That was a steady job with a half-decent salary, but the money was not nearly as lucrative as what he had earned back during the early days of the plague. He had spent most of those earnings many years earlier. And Jones learned the risks associated with a spotter's job were much greater thanks to the wild and savage outlanders who thought nothing of attacking and murdering the SE road crews.

The Systematic Expansion process was a multi-phase system. The first phase was to put together a crew comprised of dozens of road workers, highway equipment, supplies as well as a small army of well-armed well-trained spotters such as Delbert. The road workers would begin resurfacing the roadway for several miles beyond the city limits under the watchful eyes and weapons of the spotters.

Once the road had been successfully extended out perhaps two miles, the workers would back up about one hundred feet and build a temporary entrance and security gate. Then they would begin to spread out in both directions perpendicular to the road installing tall barbed-wire topped temporary fencing along the way. They would built out perhaps a mile on each side of the highway then work their way back toward the city until they connected with the main city defensive walls. This would in essence provide a two-mile wide by two-mile deep area of captured wild lands known as a buffer zone, because it would no longer be considered part of the outlands but yet it was still not officially part of the city.

Despite the fencing, the authorities could not designate these buffer zones as safe areas until Delbert and his scouts had properly cleared them. Even though many of the undead and wild outlanders usually were dealt with during the road and fence construction phase, the area was still deemed unsafe until all of the locals; both undead and living had been accounted for and properly dispatched. Then the land could be considered cleared of danger and could become incorporated into the main community.

Once that had been accomplished, the main gate to the city would be moved out to the far end of the former buffer zone, allowing for the next level of expansion to begin. This activity took place simultaneously at various roads leading into the cities in every direction. Eventually the many cleared buffer zones would intersect, merge and the newly located outer fortified barriers of the city would be properly reinforced. The result was a two mile expansion of the city in every direction. This was often a slow, time-consuming and extremely dangerous process. It could take as long as a year or more to create a complete ring of expansion around a large city and then another year to properly develop it. As harsh as it may sound the expansion was designed to slowly take back the world from both the undead as well as the savage outlanders, while systematically eradicating both in the process.

Delbert soon learned this was much more hazardous work than he had anticipated. Because he not only had to be alert for clusters of roaming zombies, but he often found himself in life and death skirmishes with bands of savage dwellers of the outlands who were violently opposed to the civilized world's attempts to encroach on what they saw as their own free territory.

He had little problem when it came to taking out the slow moving, awkward undead, but the truth was when it came to fighting against an opponent who would not hesitate to actually shoot back, he was much less of a Death Bringer and more of a Delbert Bertram. In other words he was a yellow-bellied coward. Very quickly, Delbert learned that there was often much bloodshed involved with what at one time would have been considered the simple task of road resurfacing. For the first few days on the job things had been fairly smooth sailing but when the road crew was attacked by a gang of motorcycle driving bandits with semi-automatic weapons both the spotters and the renegades suffered major losses.

CHAPTER 14

Delbert knew he had only survived that savage attack by pure luck. He and his fellow scouts were watching the woods around them in all directions when he heard the loud crack of rifle fire. He pulled his own rifle up to his shoulder and began to scour the area when it appeared the sound came from but could see nothing. He ventured a glance at the truck next to him where his partner, a man named Tom had been watching, hoping to see if he knew where the shot had come from. But to Delbert's shock and disgust he saw his friend slumped backward over the metal railing surrounding his watch station.

Tom's right arm hung down over the side of the rail and his body hung limp. Looking more carefully, Delbert could see that the force of the bullet had completely blown off the entire top of Tom's skull, and he was most definitely dead. A second later, a barrage of dozens of bullets began to shower down on the convoy of resurfacing trucks killing scouts and workers as well. As luck would have it, Delbert stepped sideways and tripped over a slight step at the base of his lookout cage and fell backwards falling ten feet to the ground. Fortunately, he fell to the side of the road where there was a soft berm of dirt leading to a deep wooded culvert. Unconscious, his body rolled down the hill and came to rest under a clump of bushes.

He would later learn when he awoke in the hospital that a gang of renegade bikers had slaughtered most of his crew. Those few survivors, who were all suffering with severe wounds, said it was the most savage slaughter they had ever seen perpetrated by living human beings. Others claimed that some of the gang of outlanders didn't even look human; that they were now something else; something that was something other than human. Authorities didn't take the claims seriously, blaming it on the stress of the ordeal or simply that the outlanders were wearing disguises to make them seem more frightening.

Delbert had been the only one who wasn't severely injured. He had a concussion from the fall but his body had been safely hidden in the brush until he awoke much later in a daze; something he would never be able to recall. Somehow, he had managed to crawl far enough up the incline in his stupor for the rescue militia to find him and haul him to safety.

The day he got out of the hospital Delbert packed his bags and headed immediately back to his home town of Ashton, now known as the Ashton Cooperative. Once home he took a job working as a member of the Dead Kill retrieval squad. It was a low-paying disgusting and demeaning job, but it was a job and was a hell of a lot safer that his previous position. His job was loading the rotting corpses of the various Dead Kills scattered around Schuylkill County into trucks and hauling them to the county morgue for possible future identification.

More often than not Delbert found himself on the verge of vomiting several times a day from the vile stench. No matter what, at least these Dead Kills didn't fight back. Occasionally he might find one that wasn't quite as dead as its slayer thought it was, but all it took was a quick stab in the ear with his Bowie knife and it was business as usual.

Delbert sighed every time when he wondered if this was going to be the state of his life from now on. He was back to being just plain old Delbert. Was he now to be condemned to spending the rest of his life scooping up rotting carcasses from the side of the road? Would he never again be able to wear the black leather suit and hat of Death Bringer Jones? Was he never again going to be able to watch the sun reflecting on his gleaming skull belt buckle? Would he never get to be Death Bringer Jones again? Was he doomed to sit alone at night reading his tattered copies of Death Bringer Jones comics, which he kept hidden in a box in his three-room apartment?

Delbert knew somehow, there had to be some way for him to return to the glory days he had once experienced as the Death Bringer. He recalled how a year or so earlier, before he had taken the job on the retrieval squad, Delbert had begun to hear rumors from people he knew who did business in the outlands. The rumors had insisted that in some obscure places in the outlands the virus had mutated. He had heard that in some extreme cases somehow the virus was activating before the time of death. The result of this mutation was a series of subhuman creatures; not exactly alive but neither were they undead. They were something else, something unique. Perhaps these creatures were actually a brand new species. He had read the official account of his own ambush given by eyewitness survivors. These witnesses swore the attackers were not human, nor were they zombies. But they appeared to be some horribly mutated form of savage creatures.

The government continuously denied these rumored mutations, especially the ones regarding mindless muscle-bound giants who could be controlled and made to do the bidding of their masters. And since the government refused to even acknowledge their existence, there had as of yet been no laws written to protect these so-called mythical creatures from being hunted. It was like the creature "Bigfoot" from the twentieth century. No one could prove whether these mutants actually existed or not. As such, no one had determined that if they did exist were they to be considered human, zombie or something else? Since nobody had categorized them, in Delbert's mind, that made them fair game.

He constantly fantasized about what it might be like to hunt down and kill one of these mythical creatures. He saw it as a way for him to regain his rightful place as the legendary bringer of death. If he could bag just one of the creatures, he could prove their existence to the world. If he could bring it back to parade in front of the media, he could also once again rebuild his reputation and become the same Death Bringer Jones children once told of in their stories, songs and comic books.

When he had returned to the Ashton Cooperative, Delbert read some stories in the local newspaper about a reporter, named Jackson Ridge who had been taken prisoner and crucified by an insane outlander psycho named Deimos. He recognized the name Jackson Ridge as being someone who had been a few years ahead of him in high school. In his stories, Ridge mentioned bagging a Dead Kill on his way to the Yuengsville office of *The Schuylkill Daily News*. The way he described the creature sounded to Delbert as if it might have been a mutant of sorts, perhaps in the early stages of mutation. It was very large, almost seven feet tall. But according to Ridge's story, that one had been dead and was most definitely a zombie when Ridge had brought it down. Still it did seem like it might have been one of the strange mutations as well.

Also in Ridge's story, he mentioned that the madman Deimos had a huge, silent body guard which also seemed to fit the description of one of the giant mutants. Ridge had said Deimos called the creature Odo. And this would have been a living mutant, not an undead creature. But the whole mutation thing had been discredited by government officials and played down to be nothing more than an exceptionally large thug who obviously worked for Deimos. Delbert had no idea why the government was so vehemently denying the existence of these creatures when he was certain they existed.

He decided, sometime he would have to pay a visit to Jackson Ridge and find out for himself what Ridge thought these creatures might really be. If they actually did exist, and if he could find a way to kill one of them without getting himself killed in the process, then he could restore his Death Bringer Jones persona once again. But from what he had heard, these creatures were not slow, clumsy and spastic like the zombies were. They were huge, muscle bound, with sharp teeth and claws and could be as savage as a wild animal. But he also heard they didn't carry guns. It was something to do with not having the brain capacity needed for the dexterity to work most mechanical devices. However, since he carried a gun, that particular fact gave him the advantage. The coward in Delbert screamed for him to forget the entire idea, but the part of him that needed the recognition and glory he felt being the Death Bringer once again told him he had no choice but to bag one of these mutated creatures.

CHAPTER 15

The two women sat across the table from each other in the Ridge family kitchen. The table was covered with a modest selection of lunchmeats, cheeses and snacks. Andrea Ridge's lunch guest was her old friend and former colleague Jyleen Wilson, who was busy talking animatedly.

"I'm so glad we were able to get together like this, Andrea. I know it's only been a few months but man, it feels like I haven't seen you in years."

"You're right, Jy. It's been way too long. How in the world did you ever manage to escape work long enough for us to meet for lunch? I know how busy you must be."

"I am for sure, especially since you left. But you know, once in a while you just gotta say 'no more' and take a little bit of personal time, you know what I'm saying?"

"Yes, I do. I'm so glad to hear you say that, Jy. And I was really glad I got to meet with you for lunch. As they say, you can only burn the candle at both ends for so long. This is especially true in our . . . I mean . . . in your line of work. An occasional chance to get away from it all is really exactly what the doctor ordered. You know what I mean, a chance to leave it all behind and recharge you batteries."

Jyleen looked at here for a second then asked candidly, "Do you ever miss it? Nursing? Do you ever wish you were still in the game?" Jyleen was known for being direct, often blunt and brutally honest. She never concerned herself with whether or not the question she was asking or the opinion she was giving was uncomfortable to the person with whom she spoke. Andrea liked that about Jyleen. She always felt she could be equally as honest with her.

Andrea thought about that question for a moment then said, "I suppose I do miss being a nurse, and I know I really miss my coworkers. But the hospice stuff and that damned zombie killing cranial device aspect of the job is something I can honestly do without. That's not why I went into nursing. Back before the outbreak, I wanted to be a nurse to help people, living, breathing sick people. I never imagined a career dominated by sessions where I had to shoot metal rods and poison into the brains of recently undead corpses."

Jyleen agreed, "Yeah, I do know exactly what you mean."

"Look, I'm sorry, Jy," Andrea apologized, even though she knew she didn't need to apologize where Jyleen was concerned. "I didn't mean to sound so negative. It's just that sometimes the hospice job made me feel so . . . so . . . frustrated . . . it was like everything I was doing was so damned futile."

Jyleen thought about what Andrea had said and replied with visible resignation, "Yeah, I guess you're right. Sometimes it does seem like that, kinda like spitting into the wind, you know? But I have a different approach. The way I look at it is like this. I figure people like us, hospice nurses, are part of the front line in a never-ending war."

"The front line?" Andrea asked.

"Yeah, the front line. And like in a war, we're part of that thin line that, you know . . . tries to hold back these horrible creatures from getting out into civilization. Us, the cops, even those regular people who get their share of Dead Kills. We do what we have to in order to keep the dead ones dead. Every patient that's destroyed by that ugly-ass helmet we carry around with us is one less dead head that might otherwise be walking the streets. Just like when a cop puts one of them down or the government pays people a hundred bucks for every Dead Kill they turn in."

Andrea recalled Jackson's episode with the Kinkaids next door just a few days earlier and only a few dozen feet away. As she spoke, Andrea stared absently out the kitchen window, "Yeah, Jy. I suppose you're right. I never really thought of the job that way. I guess I always felt like instead of helping people, I was just executing zombies. But when I think about what you said . . . about what might happen if we weren't there at their death bed . . . to . . . to finalize things . . ."

"Whenever we aren't there," Jyleen explained, "what usually happens is the old folks die anyway. But they come back with no one to stop them and more often than not they end up taking out their own families. And depending on how things turn out, instead of one old zombie geezer, we end up with a whole new bunch of 'em."

Andrea looked out her kitchen window again thinking again about Mr. and Mrs. Kinkaid and said, "I suppose I was always so busy looking at the negative side of what we did and how it wasn't my idea of nursing that I never took the time to see the good service we provided. Or for that matter, the potential for disaster that came with us not being there to do our jobs."

"Like the man says, 'it's a dirty job, but somebody has to do it.'"

"Well then . . . who knows? Maybe once all the hoopla surrounding Jackson dies down and he doesn't need me as a manager . . . maybe I'll consider going back into hospice work again, but this time I'd do so with a whole new attitude."

Jyleen smiled and said, "We'd love to have you back and I for one would definitely welcome the help."

"Thanks, Jy." Then she asked with a gleam in her eye, "So, Jy . . . I know you're very busy, but have you managed to . . . you know . . . find time to date at all? I know it's really none of my business but what the hell, I'll ask anyway. Are you seeing anyone special?"

Jyleen hesitated, taking on a coy expression then said, "Well . . . maybe . . . sort of . . . I mean . . . when we can find the time . . . I suppose I am sort of seeing someone."

"Sort of seeing someone? I've never heard that one before. How do you sort of see someone?"

"I mean . . . we've had a few dates . . . you know . . . dinner . . . that sort of thing."

Andrea smiled, prompting Jyleen to proceed, "He must be someone special if he's managed to get you all tongue-tied at the mention of the subject."

"Well . . . he is . . . and you actually know him . . . It's Sean . . . Sean Patel."

"No way!" Andrea shouted with unabashed glee, "You and Sean? Double I?

"Double Eye?" Jyleen asked pointing at her own eye. "Is that what you call him?"

"No, not me. Jackson. And it's not Double Eye like the eye in your head but Double I like the letter I. Sean and

Jackson have been best friends forever. Sean's father was from India, and his mother's ancestors were from Ireland; hence the name Sean Patel. And Jackson always jokingly refers to him by the nickname Double I . . . for both Irish and Indian."

"Oh, wow, that's a good one," Jyleen said. "I never knew that before. And I suppose I never really gave it much of a thought. Sean Patel . . . Double I . . . yeah, I suppose it makes sense."

"So tell me all about you two. Have you been dating long? Is this a serious thing? Wow! This is all really exciting!"

Jyleen said, "Well, there's not that much to tell. It's not all that serious yet. We've only been out a few times, and although we really enjoy each other's company, we both work such long hours that it's really tough to find the time. You know what I'm saying?"

"Yeah I certainly do, Jy. If Jackson and I hadn't already been married before all of this happened, we might never have met. But I'm telling you . . . you two need to find the time to get together more often. It's too important, not only for you both but for the future of the world."

"Yeah, I've seen all the government propaganda posters and heard all of the video public service commercials about how it's our duty to marry and have a ton of kids. But it's too early in our relationship to think about that; hell, we haven't even found time to do the deed yet," Jyleen laughed sheepishly. "And, honestly, Andrea, as much as it want to, I still don't see that happening for me any time soon; not with Sean or with any man. My work schedule, it overfloweth. I think I also owe it to our country to finish school and be the best damned nurse I can possibly be."

"That's probably a good mindset to have. But you can't allow your personal life, especially your love life, to suffer too much. All work and no play . . ."

"Makes Jyleen one horny little nurse," Jyleen added as they both broke into schoolgirl-like laughter.

When she regained her composure, Andrea asked, "So other than sort of seeing Sean, what else is new in your world?"

"Sadly, not so much. When I'm not popping dead heads, my world consists of going to class, doing homework, studying and taking exams. Not much time for anything out of the ordinary. . . . Although I have to tell you . . . I've been getting interested in something I've been hearing a lot about . . . it's some interesting and weird stories concerning . . . well . . . oh, never mind . . . it's all too strange . . . and that's saying a lot considering the world we live in."

"Stories? Stories about what, Jy?" Andrea inquired. "As you said, there's not much we might consider weirder than our world has been for the past decade."

"Well . . . This sort of takes our weirdness to the next level of bizarre and then multiplies it by about ten. I feel really uncomfortable even bringing it up. I mean . . . at first glance it all seemed to make some kind of sense to me but now that I'm sitting across the table from you, it doesn't seem so cut and dried. And to be honest, I'm a bit worried about looking like a fool to you."

Andrea assured, "Don't concern yourself about that, Jy. After living through a zombie apocalypse, very little catches me by surprise anymore."

Jyleen hesitated then said, "I've . . . been hearing . . . stories, tales from different people . . . well . . . about mutations."

"Mutations?"

"Yeah, mutations. I'm sure you must have heard some of the stories and rumors."

"Well . . . yeah . . . I mean I've heard things . . . just as you have, but I always assumed they were just some folk legends. I've never seen or heard of anyone having any proof or anything."

"Um . . . that's why I'm bringing this up to you. I wanted to ask you something about your husband."

"Jackson? What about him?"

Jyleen hesitated then said, "I read the accounts of his ordeal . . . what he went through with that maniac Deimos."

"Yes." Andrea said with a look of great distress crossing her face, "We were very lucky he managed to survive."

"There were two places in his book that made me wonder . . . now hang in there with me on this for a minute . . . don't give up on me yet . . . there were a few places in his book where he mentions some very large creatures which I believe might have actually been mutants."

"Seriously, Jy? I really don't think that's what Jackson truly meant to say. Which particular instances are you referring to?" Although Andrea was certain she knew exactly which sections Jyleen meant

"Well . . . the first was that Dead Kill he wrote about shooting on the morning of his reporting to that newspaper office in Yuengsville. He described the thing as being extremely large. If I remember correctly, he said it took three shots to bring the thing down."

Andrea said, "Yes, that part of the story is accurate. But the real reason it took so many shots to bring it down was because Jackson had gotten excited, and his first two bullets missed their marks. One hit the thing in the shoulder, and the other blew off its ear. Neither of those shots could bring down any zombie, whatever size it might be. The third bullet hit its mark and took off most of the creature's head. So in reality it only took one well-placed shot to do it in. Besides the Dead Kill Jackson got that morning was just that, a Dead Kill, it wasn't any living being, mutated or otherwise. Sure it might have once been a big man during its life, but as you know the Z43 virus does not discriminate about who it infects. It infects everyone."

Jyleen suggested, "But couldn't that zombie maybe have originally been one of these mutations that had died or been killed by some other method long before Jackson encountered it as a dead head?"

Andrea thought for a moment then said, "You could be right, I suppose. But if that were true, wouldn't Sean have noticed such anomalies during the identification process and wouldn't he have been required to document that sort of thing? Did you ask him about that when you last spoke with him?"

"Actually I did talk to him about it the other day when we had a lunch date. But he wouldn't even consider my suggestion. He said he doesn't believe any of the mutant stories and he has never personally examined one in his lab. He suggested Jackson's Dead Kill was nothing more than a big undead guy and nothing special."

"Well, there you go," Andrea said, assuming the conversation had run its course.

"But what about Odo?" Jyleen asked catching Andrea off guard. "Jackson described Deimos' goon bodyguard Odo in words that suggest the guy might have actually been one of these mutants. Didn't he even refer to him as 'Deimos' mutant Odo?'"

The Jyleen reached into her purse and pulled out a copy of Jackson's book, which bore the ominous title of *The Ridge Of Death*. It was a detailed account of his ordeal. She began flipping through pages marked with bent-down corners. The book looked well worn, and Andrea was certain Jyleen had to have read it many times. She also suspected if she could check it out she'd probably find many notes scribbled in the margins as well as underlined or highlighted passages.

"Here, Andrea, let me read this section right from Jackson's book," Jyleen said, not giving Andrea a chance to respond, "'The creature was massive in size and seemed to have far too much body hair for a normal human being. It—because the term it seemed more appropriate to me—was filthy dirty and glistened with gleaming sweat and was coated with grime. Its long hair was matted and it appeared to have a face, which was almost animal-like. It had incredibly huge muscles bulging from a worn, yellowed athletic tee shirt, which was also caked with filth. In fact, the only thing about it that might make someone even consider it human was its wife-beater tee shirt and its ripped and tattered jeans. I felt as if I was looking at a huge animal dressed in the clothing of a man. The thing seemed to stare at me with absolutely no expression in its dark sunken eyes, which were set deep below an overhanging Neanderthal-like brow. The rest of its face was covered with matted, grimy facial hair and those portions of its body, which were exposed, were likewise a patchwork of hair and scars. I couldn't begin to imagine what manor of man-beast this thing was. Like many people, I had heard the rumors of mutations among the outlanders but he had never seen anything quite like this creature before. Even the giant zombie I had shot on my way to work the previous day was neither this huge nor this hideous. And now that I had seen this horrifying creature I wished I could have been spared the terrifying experience . . . .' See Andrea? He practically admits the existence of mutants."

"Look, Jy," Andrea said in a calming voice, "Jackson and I had several discussions about this when he was writing the book. When he was captured, he was under a lot of stress. He had been crucified with long metal spikes driven through his palms anchoring him to a wooden crossbeam. He was also certain both he and young Sarah Stanton would be dead very shortly. And what's worse he was weak from exhaustion and blood loss. It was more than likely he was probably hallucinating. I didn't want him to play up the whole 'Monster Odo' thing in his book, but he was well-aware of how many people were out there believe these mutation stories, and he wanted to exploit those beliefs to get more book sales. So he took a little literary license in his writing. He figured it might help sell more books, which it most certainly did. We also suspect when the movie account of the book comes out, they'll play up the whole monster thing even more than Jackson did. That sort of sensationalism is what sells. But that doesn't mean that Jackson actually bought into the whole mutant idea. As I said, he was likely hallucinating quite a bit. Did you read the part at the end about his rescue and the mysterious stranger?"

"Yeah. He mentioned seeing some unidentified stranger for a brief moment before he passed out, someone he believed had saved him."

Andrea hesitated then said, "I'm going to tell you something that wasn't in the book. But, you have to promise never to speak a word of this to anyone, especially Jackson or Sean."

"Sean? What does he have to do with this?"

"Please, Jy. I can't tell you this unless you promise," Andrea pleaded. She knew Jyleen was trustworthy, and if she agreed to keep silent she would keep her word, especially when she learned the actual story.

Jyleen's curiosity was running wild, "Ok . . . ok . . . I promise. I won't say a word to Sean, Jackson or anyone. What you tell me is just between us two."

"All right then," Andrea said steeling herself. "I believe Jackson was so close to death in those last few moments before his rescue that he most definitely was hallucinating. That's why I don't put a lot of faith in his description of Odo. I think he was so out of it he might have seen just about anything. In fact, the only reason his book spoke of a mysterious indescribable stranger was that he couldn't say what he really believed he saw . . . When Jackson got home, he would have sworn an oath on a bible that the person who had come in and saved him was Sean Patel."

"What?" Jyleen exclaimed with visible disbelief. "My Sean? Breaking into that horrible monster-filled barn like some sort of superhero and shooting that zombie police chief in the head and saving the day? My Sean? No way . . . no friggin' way! Sean's a pussycat. I mean he's a wonderful guy and something of a genius; I'll be the first to admit that, but he ain't no superhero."

Andrea said with understanding, "I agree with you, Jy. But for the longest time Jackson was certain of what he had seen. In fact, for a few months things between him and Sean were a bit strained. You see every time they met, Jackson would insist that Sean had saved him, and he would be all grateful and humbled by Sean. And Sean kept insisting Jackson was way off base, and that he was actually back at his lab in Yuengsville when Jackson was rescued. It made things a bit tense between them for a while."

"So what happened? I mean . . . how did they make things right?"

"Well, they're still working on it although they've made a lot of progress. Eventually Jackson began to realize that not everything he had believed he had seen actually occurred. He began to understand just how close to death he had come and that his mind was not what it should have been. It was very possibly playing tricks on him. There were certain things that could be proven by the bodies of Deimos, Chief Holden, and Sergeant Evans, but that was about it. None of the other things Jackson thought he had seen could be proven."

"But what about Odo? I recall from Jackson's book, after Odo was shot he fell into the pit with the zombies, but couldn't they learn anything from . . . well, from the pieces?"

"No, they couldn't. By the time the authorities arrived, there was little left of Odo but fragments. Then the cops doused the zombies in the pit with gasoline and toasted them along with whatever pieces remained."

"Damn. There might have actually been something in there. You know, some proof. But it looks like that ship has sailed. Double damn . . . I guess . . . well, I suppose I was hoping . . . ah, never mind . . . it was a stupid idea anyway."

Andrea gave her an understanding smile and said, "I think I see now. You were hoping maybe Jackson would consider in looking into this whole mutation thing. Maybe doing his own investigation? Does that sound about right?"

Now looking a bit embarrassed, Jyleen reluctantly admitted, "Yeah, I guess I was . . . I hoped with his popularity and reputation that if he found even the smallest bit of proof . . . well . . . I figured people would believe him."

"Humm. I'm flattered as I'm sure Jackson would be at your faith in his ability to sort out fact from fiction and possibly get to the bottom of all this . . . but he hasn't been involved in investigative journalism since . . . well since that last incident." She pointed at the book in Jyleen's hand.

"Yeah. I guess after what he's been through you probably aren't in any hurry for him to get back into it any time soon either . . . not that anyone could ever blame you."

"Thanks, Jy. And if I'm being perfectly honest with myself what you said is a very true statement. Both Jackson and I have been so busy living in the moment, the day-to-day dealing with his celebrity, while we were also doing our best to lead as normal a life as possible. We really haven't given any thought to the future, at least I haven't. However, now that I think about it, being an investigative journalist is what Jackson loves best. If there's such a thing as a calling, that's his for sure. I guess he and I have to sit down and talk about that some time."

"I think that's a good idea." Then she said hesitantly, "Look, Andrea . . . maybe I shouldn't have said anything . . . you know . . . about Jackson investigating . . . stuff. I mean, I don't want to do something to cause any trouble between you two. I'd feel like crap if anything like that happened because of me."

"Don't worry, Jy. After Jackson got back from the hospital, we did have one very important discussion. And although it didn't involve him never doing any more investigative-type journalism, we did agree that if at some point in time he did decide to head down that road again, he would make sure it wouldn't be so dangerous. Since then we've been so busy we've simply not had any time to talk about it again, so I guess it just slipped my mind."

Jyleen looked uncertainly at Andrea and said, "Then I guess trying to track down horrible deadly giant mutant monsters might fall under that category of very dangerous."

"Only if the rumors and stories are true," Andrea countered. "And not to offend you, but I honestly don't believe they are. Maybe I'm being naïve, considering the state of the world we live in. But I think of these rumors just like the old Big Foot, Loch Ness Monster or space alien sightings of the twentieth century, not to mention the ghost investigators of the early part of this century. In all these cases, investigators generated mountains of books and stories. And let's not forget the hundreds of movies and documentaries on all of these subjects. During all those years and all those investigations, no one had ever managed to come up with one shred of proof that any of these phenomena ever existed. Also to the best of my knowledge, not a single investigator was ever killed doing his research."

"I see," Jyleen acknowledged with some hope beginning to show on her face.

Andrea continued, "So if Jackson were to tell me he wanted to start his own investigation into these myths, I probably wouldn't have any more problem with that than if he told me he was going to investigate Santa Claus or the Easter Bunny. In fact, I'm certain it would be less dangerous than investigating the real, live, breathing criminals as he's done with stories in the past. We've seen where that has gotten him."

"So . . . do you think . . . you could maybe mention something to him about it . . . you know . . . just to see if there was any interest?"

"Sure. Why not?" Andrea agreed. Then she thought about the nightmares Jackson had been having and said, "He's spent the last several months, more than half a year living and reliving his horrible experience for the press and in his book; not to mention the screenplay for the upcoming movie. Maybe this could prove to be just what the doctor ordered; a much-needed therapeutic distraction to help take his mind off the past. I'll talk to him about it, probably today or tomorrow. His schedule has been showing signs of getting lighter lately . . . you know . . . fading public interest and all of that. I'm sure once the movie comes out it will all start up again, but that's a good six months or more away. I think he might actually be looking for something different . . . who knows?"

"Oh wow!" Jyleen exclaimed with her typical enthusiasm. "If you could just say something to him . . . that would be so great!"

"Just so you understand, Jy. Just because I suggest it doesn't mean he'll be interested."

"I understand. But either way thanks for at least agreeing to talk to him about it."

Then the two women put aside their discussions of monsters, mutants and zombies to return to much more pleasant topics while enjoying their lunch as well as each other's company.

CHAPTER 16

Nathan Brody sat in his car near the side of the road wrestling with feelings of both frustration and growing terror. His hands were tapping anxiously on his steering wheel, as he looked continuously all around him. He was alone, stuck along Route 61 about five miles into the outlands south of the Yuengsville Free Zone with a flat back left tire and no idea when help might arrive. He had a good idea of where he was based on what seemed like ancient memories. If his recollection was correct at one time, a road heading off to the right from Route 61 led to a town formerly known as Cressota. What was once that thriving town was now just a series of abandoned ruined buildings overgrown with trees and vines; just so much part of what people called the outlands. The buildings were now likely home to wild savages.

The place where his car sat stranded was once the location of a small shopping mall. However, now it looked more like a forest of weeds and gigantic trees, thick with foliage. Brody was amazed at how quickly the trees had grown so surprisingly tall after only a decade of neglect. The windows and glass skylights of the mall had long since disappeared and now the tops of trees jutted ten or twenty feet above the roof of the structure. It was hard to imagine how such a dense forest could have grown in such a relatively short time. So much so that in places there was almost no sign that civilization had ever existed. Nature had taken the world back in these outlands and no matter how hard the fortified cities tried to expand outward, it seemed like a constant and never ending battle between man and nature for the rights to the world.

Route 61 the main highway itself was not what anyone would remember as the major state route and thoroughfare it had once been. No matter how often the road crews tried to maintain it, as well as those few other remaining routes, which connect the major surviving towns and cities; they always seemed to be in dire need of repair. This especially irked Nathan, as he had been certain his tires were in good shape when he left Yuengsville that morning. That is to say at least as good as anyone else's tires. There was a small vulcanizing and tire retreading business on the north end of Yuengsville, which everyone in the Free Zone used for their automotive needs. But he had to admit that the quality and reliability of the retreads were always an uncertainty. He had only purchased the latest set of retreads a month earlier. His previous tires had not so much worn out as they had dry-rotted. He seldom needed to use his vehicle in Yuengsville. Most of the time, he either walked or he used his bicycle in the warmer weather to get around.

He did, however understand that only an idiot or someone with a death wish would venture into the outlands with his tires in anything but the best available condition. The only plausible reason for the dilemma in which he now found himself was that he must have run over something, perhaps a sharp stone or maybe a nail to cause his tire to deflate. He didn't think he had hit one of the scores of dreaded potholes, which dotted the highway like a rampant case of asphalt acne. He had done his best to avoid them, as some of the holes were so deep they would have caused even greater damage to his vehicle had he hit one.

He had already placed a call for emergency assistance on his Communications Unit but had no idea when the rescue truck would arrive to assist him. A handful of vehicles had passed by while he waited a few heading in the northbound direction and some in the southerly direction, not one of them had stopped. Of course they hadn't stopped. No one ever stopped any more. That's just the way things were. It might not have seemed morally right, but it was what it was. There were no more Good Samaritans; there simply couldn't be.

He knew the highway truck would eventually arrive, maybe within an hour if he was very lucky; perhaps two or three if he wasn't. And if he was really unlucky he might find himself surrounded by a gang of insane motorcycle-riding outlanders. But he didn't want to dwell on thoughts like that. Brody was certain had he been a city official or dignitary of some sort then someone from the city would have likely dispatched a rescue crew promptly. But he was no one special; just a regular Joe with an unimpressive job working as a junior copy editor for *The Schuylkill Daily News*, known to locals as "The Skook." He considered pulling the "member of the press" card when he called for help but depending upon who the dispatcher was and how they felt about the news media, it could very easily backfire on him, so he let the idea pass. He also considered calling the Skook and asking for help, but then he'd have to explain why he was so stupid as to travel into the outlands and have car trouble. And what would he tell them anyway?

He didn't even know what he was doing out there in the first place. He wasn't out in the wild on assignment or even on some sort of noble quest. He supposed he had simply gotten bored. He had been on his lunch break and suddenly decided he needed a little adventure in his life. Just like that, out of the blue. So he figured he would just drive a few miles south and see what might possibly be out there. He realized the idea might seem a bit strange and quite possibly dangerous, but to Brody it seemed that lately his voluntary confinement to the safety of The Yuengsville Free Zone had just started to wear him down.

This wasn't to suggest that Yuengsville was any sort of prison, because it wasn't. It was just as its name implied; a free zone. It was a place of civilization with laws and rules and the safety such a place brought with it. And it wasn't to suggest that Yuengsville was small and confining either. The free zone was in terms of square miles probably two to three times the size of the original city back in the days before the plague. After the zombie wars when the city had begun to build it boarders, many of the local adjoining towns, villages and rural areas wanted to benefit from the protective boundaries and voluntarily gave up their original borough charters to merge with and become part of the city. So whether walking, riding a bicycle or driving a car, The Yuengsville Free Zone was quite vast and anything but confining.

But Brody missed the old day, the days of his youth. He longed for a time before the plague when he could just hop in his car and drive to Reading or Allentown and stop along the highway at a variety of fast food joints and mini-marts. He was only twenty-nine, but those times seemed like a lifetime ago rather than just a decade. Brody was smart enough to realize that old memories tended to be recalled in a much more favorable light than they actually had been. But he didn't care. Brody missed those days; God how he missed those days. And some days he missed them more than others. Today had been one of those particular nostalgic days.

For the past ten years, he and his fellow survivors were essentially prisoners of the cities because of the many dangers, which surround them in the outlands. And although it was true that the cities had been expanding ever so slowly this did little to relieve the feeling of confinement he often felt. Brody had heard lately that things had gotten much better in the outlands over the past several years with the populations of the undead diminishing to a fraction of what they had once been. He had also assumed the outlanders themselves had likely succumbed to the hazards of wilderness living.

Whatever the situation, Brody knew he just needed to get away for a little while; just to take a brief trip outside of the safety of the city and get out into the country; out into the real world. Such a journey was the sort of thing he had taken for granted years earlier and now was something he craved more than he ever realized he would. He knew reporters for the newspaper often travelled in the outlands, some in search of stories, but many simply traveling from city to city. Hell, lots of people did. And most of the time they seemed to make it back safely, so why shouldn't he?

As a result, he had hopped into his car after lunch, called the newspaper office and said he was taking the afternoon off, went through the South access gate to the city, past the armed sentries and headed down the highway. Now here he was, stranded with a flat tire and no idea whether or not his life was in any danger and if so, how much.

He didn't really want to risk trying to change the tire himself. It wasn't that he lacked the skills to complete the task. It was the simple fact was he was alone in the outlands. What a decade earlier would have been a relatively simple and safe task, now could be a life-threatening risk for him to take. He unconsciously reached down to his right and laid his hand on the stock of the double-barrel shotgun, which lay in the passenger seat foot well. He had already made up his mind that if help didn't arrive within two hours he was going to take the chance and change the tire himself.

Usually the road teams that came to render assistance were comprised of a minimum of two but often three or more workers. Although it might only require one to do the actual repairs, the others would be there for protection. Often these roadside crews would find themselves under attack by bands of outlaws or hoards of the lingering undead.

Brody was not overly concerned about a few dead heads, as long as they didn't manage to surprise and overpower him. But a gang of motorcycle riding savage blood-thirsty half-crazed marauders was another story altogether. He looked into his rearview mirror for what was likely the hundredth time, hoping to see the familiar yellow flashing lights of the roadside rescue truck coming down the highway but he saw nothing. He cursed himself again for his stupidity. How could he have let himself get into such a situation? No matter how much he wanted the good old days to return, he knew in his heart they never would. The past was dead. He only hoped he wouldn't be joining the past in death today.

Out of the corner of his eye off to the right, Brody saw what he thought was a slight movement in the shadows near the dense woods, which surrounded the abandoned mall. Slowly and cautiously, turning his head in that direction and then squinting carefully he tried to make out the dark shape far in the distance. Brody could see someone or something standing in the darkness cast by the tall trees. It appeared to be very, very large. He couldn't make out what it might be, but he could see that it was standing ominously unmoving as if it were watching him as well. He didn't have the impression that the mysterious being was in any way timid or afraid of stepping out of the shadows, rather it seemed as if it was simply being cautious; eyeing up the situation before deciding how to proceed. Once again, Brody reach down, seeking the comforting touch of his gun. The huge shadowed figure remained perfectly still, watching and perhaps waiting.

"Waiting for what?" Brody wondered.

At first, he thought the shape might be a zombie, but it seemed so much bigger than any typical human he had ever seen; clearly over seven or perhaps eight feet tall. Brody could tell that much even at the distance of two hundred or more yards away. The man also wasn't hunched or shambling about the forest haphazardly like zombies tended to do; instead, it seemed to stand purposefully and deliberate, watching intently.

Brody wondered if perhaps the shadowed being might be a scout for one of the gangs of outlaw renegades. Maybe he was waiting for the others of his ilk to arrive. If so, Brody was in serious trouble. Because once the watcher determined he was alone and his car was disabled, it might only be seconds until a band of roaring motorcycles came rolling out of the forest with their riders whooping like the savages they were. A few minutes after that, if he were lucky, he'd be dead. If he were unlucky . . . well, he didn't want to think about that. He knew what happened to anyone who found themselves captured by the outlanders. Death would be much more favorable to that. He looked down at his shotgun again, but this time wondering if he might have to turn it on himself rather than fall prey to a gang of psychos.

Perhaps the man, if it was a man, was considering whether to approach Brody's car himself. As he continued to watch, Brody felt his luck might be changing for the better after all. It appeared as though the creature wasn't making any obvious moves to alert anyone or to call for backup. Brody still couldn't determine what this was all about but he was beginning to feel very uneasy with the entire situation. He didn't know if he should make the first move or wait to see what the stranger might be planning. He wondered if he were to shoot over the creature's head . . . would that be enough to scare it away? Yet something inside him told Brody to forget that idea. He looked nervously again for a brief second in his rearview mirror but still saw no sign of help on the way.

This was how he supposed things were in the outlands. Two strangers encounter each other, neither knowing if the other is a friend or an enemy. As a result, there is a standoff until either a hostile or friendly gesture is introduced. Brody assumed most of the time the encounters would be unfriendly, ending in violence and likely death. Such would be true of the pure Darwinian nature of life and death in the outlands.

Brody decided he wasn't about to wait to see what this character might be planning without being at least a bit more prepared. He picked up his shotgun and leaned the barrel against the passenger door at the base of the window. He cautiously turned the ignition key to auxiliary and began slowly lowering the passenger window to a point about half way open. If the mysterious shadow decided to make even the slightest move to approach his car Brody would lower the window the rest of the way, lean the shotgun out the opening and blow the bastard to hell. He was certain this character wasn't a dead head, and something was telling him it might not be a typical outlander either. Brody suspected the stranger might be a lone wolf of sorts. Brody knew the law, and above all else, he had the right to defend himself. He was armed and if the need arose, he most certainly would do whatever he needed to do. Still, the huge, dark, hulking shape kept its distance. Once or twice Brody thought he saw the shadow looking about cautiously as if it sensed something wrong. He would have even sworn the stranger looked as if it were sniffing the air around it for trouble; if such a thing was probable.

Then Brody heard another sound, a high-pitched whining noise reminiscent of the cry of some sort of wild bird. The huge shadowed creature heard it as well because it stepped out from the shadows and stood alert now no longer looking at Brody's car but was focused off in the distance to its left. Brody understood immediately a threat was looming, something very dangerous was approaching. His breath caught in his throat, as thankfully so did an involuntary scream. He could now see the formerly shadowed creature in all of its horrifying glory. And creature was most certainly the right word. For there was no way this creature was human.

CHAPTER 17

The thing was unbelievably huge, close to eight feet tall, with massive shoulders supporting a block-like head. It wore a tattered black jacket and equally worn black pants with no shoes. It reminded Brody of a clip from a film he had seen fifteen years earlier as a kid visiting a movie museum. The clip had been from ancient black and white move adaption of Mary Shelly's story Frankenstein featuring an actor named Boris Kardoff or Karlas or something like that if Brody remembered correctly. He couldn't recall for certain. Brody noticed the monster was no longer paying any attention to him whatsoever but was looking out in the direction from which the horrifying cry had come.

Out of the woods came something so incredibly inhuman that Brody could scarcely believe he was actually seeing what his eyes tried to convince his brain he was seeing. Like the first creature, this one was big, eight feet tall or larger with an equally massive build. It had two muscular arms and two powerful legs, but that was where the similarity between them ended. This creature's head was not like a block as the first creature's was but was huge and elongated like a great ellipse resting upon its shoulders. The top of its head was hairless and covered with a dark leather hide leading back to a greasy and matted mass of shoulder-length hair. At the front of the head were two large baseball-sized segmented eyes like those of an insect. Between those horrible eyes was a pig-like snout, and below that snout was something Brody could not have imagined in his worst nightmares. The entire lower front half of the creature's face was a mass of tentacles, which were at least three feet long and were in constant motion, twisting, turning and interlacing in a ballet of horror.

Brody thought the thing resembled a large man wearing a helmet shaped like a four-foot long squid of some sort. Like the first creature, the "squid man" as Brody thought of him, was dressed in tattered remnants of human clothing but its shirt was sleeveless and its pants were hanging in rags. The creature raised both of muscular arms, and Brody could see its hands were not human in any way but had oversized, extremely long gnarled appendages with talon-like claws. The creature leaned forward with its arms above its head, and it powerful legs anchored as if in a fighting stance.

Looking back at what he now called the Frankenstein beast, Brody noticed it too had taken on a fighting posture. Before Brody had a chance to take in everything unfolding before him, the tentacle-faced thing let out another of those horrifying Godzilla-like shrieks while the Frankenstein beast howled like a crazed animal. Within two seconds, the two creatures were barreling toward each other at full bore and just a moment later they locked in combat, each creature doing all it could to tear the other one to pieces.

The Frankenstein beast was savagely pounding on the skull of the Squid-man who had its tentacles wrapped tightly around its opponent's throat, while at the same time its talons tore off the Frankenstein creature's shirt digging deep crimson furrows in its chest. There was some sort of viscous fluid, yellow-green in color spilling from a wound in the side of the Squid creature's head. Fluids of all types, recognizable as well as unrecognizable were flying in virtually every direction. Brody stared in awe at the horrifying confrontation.

"What the hell are those creatures?" he wondered in shock. They obviously weren't human nor were they even reanimated zombies. Then the realization hit him.

"Mutants!" He thought suddenly and then almost cried out. Why hadn't he realized that immediately? He had heard stories of these creatures, yet here he was looking right at two of them and he hadn't even realized it.

"You idiot!" he thought, scolding himself, "You work for a newspaper for God's sake. Pictures! Get Pictures!" He had a chance to do what no other human had ever done before. If he could take a good picture or better yet, a video of these two creatures in combat, he would be famous; maybe even more famous than that reporter from Ashton, Jackson Ridge who had been crucified a few months earlier. Brody had seen him once in the halls at the Skook months before Ridge's ordeal, but they had never met. But if Brody could get a good shot of these two, he would be on the road to riches and fame for sure.

Brody pulled out his Communications Unit and switched it to video mode. He lifted it into position and pressed record. It recorded the action for a few seconds then wham! Suddenly he felt the car rock, and the CU dropped from his hands to the passenger side floor. He tried to reach for it, but the stock of his gun was in the way. Then he felt another loud slamming sound right behind him and the car shook once again.

Turning to look out the driver's window Brody saw two filthy palms pressed tightly against his raised window. They were gray in color and some of the flesh had sloughed off leaving bone exposed. The hands slid slowly down the glass leaving a snail trail of yellow and crimson; a combination of blood, puss and whatever other disgusting fluids, leaked from its decomposing fingers.

As the rotten hands slid further down the window, a face appeared and pressed itself tightly against the glass. It was beyond disgusting. Brody had seen these undead creatures countless times before and had even put down his share of them as well. But little could have prepared him for this up close sight of the grey-skinned walking corpse with its filmed-over eyes pressed firmly against his window. Only a quarter of an inch of safety glass stood between Brody and the blackened puss covered tongue, which the creature now dragged up along the transparent surface.

Brody could see maggots crawling beneath the surface of the creature's ashen translucent flesh. As the creature pressed its face even tighter against the glass, obviously not comprehending that it couldn't get to Brody, its nose slowly crushed inward, right before Brody's astonished eyes. Even through the glass, Brody could hear the cartilage and bone cracking, splintering into tiny shards, some of which popped out through the creature's parchment-thin flesh.

Despite his almost uncontrollable revulsion, Brody gathered enough resolve to press the button to raise the opposite passenger window, just in case there was another of the wretched dead heads stumbling about. As he did, he could see the two gigantic monsters were still locked in a fight to the death. Now no longer distracted, Brody reached for his Communications Unit on the passenger side floor but still couldn't get to it. There was a steady thumping coming from behind him as the undead creature pounded its boney fists against the window. Brody knew the thing would never be able to get to him, but the sight of its sloughing flesh sliding down the glass made his stomach want to turn over. He held back his retch knowing that such a stench was the last thing he needed in the close confines of his car.

Then Brody heard something in the distance; a siren, its bellowing howl getting closer by the minute. The rescue truck was almost there. The two strange creatures must have heard the sound as well, because the noise seemed to momentarily take their attention from their battle, as both simultaneously released each other and stumbled wounded but alive back into the forest in opposite directions. Brody looked into his rearview mirror and could see the highway rescue truck getting ever closer. As it stopped about ten feet behind him, the siren died down, but the yellow lights continued to flash.

Outside the zombie continued to pound on his window for a few seconds longer until Brody heard the sharp crack of gunfire, and the creature's head exploded into what seemed like a million pieces of bone, flesh and gore. It dropped to the ground in a heap as a man from the rescue squad approached. Brody opened his door and carefully stepped over the remains of the downed creature. He stood on wobbly legs facing whom he assumed to be the leader of the road crew.

The man was dressed in a black uniform with a Kevlar vest and held an automatic weapon in his right hand. The left sleeve of the man's uniform bore the insignia of the HSRS the Highway Security and Rescue Squad and on his shoulders were the epaulets which told Brody he must be an officer of some sort. He was tall and obviously fit as were the two other crew members who stepped out of the vehicle next, weapons raised, both scanning the area for potential trouble.

"Mr. Nathan Brody?" the officer inquired. "I'm Sergeant James Scott, commander of this rescue unit. We received a call that you had a flat tire which was in need of repair." As the sergeant spoke a fourth man dressed in service technician coveralls exited the vehicle and began examining the car to see which tire was flat.

"Ye . . . yes . . . I . . . I'm Nathan Brody," he stammered. "Thank God you're here. I might have been killed."

The group leader looked at Brody with confusion, "Sir, I seriously doubt that. This creature was just one lone dead head which I'm quite certain couldn't have gotten into to your automobile. Also you seem to be armed sufficiently to handle it anyway." One of the other officers was dragging the corpse over to the side of the road by its feet.

"Can he pop open the trunk so I can get to the spare?" the serviceman called from behind the car.

"Um . . . ah . . . sure," Brody said as he turned and leaned into the car being careful not to get any of the bloody fragments of the dead creature on his clothing.

Then he said to Sergeant Scott, "You don't understand. I wasn't worried about that thing . . . it was . . . the . . . the other . . . things."

"Other things?" the sergeant inquired.

"Didn't you see them?" Brody asked. "Those other two horrible monsters?"

This statement set the two officers into action. They immediately began moving in an almost choreographed manner around the car looking everywhere for any sign of additional danger.

"What two other horrible monsters, Mr. Brody? All we saw when we got here was that one walking stink pile which is now rotting by the side of the road. What are you talking about?"

"They were . . . were over there," Brody said pointing at the abandoned ruins of what once had been a shopping mall, and now was nothing but fallen brick and trees.

The sergeant looked over and said, "Nope. There's nothing there but trees and that ghost mall."

"He mighta seen an outlander," the service man suggested, looking up from where he was changing the tire, "and you know what that could mean, Sergeant."

Sergeant Scott knew exactly what that might mean. He said to his men, "Come on, boys, let's wrap this up and make it quick. Give Willie there a hand with that tire. If Mr. Brody saw one outlander, there's bound to be others; there often are. And although we can handle ourselves in most situations, we're not geared up to go to war. So let's get this vehicle drivable ASAP. And, Mr. Brody, I'm not sure where you were heading this afternoon, but if I were you I'd turn this heap around and follow us right back to the Yuengsville Free Zone."

"Ye . . . yes . . . I have to agree. That's probably the right idea," Brody agreed. He had originally been planning to tell the sergeant about the strange mutated monsters he had seen but thought better of it. He wanted to get back home and check out the video on his CU before he started making any unsubstantiated claims. Besides, today he had experienced enough excitement to last him for another decade. Suddenly, the idea of living within the safe confines of the fortified cities didn't seem so bad after all.

When the car was ready to roll and his gun was tucked safely away, Brody reached down and picked up his CU seeing that it was still recording. He turned it off and placed it on the seat next to him. He wouldn't have time to check out what, if anything, he had recorded. He had to get back to Yuengsville first, and the road crew was already turned around and heading back up the highway. Brody didn't know what he might have filmed, but he was hoping it would be the video of the decade; actual footage offering proof positive of the existence of mutants.

CHAPTER 18

"Hey, Jackson, my friend. How are you today?" the larger than life voice boomed from the overhead speaker connected to the base unit positioned on Jackson's desk in his home office. He had his CU plugged into the docking station, which was equipped not only with state-of-the-art wireless speakers for audio, but if he chose to use the CU's video chat feature, he could display the caller on his enormous wall-mounted display screen. Likewise, he could send professional studio quality video of himself to the caller if required. In addition, he had the ability to capture both audio and video with the sophisticated system. He often did this when conducting one of his interviews in order to keep copies of them for posterity. However, he had no intention of doing any of this when conversing with the individual currently on the other end of the line; that gentleman was strictly old school and liked things that way.

That was why the call was coming over a twentieth century, landline desk phone. This particular caller swore by them. After the plague had hit and all the satellites and such went by the wayside for a time, the first sign of civilization to return after electricity was restored was the old telephone land lines which although hardly used in decades still existed in many towns and cities.

"Reliable as the day is long," the man would often say. "Reliable as old Ma Bell herself."

Jackson had of course immediately recognized the caller's voice. It was the Editor-In-Chief of *The Schuylkill Daily News*, William "Big Bill" McCleary. McCleary had been responsible for giving Jackson the assignment, which had resulted in his near death by crucifixion. In deference to the editor, it wasn't his fault Jackson had ended up in such dire straits. In fact, McCleary had planned on Jackson not being in any danger whatsoever. McCleary along with the Mayor of Yuengsville had thought they had taken all necessary precautions to insure Jackson's safety.

However, besides the fact that the Mayor was unaware his chief of police was a criminal, it was Jackson's own last minute change of strategy, which caused the operation to fall apart. Nevertheless, McCleary had felt responsible for Jackson's eventual plight and as a result had continued to keep Jackson on the payroll not only during his hospital stay and throughout the months of rehabilitation, which followed, but at that very moment Jackson was still collecting a paycheck from the newspaper. This was no minor commitment from the always-frugal McCleary of whom it was said, "could squeeze the crap out of a buffalo nickel."

In addition, it was not that McCleary was out to win a humanitarian of the year award or that he was doing this completely out of the goodness of his heart. In exchange for the steady income, Jackson had agreed to let McCleary's paper have first world exclusive rights to his story. During the weeks after Jackson's release from the Reading Hospital, McCleary had sent a reporter from *The Schuylkill Daily News* named Emmett Glenn to spend several days a week working up articles for the newspaper. They had started out co-writing articles just for the Skook, but soon their pieces also found their way onto the various wire services as well. This initial writing work only lasted for a few weeks or so before the furor and public interest began to wane. During that time, however the newspaper's circulation grew dramatically.

Once the newspaper article portion of his responsibility was over Jackson began working with Brian Arthur from the New Times Publishing Company about seven hours a day. They were working on the book version of his story for *New Times*. Andrea had managed to negotiate a deal with McCleary involving both *The Schuylkill Daily News* and *New Times* while Jackson was still in the hospital. The book took the form of a first person narrative novel told in Jackson's own words with the hopes of providing a firsthand account complete with all the same joys, sorrows, fears and other emotions he personally experienced during his ordeal. It worked better than they had anticipated and the book became a best seller with a major motion picture based on the story in the works.

"So, Bill. What can I do today for the esteemed Editor-In-Chief of Schuylkill County's most prestigious outlet for all the news that's fit to print?"

"Not to mention your patron and employer," McCleary countered making sure Jackson remembered who was still responsible for providing him with an income, "Let's not forget who's been footing at least some of the bill for your newly acquired lavish lifestyle." Although it was true the Skook was paying Jackson a salary, he had earned a great deal more money from the other creative enterprises surrounding his story.

"Ah, yes," Jackson retorted, "I've been living the life of luxury for sure, just sitting around loafing out on my patio and listening to the wind whistling through the holes in my palms. I suppose I owe you a great big thank-you, Bill."

"Ok. Ok. You win. You know I have to back down when you pull out the crucifixion card. That's a really low-down tactic to use just to win a bantering contest; if I must say so myself."

Jackson reluctantly agreed, "I suppose that's true, Bill, but you know me; whatever it takes to get the job done. So what can I do for you today?"

"Well," McCleary said hesitating, "I heard your interview schedule has been getting a bit lighter lately, and I was wondering if you might be looking for another investigative assignment."

Jackson didn't reply.

McCleary added, "Ah. I see by your lack of an enthusiastic response that perhaps you haven't quite gotten over that last experience."

"Experience? Seriously, Bill? Experience? For God's sake! What I went through was much, much more than simply an experience! And I'm sure you know that very well."

"Ok. Ok," Bill conceded again. "Enough with the guilt trips already. Jeeze! If I had a sword, I guess you'd want me to fall on it for you. Man! My point is this; I know things are slowing down for you in the interview department and will likely stop for a while, at least until the movie is released. Then you'll probably get busy all over again. But in the meantime, I was wondering if you're starting to get a bit tired of all of the recaps of your last story and might want to investigate something new; something for me. I have a particular assignment in mind."

"What sort of assignment, Bill? I certainly hope you have no plans for anything dangerous . . . you know . . . undercover type of work. Because if you do then count me out. Because even if I agreed, Andrea would probably kill the both of us before I ever got a chance to investigate anything."

"No. No. Nothing dangerous . . . nothing like that . . . I promise. Your lovely bride has made that point perfectly clear to me more times than I care to mention during the past several months. This is strictly . . . well, let's call it a bit of research . . . you know . . . gathering information and interviewing witnesses. In fact, I'm fairly certain the whole thing will go nowhere"

"Famous last words." Jackson said sarcastically.

"Perhaps so . . . but it's something I need you to do . . . well . . . I need you to do it as a personal favor to me."

"A personal favor to you, hum? Now this is starting to get interesting. And why would you need me to do you a personal favor for which you will no doubt be eternally grateful and owe me big time? If I might ask."

McCleary hesitated for a long moment then said, "Do you recall a young man by the name of Nate Brody, a junior copy editor here at the Skook?"

"Um . . . I believe so . . . yeah . . . Nate . . . a young guy in his late twenties right? As I recall, people at the paper say he's a pretty nice guy and excellent at his job. I know of him, but I don't believe I've ever had the opportunity to meet him. What does he have to do with all of this?"

"There's something about Nathan you may not know . . . Nate is actually my nephew. He is my sister Linda's boy."

Jackson said after a pause, "Ah . . . no . . . No, Bill . . . I didn't realize that. So may I therefore assume that Nate is somehow tied to your request for a favor? If so, I still don't understand where this is going."

"You will shortly, Jackson. I sent an extremely short video file to your CU. Not to the CU you're currently using but to the other one . . . .you know . . . the very special one."

"Huh?" Jackson asked confused. It took him a moment to realize what McCleary was talking about. Then he realized McCleary was referring to the Communications Unit given to him for his last assignment. "Bill. I haven't turned that CU on in over eight months. The battery is probably as dead as a doornail."

"First of all, I seriously doubt that you or anyone else for that matter has the slightest notion what a doornail is Jackson. And second, that CU won't lose its charge for at least another decade. Remember? It's special."

"Seriously? A decade? Honestly, I had no idea."

"Well, now you do. Apparently, Holden was too busy being a crook to have properly explained every detail of the device to you . . . or else . . . perhaps you weren't exactly paying attention . . . which is more than likely."

"William, you cut me to the quick!" Jackson said, feigning hurt feelings.

The Communications Unit they were discussing was given to Jackson by the Yuengsville Police Department. In fact, it was the same Chief of Police Brent Holden, who as it turned out ended up being a criminal mastermind. And as Jackson's luck would have it, Holden had been the one charged with explaining the CU's usage to him. Obviously, Holden hadn't shown him everything he needed to know; perhaps this was on purpose considering the man's ulterior criminal motives. And despite what Bill McCleary said, Jackson was certain he had not only listened carefully to the explanation, but he could still recall every detail Holden had explained to him.

It was no typical CU by any means. As McCleary has stated, this one was very special. It could be used to track the user and know where he was at all times whether the phone was turned on or turned off. The CU had a black button located on its right side which when pushed allowed the user to capture and store audio files of whatever was going on around them. The device had a built in one petabyte drive or the equivalent of a thousand terabytes. It contained enough space to record several weeks' worth of conversations. Also, as long as the user was not more than one hundred and fifty miles from the Yuengsville police station, anything that was recorded would be simultaneously sent to the police command center where it was monitored and recorded on a second even larger drive. That data could also be sent to the crucial personnel monitoring an operation's progress in the field.

The CU came with a camera that worked for both audio and video just like a typical CU would; however, having the black button with the audio-only feature was an excellent tool for surveillance. With it, the user could record someone without their knowledge. For example, if the CU was in the user's shirt pocket or lying on a table the screen remained dark and gave no indication that any recording was taking place whatsoever.

There was also a red button located on top of the unit, which could be used to call for help. If the user pressed the red button twice in rapid succession, it would alert the command center that the user was in grave danger and in need of their immediate assistance. But if the user pressed the red button only once nothing would happen as the system was designed to take into account the potential for an accidental bump.

On the left side of the unit was a bright yellow button. If the user found himself in a situation where he needed to protect himself until appropriate help arrived, he could aim the top of the CU at the intended target and press the yellow button on the side twice. Immediately, a sharp projectile would shoot from the top of the CU delivering a 2000-volt charge into the target. This would be enough to bring down most men and render them helpless. However if the user found he needed more voltage, perhaps enough to kill a man or even destroy an undead creature, he simply had to keep holding down the yellow button, and the voltage will rapidly increase up to 50,000 volts.

Jackson had found all of those features beneficial during his previous investigation, but it was not helpful enough to prevent his capture, torture and almost death. He hadn't turned the unit on since then and had no desire to do so now. But with McCleary sending the file to that unit, Jackson seemed to have no choice.

"So why did you decide to send the file to that CU, Bill? Why not send it straight to my personal unit?"

"That's simple, Jackson. Your special CU is encrypted, and only you can access it. I wanted to make sure no one but you could see what I'm sending you. Now go ahead and turn it on; it should power up with no problem."

Jackson opened a desk drawer and reached deep inside. Near the back, under some papers he found the mysterious Communications Unit. He pulled it from the drawer and stared at it for a moment, hoping the memories from those horrible days would stay away. After taking a deep breath and releasing a loud sigh, the CU powered up and as McCleary has assured him, it sprang quickly to life.

"I want you to check it out right now. Go ahead, I'll wait."

"Ok. Just a second . . . and if I lose you, Bill, I'll call you right back." Jackson was fumbling with the unit.

"Still getting used to the new system, I see."

Jackson placed McCleary on hold, at least he hoped he did, and removed his personal CU from the docking station replacing it with the special CU. The he went to the message screen. He noticed one from McCleary's personal CU number.

"It must be something really special," Jackson wondered aloud. Prior to his ordeal of a few months earlier, Jackson rarely spoke with McCleary outside of the office. Now he was getting a message from the man's private CU, and it was being sent to a special encrypted CU. This was all very unusual. Jackson felt more like a spy than an investigative reporter. He selected the file to play on the CU and the video began to play instantly on his large monitor.

The entire file only lasted for a few seconds; three maybe four seconds at best. Then Jackson saw what looked like cloth upholstery in shadows for a few more seconds then the video went blank once again. Jackson pressed the communications button on his personal CU and got McCleary back on the line.

"Ok, Bill. I played the video, but it went buy very quickly, and I really couldn't tell what it was all about."

"Did you look at it really carefully?" McCleary asked with the sanctimonious tone of a frustrated parent.

"No, actually I didn't get a chance to. It went by so fast I wasn't sure what I was seeing."

McCleary took a deep audible breath and instructed, "Ok. Well here's what I want you to do. When we're finished talking here, I'm going to hang up and let you look at it again, several more times. I also want you to make sure the audio is turned up on your video player as well. Ok?"

"Yeah, I can do that."

"Good." McCleary said, "Then after you've done that . . . not before . . . but after . . . I want you to call me back, and then I'll send you a few choice still photos I clipped from the video. Got that?"

"Got it," Jackson said a bit miffed. McCleary was very demanding and if you didn't follow his direction to the letter he tended to go into what Jackson thought of as "daddy lecture mode," which he had just done.

"But I still don't understand why all the mystery? What am I supposed to be looking for?"

McCleary explained in that same somewhat condescending tone, "I don't want to do anything to prejudice your opinion, Jackson. I just want you to look at this without any preconceived notions. Just study it for a few minutes then call me back. Ok?"

"Ok. No problem. I'll do it right away. Talk to you soon."

"Good. And Jackson, remember . . . let's keep this between you and me for the moment, ok?"

"Sure thing," Jackson agreed as he hung up the phone and prepared to replay the short video.

CHAPTER 19

This time he watched the clip more carefully knowing that its duration was so short. It still didn't appear any clearer, but from what little he could discern there looked to be a large figure, or more likely two large figures moving far in the distance. They, if there actually were two figures, seemed to be embracing. Then the video was over and the dark gray background reappeared for a few more seconds before the video went dark.

Next, Jackson adjusted the CU's video program to make the frames move at one quarter of the original speed. This meant it would take about sixteen seconds to play the viewable portion of the video. Again, he focused his attention on the screen and pressed play. He saw the shadowed figures, and he was now certain there were definitely two of them, both of which were enormous in both height as well as build. What he originally interpreted to be an embrace now appeared to be more like the posture of two huge creatures fighting. The silhouetted figure on the left side of the screen looked very much like a giant man while the one to the right seemed to be wearing some sort of mask or helmet; Jackson couldn't tell.

After a few more replays, he was certain the two actually were fighting. There was something he felt deep inside like a primal warning, which interpreted the two shadowed figures' body language and within a split-second told him there was a violent confrontation taking place on the screen in front of him.

Then Jackson recalled something McCleary had said. He had told him to remember to play the video with the sound on. Jackson had forgotten to turn on the audio feature of the CU's video program. He was happy McCleary wasn't around to see his mistake or that would certainly have been the catalyst for another of McCleary's annoying lectures. Jackson set the video program back to its original speed and set the volume to loud since the figures were off in the distance and as such he assured any sound which might have been recorded would have been done at a less than desirable volume. Regardless, he believed with the volume adjustment the audio would come through his sophisticated speakers clearly. Then he pressed play once again.

Jackson sat staring at the screen in complete disbelief as the four-second video played again. The howls he heard coming from the speakers were unlike any he had ever heard in his life. His stomach clenched as a tremor of horror shot through his body. The impression he got was that of two wild, savage beasts engaged in a fight to the death. And even when the screen went dark, the howling and screaming continued until the video was over.

"What in the unholy hammers of hell was that?" Jackson shouted in his empty home office. He was grateful that both Andrea and Kyla weren't home. Had they heard those ungodly noises blaring from his sound system they would most certainly have come running. They would have a lot of questions for which he had no answers he cared to share.

Jackson lowered the volume on his speakers significantly and replayed the video several more times, each replay making him feel as though the mystery of the strange video was just getting more confusing by the minute. Eventually he picked up his personal CU and redialed Bill McCleary who answered on the second ring.

"So what do you think now?" McCleary asked without preamble.

"Wha . . . what the hell . . . did . . . did I just see, Bill?" Jackson stuttered. "What . . . what were . . . those . . . those noises?"

"I'm not exactly sure, Jackson. That's what I was hoping your investigation might tell me."

"My investigation? Bill . . . you must have some sort of idea what that was . . . I mean the video portion was crap . . . but the audio . . . oh my God, that audio was incredible! It gave me the willies."

"I'm going to send you two or three pictures in a moment. They're single frame shots from the video as I mentioned earlier. They're the best and clearest shots I could put together although they aren't all that great. They didn't even come close to capturing what my nephew Nathan claims to have witnessed. Not that I completely believe him."

"What is it Nathan claimed to have seen, Bill?"

"Before I get into all of that, Jackson, I want you to examine the stills I just sent you. Take your time and enlarge them as you need then call me back again."

Jackson absolutely hated this sort of cryptic back and forth nonsense. It was a signature Bill McCleary tactic, and it drove him crazy. He didn't understand why McCleary insisted on this sort of pseudo-mystery game playing to make his point. Why didn't he just come out and say whatever it was he wanted to say.

"Ok," Jackson replied once again with resignation. "I'll get back to you in a bit."

He disconnected the call and went back to the special CU's mail program. He found three photo files, which again came from McCleary's personal Communications Unit. He opened the first file and stared in amazement. The enlarged photo took up his entire fifty-inch display screen. It was a cropped section of a single frame showing two shadowed figures locked in battle. Although the image was pixelated, grainy and blurry Jackson could see enough detail to cause his breath to catch in his throat.

There were definitely two huge beings darkened by shadows but clear enough for Jackson to recognize the similarity of one of the creatures to someone he had seen before. "Odo." Jackson whispered as he stared at the screen. The silhouetted creature on the left side of the screen had a block-like head, thick lips, a large nose and protruding brow very similar to that of the now dead bodyguard of the madman Deimos. When Jackson considered the size of the creature, along with what he had just seen, he realized the creature in the photo could have been an almost carbon copy of Odo. Then another thought came into his mind, one he had not even thought about previously.

On the morning when he had traveled down to *The Schuylkill Daily News* many months earlier, he scored a Dead Kill of his own when he took down a large zombie that was attempting to cross the highway. It was very big as Jackson recalled, and now that he thought back, its head and size was also very similar to both the creature in this picture as well as to the late Odo. This made him start to wonder.

He looked at the second shadowed figure and could tell it scarcely looked human at all. Its body was like that of a very large, muscular human, but that was where any resemblance ended. He wished the picture were clearer. From what he could discern by the shape of its head, the creature looked like a giant squid of some sort, with a mane of long matted hair behind it and dozens of tentacles at its front. He wondered if this might be some sort of outlander ritualistic mask. He knew from first-hand experience that many of those living in the outlands had regressed to the point of being pagan savages. Jackson had heard that some of the really wild ones could barely hold onto enough of their humanity to still speak comprehensibly and had become almost like animals. Perhaps that was the case with these two.

Then he remembered the rumors, the stories about mutant creatures being sighted in the outlands. He had never considered these rumors to be anything but fantasy. In fact, he had even taken advantage of those fabricated legends during the writing of the book about his ordeal. In his book, Jackson had referred to Odo as being some sort of mutant. He had originally done this only to sell more books and that tactic had worked very well for him. But now that he thought about it, maybe subconsciously he was aware of something. Perhaps he somehow understood that Odo really had been the result of a mutation. Now that he gave it more thought, it that seemed too ridiculous. He was a serious investigative journalist. Surely, he couldn't consider such impossible thoughts. Then again, a decade earlier he never would have believed the dead could reanimate and consume the living.

So was that what Bill McCleary wanted him to investigate? These rumors about mutations? Could he seriously be expecting him to actually do a scientific investigation into a bunch of old wives' tales? Jackson looked again at the picture displayed on his monitor. Then he checked the next two photos which were very similar.

Perhaps this really was what McCleary wanted. He dialed McCleary once again.

"Mutants, Bill?" Jackson asked. And before McCleary had a chance to reply he insisted, "Please tell me you're not going to ask me to do a serious journalistic investigation into these ridiculous claims."

"Well . . ." McCleary started to reply but not getting a chance to finish his sentence.

"What's next Bill? Big Foot? The Lochness Monster? The Jersey Devil? The Louisiana Rougarou? Why not Ashton's Devil Dan? Seriously, Bill?"

McCleary hesitated for a beat. "Now just hold on for a minute, Jackson, and hear me out. Nathan is a very serious young man with no tendencies for over imaginative thinking. Yesterday he took a drive into the outlands south of Yuengsville for God only knows what reason. Granted it wasn't the brightest thing he has ever done, but that is neither here nor there. While traveling along the highway down near what used to be the Cressota Mall, he got a flat tire and had to pull over to the side of the road. He immediately called for a rescue unit to come to his location. While he was waiting, he noticed movement down in the thick forest which you may recall has grown up around the abandoned mall."

"Yes. I recall passing the ruins on my way to the Fortified City of Reading during that last assignment."

"As Nathan waited for the rescue squad to arrive, he noticed movement in the shadows and saw that huge creature, the one in the left of that photo watching him. Then he said a few minutes later the creature seemed to sense something coming out of the woods, and that other squid-looking creature showed up and within a few seconds they were at each other's throats."

"But why is the video so short?"

"A few seconds into the filming, Nathan dropped is CU when his car was attacked by a dead head. It startled him, and the CU fell to the floor. That's the dark background you see at the end of the video. It actually went on for quite a few more minutes like that, but I cropped the video shortly after the point where the shots of the creatures ended. The rescue squad arrived and put down the dead head, but apparently it scared off whatever it was those two things were."

"And you think they were mutants, right?" Jackson asked skeptically.

"No, Jackson. I don't think anything. In fact, I doubt they were anything more than a couple of outlanders dressed in some sort of costumes to frighten people away from their woods. That actually seems like just the sort of trick those types of maniacs might try to play."

"So why the investigation, Bill? I don't get it"

"I already told you Nathan is my sister's son, and she is pressuring me to at least have someone speak with the boy and maybe interview some of the others who claim to have seen similar things. Nathan completely believes that he has seen mutants, and so now she believes it as well."

"Ah. So this is why it's supposed to be a personal favor and why we need to keep everything between the two of us."

"Ahem . . . yes." McCleary said hesitantly clearing his throat, "My sister asked for you specifically. She said she read your accounts and believes you're the best. So if you take a few days, ask some questions and then if you determine this is all a bunch of hooie, then maybe she'll back off, and hopefully we can even put all of these rumors to bed once and for all."

Jackson took a moment then said, "And what if I discover this isn't all a bunch of hooie, Bill? What are we supposed to do if I find out that mutations really do exist, what then?"

"Then, Jackson my friend, we'll have more trouble than we could have every bargained for. We'll have stumbled onto a second major investigative piece in the same year. And you may go from being simply famous to legendary."

Jackson asked conspiratorially, "But you don't really believe for one second that any of this is really possible do you, Bill?"

"To be completely honest with you, Jackson . . . no . . . not even in the slightest," McCleary agreed. "If I honestly did think such monsters existed, I'd be turning the story over to someone else. I think I put you in enough danger for one year. Speaking of which, if by some ridiculous coincidence you start to find proof of the existence of mutants, I want you to back off and call me immediately. Asking questions of witnesses and gathering information is one thing, but putting yourself in harm's way won't do. You wife would literally skin me alive if I allowed anything to happen to you."

"Ok, Bill. I'll take this one on. But I'm going to have to say something to Andrea about it. I won't mention Nathan or your sister, I'll just tell her you asked me look into a number of reports you've gotten. I'll play the whole thing down. How does that sound?"

"Yeah. Probably a good idea. If she needs any additional assurance that the assignment isn't risky, have her call me and I'll explain everything to her."

"Sounds good, Bill. I'll get on this right away. I'll speak with Nathan as soon as he's available. I'm sure you've been getting a lot of crank reports about mutations throughout the year. If so, can you pass them on to me so I can contact those folks as well? You know . . . just to keep the investigation thorough."

"No problem, Jackson. I'll have them for you by the end of the day. Keep me posted on your progress."

"I will. Talk to you soon."

Then Jackson disconnected with McCleary for the last time that day and sat back thinking about his new assignment, the video he had just seen, about the Dead Kill he had put down so many months earlier, about the monstrous Odo and about the very distant possibility that these strange stories might actually be more than just rumors after all.

CHAPTER 20

Jackson watched the video from Nathan Brody several more times in slow motion being certain to keep the volume turned off. There was no need for him to hear those horrible animal-like screams again. Listening to them once was more than enough. He was quite certain he would never forget those spine-chilling howls for as long as he lived.

When he had taken several notes in a word processing document, which he had created specifically for this assignment, Jackson stored the document on the same special CU containing video file. He wanted to make sure neither Andrea nor Kyla accidently came across either the notes, or more specifically the video; the last thing he wanted was for them to hear those ungodly sounds.

He checked his personal CU phone directory for the number for the main desk at *The Schuylkill Daily News* and placed a call. He figured the sooner he spoke with Nathan Brody the better. It was always preferable to interview a witness as quickly as possible following the event. After a few rings the receptionist answered with a bright and cheery greeting.

"Good morning. *Schuylkill Daily News*. How may I direct your call?"

Jackson asked, "Joanie? Is that you? This is me Jackson, Jackson Ridge."

"Jackson? Oh my sweet Lord in Heaven!" she practically shouted into the phone, "It's so very wonderful to hear your voice. I've been so concerned about you. How are you getting along, my boy?"

Joan Dawson was a plump grandmotherly woman in her late fifties who had been working the reception desk at the Skook for more than thirty years. During the early stages of the plague, she had lost both her husband as well as one of her adult children. She had three other grown children with families of their own scattered throughout the country and unfortunately, she had no idea what had become of them. She had not heard from them since the start of the outbreak, and as such they were now among the countless millions of lost souls; victims of the apocalypse. She never gave up hope that they might still be alive somewhere and someday they would connect again, but that wish was most likely a false hope at best. Because she had found herself alone, Joan had made the staff at the Skook her surrogate family and had taken a particular fondness for Jackson. She often had referred to him as "my boy." Perhaps it was his brown hair and glasses or his smile, he wasn't sure, but she had told him on more than one occasion that he reminded her of her son, Charles, one of those who was still listed as missing. He didn't mind the motherly affection and because of his own personal losses; he often actually welcomed it.

"We . . . we are all doing . . . fine, Joanie. How have you been?" Jackson asked a bit taken aback. He had just suddenly realized that he had not spoken with the woman since his ordeal almost eight months earlier, and now as a result, he was feeling more than a bit guilty. He was finally calling her but only because he needed something. He was wondering how he had allowed himself to become so wrapped up in his work, his celebrity and all that they entailed to have forgotten to speak with a person who truly cared for him; not as Jackson Ridge famed investigative reporter but Jackson Ridge the person. He wondered how many other people he had unknowingly slighted during the past months. The realization didn't make him feel very good about himself.

"How am I?" the woman said with surprise. "How am I? Oh Heavens, Jackson why should anyone care about an old lady like me? You're the one who just went through that horrible experience while I've been here in the safety of my desk. I've been wondering about you for months. I read all of your stories, and I ask Bill McCleary about you almost every day."

This pronouncement from the woman only served to make Jackson feel like even more of a major jerk. Here was this sweet unselfish woman who had lost her entire family, who was alone, who cared for him and who he had basically ignored for months. And when he finally called her, because he needed her help all she could think to care about was him and his family. Could he possibly feel like more of a scumbag? He didn't think so.

"I'm so very sorry Joanie," Jackson said by way of an attempted apology. "I feel like such a jerk. You are an amazing and wonderful woman. You've always been so good to me and my family, and you deserved far more respect than I've shown you. Please accept my apology for not calling you sooner."

"Oh don't give it another thought, my boy," Joan assured him in her motherly way. "I understand completely. I know you've been so busy getting well and writing all those stories. I even heard a movie if being made of your adventure. No. There is no need to bother yourself at all. As I said, I kept tabs on your progress. Now as I said don't you give it another though:."

"Still, Joanie," Jackson said now with a bit of humor, "it would mean a lot to me to have you accept my apology for being the world's crappiest friend."

Joan conceded, "Well . . . although it's completely unnecessary, if it will make you feel better, then your apology is graciously accepted. Now that all of that nonsense if out of the way, what is it I can do for you?"

"I was wondering if you could connect me with Nathan Brody."

"Nathan Brody . . . Nathan Brody . . . isn't he that young man in copy editing?"

"Yes, that's him. Could you please connect me with him?"

"Absolutely. I'll be more than happy to, my boy." Joan agreed, "and please, you be sure to take care of yourself and give your lovely wife and your darling daughter a big hug for me, ok?"

"I will, Joanie. And I'll try to call you again soon. I promise."

"No need, my boy. You have much more important things to do. But if sometime you want to waste some of your time talking to an old lady like me, I'll be thrilled to hear from you. In fact, I would love it if you were able to stop by some time. I don't believe you've been in the office since . . . well . . . since your ordeal."

"That's true, Joanie," Jackson said. "I've only recently started driving again, and to be honest, I haven't driven alone outside of the Ashton Cooperative since I've been home either. But I suppose a trip to Yuengsville is long overdue and will be imminent sometime soon."

"That's wonderful, Jackson. Just make sure you let me know when you're coming so I can be here to see you. Maybe I'll even bake you your favorite desert."

"Not your amazing homemade chocolate fudge?" Jackson teased.

"Oh, yes. That's exactly what I'm thinking of."

"Ok. You win. I'll be sure to let you know the day before I head down. I wouldn't want to miss out on that fudge, believe me."

Joanie laughed, "That's just wonderful. I look forward to your call. I have to go now, Jackson. The other line is ringing. I'll patch you through to Nathan now."

Before Jackson had a chance to reply, he heard the familiar electronic buzz, apparently at Nathan Brody's desk. After four rings, the call went to voicemail. Jackson heard, "This is Nathan Brody, Junior Copy Editor. Sorry I missed your call. Please leave your name and number, and I'll get back to you as soon as possible."

After the beep Jackson said, "Nathan, my name is Jackson Ridge. Bill McCleary asked me to contact you regarding the . . . um . . . regarding your experience in the outlands yesterday." Then Jackson left his CU number and disconnected. He hoped he would hear back from Nathan before too long.

He checked the inbox on the special CU's email program and found another message from Bill McCleary. It contained what looked to be a large document file. Jackson opened the file and saw what appeared to be a personal letter to the editor of newspaper. He quickly scrolled down through the rest of the document and could tell that there were dozens of letters, one after the other. He realized McCleary must have been collecting these letters for quite some time and storing them in this document.

Even before he had a chance to read any of them thoroughly, his quick scan told him they all pertained to alleged sightings of mutants. There didn't appear to be any photos with them but each letter did contain the contact information including name, address and phone number for each of the authors. During the scan, Jackson did stop for a moment when he saw a rough sketch someone with obvious artistic talent had drawn. It was what caught his attention enough to make him stop. The drawing, which was very detailed, looked just like the henchman Odo. "What the hell is going on here?" he wondered to himself.

Then he was startled when he heard the front door open and the skittering sound of little feet in the hall. He quickly closed the file, and popped the special CU out of the docking station then turned off his display screen.

CHAPTER 21

"Daddy! Daddy!" Kyla said excitedly as she burst through the door to his office and jumped up on his lap, wrapping her arms tightly around his neck. "We're home, Daddy. Mommy and me went to the store and got all kinds of good stuff for supper."

"Not 'Mommy and me,' Kyla; it's 'Mommy and I'," Jackson corrected.

"No, that's not right, Daddy. You weren't there. You were here at home. It was just me and Mommy."

Jackson chuckled to himself, shook his head in resignation then asked his daughter, "So where's Mommy now, Kyla?"

"She's coming," the little girl said enthusiastically. "She wanted to put the groceries away."

Eager to get his little girl far away from his latest disturbing research project, Jackson stood then took his daughter's tiny hand in his and said, "So let's go out and give Mommy a hand with the groceries. What do you say?"

"That's a good idea, Daddy," Kyla agreed as she pulled him out of the office and down the hall toward the kitchen. When they got to the kitchen, he saw Andrea busy putting groceries into their proper places in the kitchen cabinets.

"Anything I can do to help?" Jackson asked.

"I'll put these away if you'll go out to the car and bring in the other bags from the trunk."

"Will do."

Jackson walked out the back door, along the side of the house to the front driveway glancing unconsciously over at the now vacant house next door. The horrible encounter with the elderly Kinkaids from several days earlier still bothered him. He had tried to hose down their patio several times after the cleanup squad had recovered their corpses, but he doubted that anything but time and the forces of nature would successfully make all the traces from that day disappear. He knew the stains that the incident had made on his soul might be even tougher to erase.

He assumed the house wouldn't remain empty for very long. The Ridges lived in a three story single home in a town dominated by clusters of row homes. Although not attached to any neighbor, the space between the properties was only about ten or twenty feet wide, with two narrow walkways leading from the back of the property to the front. Out in the front was a single car driveway leaving limited space for a postage-stamp front yard. At the back of the property was a single car garage accessible from an alley. The Ridges never parked their car in the garage even in the winter, and as such, it became a combination workshop storage shed and depository for virtually anything they didn't want to keep in the house. The walk on Jackson's side took him right between his house and that of the deceased Kinkaids.

Jackson hoped the next owners of the Kinkaid property would be as good neighbors as they had been. Then he had a thought which he realized was quite selfish but one he nonetheless couldn't help having. He had hoped the next couple that moved into the Kinkaids home was a younger couple. Jackson knew it was wrong to have such thoughts, but right now, the last thing he wanted to worry about was another older couple, closer to the age, which might result in his having to repeat the horror he had just gone through a few days earlier. He decided it would be best if for now the just put the thought out of his mind entirely.

Within two trips to the car and back, he had managed to bring all of the groceries and gratefully closed the back door, putting a much-needed psychological barrier between himself and that unpleasant memory. Andrea looked over at him and could tell something was a bit off with him. And knowing her husband as well as she did, she was certain she understood exactly why he was feeling a bit down.

She looked over at Kyla and said, "Honey, why don't you go into the family room and play or if you want to you can watch your favorite video? Daddy and I can take care of this."

"Ok, Mommy. Can I take the cookies in with me?" They had just purchased a box of freshly made cookies from the Ashton Bakery.

"Not all of them. I don't want you to spoil your appetite for dinner." Andrea said, "You can take two cookies in with you. I'll bring in some milk shortly. Deal?"

"How about three cookies?" Kyla said, trying to negotiate a better bargain.

"How about no cookies?" Jackson suggested with a stern look knowing Kayla would understand his meaning and would settle for the original deal.

"Ok," the little girl said, "two cookies is good."

With that, she headed into the family room. When Andrea heard the video player click on, and the familiar sound of Kyla's favorite video begin to play she turned to Jackson and said, "Are you ok? You look a little stressed."

"Yeah. Well, I guess I am . . . maybe a little," Jackson admitted. "It was just . . ."

"The Kinkaids?" Andrea asked.

Jackson hesitated, always amazed at his wife's keen insight, then said, "Yeah . . . when I went out to get the groceries, I couldn't help but look over there and . . . well I guess I started feeling bad all over again. Dammit, Andrea, they were both just such nice people . . . I mean . . . I know I only did what I had to do . . . and legally I had no choice but . . . but that doesn't make it any easier."

"I do understand."

"Of course you do . . . if anyone on this planet could understand it would be you," Jackson agreed referring to her old job in hospice nursing, "Do you ever think about . . . you know . . . about going back to nursing . . . getting back into hospice work again . . . knowing everything you know about what you have to do? I know at one time it bothered you quite a bit."

Andrea smiled and said, "I don't know, babe. Maybe someday I will, then again, maybe I won't. Right now it's hard to say."

"Did you and your friend Jyleen talk about that at all when she stopped over for lunch the other day?"

"Actually that was one of the several things we discussed," Andrea admitted. "I hadn't realized before what an astute young woman Jyleen was. When I gave her my speech about my getting into nursing to heal people and not just to kill zombies, she surprised me with her attitude toward the whole horrible mess."

"Why? What did she say?"

Andrea explained, "She said she thought of her job as being every bit as important as the police, the army and anyone else who takes the initiative to keep the dead, dead. She said hospice nurses were the last line of defense and the only thing keeping the recently dead from coming back . . . like the Kinkaids did. She said she felt she was helping living people because every dying person we prevented from coming back saved their families even more heartache."

"Wow! That's absolutely right. I hadn't thought of that either," Jackson agreed. "You're right. She is a very astute young woman. In fact, thinking of things from her perspective . . . well, what I had to do the other day . . . that whole thing could have been avoided if Mr. Kinkaid had been sick and had been a hospice patient. If Mr. Kinkaid had not died suddenly and a hospice team had been on hand to do what had to be done, Mrs. Kinkaid would still be alive and everything would have been a lot . . . well cleaner and more manageable."

Andrea agreed, "Yeah. I guess I'd never thought of it quite that way before either."

There was a silence for a few minutes as Jackson contemplated how he was going to approach the subject of his new assignment with Andrea. He wanted to make sure she knew his involvement would be strictly from an information-gathering standpoint and that there would be no danger involved whatsoever. Yet he didn't want to sound as if he was trying to over-convince her. But to his relief, Andrea said something to him first which eventually eliminated his need to bring up the subject at all.

"When Jyleen was here, she also asked me to speak to you about something."

"Me?" Jackson asked. "I've never even met Jyleen. I've only heard about her from you. What could she possibly need from me?"

Andrea looked at Jackson astonished. "You still don't get it do you?"

"Get what?"

"I mean, I know you understand that you're famous now, but I really don't think you understand what that means."

"Understand what, what means?"

"Jackson, just because you don't know someone, doesn't mean that they don't know you. In fact, they may know more about you than you realize."

"Ok. Jyleen knows about my story and all of that stuff from the newspaper and the book, and she may know a bit more because of having worked with you . . ."

"And that's doesn't even take Sean into consideration," Andrea surprisingly interjected.

Jackson looked perplexed, "Sean? Sean Patel? Double I? What does Sean have to do with any of this?"

"Jackson you have to learn to start paying more attention to stuff going on right under your nose. Sean and Jyleen . . . well, they're an item."

"An item? You mean they're dating?"

"Yep. And have been, apparently for some time. I suppose Sean hasn't bothered to mention that to you before."

Jackson thought about it for a minute then said, "No, I don't think he has. In fact, I'm sure he hasn't. I certainly would have remembered something like that. But you know I haven't really spoken with Sean in a while. Maybe it's time I give him a call."

"I think that would be an excellent idea."

"Anyway," Jackson asked, "what is it that Jyleen needs from me?"

Andrea explained, "It's not so much that she needs something from you, but she wanted to suggest something to you. An idea for something you might want to consider for a story."

Jackson wondered where this was all going. Here he was about to tell Andrea about his new assignment, and now this woman Jyleen was suggesting something else for him to investigate. He was only paying half attention when he heard Andrea say, "You know your interview schedule is slowing down for a bit. I thought you might want to consider it, you know, to keep your hand in the investigative side of writing."

"I would have thought you had your fill of my investigative work by now." Jackson said suddenly realizing what Andrea was suggesting.

"Only the dangerous stuff," Andrea corrected. "I know you love doing investigative journalism and what Jyleen is suggesting, if it can actually be considered journalism is probably not dangerous at all."

"Ok. Now you've got my attention. So what is this idea which your friend and Sean's apparent girlfriend has thought up?"

Andrea hesitated then said, "Now, Jackson, before I tell you the idea, I want you to promise to have an open mind. This isn't something you might normally consider, and you'll probably think the entire idea is ridiculous."

"Oh, boy. This sounds wonderful already," Jackson said sarcastically.

"Come on, Jackson," Andrea scolded. "Just promise me you'll give the idea some honest consideration before you go and make fun of it."

"Alright, I'll do my best. Tell me about it."

"Well." Andrea said cautiously, "While doing her hospice work over the past several months, Jyleen has had the opportunity to meet up with a great variety of people from all different walks of life, just as I did when I was a nurse. But lately she has been hearing different things; stories from the families of her patients who have traveled from city to city, passing through the outlands."

"The outlands?"

"Yes. And these people have been telling her stories about strange things they have seen in the outlands."

"What sort of things?" Jackson asked feeling certain that he knew exactly what direction this conversation was about to head.

Andrea must have seen a familiar look of condescension growing in her husband's eyes because she hesitated again then said, "Now I'm warning you in advance, Jackson; don't you dare criticize what I'm about to tell you."

"I won't. I promise." Jackson knew her looks as well and any snide comments on his part would not sit well with his wife; of that he was certain.

"Well . . . people have been telling Jyleen they have seen creatures that aren't zombies, but they aren't human either . . . they are some sort of . . . mutations."

CHAPTER 22

"Mutations?" Jackson asked doing his best to appear to have been caught off guard by the proposal. "You mean to say Jyleen wants me to start investigating reports of some sort of mythical monsters out there roaming around? In the outlands, no less . . . the very same savage outlands which were not very kind to me the last time we crossed paths. And let me get this straight . . . you think it's a good idea? Don't you think it might be a bit dangerous, that is, especially if these creatures really do exist?"

Andrea looked at Jackson not sure if he was joking or not. "Jackson, you'd better not be messing with me or you'll be sleeping on the couch tonight."

"No, babe. I promise you I'm not messing with you," he said, even though in one way, that was exactly what he was doing. "It's just that I was wondering . . . I was thinking . . . what if . . . you know?"

"What if what?"

Jackson said, "What if these reports are not all just a bunch of made up old wives' tales? What if there really is something to these stories? Do you want me to go out into the woods, in the outlands looking for proof of one of these creatures? There's plenty of danger out there that has nothing whatsoever to do with mutations. As we both know very well, there are gangs of savage maniacs and still plenty of dead heads stumbling around as well."

"No. No. No. Absolutely not!" Andrea insisted. "That's the last thing I'd want you to do. All I was thinking was if you had some time you might want to talk to these so-called witnesses and gather their stories. You wouldn't even have to leave your office here in the house. All you'd have to do is call them then listen, take notes and organize your information. You're great at that . . . it its perfectly safe. Also I was thinking you could compile the stories and put them together in book form, and we could publish it right around the time the movie of your other book comes out. It shouldn't take a ton of work, and I'll bet with these supposed eye-witness reports you could probably fill several hundred pages with very little effort on your part."

"So as far as you're concerned, this would only be about a possible quick way to publish a new book?"

"Well. No, not really. That was a secondary idea. My first goal was to give you something else to occupy your time and take your mind off of the other stuff . . . you know what I mean? I was hoping the distraction might help with . . . with your nightmares."

Jackson looked at his wife thoughtfully, "I don't know. But you may have something there. So far, nothing else has seemed to work. Maybe the change of pace will help."

"And as I said, Jyleen is a pretty sharp young woman, Jackson. I doubt that she'd make a request if she didn't think there might be something to these stories."

"Mutations among the outlanders, you mean."

"Yeah. Why not? It makes logical sense, doesn't it?" Andrea asked. "I mean fifteen years ago the idea of the dead reanimating into cannibalistic creatures was the stuff of horror fiction. No one would have ever believed it could become true, yet the Z43 virus changed all of that. What makes this whole mutation thing so scary is that we all carry this virus inside of us. If what these reports are claiming is true, there's something about the outlanders that's allowing the virus to mutate and change living humans into something else; some other weird types of creatures."

"But the government denies their existence."

"Just like they denied the existence of the undead back in the beginning of the plague." Andrea argued, "Remember how they blamed the early reports of zombies as being nothing more than the rampant use of the drug Braino causing living beings to appear to be mindless zombies. That was why the plague was able to spread so quickly. Remember? Government denial?"

Jackson knew this to be true. Braino was the street name for an extremely addictive synthetic drug derived from the combinations of both crack cocaine and heroin along several other highly addictive components. Braino had been nicknamed after the old drain clog cleaner, Drano because it did an outstanding job of cleaning out the brains of its users rather quickly, rendering them essentially mindless zombies. It ate its way through brain cells like Drano destroyed clumps of hair and other drain remnants.

Unlike real zombies; Braino addicts often could be controlled and made to do the bidding of their handlers, and they, of course, had no natural craving for human flesh. In extreme cases of Braino addiction where the person had been high for several weeks, it was often difficult to tell the difference between the living addict and the undead zombie. However, the Braino addicts didn't move as slowly and lethargically as the reanimated dead but moved much faster and could often be more dangerous than a zombie. Despite the fact that these poor souls were not cannibalistic, if commanded by their handlers to eat someone alive they might actually attempt to do so.

Andrea was right in that one of the reasons the plague had caught mankind by surprise and had gotten a large lead on humanity was because for some time perhaps weeks, perhaps months, those in authority insisted that the reports about lumbering dead were not really undead cannibals just severe cases of Braino addiction. It wasn't until some of these so-called addicts were captured and were found to have no pulses or heartbeats, not to mention the fact that they were in various stages of decomposition that the authorities realized something else was responsible for their condition.

"Good point," Jackson conceded. "Being a reporter, I naturally distrust Uncle Sam to give us the truth in most situations anyway."

"So does that mean you're going to do it?"

Jackson waited a beat pretending to mull the idea over then said. "Sure. I think maybe I will. But since the Skook is still paying me, at least for the moment, maybe I should run it by Bill McCleary first, especially since he was such a big help in getting the first book published."

Jackson already planned on calling McCleary to inform him of Andrea's suggestion. He would also make sure McCleary kept quiet about being the first to offer Jackson the assignment. It was only a little deception, but Jackson knew it would be better if Andrea thought the whole thing was her idea. He also figured this way he could communicate openly with McCleary without giving away the editor's personal connection to the investigation.

"Good idea," Andrea agreed. "And tell him it was my idea so he knows I'm cool with it as well. I think I might have put the fear of God into him after that last disaster."

"If there's anyone on earth who could put fear into the black heart of Big Bill McCleary, it would most certainly be you, sweetie."

So it apparently was now official. Jackson was starting an investigation into the various mutation sightings. He already had a good head start with what McCleary had sent him, and now perhaps Jyleen would be able to provide him with additional leads.

CHAPTER 23

"Yes, it's nice to speak to you as well," Jackson Ridge said to Jyleen Wilson who was on the other end of the call. "Sorry I couldn't do this in person, but I'm sort of in the middle of a bunch of stuff. Maybe sometime in the near future we can meet somewhere to speak face-to-face."

She replied, "Yeah. That'd be great. But look, I'm sorry if this seems like I'm meddling or imposing myself in your busy schedule or anything like that. I didn't want to do that . . . it's just that . . . ."

Jackson finished her sentence, "It's just that this is something you feel is very important and something which you need someone like me to look into on your behalf. No problem, Jyleen. Andrea already explained everything to me, and I truly understand. Here's the funny coincidental part. You might as well know, there's no reason to feel bad about your suggestions, because as it turns out, my editor at the Skook has put me on a very similar assignment, so what you have for me could very well complement what I've gotten from them."

"Oh, that's good to hear. That really makes me feel better about everything."

Over the course of the next half hour or so Jyleen recounted several different occasions where family members of her hospice patients had told her of personal sightings of mutated creatures roaming about the woods of the outlands. They insisted what they had seen were not zombies, nor were they humans. She said she had compiled a list of all of those people who had reported these stories to her along with their addresses and where available, their Communications Unit numbers. She agreed to email them to Jackson as soon as their conversation had ended.

"Seriously, Jyleen, I think these names will really help add more credence to my story."

"I'm glad to hear that," she said.

Then Jackson changed the subject slightly, "So . . . I hear you've been dating my friend Sean."

"Um . . . well . . . yeah . . . we've been seeing each other a bit . . . when we can."

"That's great to hear. Sean's a good guy, and in my opinion, he needs some romance in his life. And from what Andrea tells me you are perfect for him."

"We do seem to get along very well. It's just that we're both so busy . . . you know . . . it's really hard to get time to spend alone."

"Yeah, I remember what that was like. When Andrea worked hospice, Kyla was at daycare and I was on assignments, it seemed we hardly got to spend any time together . . . and we were a family. But now since she's been working here at home, handling all my appointments, and Kyla is no longer in daycare, we get to see each other every day. We've been very fortunate in that regard."

Jyleen said, "I suppose it's good to know that something positive could come out of your terrible experience."

"Yes," Jackson agreed. "I think about that often."

Just then, Jackson's CU chimed signaling him that there was another incoming call. He looked at the display screen and saw *The Schuylkill Daily News* main switchboard number.

"Hey, Jyleen," Jackson said apologetically, "I hate to cut you off but I'm getting another call . . . one I have to take."

"No problem," she replied. "Thanks again for everything you're doing."

"No," Jackson corrected, "thank you. You've been a big help. I'll watch my email for that list of names you're sending me and I'm going to talk to Andrea about the four of us getting together sometime soon. Sound good?"

"Sounds great. I'll look forward to it."

"Ok then. We'll talk again later . . . gotta go."

Jackson disconnected the call then said into the receiver, "Jackson Ridge speaking."

"Mr. Ridge?" a soft-spoken voice said. "This is Nathan Brody from *The Schuylkill Daily News.*"

"Nathan. Good to hear from you . . . and please . . . call me Jackson."

"Ok, Jackson it is. I got your message. I assume by now you've seen the video?"

"Seen . . . and more importantly . . . heard it too. The audio was absolutely terrifying."

"Yes, it was," Brody agreed. "But not nearly as scary as being there in person."

"I can't begin to imagine. Nathan, do you have some time to walk me through all that happened?"

"You mean right now?"

"Sure . . . no time like the present. That is, if you're not too busy. If so we can reschedule it later."

"No, no . . . by all means . . . we can do it now. In fact, Uncle . . . I mean Bill McCleary said speaking with you was to be my top priority."

"Excellent! And if you don't mind, I'm going to record our conversation. It makes my reporting all the more accurate that way. Ok?"

"I don't mind at all."

Then Brody began a long and detailed description of the encounter. Periodically Jackson would stop him and ask for additional detail or clarification of specific items. He also asked how Brody was feeling at various times during the ordeal. When Brody described the "creatures," he had filmed Jackson realized that the slightly blurry video didn't provide as clear a description as Brody's eyewitness account did.

Their conversation continued for almost an hour until Jackson felt as if he had covered all the important angles. He found it a bit humorous how Brody constantly referred to the video as "The Brody Video," and how he kept encouraging Jackson to do the same, repeating the importance of "branding" the video so the public would recognize and remember his contribution.

"I could have died getting this video," Brody had said several times.

Jackson agreed, not really caring how anyone referred to the video. It was obvious to him that Nathan Brody was seeking the same sort of fame, which Jackson was doing his best to avoid. What Brody didn't realize was that Jackson was more than happy to have the spotlight shining on someone else.

"Um . . . ok then." Brody said sounding a bit dejected that the interview was over, as if he was hoping to talk for much longer.

"Unless there's something else?" Jackson asked.

"Well, no . . . I suppose that's everything," Brody mentioned. "If I think of anything else, may I call you again?"

"Sure . . . of course." Jackson replied with a less than enthusiastic response, "Call anytime. And if I think of anything else, I need to ask I'll call you as well."

In reality, Jackson had no intention of calling Brody back. He had more than enough information, and the thought of hearing Brody go on about himself for another hour was more than he cared to think about.

CHAPTER 24

Sitting alone in the almost complete darkness of his private office, Sean was troubled. The only light in the room was that from his computer monitor, which he had strategically tilted so no one happening by his office window could see what it displayed. He was examining another encrypted email he had just received from the scientists at the NCDVC. Like the others, this one was marked TOP SECRET and was addressing what steps the government might need to take to contain the further spread of rumors concerning mutations. Things had apparently gotten to the critical stage, very quickly.

Sean had personally found the initial tone of the email very disturbing. Unlike the previous emails, it didn't even suggest the possibility of acknowledging the existence of the Z43 virus mutations; instead, it focused on what to do to keep any rumors from spreading. To Sean, it seemed like he might be witnessing a planned government cover-up, which meant he had involuntarily become part of it. His stomach began to tighten, and the idea that, by the nature of his position, he might be forced to ignore a problem which could have grave consequences for humanity. But perhaps he was jumping the gun in his assumption so he continued reading the note.

Although the NCDVC was a national agency, Sean learned that the latest problem relating to mutant sightings had actually originated just outside of his home city of Yuengsville. This was bad because Sean knew it would put unwanted pressure on both himself and his boss, Wilbur Hershberger, not to mention the Mayor of Yuengsville, Frank McKinney. Sean was always able to think several steps ahead of the average person, and his mind was already anticipating the fallout from the political football which was about to be hurled directly at his city.

From what the report indicated, the NCDVC had received word that a very short video file, just a few seconds in length was filmed by someone at *The Schuylkill*

Daily News, named Nathan Brody. It was believed that the video file was currently in the hands of the Editor-In-Chief, William McCleary. Sean knew in this brave new world, the NCDVC had become one of the most powerful government agencies in the country and as such had a network of observers in all walks of society. He hesitated to use the word "spies" because that sounded so sinister, but he suspected a lot of these so-called observers were, in fact, nothing but spies and snitches.

The email reported that the NCDVC source had claimed the video contained both audio and video proof of the existence of mutated creatures. They feared it was likely too late to do anything about the video eventually becoming public since it was now in the hands of the news media, but they said suppression of the video might still be a possibility. The email also suggested that in the event the video actually did get released, there were steps that could still be taken to discredit it as being nothing more than another trumped up hoax.

That portion of the letter didn't concern Sean too much since the government had been denying all sorts of things for as long as he could remember. What did send a chill down Sean's spine was the information that followed. It was printed in bold upper-case letters to express it importance and said, "ANY AND ALL STEPS MUST IMMEDIATELY BE TAKEN TO DISCREDIT AND/OR STOP, BY ANY AND ALL MEANS, THOSE INDIVIDUALS INVOLVED IN ATTEMPTING TO PUBLISH OR WRITE ABOUT THIS VIDEO." It said that if the right steps were taken at this early stage in the process, it would be much easier to control than later when the video had become public.

And what followed turned Sean's blood to ice. The letter went on to name individuals who should be targeted to prevent the video from being released. It listed three names but said additional names might follow if required. The names on the list were, Nathan Brody, Junior Copy Editor and person responsible for filming the video; William McCleary, Editor-In-Chief of *The Schuylkill Daily News*, and Jackson Ridge, reporter assigned to the story of the sighting. Sean sat staring at his monitor.

"Jackson Ridge?" Sean said. "Jesus, what have I done?"

A million thoughts raced through Sean's mind at the same time. He was overcome with guilt. He had been the one who had used his influence with Jyleen to get her to speak with Andrea about Jackson starting an investigation. Because Sean was unaware of McCleary giving Jackson the assignment, he assumed Jackson must have spoken with McCleary after Jyleen got Andrea to convince him and gotten McCleary to ok the investigation. Then later the video must have shown up, and McCleary naturally added this to Jackson's growing storehouse of information. But video or not, Sean was convinced it had been he who had started the whole thing in the first place by manipulating Jyleen. And now his best friend was being targeted by the NCDVC and as such was in the crosshairs of one of the most powerful government agencies in the country.

Sean had no idea what "DISCREDIT AND/OR STOP BY ANY AND ALL MEANS" might entail but at the very least, it might mean his best friend's reputation was in danger of being ruined and at worst . . . well, he didn't want to think about what at worst might mean. His palms were sweating, and his legs were trembling. What was he going to do? What could he do? How could he possibly help his friend and not allow his government employers to know he had done so?

Suddenly there was a sharp knock at his office door. Sean looked up and started when he saw his boss, Wilbur Hershberger, Schuylkill County Coroner standing outside his window looking gravely serious; even more serious than what was considered normal for the dour man. Sean waved his hand signaling for Hershberger to enter.

"Hey, boss, what's up?" Sean said trying to sound much more comfortable that he actually felt. He surreptitiously wiped his wet palms on his pants, "Please . . . come in . . . please sit down."

Dr. Wilbur Hershberger was a thin, balding man in his late fifties, with one of those faces that never seem to betray whatever emotions he was feeling. These cold expressions often troubled Sean, as he could never be sure where he stood with the man. Hershberger was currently not wearing his lab coat but was dressed in a white shirt, blue sports coat with matching pants and a blue and white striped tie. So Sean assumed his boss was not there to discuss any activities relating to the lab.

Hershberger walked toward Sean's desk and sat down on his guest chair. He never broke eye contact with Sean the entire time. It felt as if the man was examining him, taking in his every movement. Sean felt like a microbe being studied under a microscope. Sean suddenly realized this had to be about the NCDVC email.

"I need to speak with you about that latest email," Hershberger said with a tone of mistrust present in his voice; confirming Sean's original supposition. "May I assume you've read it?"

"Yes . . . actually I've just finished reading it," Sean was trying to keep all inflection out of his voice. He wanted to appear as cool and in control as possible, since he was now sure where this conversation was heading.

"Jackson Ridge," was all Hershberger said.

"Yes?" Sean replied questioningly.

"He is a friend of yours, is he not?"

"Yes. We've been friends since childhood."

"Hum . . . that's unfortunate."

"How so?" Sean acted as if he didn't understand the implications of their friendship in relation to the email.

"I think you know very well how so," Hershberger replied with a bit of an abnormally rough edge to his voice. "Let's put an end to this little verbal dance, shall we, Sean?"

"Very well," Sean acknowledged. He was feeling anything but as confident as he was acting. This man wasn't just his boss but was also a high ranking official in the NCDVC and the direction Sean's future would take was about to be determined by how the next few minutes might play out.

"Ok, here's the gist of our dilemma . . . and by that I mean yours and mine." Hershberger was making sure Sean knew that this problem could affect his own standing as well as that of Sean. "You see . . . I've always liked you, Sean, and I think you do a terrific job as Assistant

Coroner, especially since you've never had the opportunity to complete your formal medical training."

"The plague changed the world for everyone, Wilbur. It made us rewrite the rules. We've all just learned to adapt as necessary. You know that. Hell, I'm proof of that." Sean could sense something more was on his boss's mind. Whatever that might happen to be he suspected he would know soon.

"Precisely," Hershberger agreed. "And now it seems we may need to . . . as you say . . . adapt once again."

"Excuse me?" Sean asked indicating his misunderstanding yet fearing what he suspected was coming.

"Well, it's like this, Sean. You've read the email, the confidential, top secret email, and I assume you understand what all of that implies. You saw the recommendation, which indicated that steps must be taken to stop this video from ever becoming public. You therefore saw the mention of discrediting or stopping those involved, including your best friend Jackson Ridge."

"Yes, I did," Sean replied honestly. He was hoping his false mask of composure was not showing the signs of cracking he was feeling, as his palms began to sweat more profusely. He could feel perspiration beginning to form and slowly trickle down the back of his neck.

"If the writers of that email had known that you and Ridge were such close friends, you never would have received it. But I suppose that is neither here nor there since you have in fact seen it."

"Ok. So I saw it. So now what?"

"Now what indeed," Hershberger pondered speaking in a manner that was much too calm for Sean's liking. He found it somewhat disturbing to hear this almost expressionless tone in his boss's voice.

"As you may have guessed, Sean, this puts me in a bit of a troublesome predicament. As I said, I do like you as a person, and I likewise respect your professional abilities." This also made Sean feel uncomfortable since Hershberger had just said that a few seconds earlier. He suspected this might be nothing more than the lubricant for the major screwing he was about to receive.

Hershberger continued, "You also have a good work ethic and are, I hope what I and the NCDVC consider a team player. I am right about that, Sean; you are a team player, aren't you?"

"Yes . . . I . . . I like to think of myself as such . . . yes." Sean felt as if he was losing control of the conversation, assuming he had ever had control in the first place.

Hershberger asked, "May I then also assume that as a team player you would never, ever consider passing on such sensitive, classified information to anyone . . . even shall we say your best friend?"

"Look, Wilbur If Jackson is in fact involved in an investigation; it has nothing to do with me. He would only do so because it's part of his job. It's an assignment, and he hasn't contacted me for any information whatsoever. I can only assume he's writing this story simply to sell papers. I can't honestly believe he'd take seriously some obviously trumped up fictional video. I know Jackson; he's very skeptical and very thorough as well."

"So you say, but I suppose that's irrelevant, isn't it, Sean? Because we both now know that mutations really do exist. So whether he believes or not, he's going to dig until he finds proof. Then he'll write the story, and he'll be linked to those releasing the video. So as a result he is in, shall we say . . . the sights of the NCDVC . . . so to speak."

"Yes . . . I suppose you're right. He is," Sean agreed reluctantly. Then he pressed both of his palm down on the top of the desk, leaned forward and said, "It's not so different from the way you and I have been forced by virtue of our jobs to be unwilling participants in this . . . this government cover-up is it, Wilbur?"

Hershberger only seemed to flinch ever so slightly, maintaining that disturbingly eerie calm, "Easy there, Mr. Patel. I don't think you want to be caught using terminology such as that. You might want to focus a bit more when it comes to controlling those types of outbursts, as well. It seems they appear to cause you to say things, I'm quite certain you truly don't mean. Because what you just said wasn't what I would consider something a team player would say. In fact, it was quite the opposite. And I certainly would hate to think that such an assumption was correct. Because if it was, it would mean you weren't one of us at all but one of them. You're not one of them, are you, Sean?"

Sean sat silently for a moment realizing he had crossed some invisible line he shouldn't have crossed. For the first time in his career, Sean was actually starting to become afraid of the man sitting across from him, a man he had thought of as a friend and mentor. But now he realized if he wasn't careful, he not only might lose his job and destroy his career, but he could find himself in prison for God only knew how long. Depending upon the whims of the government and how much of a threat they might determine he was, he could simply disappear into the system and never be seen again. Sean suddenly realized he had to be extremely careful.

"No . . . no . . . of course I'm not one of them, Wilbur. You know that very well," Sean lied, he hoped convincingly. "I know the importance of the work we're doing here, and I'd never do anything to risk either my career or our reputation as a top-notch forensic facility."

Hershberger looked at Sean carefully as if trying to determine if he were being honest. "But what about your best friend Jackson? I don't know if you realize it, but things could become quite unfortunate for him in the very near future. Quite unfortunate. Don't you feel some need to perhaps warn him? Don't you think you might want to convince him not to continue down the path he is taking?"

"Jackson's a big boy, and I know he's had to face obstacles many times before. I suppose he'll do whatever he chooses to do . . . unless . . . are you're suggesting that I say something to him? Are you suggesting that I should warn him to stop his investigation?"

"Well," Hershberger said, "you read the email. This investigation is going to be stopped one way or another. If someone convinces Jackson to abandon his research now, early in the game, he might come out unscathed. But if he follows this through to the end, whatever that end might entail, well then that might produce a completely different outcome."

"But I don't honestly see any way I could get him to change his mind," Sean admitted. "And I certainly couldn't tell him about the emails . . . could I?"

"Absolutely not! You most certainly can't say a word to him about those emails. But if you could find a way to convince him to back off it will save everyone a lot of heartache. But you must do so without involving our facility or the NCDVC. As is said earlier, he is in their sights, and that's not a very healthy place to be, especially for a young man with a lovely wife and small daughter."

Sean realized the NCDVC knew all about Jackson already, and this mention of Andrea and Kyla was meant to be a not so subtle threat.

"I see," Sean replied. "Just how bad do you think things might get for him?"

"I truly don't know, Sean. And to be perfectly honest, I really don't want to know. You read the email. To paraphrase it said discredit and stop those by any means necessary. I can't predict what the outcome of that statement will be. It might mean one thing to me and something entirely different to someone else, especially someone who is, shall we say . . . overzealous. That opens up a world of frightening possibilities, Sean. The NCDVC is a very large organization with many dedicated professionals helping to keep it great. As a result, there are many people affected by this besides you and I, Sean."

"So then you do think I should warn Jackson." This was a statement not a question.

"I think you should do whatever you need to do to both protect this office and our profession and if possible divert the attention of your friend away from his current investigation. Otherwise, all I can say is whatever will happen will happen."

With that, Hershberger stood and turned to walk out the door. Before he left Sean asked, "What about me? Are we still good? Is my job still secure?"

Hershberger took a deep breath, let out a contemplative sigh and said, "For now, Sean . . . but . . . time will tell. The day is young. There are forces at work here greater than you and I. I will do my best to keep you out of the fray for as long as I can, but as you know the NCDVC is a very powerful organization, and it may only be a matter of time. . . ."

With that, Hershberger walked out the door, letting it close behind him, not looking back. Sean had no idea what he was going to do. He believed he had been the one to get his friend into this mess in the first place, and now he had to find a way to talk him out of it.

CHAPTER 25

Nathan Brody was feeling quite good about himself, not to mention his future, as he walked home from the offices of *The Schuylkill Daily News* heading for his apartment, which he shared with a goldfish that was not so creatively named Goldie. The evening air was warm with a slight breeze, which felt good against his skin. He loved nights like this when he could use the walk home to relax and unwind after a long day.

This day had been especially long and quite eventful, and as such, the warm air felt better than usual. He had given a copy of the mutant video to his uncle Bill, and from what he could determine, McCleary had assigned the investigation to the legendary Jackson Ridge to work the story. At first, Brody wasn't sure he wanted Ridge to handle what he thought of as his story. He was concerned that his incredible discovery might be overshadowed by Ridge's fame. But he figured if that was who his Uncle Bill had chosen for the assignment then so be it. He had to trust McCleary's judgment, especially since at first McCleary had been so reluctant to even consider starting any sort of formal investigation.

"Do you have any idea how many crazy emails I have on file from wacky people claiming to have seen mutants walking around in the outlands? Hundreds, I tell you, hundreds," McCleary had shouted at his nephew, his face appearing to become redder by the second. "Half the time all they're seeing is some errant dead head or maybe an outlander who hasn't seen a bathtub or shower in years."

"But think about it, Uncle Bill," Brody pleaded. "If you took all of these so-called crazy claims and combine them with that video I gave you, wouldn't that make a great story? Although I swear what I saw was real, it really wouldn't matter if the other stories were fact or fiction. We can let the public decide for themselves. A story accompanied by stills from that video would send circulation through the roof. I honestly think we could see a better boost than even with the Jackson Ridge story of last fall."

After a number of vulgar expletives, McCleary had rudely suggested that Brody stick to copyediting and leave the running of the newspaper to him. He had also not so politely thrown his nephew out of his office. However, Brody had no intention of letting things end there. Shortly after leaving his uncle's office, Brody called his mother, McCleary's sister, Linda to complain about how poorly his uncle had treated him. Within a few seconds, she was on the phone chewing out her younger brother, giving him an earful of her Irish temper. Shortly thereafter, McCleary gave in and spoke with Jackson Ridge. Then the wheels were set in motion.

Brody realized he should have felt ashamed if not quite immature about going to his mother to rat out his Uncle Bill. He knew it wasn't only unprofessional but down-right gutless. However, in his mind, Brody felt the ends would justify the means. He had gotten what he wanted. And now the best and most famous investigative reporter in the state was on the case. Very soon, that few second video was going to make Brody just as famous as Jackson Ridge. Sure his uncle might be angry with him for a while, but once the newspapers started flying off the newsstands, McCleary would calm down. This was a business, and McCleary was a businessman first and foremost.

Brody had already been referring to the video as "The Brody Film," and the name had already begun to stick. When he had spoken to Jackson Ridge later that day, he had made sure Jackson understood the importance of that name. Brody figured once "The Brody Film" became known to the public, everyone would start calling it by that same name. In his mind this video was as important if not more so than the legendary "Zapruder Film," the one which captured the assassination of President John F. Kennedy back in the previous century. He was certain once the film hit the media outlets, "The Brody Film" might actually surpass the level of fame of that ancient piece of history. It might even earn Brody his own place in the history books as the man who played a vital part in the most critical discovery of the Z43 Virus era.

He realized his Uncle Bill would probably be angry with him for some time over the sleazy tactic he had taken, but it was too late for him to worry about that. "The Brody Film" was something so special, so monumental, he couldn't let anything stand in the way of its release. Maybe it was a bit blurry and grainy, but the audio portion was incredible. Every time he thought about hearing those cries in person, it sent chills racing down his spine.

That was exactly what he had told Jackson Ridge when Ridge had called him to discuss the video. His uncle had forwarded a copy of the video file to Ridge who had watched and listened to it. Ridge had called and left Brody a message and he had returned the call catching the reporter in his home office later that same afternoon. As Ridge listened, asked questions and took notes, Brody went into extremely descriptive detail of every minute of his encounter. He was glad to learn Ridge was recording the interview as well, that way every nuance of his story could be captured for posterity.

Brody made certain Ridge understood that he wanted the video referred to as "The Brody Film" whenever possible. He stressed the importance of getting that tag line out in the public quickly and often. He wanted to make sure the name stuck. He did get the impression that Ridge might have been getting a bit angry with him over his constant instance, but Brody was certain of his strategy, and if Ridge didn't like that then too bad. Brody did his best to describe all of the feelings of horror he'd experienced without actually sounding as terrified as he truly had been. He thought it would be better if when the story came out, he was portrayed as perhaps more fearless than frightened.

Ridge had asked him dozens of questions, and their entire interview had lasted almost an hour, much longer than Brody's entire encounter itself had lasted. Before Ridge had contacted him, Brody had already begun writing an account of the ordeal himself in anticipation. He was not a very proficient writer, but he could get the facts down in a logical progression, which he felt would only help the reporter. Then after their discussion, he emailed a copy of the document to Ridge, in case there was something important he might have left out. Brody didn't want to take any chances with the possibility of missing out on even one ounce of credit for his part in the story. He could just imagine the general public giving credit for everything in the story to Ridge, since his was the name they already knew. He wanted to be certain his would be the new name on everyone's lips from that day forward.

Brody had not planned to work as late as he did, but this opportunity was one he felt deserved the extra time. He especially wanted to get the written account documented while it was still fresh in his mind. As a result, he didn't leave his office until after dark. It didn't matter to Brody because the night was warm and perfect for a walk, and Brody needed some fresh air to help clear his mind. The last thing he wanted was to find himself up all night reliving the events of that terrifying encounter. The street lights in that part of town left something to be desired as most of them were broken and those few which were lit were at best dull, casting very little illumination.

As Brody turned the corner heading down the sidewalk toward his apartment, he noticed something out of the corner of his left eye. He slowly turned and saw a nondescript mostly black panel van pulling up alongside him. Before he had a chance to fully understand what was happening, the side door slid open and several men dressed in black wearing dark hoods emerged from inside the van. They grabbed Brody and unceremoniously pulled him inside the van. The door slid shut, and Brody could hear the van's engine revving and its tires squealing as the van pulled away with him inside. Strong arms held him down while others secured him with ropes, a blindfold and a ball-gag for his mouth.

Brody was too shocked to think about what might be happening to him, and after a few minutes of struggling he felt the sharp crack of something hard against the side of his head, and he lost consciousness.

CHAPTER 26

"Mr. Jones? This is Jackson Ridge. I got a message that you wanted to speak with me. What can I do for you?"

Jackson had received a voice message from Joan at *The Schuylkill Daily News* informing him that a Mr. D. B. Jones had needed to speak with him about an urgent matter, one which he needed to address as soon as possible.

"Jackson?" The voice replied, "You . . . you probably don't remember me. This is D.B. Jones . . . from Ashton High . . . I was a couple of years behind you in school."

"D.B. Jones . . . D.B. Jones . . . I'm sorry," Jackson apologized. "That doesn't ring a bell with me."

Jones explained, "How about the name Delbert Jones? I think we might have played little league baseball together for a year or two when we were kids."

"Delbert Jones . . . Delbert . . . Yeah . . . Delbert Jones . . . you were that skinny little guy . . . you could run like the wind as I recall. Yes, I do remember you."

"Maybe I could run like that once upon a time. Now I'm not so young, not so skinny and not so fast either. And these days I go by D.B. Jones, my first and middle initials. I learned the hard way that Delbert Bertram is a tough handle to carry around."

"I suppose it would be," Jackson said as if contemplating. "So how can I help you Delb . . . I mean, D. B.?"

Jones hesitated briefly then replied, "Well . . . um . . . Jackson . . . you see . . . I'm not exactly sure . . . but . . . I read your book as well as your newspaper articles about what happened to you . . . you know . . . in that whole Deimos thing."

"Unfortunately, as I'm sure you realized that 'Deimos thing' wasn't a very pleasant series of events at all," Jackson stated emphatically.

"I'm sure it wasn't. And please forgive me . . . I didn't mean to make light of that situation. Well . . . here's the deal. What I'm looking for is . . . is some information relating to that event."

"Information? I was pretty sure I put everything in my stories, but ok, what sort of information are you looking for?"

"Um . . . you know what? I probably should explain a few things first . . . it might help what I'm going to ask . . . maybe make a bit more sense."

Jackson agreed, "All right then, D. B. Go right ahead. Because if it can help I'm all for it. But right at this moment I'm at a bit of a loss here."

"Sorry. I'm not very good at explaining myself sometimes. I tend to get confused when I'm excited about something. But I'll give it the old college drop-out try. Um . . . did you ever hear of someone called . . . the Death Bringer?"

Jackson thought he recognized the reference, "You mean that comic book character that was popular during the height of the zombie wars a few years ago? As I recall there were like tons of graphic novels written about him. The Death Bringer . . . yeah . . . Death Bringer Jones, I believe his name . . . hey wait a minute! Are you trying to tell me?"

"Yeah. I suppose I am. Those graphic novels were roughly based on stuff I did back when I was a zombie slayer and actually went by the name Death Bringer Jones for a time . . . get it? D. B.—Death Bringer?"

"Sure, I get it. But honestly I had no idea those things were based on a real person let alone someone I had once known. I figured it was all fictitious. Wow! It's all sort of strange to learn the truth."

"Yep. That was me . . . it seems like . . . such a long time ago," Jones lamented.

Jackson asked, "But what about the uniform . . . didn't the character have like a superhero costume with a belt buckle depicting a skull head? And what about those giant muscles in the graphic novels? You were always such a skinny little kid. Where did they come up with the superhero body?"

"The way they drew the uniform is pretty accurate. It looked a lot like the one I came up with for myself," Jones explained. "The muscles might have been exaggerated a bit for the novel . . . you know . . . for effect. I was in top shape back then but not nearly as buff as the comics made me look." Then he laughed, "But it did help to sell a lot of comic books and made me some good money . . . for a while. Too bad I spent all of it." This was followed by a nervous chuckle.

The phone went silent for a moment as Jackson suddenly got an idea. "You know D. B. your story might still make interesting reading sometime. I think a lot of people, especially young adults who grew up reading your comics might be interested in learning about what you've been up to. You know . . . a sort of 'Where are they now?' type of thing."

"I doubt that very much," Jones said. "I can't imagine people wanting to know that the great Death Bringer Jones is now nothing more than a grunt working on the Dead Kill retrieval squad. The former Zombie Slayer has become someone who scrapes up rotting corpses off the roadways for peanuts while the lucky sap that shot the thing gets a hundred bucks . . . not a lot of real superhero excitement there that's for sure!"

"Oh. So that's . . . um . . . that's where you work now? I'm sorry. I didn't know." He had a flashback again to the day when he had to call the Dead Kill retrieval squad to remove his former neighbors. He wondered if Jones had been on that call. He decided not to ask; he really didn't think he wanted to know. All of this was a bit too coincidental. Jones was after something.

"Yeah. Unfortunately, that's where I work now," Jones admitted. "How far the mighty have fallen. Right?" Then he let out a sardonic laugh.

"I suppose we all do what we can to help the greater good."

Jones said, "That's what the government propaganda machine wants us to believe. It's all for the 'greater good' . . . as they like to say . . . it's no longer about the needs of the individual any more . . . we all must make sacrifices . . . but you know what, Jackson? I've never once seen one of those high and mighty government types dragging a stinking rotten carcass across a roadway leaving a trail of brains behind it . . . huh . . . so much for sacrificing for the greater good . . . but enough of that . . . I didn't call you to bellyache about my personal problems. And I certainly wasn't looking to have you write any story about me. But I did call so I could ask you about something."

"Sure. Go ahead D. B . . . ask away." Jackson felt as if he had already asked Jones several times what he wanted. He was beginning to get impatient.

"Odo," was all Jones said.

"Odo?" Jackson replied uncertain he had heard the man correctly. He was stopped cold. He could feel the hair on the back of his neck beginning to rise at the mere mention of the horrible creature's name. He wouldn't have expected to have that kind of reaction.

"Yeah, Odo. From your book. Deimos' mutant lackey. I'd like to know everything you know about him and about his kind."

Jackson realized suddenly what Jones was asking. "His kind" meant Jones wanted to know if Odo really was a mutant as Jackson had described him in his book. Jackson no more knew the answer to that now than he had all those months ago. So he chose to be honest with Jones.

He regained his composure as to the best of his ability then replied, "First of all, D. B., I honestly can't say . . . that Odo was . . . you know . . . a mutant. That was just how I described him . . . to be honest . . . to sell more books. I'd heard all the stories about alleged mutant sightings, so I figured why not get in on the scam and move a few more books at the same time." However, now all these months later based on what he had seen in Brody's video, Jackson wasn't so sure that what he was saying was true.

"But . . . but the way you described him . . . his physical appearance . . . the block head . . . the caveman brow . . . it sounded exactly as I would have imagined such a mutated creature would look. I've heard many stories about them and what you described was exactly the same."

Although Jackson was still a bit off balance at the memory of Odo, he sensed where Jones was going with this and figured it would be better if he didn't encourage the man to continue down that road. He tried once again to explain, "Look, D. B., I'm a writer. It's my job to provide enough detailed descriptions to paint a scene for people. I could just have easily written about Santa Claus, the Easter Bunny or Bigfoot, and I would have made the descriptions just as convincing. It's my job . . . it's what I do."

"But . . . but . . ."

"That whole mutant rumor thing has never been proven by anyone." He suddenly thought of the horrifying howls and screams in the video from Nathan Brody and had to hold back an involuntary shudder.

"But, Jackson. What if they were real . . . and . . . .what if I managed to bag one of these things. That would be incredible." Jones was now speaking even more excitedly, "If I could do that I'd probably be even more famous than you are. I could even go back to being Death Bringer Jones if I wanted to. I suppose I'd have won that right. I'd be 'Death Bringer Jones: Mutant Slayer.' I might be able to make some real money and not have to be just another corpse slinger. Man, I could actually matter again."

"D. B. listen to me," Jackson said trying to reason with the man thinking of what information Brody had relayed to him. "I know this is really important to you . . . but you have to listen to me . . . if these stories somehow were true . . . these things would be monsters . . . not the awkward slow zombies we are all used to but huge, very strong, very fast and deadly predators. No mere human man might even stand the slightest of chances against such a creature."

Jones seemed to think about it for a beat then said, "Maybe so in a one on one confrontation, Jackson. But these things are no longer human . . . they're more like animals . . . and we have the advantage of a human brain."

"And wouldn't they still have at least part of a human brain remaining as well? Maybe they'd be animal-like, savage and perhaps a bit reckless but part of them would still have the cunning of a human being. Besides, you have to think about the consequences if you were successful. If they were determined to still be part human, only a sort of impaired human, you'd likely be charged with murder. Don't you see that?"

"I'd be willing to take those chances . . . for one more shot at being that guy again . . . Death Bringer . . . the hero children spoke about in stories, the one featured in those graphic novels. For just one more chance . . . I think it would be worth it."

Jackson realized he was wasting his time trying to change Jones' mind. The man was apparently determined to return to his glory days no matter what the personal cost. Yet he nonetheless tried once more saying, "Besides, D. B., there has yet to be any reliable proof that these mythical creatures even exist."

"But what about that so-called Dead Kill you brought down at the beginning of your book, the one you got on your way to the Skook that morning? You mean to tell me you don't believe that was a mutant too? You shot that thing right in the head, but were you charged with murder, Jackson? I don't think so. And that's because it was a mutant."

"Now wait a minute, D. B. You're way off base on that one." Jackson insisted. "The creature I shot was most definitely a dead head. And as far as I could tell it was nothing more than a large Dead Kill. No mutant."

The truth was Jackson had been starting to wonder the same thing Jones had just questioned, but he didn't want to acknowledge such an idea over the phone to someone who was practically a stranger. However, he still wasn't completely convinced that mutants even existed, and he needed to believe the creature he shot had in fact, been dead already. His conscience wouldn't allow him to acknowledge any other possibility.

"Look, D. B., I swear to you, no matter what I may have suggested in my book to make the story more interesting, the thing I shot was a zombie. It was not a mutant. Odo was no mutant either. They were just big ugly guys, one dead, one alive. End of story."

Jackson heard Jones breathe heavily into the receiver, "I can see you have no intention of acknowledging any of this, Jackson. And that's fine. I understand. I was just hoping you might be able to help point me in the direction of where I might find one of these things. But I can see you don't even believe they're real. And I suppose that's too bad."

"Well . . . I'm sorry, D. B., but I suppose I can't help you. I'll tell you what. I'll make a deal with you. If you ever want me to do a story about you and your alter ego . . . you know a history piece on Death Bringer Jones . . . I'd be more than happy to get the true version of your adventures directly from you. I think it would make a great book, a biography. We could combine your story with some of the illustrations from the graphic novels, and I think it would be a big seller. It might earn you enough to get you out of that job you hate so much. And honestly, isn't that what you really want?"

"It might at that," Jones seemed to consider. "But no, I don't think so. That's old news, the past. When you do decide to interview me, I want it to be because I bagged one of those mutants. Then you would be writing a story on the real Death Bringer Jones; a reborn Death Bringer Jones. Now that would be a story worth writing."

As Jackson said goodbye and disconnected the call, he was certain any story he might be writing about Death Bringer Jones would not be about his bringing down a mutant but more than likely it would be the man's obituary.

CHAPTER 27

Nathan Brody slowly opened his eyes, unsure of where he was or what had happened to him. In fact, he had no idea what time or even what day it might be. The last thing he could recall was seeing the mostly black colored van pull up next to him on the street. Like most vehicles, it had patches of other colors but all those were dark colors as well. His head ached with pain, and he was beyond disoriented. Trying desperately to make it back to the conscious world, he attempted to take in his surroundings.

The room he was in was cloaked in darkness save for a bright spotlight which was shining right into his eyes preventing him from seeing anything of any significance. He sensed someone was sitting somewhere back behind the light, and that someone was waiting for him to awaken.

"Mr. Brody. So nice of you to join us," a strange voice said from the darkness.

He tried to formulate some words but was unable to do so. It was as if his thought process was out of sync with his ability to speak, as if his lips were several seconds behind his brain. All he was able to eke out was a meager, "I . . . I . . . whe . . . where . . ."

"Ah, yes," the voice interrupted. "The proverbial question . . . where am I? If I were a betting man—and I'm not—I would have bet the farm that would have been the first thing out of your mouth, Nathan. May I call you Nathan? Of course I can . . . I can call you anything I want. In fact I can do anything I choose to you, and there's not a thing you can do about it."

Nathan was starting to come to his senses and suddenly realized his hands and feet were bound, and something was also pulled tight around his waist and chest. As he became more alert, Nathan lifted his head and felt the back of a tall chair of some sort against his head. His skin felt damp, and when he sampled the air around him, it had a dank cellar-like smell. He tried to struggle, but the chair wouldn't move, either because he was too weak or the chair was too heavy.

"Save your strength, Nathan," the voice assured. "You'll never move that chair or break free. The chair is both extremely sturdy as well as heavy. I secured your bindings myself. Besides, even if you did manage to get yourself free, I'd just have to shoot you in the head, and that would be the end of that. We'd miss any opportunity to chat. That wouldn't be very much fun, now would it? So do us both a favor, relax a bit, and let me explain the situation to you. I promise if you do exactly as I ask, you won't be harmed any more than is necessary. If you resist . . . well . . . let's just say you really don't want to fight me on this point."

"Wa . . . wa . . . whadda you want?" Nathan managed to slur.

"There now, I think that's a much better question. Now we're getting somewhere."

Nathan could see something glowing in the darkness; a small red ember like the end of a cigarette or cigar. He breathed in through his nose and noticed the smell more clearly; it was definitely a cigarette.

"We're going to play a little game, Nathan. It's called . . . um . . . oh, well, it doesn't actually have a name, nor does it need one. It's just a barrel of fun, at least for me. The rules of the game are simple: I ask a question, and you provide the answer. Is that simple enough for you? I hope so, or things might get a bit unpleasant in here very quickly. Now nod your head if you understand the rules of the game."

Nathan remained silent, staring out into the bright light with his eyes squinted. He wanted to nod his head, but for some reason he couldn't quite figure out how to do it. He truly wanted to cooperate with this lunatic. He hoped if he did as he was told he might actually get out of this mess in one piece. Since he hadn't seen his captor, he figured the chance of freedom might at least be a possibility. But he couldn't get his head to move.

Suddenly the spot light went dark, and he heard his kidnapper screaming like a wild man, "I told you to nod your head, you idiot! You must do as I say. That is the only rule. How much simpler can it get? Do as I say!" He saw the red ember coming directly toward him in the darkness.

Nathan suddenly felt a searing pain in the center of his forehead and could smell his own flesh burning. He realized the maniac had put the hot end of the cigarette right into his flesh. He opened his mouth and screamed with agony. At first all that came out was a slight moan, then a full-blown howl of a scream. He dropped his head to his chest and could hear the footfalls of his captor walking back to his original position. Once again, the spot light came on, and he was blinded by its brightness. He didn't know which was worse, the blinding light or the fiery pain in his forehead.

"All right then. I think I did a fairly good job of re-explaining the rules to you, Nathan. Now, once more with feeling . . . if you understand the rules of our little game, please nod your head."

Although the pain was still excruciating, Nathan nodded his head to the best of his ability. It was a weak nod, but a nod nonetheless.

"Very good, Nathan. Now we're getting somewhere. So now for the next question. The video you shot down at the abandoned Cressota Mall; tell me about it please."

"I . . . I . . ." Nathan mumbled.

"Take your time, Nathan . . . but not too much time. I don't think you want me to grow impatient with you again, now do you?"

"N . . . n . . . no," Nathan whimpered. "I . . . I'll tell you . . . I was bored . . . so I went driving . . . and . . . and . . . I got a flat tire."

"A flat tire?"

"Y . . . yes. At . . . at the old Cressota mall."

"And you decided to shoot a video?" the voice asked skeptically.

"No . . . no . . . I didn't . . . I mean . . . not at first . . . I called for help and locked my car . . . I was waiting . . . for . . . for the truck. Then I saw something down at the mall."

"You saw a mutant? Is that what you're trying to say?"

"Yes . . . but I didn't know what it was." Nathan's voice was starting to sound weaker.

"You're not going to fall asleep on me are you, Nathan? If you're starting to become bored, I'll be more than happy to provide you with some additional stimulation."

"No . . . no . . . I'm ok," Nathan assured. Then he went on to describe about the arrival of the second mutant, the fight, his shooting the video, the attempted attack by the zombie and finally his rescue.

"So what did you do with the video? We have your CU which contains the original video, but who else has copies?"

"I gave a copy to my Uncle, Bill McCleary at the Skook."

"Bill McCleary is the editor at the newspaper, is that correct?"

"Yes," Nathan replied weakly.

Then the voice asked, "And what do you suppose McCleary is going to do with that video?"

"I . . . I don't know. Probably nothing. He . . . he doesn't believe . . . in mutants." Although it was true that McCleary didn't believe in mutants, the idea of him sitting on a video story like the one Nathan brought him was ridiculous. Nathan was sorry he had said the words and realized he had made a major mistake as soon as they left his mouth.

For a moment, the voice didn't respond. Then it said, "Nathan, oh, Nathan. I asked you to tell me the truth."

"B . . . b . . . but . . ." Nathan stammered.

"No buts, Nathan. It's too late for that."

Once again, the spotlight was extinguished, and Nathan saw the glowing red ember coming ever closer. Then something else happened. A small light appeared like the beacon produced by a flashlight. It seemed to hover in the darkness about the height of a man's head. Nathan realized his captor was wearing some sort of head-mounted light so he could find Nathan in the darkness. He must have had it on when he made his initial attack with the cigarette, but Nathan hadn't noticed it earlier. Now he saw both lights coming toward him, and he braced himself for another cigarette burn.

Nathan very quickly and unfortunately learned two things. The first was that you could never prepare yourself to have the flesh burned from your face; the pain was just too excruciating. Unfortunately, that wasn't the worst thing he learned. The next thing he discovered was how while he was screaming in agony wide-mouthed his exposed teeth became vulnerable as well. His attacker first sunk the burning ember into Nathan's cheek searing his flesh. When he opened his mouth to cry out in pain, the man placed a plyer of some sort on one of his front teeth and with a flick of his wrist yanked the tooth from its gums in a shower of blood as Nathan howled even louder just seconds before he passed out.

After an indeterminate amount of time, Nathan awoke to find the spotlight shining back into his eyes once again. His face felt as if it was on fire, and he suddenly realized that his captor had burned him many more times while he was unconscious. Likely so that when he awoke, he would do so in extreme agony. His mouth tasted coppery and ached terribly. After moving his tongue around, he discovered he was missing some additional teeth. He wondered what this man's game was. If he wanted to torture Nathan, wouldn't he have waited until he was awake to inflict more damage? Not that Nathan wasn't grateful he had apparently been unconscious through the worst of it. He was still in pain nonetheless.

"Oh, good. I see you've returned to us once again," the voice said. "You may have noticed some additional facial burns and several more missing teeth. I did that while you were asleep to save some time. Now, Nathan, it's very, very important that you tell me the absolute truth. You see, you have quite a few open sores on your face and inside your mouth, and one of the worst things I can imagine doing at this point would be do douse you with salt water. Don't you agree?"

Nathan's eyes grew large with horror. The only thing worse than the pain he now had would be if the pain was multiplied by the addition of salt water to his wounds. "I . . . I agree." He slurred due to the missing teeth.

"Good to hear. So I know you have a copy of the video and your Uncle Bill McCleary also has one. What I need to know is who else might have one. And keep in mind, Nathan, I rarely ask a question I don't already know the answer to. So if you confirm what I know, all the better. If you try to lie to me, I will know and . . . well . . . you can just imagine how perturbed I might become."

"Are . . . are you going to kill me?" Nathan asked directly. He suddenly realized his captor really didn't need his information. He already knew everything. He was just playing some sort of twisted game. He might pretend to be verifying his information, but Nathan knew this was about something else. Perhaps about making an example of him. Yes, Nathan realized he was as good as dead.

The stranger hesitated for a moment out in the darkness then replied, "Yes. I'm terribly sorry, Nathan, but I am going to have to kill you after all. It's just a matter of whether I kill you quickly or if I let you suffer for a while. Maybe I'll leave the decision up to you."

Nathan looked out into the darkness behind the spot light and said, "If you're going to do it eventually . . . please . . . just do it now."

"Not to worry, Nathan . . . I will . . . possibly soon, but it seems I have just one more question. It's an easy one, a simple yes or no question. Did McCleary assign the story of the mutants to Jackson Ridge?"

"If I tell you the truth will you please end this for me?" Nathan pleaded.

"Perhaps," the man replied. "But I'll tell you one thing for certain. If you don't tell me the truth, you will be suffering for many, many more hours. So the choice is yours."

Nathan hesitated for a moment then said, "Yes . . . He . . . he . . . gave the video and the assignment . . . to . . . to Jackson Ridge."

"Very good, Nathan. That's absolutely correct. I knew he had passed on the assignment to Ridge, and you just confirmed that for me."

Nathan asked, "But . . . but if you knew that . . . why am I here? And why are you doing this to me?"

"That's simple, Nathan. I'm doing it because I want to."

With that, the man walked through the darkness toward Nathan once again. Nathan flinched but then noticed there was no glow from the cigarette just the light on the top of his head. A second later, Nathan was drenched with a bucket of water, salt water. The pain shooting from his many wounds was beyond imaginable. Then a second before he was about to pass out he felt the point of something sharp piercing his chest. The last thought he had in life was imaging his chest pierced by a cold steel knife blade.

CHAPTER 28

Jackson heard the doorbell ringing. Then a few seconds later it rang again and then again revealing the obvious impatience of the visitor. He was surprised by the incessant ringing since it was only eight-fifteen in the morning. Jackson had of course, been awake since around five having once again experienced his horrifying reoccurring nightmare. He had hoped that by being distracted by his latest project, he might have found a way to subconsciously cause the nightmares to cease; but so far, the dreams continued. As a result, he had been awake, showered, dressed and working in his office, reviewing the document containing a collection of emails from people claiming to have seen mutants.

Sadly, Jackson realized why Bill McCleary had chosen not to write any stories based on the submissions. None of them offered an ounce of proof and even taken as a collection the letters were essentially useless. They spoke of strange creatures so bizarre that no one would ever believe them to be real without additional photographic evidence to back them up. And many of the notes were written so poorly they scarcely resembled English.

However, a few of them did offer vivid descriptions of creatures, which in many ways paralleled the two images seen in Brody's video. That could prove to be a good thing. Jackson believed if his story tied these letters dated months earlier to Brody's recent video, he would be able to present a very convincing story; not even close to anything resembling scientific proof, but at least convincing enough to share with the general public. He suddenly realized that after just several days of researching he was actually starting to believe himself that such creatures might actually exist. The skeptical reporter side of his brain was still questioning the authenticity of the video. He also doubted Nathan Brody had tried to fake the video. He seemed too excited about the video to be responsible for such a ruse. Jackson didn't personally possess the equipment or technical ability to analyze the video, but he knew before he agreed to attach his byline to any story, he would have the video thoroughly tested by someone who did.

Yet another part of him, the creative and imaginative part of Jackson Ridge wanted the video to be authentic. Although he realized such a fact could mean potential catastrophic results for an already beleaguered humanity, he also knew that breaking such an amazing story would be even more incredible than his last adventure and subsequent story had been. He did his best to curb his creative enthusiasm and focus on his skeptical, analytical side. He knew it was the only way to make sure his investigation remained as objective as it had to be.

Jackson pushed back from his desk and stood as the doorbell continued its annoying ringing. He turned and went to see who was so insistent on seeing him. The house was empty as Andrea and Kyla had left early that morning to go visit Kyla's little friends at her former daycare. When he had been freelance writing and Andrea had been a hospice nurse, Kyla attended the Ashton Cooperative Happy Home Daycare where she had made a lot of friends. But now that Andrea was managing Jackson's career, and they were both working from home, there was no need for daycare; at least no need on their part. But Kyla missed her friends and asked about them often. As a result, Jackson and Andrea agreed that one day a week Kyla could still attend the daycare and hang out with her friends; especially now that the daycare had relocated to the center of the Ashton Cooperative where it was at a much safer location.

In fact, the catalyst for the daycare's move had been a near miss encounter Kyla had experienced with a group of zombies when the daycare had been located along the outside border of the Ashton Cooperative. Luckily, no one was hurt during the encounter and the dead heads had been safely brought down thanks to the quick actions of the school's custodian, Mr. Schwartz. That single event gave the daycare's supervisor, Mrs. Johnston, enough leverage to demand the much needed relocation from the town council. After months of foot-dragging, once the town council learned that the child who was almost killed had been the only daughter of the now famous investigative reporter Jackson Ridge, the motion to relocate the daycare was promptly and unanimously ratified.

As Jackson approached the front door, he looked out through one of the sidelights and could see his friend Sean Patel standing on his front porch pacing nervously and pressing on the doorbell every few seconds. Jackson opened the door.

"Double I! My man! What are you doing here this early in the morning? Shouldn't you be at work? And what's with all the doorbell ringing?"

Sean seemed to not hear Jackson as he walk past absent-mindedly. Jackson could have sworn Sean was muttering incoherently to himself under his breath. His eyes seemed to dart back and forth nervously and he was anxious for Jackson to close the front door. He seemed to be preoccupied with something. This in itself wouldn't be considered out of character for Sean since he was often preoccupied. But today there was something else about his body language which told Jackson something was very wrong with his friend indeed.

"Sean? What's going on, man? You look . . . well you look like crap!"

"I . . . I . . . I don't know . . . I mean . . . I know . . . but I don't know . . . where to start . . . I have to . . . have to tell you something . . . but . . ."

Jackson led his friend by the arm to the sofa in the living room. He could feel that Sean was trembling beneath his grip. Jackson picked several of Kyla's toys off of the sofa and tossed them onto a nearby empty chair. As soon as Sean sat he seemed to melt down into the sofa. He was hunched forward staring down at the floor muttering as his arms hung limp by the sides of his legs.

"Sean . . . buddy . . . what the hell is going on?"

Sean shook his head several times as if in conflict with some unseen inner demon, "I . . . I have so . . . so many things . . . I have to tell you . . . I'm so sorry, Jackson . . . I should have come to you . . . much earlier . . . but I couldn't . . . I mean I could have . . . I should have . . .

but . . . but dammit I didn't . . . and now . . . Oh God, I'm so sorry, Jackson."

"What in the world are you talking about, Sean? You're not making any sense."

"I . . . I . . . have to come clean, Jackson . . . about everything. I owe you that."

Realizing he had to do something to get Sean to relax, Jackson told him to sit quietly for a moment until he returned. Jackson went to the kitchen and got a cordial glass, adding three ice cubes. He returned to the living room to see Sean still in the same spot and in the same condition. Jackson walked to a cabinet, opened it, selected a bottle and poured whiskey over the ice cubes.

"Here, Sean. I know it's early, but drink this. It'll help you relax a bit. Then you can tell me whatever it was you came to tell me.

Sean took the glass from Jackson, nodded then and practically guzzled the entire contents in one gulp. This was amazing, since Sean wasn't much of a drinker. He coughed a few times then shook his head. The whiskey warmed him from head to toe. He sat silently for a few seconds more then took a deep breath and blew out a long whiskey-scented sigh.

"All right. I . . . I think I'm ready . . . here's the thing, Jackson . . . I have several different things I need to talk to you about . . . I need to explain . . . about many . . . many secrets . . . things I've kept from you."

Jackson had no idea where this was going but he knew it was important to his friend. "Ok, Sean. You know you can tell me anything. We've been friends since . . . well, since forever. And you don't have to apologize to me for anything that you may have told me or neglected to tell me. We'll work it out, man. We always do."

Sean took another deep breath then finally said, "Ok . . . First of all . . . I lied to you about something very important. I honestly did have my reasons . . . and still do I suppose . . . but regardless . . . you have a right to know . . . you need to know."

"Ok, Sean. Go ahead." He could tell Sean was conflicted, torn about what he was going to say.

"Remember how I told you that it wasn't me who you saw that day when you were rescued from crucifixion that horrible barn?"

"Yes, of course, I recall." Jackson looked down at the pink scars in the palms of his hands, "I thought I saw you and someone else, but you said you were in Yuengsville at the time and that I must have imagined everything."

"Well . . . I lied to you Jackson . . . you were right . . . I was the one . . . I was there . . . it was me . . . I'm so very sorry for lying to you . . . and I'm especially sorry I managed to convince you that you were hallucinating . . . that you had imagined everything. You swore it was me and rightfully so . . . when I told you I was back at my office at the time were rescued . . . that too was a lie."

Jackson just stared silently at his friend in amazement.

"It was me, Jackson . . . I was the one who shot the zombie incarnation of Police Chief Holden . . . me and a young Yuengsville policeman who assisted me. And I'm sorry, Jackson . . . but I can't reveal his name . . . he must stay out of this . . . for obvious reasons.

Jackson looked on still speechless. He had always been certain of what he had seen that day but had allowed himself to be convinced otherwise. He finally said, "But . . . but why . . . why didn't you just tell me before, Sean? You could have trusted me to keep your confidence . . . you know you can always trust me . . . I don't understand . . . I also can't figure out why you didn't want to accept the credit for saving my life? I mean . . . Jesus, Sean . . . that was an incredible thing you did."

"I couldn't," Sean insisted. "In fact . . . I still can't . . . at least not publicly. It has to remain a secret . . . it might mean the end of a career for that policeman who helped me."

"But . . . but how did you two ever find me in the outlands?"

"My partner in the rescue had been suspicious of Chief Holden for a long time . . . he didn't know what Holden was up to . . . He had no idea that Holden was the ring leader . . . but he suspected the Chief was up to something illegal . . . then when you went missing Holden told the mayor he wanted to take his Sergeant Evans with him to try to find you . . . My friend suspected he was up to no good . . . He managed to place a tracking device in Holden's jacket . . . He knew I was upset after learning of your disappearance . . . He and I had been involved in several cases together in the past . . . He from a police standpoint . . . and me from the forensic side . . . He came to me and told me of his plan to nail Holden . . . and how he believed Holden might lead us straight to you and Sarah Stanton . . . We tracked Holden to the outlands surrounding Reading and . . . well, you know what happened after that."

Jackson was stunned. "So you really did save me after all, Sean. That's incredible. I still think you should have told me . . . but I think . . . I mean. I believe I understand what you're saying and why you did what you did, especially if the whole operation was off the grid. Am I right about that? I assume it was an unsanctioned action. And since it eventually led to the death or I should say re-death of Chief Holden, I'm sure neither of you needed to deal with the sort of heat such an exposure would generate. So you two chose to make it seem like no matter what I thought I saw, neither of you were there."

"Yes . . . I'm sorry to say so," Sean confessed.

"Ok," Jackson said taking a deep breath. "I suppose I can live with that . . . and I'm glad you chose to come clean . . . See, Sean? That wasn't so bad now was it? You told me now and I'm cool with it. No harm, no foul. Getting the truth out there is a good thing. Right? It makes you feel better."

Sean hesitated then replied, "Yes . . . yes, it does . . . but there's more . . . there's . . . there's something else."

"More? I assumed that was everything. But . . . ok . . . hey, go for it."

"It was . . . sort of everything. I mean . . . at least as far as the whole rescue was concerned . . . but there's more I have to tell you . . . about an unrelated subject . . . and it has me extremely upset. I . . . I really screwed up, Jackson . . . I may have put the wheels in motion for a real mess . . . and I may have inadvertently put you . . . in harm's way."

"What are you talking about, Sean? I'm not in any danger. As you can plainly see I'm just sitting here safe and sound in my own home. No problem."

"You don't understand, Jackson . . . I have to explain what's going on. And . . . you see . . . simply by passing on this information to you . . . I could end up behind bars myself . . . Do you understand what I'm saying . . . and how dangerous all of this is?"

Jackson hesitated, "Ok . . . ok . . . I think I understand . . . you feel you have to tell me something that you really aren't supposed to, and it's most likely something I'm not supposed to know about. Right? And if word ever gets out that you were the one who told me whatever this is you want to tell me, you'll find yourself in deep doo-doo. Does that pretty much sum it up?"

"Yes . . . most definitely," Sean confirmed. He was too stressed to even notice Jackson's cavalier attitude, "You see, Jackson . . . in my capacity as assistant coroner . . . I am . . . or I should say I was privy to . . . classified top secret encrypted email messages from the NCDVC, messages that only myself and Dr. Hershberger were permitted to see."

"Ok. That makes sense. I get it. So what?"

"The 'so what' is this . . . I recently came across some information that . . . I thought you needed to see or at least learn about . . . However, I was forbidden from sharing it with you . . . or with anyone else."

"What sort of information, Sean? What were these memos about?"

"I'll get to that in a minute. In order to get you interested . . . in what coincidently ended up being the subject of these memos . . . I had to find someone else to . . . to motivate you . . . without having any ties directly to me."

"Ok. I think I get that. But I still don't know what the hell you're talking about."

"Jyleen!" Sean said with visible frustration and embarrassment. "I . . . I tricked . . . No, I deceived Jyleen into speaking with Andrea . . . I got her to ask Andrea . . . to talk to you . . . Don't you see? That means I mislead Jyleen and Andrea as well as you."

"Do you mean about investigating those stupid mutant stories, Sean? Is that what has you so upset? Seriously?"

"Yes . . . your involvement . . . in this mutant investigation . . . It's all my fault . . . it's all my doing . . . It's the direct result of my deception . . . I'm so sorry, Jackson."

Jackson suddenly felt relieved, "Sean, I think maybe you're overreacting. I need to set the record straight about something. First of all, before Andrea every approached me on behalf of Jyleen, I had already been offered the assignment by Bill McCleary at the Skook. Any sort of clandestine involvement you might have had, only helped make things easier from the standpoint of my dealing with Andrea. As far as she is concerned, having Jyleen talk to her made it all seem like it was her idea. You see . . . you were actually beneficial. Look, Sean, this is a no sweat situation. And, between the two of us, if you don't spill the beans to Andrea about me, I'll make sure Jyleen never knows what you've just confessed to either. Deal?"

"But there's more, Jackson . . . .more you don't know about."

"Then tell me, Sean. I promise I'll make sure your name never comes up. You know I can do that."

"Once that would have mattered to me . . . perhaps more than anything else in the world . . . but not now . . . not ever again . . . This is all too important."

"For the last time, Sean, what is it?"

CHAPTER 29

It was still dark as the sun was just beginning to come up over the eastern hills of Yuengsville where two Dead Kill retrieval squad workers, Nick O'Hara and Ryan Nolter were busy getting their utility truck ready to start another workday. Their job was not a glamourous one by any stretch of the imagination, but the work was steady, and it earned them a half-decent living. They liked to think of themselves as being akin to their counterparts; the workers who manned the city's trash trucks. However, instead of hauling away rubbish, the refuse of humanity, they hauled away the refuse that once was humanity, the remains of Dead Kills found along the highways of Schuylkill County. Also, instead of being confined to the safe perimeters of the enclosed cities, O'Harra and Nolter's truck traveled throughout the entire county primarily taking in the wild and unsafe outlands between the cities.

Occasionally they would get a call from within the walls of one of the fortified towns when someone died then had returned from the dead and had to be put down. In fact, just a few days earlier they had to travel up to the Ashton Cooperative and retrieve the carcasses of and old man and old woman who were put down as Dead Kills by the famous investigative reporter Jackson Ridge. The old couple apparently had been his next-door neighbors. Nolter and O'Hara were surprised that particular story had stayed out of the paper, but they supposed Ridge had his connections. Besides, all of that was irrelevant to the team because for them those two old people were nothing more than a couple of dead heads waiting to be scraped off the ground and thrown into the back of their truck.

"Hey. Where da hell is Jonesie dis mornin?" Nolter suddenly asked. "What is dis? The guy only shows up whenever he feels like it? So dats how it goes, does it?"

The Dead Kill Retrieval teams usually consisted of a minimum of three and sometimes four members; one to drive the vehicle and the rest to handle the tasks required to load the carcasses onto the truck. Usually the driver and an assistant if available would also serve as sentries while the loading process was taking place. Retrieving in the outlands the job often proved to be quite dangerous. As a result, team members would switch off duties daily with loaders and drivers trading responsibilities. However this team was one of the leaner teams with only three standard members and now with Delbert Jones not showing up for work, Nolter and O'Hara knew they would have a rough day ahead of them. With Jones missing, they'd have to load any bodies without the benefit of an armed spotter watching out for other outland dangers, and they'd also have to be on their toes at all times.

"Who da hell does dat lad tink he is, comin' and goin' as he dam well pleases? Don't he know we got a friggin' job ta do?" O'Hara added.

Nolter said, "Mebby he tinks dat he's too good ta work wit da likes 'a us on da bod squad."

"Could be. He does go around sometimes wit his nose in da air like his crap don't stink er somtin. Da udder day when he was wit us on dat Kinkaid retrieval up in Ashton, he seemed to spend more time staring over at dat Ridge lad's house den he did helpin' us."

"Yeah," Nolter agreed, "I didn't know wat his problem was. Maybe he's lookin' ta make a name fer himself . . . you know . . . hopin' dat dere reporter would write about him in da paper 'er sometin. I heered way back before he took dis job he was onea dem big time zombie hunters."

O'Hara replied, "Well, I don't give a rat's rosy red arse wat he was. Wat he is now, is nuttin more den a carcass hauler just like da resta us, an da sooner he gets that tru his tick head da better."

"You gonna report him to da boss?"

"I gotta. Got no choice. Not that I really care what happens to him anyway . . . he ain't like you an' me, Nick. He ain't no team player."

"No, dat he ain't fer sure," Nolter replied. "So I guess it looks like it's just gonna be you an' me t'day."

"Yeah . . . I 'spose. So we better get headin' out," O'Hara insisted. "Da dispatcher says we got a dead 'un ta pick up first ting along da highway between Yuengsville and Saint

Clara den another one up along Route 61 between Ashton and Franksville."

Just then the pair heard a low guttural growl coming from somewhere out in the morning darkness accompanied by the shuffling of feet along the roadway.

Nolter asked, "Is dat wat I tink it is?"

O'Hara looked out into the shadowed darkness squinting to see what was making the sound. "Yep. I believe so. Dis has gotta be a first, Ryan. Usually we haffta go out and get dem, but it looks like we got ones comin' ta us. Do me a favor and han' me dat metal hook would ya?"

"Sure ting, Nick."

Nolter reached into a compartment on the side of the utility truck and withdrew a three foot long metal bar which at one time might have been a poker for a fire place. It was black and had a handle on one side and a spear-like point on the tip. It was solid and heavy and was more than capable for doing the job at hand.

The growling grew louder, and the shuffling more pronounced as whatever the creature was that was lurking in the darkness slowly made its way into the early morning light. Although accustom to seeing dead heads on a daily basis, there was something about this creature which the pair found extremely disturbing. They could tell it was a fresh one; it had to be as there were only the first signs of decomposition beginning to show in its sallow cheeks. No it was not typical decay they were seeing; it was something else much more disquieting.

The creature appeared to be a young man who was almost completely naked save for a soiled pair of undershorts, tighty-whities, but they were no longer either tight or white. They hung loosely as if haphazardly worn and they were stained with shades of gold, brown and crimson, the source of which Nolter and O'Hara preferred not to know. The creature drug a pair of pants which seemed to be attached to its right leg. Under other circumstances, this might be considered humorous, but there was something very wrong about this scene.

O'Hara realized what was strange was the creature's flesh. All along the creature's face and arms were round burn marks as if made by someone pressing lit cigarettes deliberately into its flesh. The same marks could be seen in its chest and on its legs as well.

As the creature got closer it opened it mouth to once again let out a horrifying howl, and O'Hara could see that several of its front teeth were missing and based on the open red and blackened bleeding gums, he knew they had only recently been extracted. He immediately knew this was not going to be a typical Dead Kill situation. He had seen enough in this new world to know that the zombie coming toward him had not been someone who met with a natural death. Something very bad had happened to this man shortly before he died, and team members were trained to watch out for such things. Many times during the past decade, murderers had tried to get away with their foul deeds by killing their victims then leaving them to return as zombies with the hopes that some well-meaning citizen days or months later might blow their heads off leaving the bodies unidentified and their crime undiscovered.

"Forget da poker, Ryan. Gimme da needle."Nolter reached into the utility cabinet and extracted a long thin metal rod about a foot long with a rubber grip handle. It resembled an extended version of a carpenter's awl. He handed it to O'Hara and asked, "Why dija change, Nick? You coulda bashed his head in wit dat poker."

"Look at da guy, Ryan. Look at his skin," O'Hara said. "Dis ain't no normal dead head. Somebody kilt dis guy . . . probly last night. An look at dem marks on his arms, Ryan. Dis guy was tortured fer a long time, I tink. It looks like day even ripped out somma his teet. I gotta take him down wit da least damage I can do."

This was the one aspect of their job both O'Hara and Nolter hated the most. It was bad enough dealing with hauling the rotting corpses away every day, but when they got called to pick one up and it was still moving, they had to put the creature down. They never thought this was fair because whoever called in the Dead Kill already received $100 placed into their bank account even though in reality the thing was not yet properly dispatched. And because it was deemed to be part of their job neither of them could claim the money for the Dead Kill, regardless of the fact that they were the ones to put it down. They and their co-workers had complained numerous times to the local governments about this flaw in the system, but nothing was ever done to remedy the situation. As a result, they carried a variety of tools for up-close disposal of such creatures should the need arrive.

The creature was now just a few feet away from O'Hara coming deliberately at him, all the while a mixture of saliva and blood trickling down over its split lips from its ruined mouth. O'Hara knew the beast probably still had enough teeth remaining to nonetheless make it a significant threat. When it got closer, the creature raised its arms to grab O'Hara, but the man was much quicker than the wretched beast and with one quick thrust he drove his long sharp pick into the creature's eye, sinking it deep into its brain. Just as quickly he pulled the tool out taking with it blood and fragments of gray matter along with the creature's shattered eyeball. The zombie fell to the ground in a heap. Its pierced eyeball hung on the thin shaft of the needle with several strands of crimson muscle still attached and dangling in the cool morning breeze.

"Well den, I guess dat settles dat," Nolter said.

"Yep," O'Hara agreed. "I wonder who da hell dis guy is an how he ended up in dis shape, da poor bastard."

"We probly should be callin' da cops dontcha tink, Nick?"

O'Hara agreed but decided he should check the zombie's pockets for identification. Since the pants were on the ground having been dragged by the creature's leg and not close to the body he figured it would be ok to look for and ID without disturbing the scene. He reached into the pants pocket and discovered a wallet. He pulled out the wallet and found a driver's license which he held up to the morning light from the rising sun.

O'Hara said, "The license says this guy is somebody named Nat'n Brody."

"Never hearda him," Nolter said. "You?"

"No," O'Hara replied. "Me needer. Dis one will be for the cops ta figure out."

CHAPTER 30

"The mutants . . . the rumors of these mutations . . . they're all true, Jackson . . . Those horrible creatures we've heard about really do exit . . . and there is now scientific proof to support it," Sean Patel said to his friend.

Jackson was dumfounded, "Wha . . . what are you saying Sean? Are you suggesting you can prove these things are real? You have definitive and indisputable proof?"

Sean hesitated then said, "Well, no . . . not really . . . I don't . . . but I did . . . I've seen the reports, Jackson . . . top secret reports from the NCDVC . . . They say that the Z43 virus is mutating . . . apparently not in the towns and cities but only among the outlanders for now . . . and, Jackson . . . the reports are saying the mutated virus no longer needs to wait for the host to die. It can activate inside of a still living body . . . and it . . . it changes them physically . . . and mentally . . . the NCDVC suggests that the virus is mutating naturally to insure its own survival. We've been so effective at wiping out the undead; we've unintentionally caused the virus to mutate."

"Oh my God, Sean!" Jackson exclaimed. "Are you telling me the government knows all about this? I . . . I . . . can't believe it. Do you still have those emails? Did you make copies of them?"

"No, Jackson. I couldn't. You see, the messages . . . were what we call R.O.S.D. which stands for Read Once then Self Destruct. Once the reader opens the email he only has a limited amount of time to read it before it destroys itself. During that time the reader can't make any sort of screen image capture either. The encryption prevents it. Plus they monitor the messages to see if anyone tries. So now all we have here is my word . . . no physical proof which is exactly how the NCDVC wants things to be."

"So you're telling me the government knows about these creatures, and they're still denying them publicly?"

"Yes. And that shouldn't come as any surprise to you . . . since that's exactly what they did at the start of the Z43 outbreak as well. It's the exact same crap all over again."

"Those bastards!" Jackson exclaimed.

"And I, Jackson . . . I was one of them . . . I was supposed to go along with their cover-up . . . not saying a word to anyone . . . so I'm practically as bad as they are."

Jackson looked at his friend and said, "Well, if makes any difference, Sean, I do understand. You're like me, just another cog in the wheel. I don't run the news outlets I work for and neither do I completely control what my story will look like when it hits the pages. I can't tell you how many times I've taken heat from the public for changes which were made to my stories without my knowledge or approval. You have a very important job to do, a job society urgently needs, and I do understand that divulging classified government secrets, especially to a reporter like me, could have very serious ramifications. In fact, I have no idea why you're even telling me this now come to think of it. Are you out of your mind, Sean? You know I can't possibly sit on a story like this!"

"I know you can't . . . and perhaps I am out of my mind . . . but the truth is . . . after what I read yesterday . . . after what happened . . . I can no longer care about such things. I . . . I have to do what is right . . . and to . . . to warn you."

"What happened yesterday, Sean? What do you have to warn me about?"

Sean recounted the contents of the last email he had read. He told Jackson how the government not only had no intention of going public with their mutant information, but they were planning to "discredit" or "otherwise stop" him "by any and all means possible."

"Discredit or otherwise stop?" Jackson asked. "By any and all means possible? Wow, Sean! That sounds a bit ominous, don't you think? Any idea exactly what that mandate is supposed to include?"

"No idea, Jackson. But my guess is that the memo was deliberately vague so no matter what happened the execs at the NCDVC will have plausible deniability. They can say they never specified what actions anyone should take. That way if someone further down the food chain gets a bit overzealous and choses to take less than desirable actions the officials at the NCDVC can back away and say they didn't authorize any such activities. They'd also be able to claim that they disapprove of such actions while simultaneously disavowing any knowledge as well. However, I certainly could imagine what might happen. And what I'm imagining is not very pretty, especially in light of what happened to me next."

Sean went on to tell Jackson about Hershberger's visit to his office. He explained how Hershberger had made a number of veiled threats and how he asked Sean if he was on the side of the NCDVC or if he was planning on taking his friend's side.

"Are you one of us or one of them," Jackson repeated Hershberger's words according to Sean, not as a question but as a statement; one he could scarcely believe.

"I thought I had done a convincing job of making him believe I was still on his team, but when I returned from lunch, I was unable to log onto my office computer. A few minutes later, Hershberger arrived with a security guard and walked me over to the personnel office. Once there, I was not so politely told that my services were no longer required and that my employment was terminated."

"What? They canned you? Are they insane? Don't they realize you've been running that place? Hershberger hasn't the slightest idea how to manage a lab. He's just a paper-pushing bureaucrat, for God's sake."

"Perhaps so. But I have nonetheless been sacked. And I've been warned that if I divulge any of what I know to the media and it gets back to them . . . there will be hell to pay."

"But as you've said, all you have is your word . . . no proof."

Sean nodded, "But I don't even have my word since at the time of my hiring, I signed a nondisclosure statement, agreeing to remain silent under penalty of law with the potential for incarceration."

"Hummm . . ." Jackson contemplated letting the expression trail off. His eyes seeming to stare off into space.

"What are you thinking, Jackson? I can always tell when you're concocting an idea or some sort of scheme. It's like I can see the wheels turning and the gears meshing inside your head."

Jackson replied, "But . . . what if I had actual proof . . . some video proof? How could they dispute that?"

"If you're referring to the notorious Brody Film, then you might as well forget it."

"How . . . how did you know . . . I mean . . . about that video?" Jackson asked, completely surprised by this revelation.

"Jackson . . . don't you get it? That's why I'm here . . . to warn you . . . the NCDVC knows all about the video. They know all about Brody and all about you. That's what the last email I read was about. It mentioned McCleary, Brody and you by name. They're targeting the three of you, Jackson."

"So let me get this straight. Brody takes the video and gets McCleary involved. Then McCleary calls me. Now we've all suddenly made it to the top of the NCDVC's persona non grata list. And because of that they're going to try to discredit the three of us?"

"Yes," Sean replied with embarrassment, looking down at the floor and shaking his head in shame.

"Sean, you don't honestly think they would resort to violence do you?"

Sean hesitated for perhaps a moment too long for Jackson's taste and said, "Two days ago I never would have considered the possibility, but today . . . well . . . I just don't know what to think."

"But the video and still pictures aren't even all that great," Jackson said as he turned on his computer monitor. His computer was still active and his special Communications Unit was still plugged into the docking station from the previous evening. "I mean . . . I'm going to have to do a lot of creative and persuasive writing to convince anyone that what the video shows might actually be a mutant. Thank goodness the audio is so disturbing or I might not even have a shot at making this work, Sean. Since you've come this far in the game . . . you might as well check out the video and see what all the fuss is about."

Jackson navigated to the sub-directory marked mutant research and looked for the video file. But it wasn't where he knew had stored it. In fact, the entire subdirectory was empty.

"What the hell?" Jackson wondered, "I'm sure I put the file in there. Hmm . . . No problem. I'll just open the original email from Bill McCleary and save it again." But when he checked his email inbox, all of the correspondence from McCleary was gone.

"This is impossible, Sean!" Jackson said in astonishment. "The video file, the still pictures, the letters from witnesses, my own notes and research . . . it's like they never existed. But that's simply not possible. This CU is secure and encrypted."

"You mean it WAS secure and encrypted," Sean replied, "but now it seems that your files have mysteriously disappeared. Even with the video you would have had trouble convincing many people this was nothing more than another trumped up big-foot type of report. But without the video, Jackson . . . well . . . if you tried to write any sort of news story . . . you and Bill McCleary would most certainly be laughed out of the business."

Jackson looked in surprise at Sean and said, "Yes . . . just like you said the NCDVC wanted us to be. But for the life of me I can't figure out how they might have gotten to my files. Maybe they didn't. Maybe I accidently deleted them. Oh, crap! What if I did? Wait till Bill McCleary finds out. He'll be furious." Then he suddenly remembered, "McCleary! That's right! Bill is the one who sent the file to me. That means he still has his copy."

Jackson retrieved his special CU from it docking port and dialed Bill McCleary's personal CU number. He knew McCleary would be in his office as he was an early riser and was always at work before seven. Jackson would have to explain that somehow he had lost his files. He knew the man wouldn't be happy but what else was he supposed to do? Then to his surprise, McCleary answered on the first ring. Before McCleary had a chance to speak Jackson said, "Bill . . . something's wrong . . . I don't know what happened . . . but I somehow lost the video file you sent me along with all those letters. I know you're gonna be angry . . . but I just . . . I just don't know what happened. I mean you know me, Bill . . . I'm always so careful, but now when I check, the files are all gone . . . I'm so sorry, Bill. Can you resend them to me?"

"J . . . Jackson?" McCleary's voice replied tremulously, not sounding angry in the least, but sounding incredibly upset, "There is a problem . . . a much bigger problem then you realize. You didn't lose your files. All of my files are gone as well. We've been hacked . . . and Jackson . . . it's much, much worse than that . . . I just got a call . . . from . . . from my sister."

Jackson's stomach clenched. He couldn't believe the unfamiliar weakened tone of the normally powerful voice of his editor. The man sounded devastated, as if he were about to break down and cry, "Jackson . . . it's Nathan . . . he's dead."

CHAPTER 31

"What? Oh my God, Bill! What are you saying?" Jackson asked scarcely able to believe what he had just heard. He looked across the room and saw Sean frozen in anticipation, aware that something very bad had just happened. Jackson mouthed the words, "Nathan Brody's dead." Sean's eyes grew wide with disbelief.

Jackson asked into the CU, "Nathan? Dead? I mean . . . how did it happen? Was there an accident?" Sean was now at full attention trying to follow the developing story based on Jackson's side of the conversation.

McCleary took a deep breath on the other side of the line trying to collect himself then said, "We don't really know all that much at this time, Jackson . . . but it looks as though he had stayed here late at the office last night . . . then sometime after he left and was walking home . . . he was kidnapped . . . and then murdered."

"Murdered?" Jackson asked now even more shocked the previously. He couldn't believe what he was hearing.

Jackson heard Sean's breath catch in his throat as saw him shake his head and heard him whispering, "Oh my God, no. How could they have done such a thing?" Jackson realized Sean was recalling the NCDVC memo, and Jackson was thinking of the same thing.

Sean began pacing anxiously back and forth across the room. He then heard Jackson ask, "Tortured? Did you just say he was tortured, Bill? Oh, sweet Jesus! This is unbelievable! I'm . . . I'm so, so sorry Bill . . . Poor Nathan . . . Oh my God! That poor man." Jackson looked over at his pacing friend in shock, suddenly realizing what this might mean to him personally.

After a few more minutes, Sean could tell Jackson was wrapping up the conversation with McCleary. "Bill, if there is anything . . . I mean anything whatsoever, Andrea and I can do for you and your family . . . please . . . please don't hesitate to call me. Even if you just need to talk. You know I'm just a phone call away," Jackson assured McCleary.

Then he said, "I will, Bill . . . and you please be careful as well."

As Jackson disconnected the CU, a look of shock was still etched on his face. Sean walked over to him and asked, "What the hell happened, Jackson? That sounded . . . bad . . . that sounded really bad . . . absolutely horrible."

"It was, Double I . . . It was worse than anything I could have ever imagined." Now Jackson walked slowly over to his liquor cabinet and poured himself a shot of the same whiskey in the same glass he had given to Sean earlier. He drank it down in one gulp then poured another which promptly joined its mate on the way to his stomach. It burned as it flowed through his body, but the burn felt good to Jackson. It reminded him he could still feel . . . and he was still alive . . . which was more than he could say for Nathan Brody.

He took a deep breath, steeling himself then said, "Nathan Brody was found dead this morning. His reanimated corpse was discovered walking around the streets of Yuengsville. Thank goodness two Dead Kill recovery workers found it and put the creature down before it could hurt anyone. They identified him from his driver's license in his wallet."

"What a degrading thing to do to someone!" Sean exclaimed. "As if it wasn't bad enough to murder someone; but to leave him wandering about as one of those wretched creatures is beyond deplorable."

Jackson said, "But that's not the worst of it, Sean. Not only was Brody murdered, but it was obvious from the condition of the corpse and the various marks on the flesh that he had been extensively tortured before he died."

"Oh my God!" Sean exclaimed.

"Sean . . . from what I heard, Brody was a good man," Jackson explained. "He wasn't a major player at the Skook. He was only a junior copy editor for God's sake. He stumbled onto this video accidently. I'm told he was well-liked at the newspaper and didn't have an enemy in the world. What sort of animals could do something like that? Are these the sort of people you worked for, Sean?"

The room was suddenly eerily silent as if all of the life had suddenly been sucked from the place leaving behind a vacuum where no sound could ever hope to exist. Sean hesitated for a moment then said, "I most certainly wouldn't have thought so before . . . but now . . . I think maybe I was very wrong."

Jackson said, "I can't imagine any other reason why Nathan would have been kidnapped, tortured, murdered than for his involvement in the video. When McCleary has his head screwed back on straight he'll come to the same conclusion as I just did. Then God help the NCDVC. McCleary will do his best to come down on them with the full force of the press. He'll be out for blood. They'll probably have to kill him as well because that'll be the only way to stop him. My God, Sean what kinds of people are running the NCDVC? I mean, this is supposed to be a government organization . . . our government. You mean to tell me our own government is running around torturing and killing its own citizens? Please tell me that isn't true, Sean."

"Look, Jackson . . . despite what's happened I sincerely doubt that those at the highest level of the NCDVC are even aware of this horrible event."

"How could they not be?" Jackson countered. "You told me just moments ago about the emails you read. You told me about the line, 'discredit or otherwise stop by any or all means possible.' I think I just figured out what that line referred to, Sean. It means murder."

"I'm sorry, Jackson, but you'll never convince me that our government officials would condone the kidnapping and torture of a citizen for any reason, let alone doing so simply to stop a story from being written. I think what may have happened is just what I feared might happen. Maybe some lower level employee with a deranged sense of loyalty to the NCDVC took it upon himself to do this horrible thing and the government had no idea what was going on."

"Sounds a lot like the plausible deniability theory you suggested earlier Sean . . . still the company man to the bitter end." Jackson said frustrated, 'Even after they fired you and tossed you out in the street like so much garbage? I don't get that Sean."

"I'm just saying I don't buy into the idea of their involvement in the murder. Look, they have all sorts of cyber geeks at their disposal. I believe they would be willing to hack someone, to steal some files to discredit someone, but no . . . I can't believe they would condone cold-blooded murder and torture, Jackson."

"Well," Jackson said, "you're probably at least partially right. Because according to McCleary, in addition to getting Brody's CU containing the original video file, McCleary's office computer has been hacked, and his copies have been stolen as well."

Sean said, "So not only are your files gone but Brody's original was taken and the Skook was hacked. So all of the files in existence have been destroyed?"

"Yes, .and I find that incredible! These people . . . the NCDVC . . . obviously have resources the likes of which I had never even imagined."

"Apparently so," Sean agreed. "More than I had realized as well."

Jackson waited a beat then said, "Yet you still doubt that they would have been willing to kill for the video."

"I honestly do, Jackson." Sean repeated, "Look at how easily they hacked into your secure files. Do you honestly think an organization powerful enough to do that would need to result to murder?"

"They tortured him, Sean," Jackson reminded. "Maybe they wanted to make sure he told them just how many copies were out there and who had them? Sure they knew about Brody, McCleary and me. You got that from that email. But maybe they wanted to make sure no one else was involved. You know . . . clean sweep."

"But doesn't that sound like some sort of plot from a bad novel or cheesy movie?"

"Maybe so," Jackson agreed, "but sometimes what seems the least possible ends up being exactly what happened. You know what, Sean? I'm starting to wonder if I have to worry about Andrea and Kyla's safety. Do you think they could be in danger as well? What are the chances these psychos might go after them to get to me?"

"I . . . I don't know, Jackson . . . I don't think so . . . I think both you and McCleary are too well-known to dispose of. They couldn't kill either of you without it making a major story. Brody was an unknown. He would be easier for them to deal with."

"But what about my family?"

"I doubt they are at risk . . . but . . . I honestly don't know. Maybe you better call Andrea and make sure she and Kyla are alright."

Jackson pressed his speed-dial for Andrea, and she picked up after two rings. "Hey, babe. What's happening?" she said with absolutely no concern whatsoever present in her voice.

"Oh, thank God. Where are you, Andrea? Is Kyla still with you? Are you both alright?"

"Easy, Jackson. I'm fine . . . we're fine . . . Kyla is at the daycare playing with a few of her old friends, and I'm down at Edna's with Jyleen having a cup of coffee and chatting away."

Edna's was a small café and breakfast nook just two doors down from the new location of the daycare. The place was owned and operated by an elderly and, more often than not, cantankerous widow named Edna Jamison. It was a two person operation with Edna taking care of customers in the front while her short order cook Charlie Murphy worked in the kitchen. It was no secret that Charley and Edna hated each other and often were seen arguing openly in the café like an old married couple. They were actually distant cousins and co-owners of the place. Many people who were unfamiliar with them assumed they were a couple, although nothing could be farther from the truth.

"You're with Jyleen?" Jackson asked.

Andrea said, "Yeah. She called this morning and I told her to meet me here between assignments. By the way, Jackson, Jyleen is really grateful for your taking a look into the mutant sightings she suggested. She was worried that you might not think it was important enough, and she really appreciates that you didn't just blow the whole idea off."

Jackson was still thinking about Nathan Brody being tortured and murdered over his video and realized he couldn't say anything to worry Andrea. He knew he should tell her, but he wanted to protect her from the reality of what happened for as long as possible. He knew if she found out she would want him off the story immediately, and he was in no way ready to do that.

"What's all the concern about?" she asked.

"Nothing. It's just after what happened this week . . . you know . . . with the Kinkaids . . . well . . . maybe I'm just a bit jumpy and over protective."

"You can relax, Jackson. Everything's fine. We'll be hanging out here for a bit then I'll go back and get Kyla, and then we'll head straight home. Don't worry. We'll be just fine."

"Alright then," Jackson said. "I'll see you later . . . please be careful."

"We will. Love you."

"Love you too," Jackson replied. Then he disconnected the call.

"Ok, Sean. Now, you've got my full attention. What in the world are we supposed to do now?"

Sean hesitated then suggested, "I have an idea. You might not like it, but I think it's the only option we have."

CHAPTER 32

"Was that Jackson?" Jyleen asked seeing Andrea's concerned expression.

"Um . . . yeah . . . I suppose," Andrea replied. "He was calling to make sure Kyla and I were safe."

"That's a bit unusual isn't it? Or does he do that often?"

"No . . . not really . . . in fact this is the first time he's ever called out of the blue to check on us like that. Maybe he's still a bit shook up and feeling a bit spooked over that incident with the Kinkaids earlier in the week. It seemed to have weighed on him big time."

"Yeah, I suppose that was tough. I mean we've all had to put down dead heads at one time or another, but it's rough when they're friends or relatives."

Andrea agreed, "Your mind wants to believe the person you knew and loved is still in there somewhere. But of course they're not."

"I assume you guys were close with the Kinkaids." Andrea had told Jyleen about the incident earlier, and Jyleen sensed from the way she told the story that the elderly couple were more than just neighbors to the Ridges.

"Yes . . . we were. Since both of our parents are gone the Kinkaids sort of became surrogate grandparents to Kyla."

"Wow! No wonder it's bothering Jackson so much. How is Kyla doing with it?"

"Surprisingly. She seems to be fine. She's asked about them once or twice, and we lied and told her they moved to another town far away where lots of old people lived so they could get the care they needed."

"And that was that?" Jyleen asked.

"Yep," Andrea replied. "Pretty much . . . That was that. I suspect someday she may ask if we can go visit them or something along those lines."

"What will you do then?"

"I'm not sure. I suppose I'll need to have some sort of excuse at the ready when that day comes."

"I guess kids are as resilient as I've heard they are," Jyleen suggested.

Andrea said, "Under normal circumstances children do tend to be quite hardy but in the world we now live they must unfortunately be even more so."

Jyleen agreed. "You're right about that."

"Sometimes it really scares me a lot, Jy. We live with so much violence, death and hardship and these kids—the kids the government is so eager for us to have—have to grow up in such a horrible environment. All of us adults lived in the time before when we thought the world was crazy but had no idea what real craziness could be. As bad and as dangerous as it was back then it was still a thousand times more civilized than it is today. These poor little kids will never know how things were before. I often wonder what affect it will have on them. Will it make them harder, less caring or maybe, less humane or worse less human?"

Jyleen said, "I suppose it'll make them whatever will be required to survive and grow in the new world. They'll probably be a lot different than we were, than we are, and we might have some trouble dealing with that. But I believe nature will do whatever is necessary to make them into what they must become."

"Jy, if that was meant to make me feel better . . . it failed miserably. In fact what you're proposing is exactly what I'm afraid will happen."

"I wasn't trying to make you feel better. I was only stating the fact that no matter what you may want for your kids . . . well . . . what will be, will be. It's not in our control. The kids will adapt and do whatever it takes to become part of the new world. That's how it's been for thousands of years. Even if the apocalypse never happened and the world moved on its natural course, it would be a different place than when we were kids. Now it's just a lot different but it will be all the next generation of children will ever know. So I suspect they'll do just fine."

"I suppose you're right. The world has been irreparably changed forever and as we've seen, only a fraction of what was once humanity has managed to survive. These kids, these post apocalypse kids are the future of humanity."

"So . . . on that happy note . . ." Andrea smiled understandingly and said, "Wow. I had no intention of going off on such a depressing tangent. I'm so sorry, Jy. I don't know what's gotten into me."

"Likely the same thing that has gotten into all of us." Jyleen replied. "We lived through what was by far the worst time in human history. We survived, and now we're attempting to rebuild. I'm sure future history books will have some amazing things to say about our generation. I think that sort of gives us the right to have a few down days. Don't you think?"

"Yeah. Maybe you're right." Then they heard a loud thumping sound like something heavy hitting the floor.

"What do you suppose that was?" Andrea asked. "It sounded like someone dropped something heavy."

"Dunno," Jyleen replied. "It was probably Charlie dropping a pot or something out in the kitchen."

"You're probably right, Jy. So are you enjoying your coffee?"

"I most certainly am, but I sure could do with a piece of Edna's delicious homemade apple pie. It's the best in town."

"We'll have to order two slices when Edna comes by," Andrea noted. "Have you seen her lately?" The café was empty with Jyleen and Andrea the sole customers.

Jyleen said, "A few minutes ago I saw her go into the ladies room. I'm sure she'll be out in a minute."

Andrea asked, "Say . . . do you suppose it was Edna we heard falling before do you? She's no spring chicken. Maybe one of us should check on her. What do you think?"

"I think we should let her finish her business in peace. We don't want to risk souring her already miserable disposition."

"I hope when she comes out she's in a more pleasant mood than she was earlier," Andrea suggested.

"Don't count on it. She's like seventy-nine years old and as crotchety as you can get. I think she enjoys being miserable to her customers. And what's worse, I think her regular customers like it as well . . . weird . . . really weird."

Andrea looked around the café, "So why we are the only two customers this morning?"

"Who knows? Maybe we just hit the place at the right time, or maybe the novelty of Edna's grumpiness has worn off. But despite Edna's abrasive personality, wait till you get a taste of her apple pie. It'll make everything else worth the trouble."

"If you say so," Andrea said uncertainly.

As they continued to chat, Jyleen saw the door to the ladies room open and noticed old Edna staggering out clumsily.

"Oh, crap!" Jyleen exclaimed.

"What's wrong, Jy?" Andrea asked seeing the look of concern on her friend's face.

"We got trouble, Andrea." Jyleen was nodding her head in the direction of the rest room area.

Andrea turned, and her breath caught in her throat. Apparently grumpy old Edna had chosen that particular morning to go into the ladies room and drop dead because what was now dragging itself across the café toward them was an undead version of what the old woman had been only minutes earlier. Her eyes were fixed in a blank stare, and she twitched and convulsed as if not yet accustom to her new resurrected form. Her mouth hung slack-jawed and a steady stream of crimson drool ran from the lowest side trickling down the front of her pink and white work shirt making the embroidered name "Edna" on her breast pocket now appeared to read "Ed." The remainder of her name was hidden by thick coagulating blood. As the Edna creature slinked across the room convulsively shuddering, Andrea looked down at her place settings for something she could use as a weapon. All she had was a spoon for her coffee.

"Don't worry. I got this," Jyleen said as she reached into her purse and pulled out a thirty-eight caliber revolver, "I really hate to do this in a small place like this. It's gonna be loud, and it's gonna be messy."

"Don't you have your hospice kit with you?" Andrea asked referring to the tools hospice nurses used to put down their charges after they passed on.

"It's out in the car . . . no time."

But as Jyleen took aim and was preparing to pull the trigger, she saw the shambling Edna creature stop in its tracks as its face suddenly split down the middle, each half falling off in either direction. Sticking out of the mess of gore and grey matter was the business end of a meat cleaver. As Edna's corpse fell to the ground with a thud the pair saw Charlie Murphy, Edna's short order cook and business partner standing spread legged, his white apron splattered with blood and soaked with sweat. He was breathing heavily with a wild look in his eyes. The door to the kitchen was still swinging on its hinges. He bent down, pulled the cleaver free of the carcass and wiped the blade off on his blood-splattered apron.

"Alright then," Charlie said with a grin. "I've wanted an excuse to do that for years. The miserable old sow, and now she finally gave me my chance . . . legally . . . Plus it will earn me a hundred bucks in bounty . . . Life don't get much better than that."

Andrea and Jyleen just looked at each other in shock not quite sure what to do next. They could think of nothing to say so they just turned and stared at the corpse and the cleaver wielding cook with their mouths agape.

"Not to worry, ladies. I'll call it in," Charlie said casually. "I always figured the old goat would likely end up croaking at work, and lately she hasn't been looking so good. I happened to look out the porthole in the door in time to see her come out of the can. At first, I wasn't sure she really was a dead head 'cause lately she's kinda looked like one most of the time anyway. But once I realized it had finally happened, I figured I had better take care of it and save you girls the trouble."

He looked down at the gun Jyleen now held at her side and said, "Nice piece you got there, young lady. What is that . . . a thirty-eight?"

Jyleen was left speechless by the man's calm demeanor and just nodded her head in weak acknowledgement.

"If you two could both be so kind as to leave your contact information here with me in case the law feels the need to talk to witnesses, I'd greatly appreciate it. You see, me and Edna . . . well, we weren't exactly what you would call friends. And most of the local cops know that from the number of times they were called in here to . . . well, to break up our little spats. So you see I might need someone to . . . well . . . to corroborate my story, so to speak. And I'll tell you what. Coffee's on the house. My treat. Since I'm the only surviving member of this here business partnership, I'll be taking over the place now that Edna's gone. Give me a few days to show my respects and clean the place up a bit then feel free to stop by. I'll make sure I have some of that apple pie on hand. I know Edna's recipe. Hell, I'm the one who's been baking it for years."

The pair nodded mutely once again. Jyleen fumbled in her purse and pulled out a business card. Andrea did the same finding one of her old cards from back when she was a hospice nurse. It still had her personal CU number on it. She laid it on the table with a trembling hand then turned to leave. Jyleen finally managed to put her gun back into her purse without having it discharge accidently; quite a feat considering she had forgotten to put the safety back on, and her hand was trembling. The pair staggered out of the front door at first not looking a whole lot better than the late Edna did, but soon they were revived by the fresh morning air.

"This is the world we live in now," Jyleen said.

"Yeah," Andrea managed to get out. "We ain't in Kansas anymore, Toto."

"Nope, we ain't," Jyleen said then she broke out in a fit of nervous laughter.

Despite her disgust and revulsion over what they had just witnessed, Andrea soon found herself joining Jyleen in almost uncontrollable laughter as well. It was something they had experienced before, the joint release of pent up stress that found its way out of their bodies any way it could manage to. The simple fact that laughing was the most inappropriate reaction to express just seemed to make the irony of situation even funnier.

"So, Andrea," Jyleen said with tears of laughter streaming down her face, "we coming back in a few days for some of that apple pie?"

"Hum . . . let me think about that," Andrea chuckled sarcastically. "Not only am I never going back there for as long as I live, but I may never eat another piece of apple pie again."

"I may have to join you in that plan," Jyleen said.

After a few more minutes, the laughter slowly began to die down and, they regained control allowing the conversation to once again take on a much more serious tone. They could hear the sound of a police siren in the distance, obviously called by Charlie.

"So, Jy, I guess you have to get back to work."

"Yeah, I suppose I do," Jyleen said leaving out a long sigh. "Not sure I feel much like dealing with any more of those creatures today though."

"Maybe you'll get lucky and no one will pass today," Andrea said hopefully, knowing that with the job of hospice nurse in this brave new world, death could come to her patients at any time, and it would be up to Jyleen and her assistant to see that their patient remains dead.

"Maybe," Jyleen said tentatively. "But who knows? We gotta do what we gotta do. We gotta keep on keeping on. We gotta put one foot in front of the other . . . blah . . . blah . . . frickin blah."

"Best of luck today, Jy. I'll call you tonight and see how you're doing."

"I'll be fine. And so will you. And come to think of it, so will Jackson and Kyla. We'll all be fine because we have no other choice."

Andrea realized just how profound that statement was.

CHAPTER 33

"What the hell are you suggesting, Sean?" Jackson asked not quite believing what his friend had just said.

"I'm suggesting that you and I go out there into the outlands and get the proof we need," Sean repeated, "Look, Jackson, we know these things exist for real now, and all the proof you once had is gone. What other choice do we have?"

"But you don't understand, Sean. These things . . . these mutants are no longer human. They're massive in size and strength, and they have absolutely no emotions." He recalled the giant, Odo and how when the man had only been a few feet from Jackson, it had stared at him with eyes as soulless as that of a zombie. Jackson had thought at the time Odo had been stoned on Braino, but now he understood the man had not been a man at all but a mutant.

"I understand that, Jackson. But people have to know that these creatures are real, and we have no proof."

"I know, Sean, but . . . these NCDVC people . . . they killed Nathan Brody over this. I'm sure of it! These people . . . the people you used to work for . . . are obviously insane, and they mean business. They're not messing around here, Sean."

"That's all the more reason for us to go out there and get the proof ourselves," Sean insisted pointing at Jackson's front door. "We can't let them get away with this sort of thing."

Jackson hesitated for a moment then said, "Ok. Let's just think about this for a minute. Suppose somehow we do manage to go into the outlands, and we do get new video or photographic proof or whatever . . . something to show the existence of these mutations. And suppose somehow miraculously we manage to make it back alive, what's to stop the NCDVC maniacs from killing us to cover up the new proof? As soon as we mention it to anyone, they'll be all over us. They apparently have spies everywhere, Sean."

"You're probably right about that," Sean agreed. "Let me think about that for a moment."

"That's probably a good idea, Sean. In fact, I think we better think about that for a lot of moments, since not doing so might result in us either being torn apart by mutants or murdered by a government goon squad."

Then Sean appeared to get an idea. This revelation didn't make Jackson very happy. He asked reluctantly, "What, Sean? I can see you have some sort of brainstorm. What are you thinking?"

"Well, from what I can tell, the reason they found out about the Brody video was because the NCDVC obviously has a spy or several spies in the offices of *The Schuylkill Daily News*. Do you agree?"

"Yes," Jackson said, "that makes sense to me."

"So let's assume for a moment we successfully come up with our own video. We wouldn't want to take it anywhere near the newspaper office or tell anyone working there except for maybe Bill McCleary that we have it because word would surely get back to the NCDVC through their spies. Right?"

"Yeah . . . that seems logical enough as well."

"Now . . . I assume the Skook has its own web site . . . doesn't it?"

"Yes, of course they do," Jackson agreed. "Most businesses do now that the web is back in operation again."

"Can I also assume that their website has links to all the national news outlets as well?"

Jackson hesitated then said, "Yes . . . I believe it does. I often see national stuff displayed on their site, and I've seen items from their site picked up by other news outlets nationwide and worldwide as well. There are still a lot of places in the world that haven't made it back onto the web, but every day it seems like more of them do. Also I've seen links to the Skook's stories show up on a bunch of other social media type sites."

"Ok. Then here's my idea. What if there was a way for us to load a story and a video directly onto the Skook's website? I mean we wouldn't want to have to contact anyone to load it for us. We would have to do it secretly and directly before anyone was aware it was happening. If that were possible then within a fraction of a second, the proof would go out to every other site connected to the newspaper's website. They all have their own links to other sites too, and my guess is that within an hour this thing will go viral . . . no pun intended. Then within a few hours most of the surviving fortified towns and cities of the country and world will know the truth."

"Maybe so. but you know the NCDVC will simply deny, deny, deny and declare everything a hoax. And although it might be too late for them to bother trying to kill me, they'll probably still try to discredit me and the story."

"I'm sure they will, but I honestly think with your worldwide fame they won't stand a chance. Your reputation is impeccable; the public would believe you, I'm sure. And if we somehow were able to get the right sort of video proof there would be nothing to dispute. You could also quote me as an unnamed source and former employee of the NCDVC."

"I'd prefer to keep you out of this, Sean. You already lost your job over this, and if I can keep you out of this mess at least publicly, you might someday have a chance at getting it back. If anyone even suspects that you were a source . . . well, they'd never hire you back."

"But don't you see? I don't care about that anymore, Jackson. All I care about is getting this truth out there. The people need to know. Think about it, Jackson, the Z43 virus lives inside of all of us. We need to know what's preventing the virus from mutating in us as it has with some of the outlanders. Otherwise, there might be nothing keeping us from someday becoming one of those wretched beasts."

"I guess I hadn't thought about that," Jackson admitted, "but you're right. If the virus is changing why haven't you and I become mutants? Surely you would have thought that someone . . . at least one person . . . somewhere in the fortified cities of the world would have experienced some form of the mutation. Right?"

"Yes. Exactly my point," Sean agreed. "Statistically speaking, unless this phenomenon is reserved for only those living like savages, surely someone within the city boundaries should have succumbed to the mutation. But they haven't; not a single person. It truly makes me wonder. And maybe there's someone out there who could help find the answers if he only knew about the problem . . . you know . . . that it actually was happening. People need this information Jackson."

"Maybe so, Sean. And if there's any way to prove the existence of these mutations and at the same time allow me to help you get your life back, I plan on making that happen. Especially now that I know for certain that it was you who saved me from death. I owe you big time, buddy."

Sean was speechless. Whether or not Jackson could help him no longer mattered to him. He was simply grateful for the fact that he had a friend as loyal as Jackson Ridge.

"So. You've worked out how we can beat the NCDVC and get our information out there . . . by the way . . . I'm sure you realize I'll have to clear all of this with Bill McCleary."

"Of course. I'm certain he'll be behind us all the way," Sean said.

"I'm sure he will be too, although I'm hesitant to contact him right now with everything his family is going through."

"I understand. But we need to make sure this is all do-able or else we're risking everything for nothing. We need to find out what we have to do to upload the information then send it on its way. That part shouldn't take but a few minutes."

"Ok. I'll have to get in touch with McCleary and find out the logistics of making this happen. But what about how we're going to manage to get the necessary proof for me to write the story? The video was the most convincing aspect of the last attempt and we have no video."

"Well, then," Sean said as if it were no big deal, "I suppose we'll just have to get our own video."

Jackson looked at him as if Sean had just announced he was an alien from another planet. "Oh, is that all? You gotta be kidding me, Sean. How in the hell are we supposed to get our own video? Do you have any idea what the odds were of Nathan Brody stumbling onto the video he filmed? They gotta be a million to one. And you honestly think we can make lightning strike twice? Too bad they still don't have the lottery game system; I'd tell you your chances might be better at winning that than getting another video."

"Well . . . maybe so . . . but I was thinking we could always go down to the same area where Nathan filmed his video and hope those creatures show up again."

"Oh . . . I see. Yeah. That should be easy," Jackson said sarcastically. "Maybe we could park by the side of the road and walk around wearing signs reading, 'Mutants Wanted —Apply Within.' Think that might work?"

"Ah, yes, the Jackson Ridge sarcastic wit. Oh, how I missed the way it manifests itself at the most inappropriate times," Sean chided.

Jackson thought about that for a moment then said, "Sorry . . . yeah . . . you're probably right. You know how it comes out sometimes when I'm stressed; most of the time I don't even realize it. But, seriously, how can we possibly expect to duplicate what Nathan did?"

"I guess the honest answer is . . . I really don't know," Sean admitted. "But I feel like we have to do something and maybe, just maybe, the same creatures Nathan saw might still be nearby and show themselves again. All we need is a few seconds of video. If we do get a good shot all you would have to do is to write a paragraph or so explaining what the video is about. Then we can claim to have proof of their existence, and you could publish an anonymous email address where people will be able to send their personal accounts of sightings. Once we upload our video it'll be too late for anyone, even the NCDVC to do anything about it."

Jackson said, "And if we get email responses after the video hits I can immediately start writing stories based on what will likely be more accounts of sightings than McCleary originally sent me."

"That's exactly what I was thinking," Sean agreed. "So are we going to do this or not?"

"Um . . . yeah . . . I guess we are," Jackson said less than enthusiastically. "I'll have to send Andrea a text letting her know I went somewhere with you. I'll tell her we're just out catching up or something. Or maybe I'll call her. That way she won't worry too much or get suspicious. She may not be crazy about me traveling down to Yuengsville because of the dangers between the cities in the outlands. I haven't made that trip since . . . well, since October, but I've done it many times before, so I think she might be ok with it. But who knows?"

Sean added, "She won't know I've been sacked yet, so you can tell her I called and asked you to stop by for an early lunch and you asked if I could give you some forensic information which might help you with the accuracy of your article. If she asks, just tell her I don't believe in such things as mutants, so my info will be strictly scientific and factual in nature."

"Yeah. I like that idea. So what all do we need to take with us?"

"Your Communications Units; both of them and whatever else you think we might need."

"But they hacked into my special CU before," Jackson said.

"I don't think so. Your CU was plugged into your docking station. I think they hacked into your base unit, and since the CU was plugged in, they were able to get into it as well. I seriously doubt they can do anything to get into a CU that isn't connected, especially one as sophisticated as that one. In fact, I believe if you had backed up the files on your portable hard drive then unplugged it and removed the special CU, you might still have the original files."

"Damn," Jackson realized, "you're probably right. Why didn't I think of that?"

"Don't beat yourself up over it. What's done is done. Let's just hope the NCDVC doesn't think of that or they might come after you personally to find out if you did have any backups. That's just another reason why we have to get moving on this quickly. It's now our job to find something even better."

The duo gathered up everything they needed for the trip. They decided they'd drive separately until they got to

Yuengsville, then Sean would park his car in a public lot and ride south with Jackson. They still hadn't formulated a strategy for getting the video proof, but they hoped an idea might come sometime along their travels. Neither of them had bothered to look out the front window onto Jackson's street or they might have noticed something, which was not quite as it should have been.

CHAPTER 34

Outside the Ridge home, a car was parked on the street about a half block away. It was a weather-beaten old 2025 Matzura Sedan. Like most of the vehicles on the road in 2054, it was inconspicuous with its a variety of colors, the result of a collection of dozens of salvaged parts from many different automobiles all stuck together, puttied, primed and painted with whatever color happened to be available at the time. There were few, if any vehicles in operation that didn't appear as if they had just driven out of some junkyard. That suited the person hunched down behind the steering wheel just fine.

He knew who lived in the home just down the street from where he watched unseen. It was Jackson Ridge, freelance writer and investigative reporter. And although that was of interest to the driver, he was more intrigued by the person he had followed from Yuengsville to Ridge's home; that man being Sean Patel, former assistant medical examiner for Schuylkill County.

The driver knew Patel had been fired from his job the previous day; however, he hadn't known that Ridge and Patel had been acquainted, let alone that they had been such close friends. He wondered exactly why Patel had driven all the way north to Ashton and why he was speaking with Ridge at such an early hour of the morning. He had shadowed Patel with the hopes the man might lead him to what he so desperately wanted, but so far all he had done was lead him to Ridge. But perhaps that wasn't a bad thing after all. Maybe there was something to this meeting he hadn't previously considered.

Could it be that Patel and Ridge were working on something together, something which would eventually produce the results he so desired. He decided to lay low and play it cool for a while to see what transpired. He was grateful it was so early in the morning, only 9:20, and Ridge's neighborhood was still surprisingly quiet. He knew soon the neighbors would be getting started on their morning rituals, running, walking, gardening and whatever. When that happened he would have to drive away as not to be noticed. He hoped if Ridge and Patel were planning something it would happen soon, and if so, he would be ready.

Then as if summoned by his mental commands Jackson Ridge and Sean Patel walked out the front door. They each headed to their own cars and without preamble, pulled out with Patel in the lead and Ridge following. The stranger knew whatever was happening between them, it was going down now so he cautiously pulled out into the street and followed an inconspicuous distance behind the pair. He was glad he had thought ahead and placed a tracking device on Sean Patel's car earlier that morning back in Yuengsville. He knew if he tried to follow closely behind them he'd be made in an instant. There were simply too few cars on the road these days to be able to try to get away with such a thing.

He wondered where they might be going as they slowly made their way out to Centre Street, the main street in Ashton heading east then turning right at Third Street to head to the southern border.

"Yuengsville," the driver said to himself.

They were heading right back to where his day had started. He realized something very important must be taking place, otherwise why else would Patel have driven all the way from Yuengsville to Ashton to talk to Ridge then travel right back an hour or so later when he could have simply called on his CU. Obviously whatever was happening hand been too crucial to be handled over the phone. He started to get a tingling sensation down the back of his neck feeling certain that he had made the right decision in following Patel.

The cars made their way along Route 61 through the southern sentry station of Ashton then into what was formerly the community of Mountain Springs, now part of the outlands between Ashton and Franksville. What were once lovely suburban homes were now deteriorating ruins overgrown with trees, tall weeds and invasive vines. Jackson hadn't made this trip in more than six months but wasn't surprised to see the roadways still in treacherous condition. Road crews did their best with little supplies to keep the roads passible. However, winter in Schuylkill County was rough and took their toll on already damaged asphalt.

As they proceeded, the driver was careful to keep a good distance away from the pair so they didn't suspect him to be anything more than a fellow traveler along the treacherous pot-hole pocked highway. The sun was now at a point in the eastern sky where it was shining brightly into his car and practically blinding him with its brilliance. He reached down into a space in the console and retrieved a pair of dark sunglasses. Yes, that was better. He could see once again.

Up ahead he recognized the familiar flashing beacon mounted atop a Dead Kill recovery truck parked along the highway. Two workers were bent over the rotting corpse of a Dead Kill. Wearing protective gloves, one of the workers had gripped the dead creature by its hands while the other had it by its feet. They began swinging the corpse slowly back and forth getting ready to toss it onto the back of the utility truck. He could see there was already one body in the back.

"You two must be having a busy day," he said to himself, smiling.

Then as he got closer, something happened which he hadn't expected. The pair was preparing for what he assumed would be their final swing getting ready to release the body. While the body was at the apex of the swing one of the creature's decomposed arms tore loose from its torso. This caused the corpse to twist and turn erratically catching the pair off guard. They let go of their grips and the carcass flew about ten feet further away from the truck landing on the gravel with a dust-raising thud.

"Losers," the driver said to himself from the safety of his car as he drove past the pair. For laughs he honked his horn as he went by and the two recovery workers shouted angrily back at him waving their fists and flipping him the bird.

The driver continued along his way up the mountain into Franksville then through the town and out the southern security gates heading down the winding highway toward what was once St. Clara but was now part of The Yuengsville Free Zone. Ridge and Patel's vehicles were no longer in site. He checked his GPS device and could see they had passed through the northern security gates at Yuengsville and were still traveling south along Route 61. This caught him by surprise. He thought they would have turned off at the side street leading up to Sean Patel's apartment, but they seemed to just be passing through the city. As he cleared the northern security gate and continued through town he could see the beacon had stopped.

"What the hell?" he wondered aloud. He slowly approached the spot where the GPS had said Patel's car was stopped and saw it was parked in the public parking facility. He instantly realized what had happened. They must now both be in Ridge's vehicle.

Where were they heading? Had they continued on and passed through Yuengsville? Were they now traveling into the southern outlands? If they had and if they stayed this course, they would eventually end up in Berks County and the Fortified City of Reading. He doubted that was their destination, especially since Jackson Ridge had recently survived a horrifying ordeal in the western outlands of that city. In fact, the driver was surprised at the idea they might even leave Yuengsville, yet he felt certain that was exactly what they were doing. Then he decided to travel a bit further and see if he could pick up their trail. He wouldn't go far outside of Yuengsville, perhaps as far as what was once the town of Cressota. Then if he didn't see Ridge's car he would accept defeat and assume he lost them. He decided he could always go back and stake out Patel's car and wait for them to return.

A few miles south of Yuengsville, near what a decade earlier had been the Cressota Mall he noticed a car pulled over to the side of the road. It was Ridge's car, he was certain. The driver knew the mall was now nothing but a deteriorating shell of a structure, overgrown with trees. Yet there was obviously something there which interested the pair. Maybe this was not going to turn out to be a wild goose chase after all. Maybe the pair would lead him right to what he needed most of all.

He slowed his vehicle and pulled it off to the side of the road several hundred feet back from the former mall location. He decided to wait a bit then to proceed south on foot. If what he suspected was right they would be leaving their car by the side of the road and proceeding on foot as well. If that was true then he could sneak up on the pair without their even realizing it.

CHAPTER 35

Jackson pulled his car over to the side of the road a few hundred feet south of where Nathan Brody had shot his video. Sean was sitting quietly in the passenger seat as Jackson finished his conversation with Andrea. Sean had been silent for the most part since entering Jackson's car. When he originally sat down, Jackson was already on his CU speaking with her.

Prior to calling Andrea after passing through the southern security post at The Ashton Cooperative, Jackson had been on the phone with Bill McCleary telling him about his and Sean's plan to try to duplicate the video. Jackson told McCleary how if they were successful they would need some way to get the video along with a brief explanation up onto the newspaper's website and quickly disseminated to any connecting links.

He stressed the importance of getting the information out on the web before the NCDVC got wind of it so that it would be impossible to stop its spread. McCleary agreed wholeheartedly and provided Jackson with a special link, which he could use to bypass all *The Schuylkill Daily News's* firewalls and place his video and story directly onto the newspaper's website. McCleary told Jackson this was his, McCleary's own personal link for occasions just like this and Jackson would only be able to have access to the link once. As soon as the video was uploaded and began spreading around the web, the link would be disabled and McCleary would be provided with a new secure link.

McCleary explained if Jackson and Sean were successful, there would be no need for Jackson to have another such link. With the story and video spreading all around the world at the speed of light, the NCDVC would have to give up any attempt to stop them. He said they'd be too busy "covering there cowardly arses" to bother with such trivial things.

Jackson also told him about Sean getting fired and how he, Jackson, suspected it was very possible that Sean's former boss, Wilbur Hershberger, might actually have had something to do with Nathan's death. Jackson told him he had no proof, but he was certain Hershberger had to be involved in some way.

"Maybe he didn't do the kidnapping himself," Jackson said, "but I think he orchestrated it. Maybe he hired some goons to do the job or perhaps even some of Sean's former co-workers at the lab. From what I can tell, Hershberger wields a lot of NCDVC authority locally, and if I were going to start looking anywhere, it would be with him."

Needless to say, McCleary was livid, and was planning on pulling out all the stops to get every bit of dirt he possibly could on not only the NCDVC but on their local office, Hershberger and all of its remaining employees. McCleary suspected Jackson was right with his theory, but even if the investigation led nowhere. Jackson was certain it would be therapeutic for McCleary to feel he was at least doing something to try to catch his nephew's killer. McCleary wasn't the sort of man to sit idly by and do nothing. Now with this possible lead, he'd be like a dog with his teeth around a juicy soup bone. Jackson realized he wouldn't want to be Wilbur Hershberger or any NCDVC cronies now that McCleary had a scent and was on their trail. After disconnecting with McCleary, as he approached the northern security checkpoint of Yuengsville, Jackson called Andrea and had been speaking with her when Sean parked his car and joined him.

"I can't believe you're in Yuengsville, Jackson," Andrea said. "You haven't left Ashton in months . . . ever since . . . well ever since you came home . . . you know . . . from the hospital."

"Yeah, I know. But Sean said he needed to show me something important he discovered in his lab."

"Do you think it has anything to do with your story . . . you know, about the mutants?"

"I sincerely doubt that," Jackson lied. "Sean doesn't believe in anything which can't be scientifically proven. If he has anything to show me regarding mutations, I suspect it will be something to contradict the idea rather than support it I'm sure."

Jackson looked over at Sean who gave him a thumbs-up gesture to indicate his approval.

Then Jackson asked Andrea, "So how are you doing? Still ok?"

"Yeah I'm fine," but suddenly Jackson noticed something wrong in her voice.

"You don't really sound fine to me. Has something happened?" Jackson was now starting to sound worried again, "You and Kyla aren't in any trouble are you?"

"No, honey. Not at all. You can relax. It's just something unfortunate happened today when Jyleen and I were at Edna's."

"What . . . what happened?"

Andrea recounted the story of their close encounter at Edna's restaurant.

"Oh my God!" Jackson exclaimed. "That was way too close. What if Jyleen hadn't seen her coming? What if Charlie hadn't come out in time?"

"It's ok, Jackson," she said. "Jyleen saw her in plenty of time. In fact, right before Charlie showed up swinging his meat cleaver like a maniac, Jyleen already had her revolver out and was taking aim. As gross and disgusting as the cleaver was, it was likely less messy than if Jyleen had shot her."

"See? That's why I think you should carry a gun, even when you're in town."

"I know," Andrea conceded, "but since I left hospice work, I've really tried to pretend all of this horrible stuff doesn't exist anymore. I know that's a ridiculous idea; today proved that better than anything could have, but I still don't want to carry a gun."

Jackson hesitated then said, "Alright. Maybe we can agree to come up with some alternative sometime, but right now over the phone really isn't the time."

"I agree. Anyway, well . . . I guess I'm glad you finally are back to your old self again."

"What do you mean? My old self?"

"Well . . . for a while I was wondering if after your ordeal in Reading last year . . . the way you were staying so close to home . . . I was afraid you might never get back to your old independent ways again. I'm starting to think maybe it was good Sean called you and motivated you to get out of the house and out of town again."

"Yeah. Me too," Jackson lied. He was feeling very guilty not telling Andrea the real reason why they were about to venture beyond Yuengsville, but he knew she'd only worry and rightfully so. He was starting to think this whole idea was insane. Yet, at the same time, part of him knew that somehow he and Sean had to find a way to prove that the Z43 virus mutations were real. He didn't intend to do anything to risk his life but then again he never did. Past experience told him that this fact alone did little to prevent his life from falling into in grave peril time and time again. He wisely decided to change the subject.

"So what are you doing for the rest of the day?"

"I'm going to walk back to the daycare and pick up Kyla. Then we're stopping at the cooperative store for a few things, and then we'll head home. I have a few calls to make to arrange for a few additional interviews for you."

"Ugh," Jackson moaned.

"Don't worry. They won't be any hard-ball interviews. Easy stuff and good for book and movie promotion.

"Always thinking," Jackson told her. "Thank goodness."

Andrea replied, "That's my job, sweetie. I AM your publicist and booking agent after all. Who knows, after you finish your articles and possibly a book about the mutant sightings maybe we'll have a whole new slew of interviews to schedule."

Jackson realized just how insightful that statement was. If he and Sean were somehow able to get the proof they sought and he managed to blow the lid off the mutant cover-up at the NCDVC, the demand for interviews would be ten times that of his previous adventure. It would likely last for years depending upon how many people in the NCDVC he and McCleary managed to bring down as well. He kept his voice neutral not wanting Andrea to realize he wasn't being completely truthful with her.

"Anyway. I should have this all wrapped up and be back home by dinner if that works out for you."

"Yes, that should be fine. I'll see you then. Love you."

"Love you too, sweetie," Jackson replied sounding as confident as he possibly could under the circumstances.

CHAPTER 36

Jackson turned off his ignition and carefully opened the door looking around to make sure it was safe outside. They were at the site of the former entrance road leading down to what had once been the Cressota Mall where Nathan Brody said he had shot his video. Now the roadway was nothing more than a pot-hole riddled mess, with weeds growing more than five feet tall, shooting up from the countless cracks in the deteriorating asphalt. There were also dozens of saplings from a few feet to trees more than thirty feet tall making the road impassable. There would be no way for them to drive Jackson's beat-up 2010 Toyota Corolla down such a tattered roadway.

"Unfortunately, we're going to have to hoof it from here." Jackson told Sean, "The road's a mess."

"D . . . do . . . do you think that's wise?" Sean stammered. "I thought perhaps we could stay up here . . . and maybe try to film from the roadway as Nathan had done."

"Look, Sean. Nathan getting that video was a lucky shot . . . you know, a one-in-a-million occurrence. We could sit here for hours or days and never see anything. If we truly want to try to get the proof we need . . . sitting here won't cut it."

"I understand . . . but what if we do find something . . . I mean . . . if we're down there in . . . you know . . . their territory . . . what are the chances of us making it back to the car safely?"

"I don't have the slightest idea, Sean . . . but I also don't see that we have any choice here. We're either going to do this or we're not . . . If you've changed your mind and want to just forget the whole thing and head back to Yuengsville, you won't be hurting my feelings in the slightest. As you know, my history in the outlands isn't a very pleasant one. I'm not exactly wild about the idea of getting anywhere near that mess down there or encountering one of those mutated things. I had actually hoped we'd be able to drive closer, but by the looks of that road, we're out of luck. So, if my vote counts for anything, I vote we go back home and forget the whole thing. Maybe we'll get lucky and learn of somebody else who was fool hearty enough to shoot his own video and who would offer it to the Skook to write about."

"But what about this story? What about Nathan?" Sean asked. "Nathan Brody died trying to bring his video to the public. We agreed we owe him some justice."

"True," Jackson agreed. "He does deserve justice, but I have no intention of getting myself killed in the process. So what'll it be? Do you have some sort of plan in mind, Sean? Because right now we're safe and sound, that is providing no dead heads stumble onto us. However, those mutated creatures are probably somewhere deep in the woods down there. Not to mention the fact that there could be gangs of psycho outlanders hanging around nearby as well. So if you want us to make this happen, what's the plan? Because right now, I got nothing."

"Unfortunately, neither do I. But there must be something we can do . . . and still manage to stay safe at the same time."

Jackson stared at the devastated ramp leading downward. He shook his head in frustration, sighed and said, "Look, Sean . . . if we're gonna to do this . . . then we have no choice. we have to go down there on foot . . . not my first, second or third choice . . . but I think we can be careful . . . you know . . . we can keep our eyes peeled for trouble . . . and be ready to run back up quickly if we need to."

"Yes . . . I suppose that's possible," Sean agreed. "We should be ok . . . with two of us watching out for trouble."

"Agreed. Can I assume you brought your gun with you?"

Sean said, "Of course. And you have yours was well?"

"Don't leave home without it." Jackson snickered showing Sean his forty-five, the same one which had brought down the huge dead monster many months earlier.

Jackson reached into the car and pulled out two backpacks. They contained many of the supplies the pair thought they might need for their excursion.

"I'm going to put my gun in the backpack. It'll still be easily accessible if need it yet safely tucked away so I don't fall and accidently shoot myself in the foot or something.

"Good idea," Sean agreed. "I'm not big on handling guns either. I'll put mine in my backpack as well. If we find ourselves wounded out here, we're as good as dead."

"You seemed to be able handle a gun pretty well that day in the barn when you rescued me."

"That was an unfortunate necessity, Jackson. And if I had to I would do it again, but the truth is I would rather leave gunplay for the police or the military. It's not really my thing."

Then whether it was an excuse to delay their next action or because it was on his mind and seemed like the right time, Jackson asked, "Sean . . . that Dead Kill I nailed that morning back in October . . . the big one? I've been wondering if maybe that might have actually been a mutant. What do you think?"

"Hum . . . I honestly don't know, Jackson. I treated that body as I would have treated any other Dead Kill. I assumed it was just a big fellow who had died and come back. I hadn't even been considering the possibility of mutants back then."

"So you're sure he was already dead when I shot him?" Jackson asked.

Sean looked at him at first with confusion then suddenly realized what Jackson was asking, "I see. You're concerned that you might have actually killed a living mutated creature rather than a zombie. Is that correct?"

"It's something I've been wondering about since I started suspecting that these things might really exist. Before then I never considered it, but now . . . well . . . it really concerns me."

"Rest assured, my friend. That thing you shot was a reanimated corpse. It was in an obvious state of decomposition and had been dead for many weeks."

"Thank goodness."

Then Sean explained, "That doesn't mean that it wasn't still a mutant before it died from whatever had initially killed it."

"What?" Jackson asked.

"I'm suggesting that based on its size and physical appearance, it could have very well been a mutant which had either died of natural causes or had been killed weeks before you ever encountered it. Then it came back as a very large zombie. But whatever its prior status, it was undead when you shot it."

"But, shouldn't something so huge have gotten your attention?" Jackson asked, "I mean . . . and I'm not telling you how to do your job or anything . . . but I would have thought with all the alleged mutant sightings, this creature would have stood out."

"Based on what we now know, perhaps it should have. Maybe you're right, Jackson. But at the time it never occurred to me. Blame it on my busy schedule or too much work and too little sleep; all valid and accurate excuses. But whatever the reason, that Dead Kill was just treated like any other. Maybe I missed it. Maybe I dropped the ball."

Jackson really didn't care if Sean had missed it or if the creature was or was not a mutant. He was just satisfied that Sean had confirmed that he had not accidently killed a living being. Then he suddenly thought of something else and asked, "The identity of that Dead Kill . . . Did you ever find out who he was in life?"

"No. That one was never identified. The remains went into the cooler for a month then eventually were cremated."

"So there's no chance to ever nail the guy's identity down now?"

Sean said, "None, Jackson. I'm afraid not. But to be honest, now knowing that mutants are real, I would love to have that beast's body on my table again. That is to say if I still had a table or a job for that matter."

"Well, maybe when this is all out in the open we might at least find some way get your job back," Jackson suggested.

"Not likely . . . at least not with Hershberger still in charge."

"Perhaps when the airborne defecation hits the oscillating ventilation my friend . . . maybe Mr. Wilbur Hershberger will find himself behind bars. I think we both agree he could very well be the man behind Nathan's murder. I haven't figured out how yet, but I promise you we'll find a way. With McCleary on his trail, there's likely going to be all sorts of dirt dug up. And believe me, if he's involved he's going down for this."

"McCleary? So you've told him about what we uncovered?" Sean asked.

"I spoke with him earlier about my suspicions regarding Hershberger and he's eager to start an investigation and if my gut is right he'll find something."

"If he is involved," Sean said, "then he should pay the price for his crimes. If McCleary can prove Hershberger is tied into this, there might actually be some distant possibility of me getting my position back. Then again, that may be nothing more than my wishful thinking. Well. then . . . I suppose if we're going to do this . . . we'd better be on our way."

"I agree," Jackson replied.

The pair slowly began to walk through the tall undergrowth along the roadway, easing their way toward the ruins of the Cressota Mall and the forest which now occupied its skeletal hull.

CHAPTER 37

About half way down the incline, Jackson and Sean suddenly were stopped in their tracks by a shrill screeching sound coming from the south. It was a blood-curdling cry that immediately raised goose-bumps on their arms.

"Wha . . . what was that?" Sean asked shakily.

"Don't know," Jackson replied. "Not sure that I want to know either."

The pair stood stock-still for a few more seconds. They noticed it had gotten completely silent except for a slight lapping sound in the distance. Then Jackson asked quietly, "Do you hear that?"

Sean whispered, "No. I don't hear anything now."

"In the distance off to our left; sounds like water running."

"Yes, that's possible. The Schuylkill River runs along the side of this place. Over there behind all those trees." Sean pointed off to the left at a thick forest consisting of what seemed like every variety of tree imaginable which had grown up through the asphalt of what had once been the parking lot for the abandoned mall. "There's a good chance one of the creatures Brody filmed is down there right now drinking from the river."

Jackson, being Jackson, chose this moment to make another of his signature sarcastic remarks having no idea how prophetic it would prove to be, "If outlanders are drinking straight from the Schuylkil, then it's no wonder they're mutating. Even before the outbreak people knew enough not to drink directly from that river."

"Regardless," Sean said, "it's possible if we head in that direction we might find what we're looking for."

"All the more reason to head back in the direction we just came from," Jackson said. "After hearing that God-awful sound, I think maybe this isn't a very good idea after all, Sean."

Sean seemed to think for a moment then suggested, "What say we just slowly head over in that direction? As I recall, the river actually runs twenty or thirty feet below this area so we should be able to sneak safely through the woods and look down on whatever is there. If it is one of those things, we can film it and it might not even know we're there."

"Might?" Jackson asked nervously. "I think I need a bit more assurance than might, Double I."

"Sorry, my friend, that's about the best I can do. We're well armed, Jackson, but to be honest with you, I think these creatures are more timid than we realize. I suspect that's why no one has successfully filmed them before Brody did."

"Did you ever stop to think, Sean that maybe the reason we've never gotten good video before is because the people trying to get said video might have been ripped to pieces and eaten?"

Sean hesitated, swallowed hard then said, "Ok. Point taken. So now what?"

Jackson looked around them then looked back at the car as if judging how long it might take him to run back if he needed to and said, "Ok. Let's go a bit further and see what happens." Then he added sardonically, "And remember, Sean . . . I don't have to be able to outrun any mutant . . . I only have to outrun you."

"But . . . what . . . do you . . ." Sean stammered. Then seeing the sheepish grin on his friend's face he realized Jackson was making one of his stale old jokes. At least Sean hoped he was joking.

As the pair made their way through the tall weeds approaching the edge of the thick forest, they heard a scraping sort of sound off to their right. They both turned simultaneously to see the tops of some of the weeds moving about ten feet away. They could tell that something was crawling low to the ground in the grass, and it was heading slowly toward them. Jackson took off his backpack, pulled out his revolver and pointed it directly at the shifting weeds, ready to blow a hole in whatever was coming.

Sean put his hand on Jackson's gun, signaling him to lower it. He looked at Jackson, made the universal finger on the lips sign for quiet and mouthed the words, "I got this."

He reached into his own backpack and withdrew a long knife with a glimmering blade attached to a wooden handle. Jackson looked at him with uncertainty as whatever was moving in the weeds seemed to get closer. Then Jackson heard what Sean must have heard before him. It was a low, guttural growl not of an animal but of the undead. Just as he realized a dead head was making its way toward them, the thing came creeping into view.

As soon as it broke through the weeds Jackson realized why it had been crawling and not walking in the typical awkward gate the creatures all had. To say the creature was incomplete would have the understatement of all understatements. It consisted of just a head, neck, one arm and just part of its torso. Below what was left of the body trailed a partial ribcage with bits of flesh still clinging to bone and the remainder of its long spinal column, which seemed to snake back and forth behind the creature. Jackson was instantly reminded of what had happened to Mrs. Kinkaid earlier that week, but this horrible creature was in much worse condition than she was. She had been a fresh kill . . . this thing was rotten, probably decomposing for months. The stench of the thing even at their distance was nauseating.

Looking more closely at the creature, Jackson realized it was not much more than a skeleton with some of its flesh still clinging futilely to its bones. Yet it was still moving and apparently it still had that same insatiable hunger all such creatures had. It was laboriously advancing itself by grasping clumps of weeds with the bony fingers of its single arm, then pulling its rotting carcass forward. It repeated this action one painstaking foot after another. And despite the decayed condition of its gaping mouth the creature appeared to have enough teeth remaining to accomplish its desired goal. It continued to inch its way ever closer to the pair.

Sean walked quietly over to the pitiful thing and drove the blade of his long knife deep into the creature's skull. Jackson heard a sickening sound as the blade passed through bone and into the thing's rotted brain. The pong surrounding the putrefying beast at such a close proximity was worse than anything he could have imagined. The creature twitched a bit more, its single arm grasping hopeless for Sean's foot. Then Sean twisted the blade, and Jackson heard the zombie's skull crack in two. It stopped twitching and lay still. Sean stood upright, leaving the blade sticking out of the shattered skull.

"Aren't . . . you . . . I mean . . . don't you want that back?" Jackson asked indicating the knife.

Sean looked at it for a moment then shook his head and said, "I have no intention of ever touching that disgusting blade again."

"Probably a good call," Jackson agreed, shaking his head in revulsion. He returned his gun to his backpack then strapped the pack securely in place once again.

The pair turned without saying another word and made their way into the dense forest of trees ahead of them. As they did, they heard the sound of the Schuylkill River getting louder and they knew they were getting closer to the end overlooking the river. They began to walk more carefully as they both assumed they were almost there. If what Sean thought was correct, there would be a long drop to the river below and the last thing either of them needed was to fall or become injured in the outlands.

Up ahead, they could see the end of the woods as light was peaking in through the last remaining trees. There was a small clearing. Sean stopped and got down on his stomach. Jackson did the same as he crawled up next to Sean who was looking down over the edge of the thirty-foot high precipice. They could see the Schuylkill River running rapidly below them and also noticed a small plot of land next to the river bank. They both realized they were far too deep in dangerous country to speak aloud so they chose instead to scan the area below in silence.

Suddenly Sean noticed something off to his right slinking along the gravely river bed. It was unlike anything he had ever seen in his life. He held back a horrifying scream which wanted to escape from his throat. Jackson noticed the terrified look on Sean's face, and he followed his line of site until he too saw the unbelievable thing below. He recognized it immediately as either being the same creature from Nathan Brody's video or one very similar. Although the video didn't allow for a detailed look at the creature, Jackson could instantly tell it was shaped just like one of the two blurry images. It was the one which had been so horribly deformed as not to be mistaken.

The hideous beast was squatting hunched on the river bank apparently bent down and scooping water from the rushing waterway. As its hand came up out of the water, Jackson could see it was massive, probably three times the size of a human hand, and in its cupped palm it must have held more than a gallon of water. Its fingers were long and perhaps two inches around with talon-like claws on the ends. It raised its bucket-like hand to drink. As it drank, it turned its head slightly to the side. Jackson and Sean saw for the first time just how incredibly inhuman the thing was.

In profile the creature's head was long and elliptical in shape with a bulbous skull leading back to a mane of long, dark matted hair which hung far below the thing's shoulders. It was dressed in human clothing but that was where the similarity to any human ended. Even in its hunched pose Jackson could tell the thing was huge and its arms and legs were bulging with extraordinarily large muscles; its flesh glimmering with sweat and caked with grime. It was dressed in a wife-beater tee shirt and jeans, both of which hung in tattered rags. Toward the front of its skull atop a slick fleshy surface were two huge segmented eyes, like those of an insect. Then at the front of the head were long squid-like tentacles which all seemed to wave madly in the air like the mythical snakes which made up Medusa's hair.

But Jackson intuitively understood that these seemingly random tentacular movements were not as haphazard as they initially seemed to be but each served a purpose. He suspected they were equipped with some sort of sensors which sampled the air, testing for the presence of danger. Their slithering motions were much too calculated to not be serving some useful purpose. The thing cocked its head further to the left and lifted it slightly. Jackson saw holes in the side of its skull that he suspected must be what the thing used to hear. These holes pulsated as if desperately searching for the sounds of potential danger. Likewise, several of the flopping tentacles were reaching in Jackson and Sean's direction as if they might have heard some miniscule sound the two had made. Jackson wondered if even at this distance the creature could smell their scent or perhaps hear their frightened breathing.

Jackson reached carefully into his shirt pocket and removed his special Communications Unit. He hoped the barely audible sound of the video record screen icon would not be picked up by the creature below them. If so, they would be in real trouble. Hoping for the best, Jackson began recording the creature drinking from the river.

As he zoomed in for a closer more detailed shot, Jackson noted how although the creature looked a lot like the silhouetted creatures in Nathan Brody's video, he had no idea just how hideous the mutated thing was. Now he could see all of the horrifying details of the beast. It was incredible. From the center of the nest of snake-like appendages at the front of the creature's head, Jackson saw a tubular fleshy thing extend outward to meet the raised clawed bucket of a hand. The water in the thing's palm was quickly sucked in through the slime-covered tube as the tentacles continued sniffing the air around them. He also noticed the creature's segmented eyes were likewise in constant motion, searching the area while it drank.

Apparently these creatures knew of the dangers in the outlands and as such understood the need to be alert at all times; something which Jackson suddenly realized he and Sean had momentarily forgotten in their excitement to get such amazing video footage. He decided now that they had what they needed, and it would be a good idea to back away slowly and return to the safety of their car. That was when he noticed the strange smell.

CHAPTER 38

The scent was deep, damp, woodsy and feral; something Jackson's instincts told him were animal-like smells. And there was something else; something he recognized as being somewhat familiar. It was an odor he had smelled a half a year earlier but one he would never forget. It was when he was in that barn, captive, hanging helplessly, nailed to that crossbeam.

"Odo," Jackson suddenly thought. That scent was similar to the stink that surrounded Deimos' mutant henchman Odo. And yes, Jackson now knew with certainty that Odo had been a mutant.

He slowly turned his head to look behind him as Sean intuitively did likewise. A blood curdling scream lodged in Jackson's throat as the sight before him. He heard Sean let out a keening high-pitched cry like that of a bleating lamb. Standing directly over them was a massive creature, a real mutant.

Time seemed to stand still as Jackson took in the unbelievably terrifying sight above him. Unlike the creature at the river, this one actually did resemble Odo but was even much more hideous. Jackson suddenly understood that Odo must have only been in the early stages of mutation, or perhaps his body had taken an alternate course of mutation. This beast however was much further removed from humanity than the monster Odo had apparently been.

The thing stood at least nine feet tall with shoulders between five and six feet wide. It amazed Jackson how something so huge could have sneaked up on them without making even the slightest of sounds. Its head was a giant cement block of a thing with long, matted dark hair and a bushy equally matted black beard. It had a thick single line of hair stretched across a protruding Neanderthal brow. It had a wide ape-like nose with flaring nostrils. Its hooded red eyes stared angrily and what was worse, hungrily from deep dark sockets. These were the eyes of a predator and hunter, Jackson knew immediately. Those eyes were cold, calculating and completely void of emotion.

The creature wore a tattered tee shirt bearing the logo of some rock band, the name of which Jackson could no longer remember. The sleeves were gone, giving Jackson a view of the beast's enormous, long ape-like muscular arms, which were riddles with scars and thick raised veins. The surface of the thing's skin was leathery, glistening with sweat and caked with filth. Swarms of flies surrounded the creature, yet it seemed to pay them no attention. All of its focus was on Jackson and Sean.

At the ends of the long arms hung two colossal hands with razor-sharp claws, extending out from the tips of its thick fingers. Below the waist the thing wore the remnants of a shredded pair of black jeans. It had no shoes and its hairy feet were as deadly looking as it hands with their own set of brownish-yellow claws.

"What . . . are we going . . . to do now?" Jackson heard Sean whisper in a trembling voice from the corner of his mouth.

"I . . . I . . . I . . . think we're going to die, Sean," Jackson said honestly.

Just then the creature took in a large gulp of air, expanding its chest to the maximum and pulling back his muscular arms. It let loose with an extraordinarily ear-piercing roar, the likes of which either man had never heard before. It was a thousand times worse than what had been recorded on Nathan Brody's video. Perhaps it only felt that way because this was happening just a few feet in front of them and they were both trapped with no chance of escape. A revolting stench like that of rotting meat accompanied the howl permeated the air and making the two men instantly nauseous. Even Sean, who dealt with decomposing zombie corpses on a daily basis, was sickened by the putrid reek.

Through squinting eyes Jackson saw the thing's wide open maw. It was filled with wolf-like yellowed fangs creating a weapon Jackson knew could easily rip them to shreds in seconds, which he assumed was about to happen. In those last few precious moments, which

Jackson understood would be his last on earth he thought of Andrea and Kyla, and how he had failed them both yet again. Only six months earlier, he had barely escaped death by crucifixion, and now he was going to be devoured alive by a mutated freak of nature.

Lying on their backs, neither Jackson nor Sean could access their backpacks where their guns were stored. Not that it mattered much, as he was certain there wouldn't be time to kill the thing before it was on them anyway. Still Jackson wondered if he should at least try to reach for it. But every time he made the slightest movement the creature tensed as if it were about to attack. He wasn't sure why it hadn't fallen upon them yet, it was as if the creature were waiting to see if it needed to defend itself. It was like the thing was analyzing the pair to determine their threat level.

Then Jackson thought about his special Communications Unit. He recalled how he had been instructed that the unit could be used as a Taser, capable of outputting enough voltage to kill a man if necessary. He had even used it once on a low setting to incapacitate the irate proprietor of an outland trading post. But he had no idea where his CU was. He must have dropped it somewhere on the ground when he saw the creature looming above them. If he could find his CU maybe he could shoot the thing with enough electricity to stun it. He doubted it would be enough to kill a beast of this size, but it might disable it long enough for them both to get away. Unfortunately, he couldn't make any sudden movements to try to feel around for it. He knew then that he and Sean were surely dead men.

Jackson suddenly noticed how everything around them had gone deathly silent. He could hear Sean tremulous breathing next to him and the deep windy sounds of the creature's inhalations above him, its block-like skull acting like an echo chamber. The silence seemed to go on for an eternity when in reality it was only a few seconds.

Suddenly the silence was shattered by an incredible explosion. Jackson and Sean were staring up at the loathsome creature waiting for their impending doom when the thing's face exploded outward showering them with bits of flesh, bone and gore. The body of the mountainous beast crashed to the forest floor with a rumbling thud powerful enough to shake the earth beneath them. The it tipped forward and landed between the pair as blood pumped from its tattered neck stump for a few repulsive seconds before slowing down to a light flow then a crimson trickle.

Jackson heard a retching sound and turned to see Sean on his side vomiting uncontrollably. Jackson had no idea why he hadn't thrown up as well, but was glad he had been able to hold it together. Now he knew it was time to get out of Dodge as there was no way that other creature down at the river bank hadn't heard the commotion. Jackson had no idea if the gunshot would scare the other creature away or would bring it running to attack, but he had no intention of finding out. He only hoped that whoever it was who destroyed the mutant, was friendly and not some psychotic crazed outlander. If that were the case then they had gotten out of the proverbial frying pan only to land in the fire.

He shook Sean indicating it was time for them to go and as he started to get up he saw a figure coming out of the trees, occupying the space where the mutant had been. It was a man holding a double-barrel shotgun; its barrel still smoking from the blast which so efficiently dispatched the creature. The man was dressed in a pair of black leather pants with snakeskin boots. He wore a black silk shirt under a black leather vest. On his head he wore a dark leather cowboy hat with a brown hatband and a silver belt buckle of a grinning skull with ruby eyes. He wore a similar style buckle and the name Death Bringer was carved on both sides of the belt.

"Delbert?" Jackson asked astonished.

The man replied, "Not Delbert any more, Jackson. Now and forever I'll be known as 'Death Bringer Jones—Mutant Slayer.'"

CHAPTER 39

"Who . . . who . . . in the . . . hell . . . is that?" Sean adked in a quavering voice.

"Sean, I'd like you to meet Delb . . . I mean Death Bringer Jones, Mutant Slayer," Jackson said, not wanting in any way to slight the man who just saved their lives.

Sean hesitated then asked, "You . . . you mean the guy . . . from the comics? That guy?"

"Yeah. The one and the same."

"You mean to tell me there really is a Death Bringer Jones? I always thought that was just something someone made up for the graphic novels."

"Nope, he's real," Jackson said hurriedly. "I'll tell you all about it later. Let's just get the hell out of here! All right?"

Jackson bent down and picked up his Communications Unit, which he found sitting at an angle leaning against the base of a small scrub tree. He noted the thing was still filming. He must have forgotten to turn it off. He clicked the stop icon to stop the recording.

"Does that CU have a video recorder?" Jones asked. Jackson suddenly realized Jones appeared much more menacing in full Death Bringer uniform than Jackson suspected he would have looked when dressed as a member of the Dead Kill Retrieval Squad. Apparently, Jones had managed to put on a good deal of muscle over the years. Maybe he wasn't quite as huge as the comic books depicted, but he was certainly no longer the scrawny kid Jackson had known.

"Yeah . . . yes, it does . . . but look . . . we don't have time for this, we need to get out of here," Jackson insisted.

"No . . . Not just yet," Jones said calmly. "I want you to do something for me first."

Jackson asked, "What are you talking about? This is no place to hang around having a conversation. Let's go back up to the car . . . we can talk there."

Jones looked at Jackson sternly and said, "First I want you to video tape this dead mutant with me standing over him. You told me the other day when we spoke on the phone you wanted to do a story about the legendary Death Bringer Jones. Well . . . here it is. This is the money shot for that story."

"But . . . but . . . seriously? You really think this is the time and place?"

"It's exactly the time and place," Jones argued, "It won't take you more than a minute to film . . . so the sooner you get started the sooner we can leave." Then Jones surprised Jackson by changing his tone of voice to one more humble and said, "Jackson, you know how important this is to me . . . I told you . . . I've wanted this for so long."

Reluctantly Jackson quickly switched on the recorder once attain and began panning the lens over the dead, headless mutant working his way along the body. When he saw Jones' snakeskin boots entering the picture, he began to pan upward. As Jones' full body shot was visible, Jackson noticed the man had struck a pose very similar to one Jackson had once seen on the cover of an old Death Bringer Jones graphic novel. Then Jones' face was in the shot along with the upper part of his body. The would-be superhero took on a serious expression and spoke directly into the camera lens.

"I am the legendary Death Bringer Jones. I've been known throughout the years as an incredible zombie killer. But now with this video as proof I have returned and am a slayer of mutants." Jones raised his arms high into the air, one holding the shotgun and the other clenched in a fist. Once again, Jackson was reminded of a pose from some comic book cover. Despite the fact that he was terrified and wanted to get back to the safety of his car as quickly as possible, Jackson did find the display a bit humorous. That was, until everything suddenly went horribly wrong.

Jones was in the middle of re-chanting, "I am Death Bring . . ." but stopped suddenly, his eyes growing wide with shock. As Jackson recorded the scene and Sean looked on, they saw the area around Jones' stomach extend outward like the distended abdomen of a pregnant woman. Then it suddenly exploded in much the same way as the mutant's head had done. But Jackson could tell this was not a gunshot which caused the eruption of blood, flesh and innards since an enormous clawed hand now protruded completely out of Jones' stomach, holding his bloody intestines in its grasp like a child playing in a bowl of thick spaghetti.

Death Bringer Jones looked down in astonishment at what was happening to him. It was just like his terrible dream, that horrible repeating nightmare. In those nightmares, he had always forgotten to check to see if the mutant was alone. In his nightmares the mutant always had a mate. In his nightmares, the mate took revenge and killed Jones. Now the nightmares had become reality. The last thing Jones saw was the horrifying hand retracting back through him. The last thing he felt, however, had been the cracking of his spine as it was torn out of his body. Then there was only darkness and thankfully, no more pain.

Jackson stood staring dumbfounded as the monstrous hand pulled back through Jones, whose body was convulsing uncontrollably. Then Jackson heard a sharp cracking sound and the dead body of Delbert Bertram Jones fell atop the headless corpse of the slain mutant. What he saw next was beyond his comprehension and chilled him to the very core of his humanity.

Standing over the corpses was another mutant, not quite as large as the first and most recognizably female. Its head was large and bulbous with long matted hair and similar facial features to the now dead headless creature lying on the ground. It wore tattered blue jeans and was shoeless. In addition, this creature was shirtless and Jackson stared at eight pendulous hairy breasts which hung down from the thing's leathery chest, resting on its distended stomach. It was most definitely a female and appeared to be very pregnant.

Jackson wasn't moving, gazing awestruck at the horrifying spectacle before him. He had apparently forgotten the fact that he was still trapped with his back to a deadly drop-off while a hell-spawn creature blocked his only escape route. Or else he was just in shock. He still held his Communications Unit and was still filming everything. A moment later, he felt a sharp tug on his backpack followed immediately by the roar of two guns blasting away next to him. It was Sean. He must have recovered from his nausea and was now peppering the wretched beast with a hail of bullets.

The creature's naked breasts were torn to pieces by shot after shot from the two pistols. Sean looked like a wild bandito from some ancient western movie with guns blazing and a look of savage determination etched on his face. But despite the severe injuries the creature had taken it somehow miraculously still stood its ground.

"The head, Sean! Aim for the head!" Jackson shouted. He figured head shots worked for zombies, and it had taken down this creature's mate so why not try it again? Sean raised both guns and fired, but they clicked uselessly, now out of ammunition.

"I'm out, Jackson," Sean shouted, stating the obvious. "I got nothing." Although they had brought their guns, they had not planned on going to war so they hadn't brought extra ammunition.

The she beast began to lurch clumsily toward them. That was when the bushes next to them were thrust aside by yet another hideous creature. Jackson recognized it as the squid-thing which had been down by the river. It must have heard the commotion and come up to investigate. Seeing one of its natural enemies dead and its mate wounded, the thing must have decided to take advantage of the situation. It grabbed the she creature by its neck with one huge clawed hand and began scraping and tearing at its already tattered breasts with the other. It was obvious to Sean and Jackson which mutant would win the conflict, so Jackson signaled to Sean for them both to try to sneak past the pair while they were preoccupied in a fight to the death.

Just as they began to inch their way around the fray, Sean felt something grabbing his ankle. It was Jones; not the living Jones who had saved their lives but a zombified version of Jones who had just returned from the dead. It crawled along the ground with its jaws snapping, eager for human flesh. A gaping bloody hole was present in its back where the she creature had ripped out his lower spine.

Because of Jackson's position in relation to Sean, he was unable to do anything to help him.

Sean bent over, grabbing his gun by the handle with two hands and with all of his might thrust the barrel downward sending it straight into the top of the zombie's head. Jackson heard a horrible cracking sound as the barrel penetrated the creature's skull then sickening squishing sound as the weapon sunk deep into the undead thing's brain. The Jones thing twitched and shuddered for a few seconds as Sean twisted and pushed the barrel deeper into its skull before it finally jerked one more time then lay still. Death Bringer Jones was gone forever, never to rise again.

Sean got back to his feet and exhaled deeply nodding to Jackson to indicate it was time to move on. In front of them the battle between the mutants was winding down; the she beast was almost dead, being no match for the stronger foe. The squid thing had suffered some serious wounds but would still be just as deadly to Jackson and Sean regardless. As the pair inched past the mutants, the squid beast raised its hideous head and its huge segmented eyes stared directly at Jackson. He knew if they tried to run the creature would be on them in just a few seconds. The she beast fell to the forest floor dead, and the squid thing now focused completely on Sean and Jackson. Once again it looked as if they would not survive the next few minutes. Then Jackson remembered his special Communications Unit as well as how it was equipped with those defensive features.

The beast began to step over the corpse of its vanquished foe and was just a few feet in front of them. Jackson could see right into the front of its terrible maw as it roared in anger. Its tentacles were thrashing madly though the air in all directions and that incredible feeding tube was beginning to inch its way out of the creature's mouth toward him.

Jackson raised the CU, pointed the front directly at the creature then pressed the yellow button on the left side launching a wired electric projectile from the CU, sinking it right into the creature's extended feeding organ. He held the button down as he had been instructed to do shooting the maximum of 50,000 volts of electricity into the beast. The creature stood in place twitching and convulsing uncontrollably. A thin stream of smoke began to pour from the tips of its tentacles and a moment later both of its segmented eyeballs exploded in a shower of gore. The creature fell dead, landing on top of the body of the she creature.

"Is . . . is it dead?" Sean asked.

"Don't know, Double I . . . don't care," Jackson replied. "Let's just get the hell out of here."

The pair disregarded any previous attempts at stealth and ran like they had never run before. They raced through the thick trees, branches scratching their faces and hands as they fled. Soon they could see the ramp leading up to their car. They shot up the ramp in seconds and soon were safely at Jackson's car. That was when Jackson noticed another car pulled over several hundred feet behind them.

"That must be Jones' car," Jackson said "He must have been following us."

"We can report the car as abandoned when we get back," Sean said.

"What about . . . his . . . the body, Sean?"

Sean thought for a moment then said, "When we eventually tell our story we can see if the authorities want to send the retrieval squad. But I suspect once they learn what we discovered and what happened, they'll probably send a team of investigators in to pick up all the remains for study."

"Poor Delbert. He finally got what he wanted in life and then it was all instantly snatched away from him.

"Not so fast youse two," a voice said from behind them.

Jackson turned and saw a strange looking little outlander, dressed in rags standing behind them pointing some sort of homemade knife at them, which reminded Jackson of a prison shiv. He was only about four feet or so tall and was slightly built. He wore a tattered leather vest over a filthy yellowed stained tee shirt. Rainbow striped suspenders held up a pair of green plaid Bermuda shorts. He wore no socks and two mismatched sneakers. He was filthy and caked with as much grime as the mutant creatures had been. It took Jackson a moment to determine that the little man was in fact, a human and not some other form of mutation.

"Doncha go makin' any sudden moves needer," the outlander demanded, "Er else I be guttin' ya likes a hog."

Jackson and Sean looked at each other as if wondering how much more weirdness they might be expected to deal with on this already bizarre day.

"You dere!" the short man demanded pointing at Jackson. "Open up dat trunk an git in. An you . . . dark meat . . . you git in dere too." He was pointing his blade at Sean now.

"Look," Jackson said trying to avoid any more conflict, "if you want the car just take it. We'll walk back to Yuengsville or call for help. Just leave us alone, OK? We've already had a bad enough day."

The little man snickered as if he was privy to a joke neither Jackson nor Sean was aware of, "But it ain't jes da car I wants. Me an me boys gonna be feastin on sum delicious long pork t'night, boat wite meat an dark."

"Long pork?" Jackson said with confusion. Then he looked over at Sean and asked him, "Do you have any idea what this guy is talking about?"

Sean looked at Jackson seriously and said, "Yeah, Jackson. I know. I'm surprised you don't, being a history buff and all. Long pork is a term used to refer to cannibalism. He's planning on taking us back to his tribe of outlanders and serving us up for dinner."

"What?" Jackson exclaimed looking back at the outlander. "You can't be serious."

The outlander lifted his knife closer to Jackson and demanded, "Git in dat dere trunk . . . boata youse. An do it quick er I'll field dress ya here an now."

Jackson was more amused than frightened and said, "Look, little fella. There's two of us and only one of you. And all you got is that crappy little knife. Do you really thing this is a good idea?" Jackson was carefully reaching for his CU with the intentions of giving the dwarf a nice jolt of electricity.

"I a sabbich killa wit no root," the strange man said cryptically as he continued to wave his knife.

"What did he say?" Jackson asked Sean.

Sean thought about it for a moment then said, "I got part of it. I think he said he's a savage killer. But I didn't get the last part." Sean addressed the little man, "Excuse me, what was that you said again?"

"I a sabbich killa wit no root," the dwarf repeated.

"Wit no root?" Sean said contemplating, "I wonder what that's supposed to mean."

"Maybe he has no relatives . . . you know . . . know roots and maybe he thinks that means he has nothing to lose."

"No . . . no . . . I don't think that's it." Sean said, "I've studied outlander dialects from time to time and one thing everyone forgets about is the way they tend to not pronounce the "th" sounds. You know . . . the word think becomes tink and so forth."

"So you think he's saying he's a savage killer with no rooth?" Jackson asked. "That makes even less sense."

Sean thought for a second then his face lit up with realization, "I've got it! He's trying to tell us that despite the fact that he small and appears relatively harmless he is actually a savage ruthless killer. Get it . . . ruthless . . . no ruth . . . or in outlander speak 'sabbich killa wit no root.'"

"Yar . . . I a sabbich killa wit no root," the dwarf said for the third time. "Now you . . . wite meat an you . . . dark meat . . . get in da trunk er die now."

Sean expression changed to a look of complete frustration. He had apparently reached the limit of what he could tolerate in one day. He said loudly, "I really don't need this. You've wasted enough of our time today." Then in a very un-Sean-like move he walked right over to the tiny outlander, punched him square in the jaw and instantly cold-cocked him, rendering the dwarf unconscious.

"Holy crap, Double I!" Jackson shouted. "I . . . I never knew you had that in you. Gandhi wouldn't have approved."

"Maybe not," Sean said, shaking off the pain in his hand, "but Jack Dempsey would have. And I am half Irish after all."

All Jackson could do was look down at the unconscious outlander with his mouth hanging open in surprise.

"Let's go, Jackson," Sean said. "We have a lot of work to do."

Then the two dragged the outlander over to the side of the road, out of the path of their car. The pair got into the car and simultaneously let out a sigh of relief, then locked the doors. Jackson did an abrupt U-turn and headed back toward Yuengsville.

CHAPTER 40

"My God! This footage is incredible," Sean said from the passenger seat. He was reviewing the recording Jackson had made just minutes earlier. "Jackson, you got everything. And I mean absolutely everything!"

"It was nothing but pure luck, Sean. I noticed when I picked up the CU that it still had been recording, but I didn't know if it had gotten anything good or not."

"It most certainly did. It took a perfect shot of not only the mutant down by the river, but the one that sneaked up on us. As Sean continued to study the video, Jackson heard a distant gunshot and realized his friend had come up to the point on the video where Jones had destroyed the mutant. He asked, "Was that . . . ?"

"Yes," Sean replied. "That was when Jones blew the thing's head off . . . Ok, now it stopped recording . . . no . . . Now it's back on again."

Jackson said, "Yeah. That was when I realized it had been recording, and I shut it off. Then Delbert asked me to turn it back on again."

Sean looked down at the screen and Jackson could hear Jones' voice distantly in the background. Sean said, "Jones is posing over the corpse . . . I think I'll stop here . . . we know what happens next and I really don't want to see him killed again."

The two sat quietly for a few seconds as if both participating in an unscheduled moment of silent remembrance. Then Jackson asked, "So up to this point is all the footage clear and detailed?"

"Very much so." Sean replied, "Perhaps too much so . . . you will have to do a bit of editing before posting this . . . it's far too graphic . . . even for our road-hardened sensitivities."

Jackson said, "Here's what I'm thinking we should do, Sean. As soon as we get back to my place, I'll put a short video presentation together with text explaining what the viewer is going to see on the video. Then at the end I'll add that anonymous email address we put together and ask people to send us stories of their personal mutant sightings. I'll only include images of the creatures with none of the gory stuff for now. Then we can post it immediately up on the Skook website with some title slide saying 'Mutants Exist—Proof Positive' or something like that. We could even add a subtitle like 'What The NCDVC Doesn't Want You To Know.' What do you think?"

"I think that's a great way to get the ball rolling," Sean agreed.

Jackson said, "Once the video is spread worldwide and the publicity starts, we can put together other more detailed videos with a voice over narrative. Maybe if we're lucky, and I think we will be, one of the national broadcasting channels will want to do a professional television special on what we've uncovered."

"That would be great. Then he hesitated for a moment and asked, "What about Delbert Jones, Jackson? That poor man gave his life after saving us. He should get the recognition he deserves, even if it is posthumously."

"Agreed. Many people may not know that Death Bringer Jones was actually a real person. I know I didn't, nor did you. And even fewer, if any, knew his real identity. We can do that for him. I was just thinking . . . we should probably permanently delete the scene from the video where Jones was killed. Besides being horrible to watch, it would be demeaning to his memory."

Sean nodded his head and replied, "Yes, of course. There is no reason to make a spectacle of a true hero who saved us both."

They passed through the southern security gate of The Yuengsville Free Zone and headed straight to the public parking lot where they had temporarily left Sean's car. Sean got out of the car, and before he closed the door, he bent down by Jackson's window and said, "This is going to be major, my friend; bigger than anything you've ever done so far."

"I know, and if I told you I wasn't concerned about that, I would be lying. That's one of the reasons I want to make sure we do this right."

The pair agreed to work on the editing together right away, so Sean followed Jackson back to his home in the Ashton Cooperative. As he drove, Jackson picked up his personal CU and called Andrea.

"Hey, babe," Andrea greated, as she answered the call, "are you on your way home?"

"You bet and if it's ok with you, Sean will be joining us for dinner tonight."

"Sean? Sure, anytime . . . it'll be nice to see him again. You sound very excited about something, Jackson. Is everything ok?"

"Yeah . . . I suppose you could say that. In fact to be completely honest, it's way better than ok. It's actually pretty amazing . . . Look, honey, the reason Sean is coming is to help me put together a video piece that is going to be earth-shattering. Something we have to get out to the public as soon as possible."

"That sounds . . . well . . . it does sound pretty amazing."

"Believe me, it is. But I'm going to have to ask you to be a bit patient with me on this one, sweetie. I don't want to get into it over the phone. It's a long story, and I think it would be best to explain everything to you when we get home. In fact, as soon as we get there we have to do the video, so it might be dinner until I get a chance to go over everything with you. I hope you'll understand."

Andrea hesitated for a moment then replied; "Now you're really starting to worry me, Jackson." She knew her husband well, and when he held things too close to the vest, she knew danger was involved in one way or another.

Jackson explained, "Don't be concerned. There's nothing to worry about. It's just that I have a lot to tell you and would rather do it in person."

"Ok. I suppose," Andrea replied reluctantly. "I guess I'll have to wait."

"And one other thing I just thought of. Can you get in touch with, Jyleen? She's going to want to hear all of this too. You can mention that Sean will be there, and my guess is she'll be thrilled for the invitation."

"Now you've really piqued my curiosity Jackson. Is by any chance about . . ."

"Don't say it, honey. Not over the phone. But . . . yes it most certainly is, and as I said it's big . . . I mean really big . . . what I've been researching . . . there's proof, but I can't risk saying any more. Things have gotten . . . way to . . . um . . . serious . . . and I have to admit, potentially dangerous."

"Jackson, you're scaring me. Do you think someone's listening to our conversation? Are our CU's being monitored?"

"I don't believe so, but I don't know, and this has gotten too big to take any chances. I just want to be extra careful. I don't want you to be scared . . . just please be cautious. Just stay home with the doors locked until I get there. Don't let anyone in, especially someone you may not know well. Once Sean and I get home and take care of what we have to do . . . the danger will be all over . . . then I can tell you all about it."

"Ok. If you say so. In that case, when can I expect you?"

"I should be home within the hour. We just passed through the north gates of Yuengsville. It's about two o'clock now which means if we don't have too many slowdowns getting through the gates at Franksville and Ashton, we should arrive by three. It shouldn't take Sean and I more than an hour to do what we have to do then we can tell you and Jyleen all about it. That way we only have to go over the story once. For now, that is. I'm sure once the story breaks, I'll be telling it time and time again. In fact, you'll probably be busier booking interviews as well as book and movie deals than you were before."

"Really? Wow! Now I can't wait to hear this."

Then Jackson suddenly remembered, "Kyla! I don't want Kyla to hear this . . . It's really not something she should hear about, at least until we have a chance to figure out how to address it with her."

"Maybe we should save the discussion for after dinner Jackson. I can put Kyla to bed, and we can take out time when she is out of ear shot."

"Yeah. That's probably a good idea. Ok. I'll be home soon, babe . . . I'm dying to tell you about what I've found. This is big . . . I mean really, really big."

Andrea said, "So you keep telling me. I'll call Jyleen right away and we'll see you both soon. Love you."

"Love you too. Bye."

Both Jackson's and Sean's cars pulled into the Ridge driveway just before 3:00, and the two men raced up the walkway and through the front door. Andrea was waiting with a look of anticipation.

"So?" Andrea asked anxiously.

Jackson walked over, took her in his arms and after a brief hug and kiss said, "They're real babe. The mutants exist, and I have video proof."

"Oh, my God," she exclaimed gasping, "Can I see it?"

"Soon. Not just yet. Sean and I have to edit it a bit . . . right now it's really bad . . . disturbing . . . really very graphic."

"I . . . I don't understand Jackson. Graphic?" Andrea asked with alarm. "What are you talking about graphic?"

"I'll explain it all later, I promise." Jackson assured, "Some things happened . . . some unpleasant things . . . but as you can see, Sean and I are fine and unharmed."

Andrea noticed the scratches on both men's faces and hands and said, "You don't look fine. What are those scratches?"

"They're nothing, Andrea," Sean explained. "Just scratches from brush and bushes. We had to do some filming in the woods and had to leave in a hurry. But as you can see we're both unharmed."

Trying to change the subject Jackson asked, "Did you call Jyleen? Is she coming over?"

"What?" Andrea said distracted. "Jy . . . um . . . yes, I did. And she's coming over. She should be here by four."

"Good . . . good," Jackson said keeping things moving, "That should give us time to do what we need to do. Sean and I will be in my office editing and putting a brief presentation together for the next hour or so. As soon as we're finished, I promise we'll tell you all about what we've learned and show you the video. Ok?"

Looking a bit shell shocked Andrea reluctantly gave both Jackson and Sean a look of disapproval then said, "Well . . . I suppose I have no choice."

"Thanks, sweetheart," Jackson replied giving her another quick peck on the lips. "I promise you won't be disappointed."

"I'm already disappointed. It'll be your job to make me forget my disappointment."

"I will. You'll see . . . this will be monumentous."

Then he and Sean hurried to Jackson's office where they began editing the video, preparing it for uploading. By four-fifteen, the video presentation was completed and had been successfully loaded onto *The Schuylkill Daily News's* website via the secure link provided by Bill McCleary. Jackson had called McCleary and told him to check out the posting. The editor said he was amazed by the video and that he had never seen anything like it before.

"My God!" McCleary had shouted. "This video is much clearer than Nathan's, and this is the real deal. It makes the video he took seem insignificant. I hate to think that poor man gave his life for nothing."

"Not for nothing, Bill. If he wouldn't have insisted on doing a story on his video, none of this would have even happened."

"Maybe not, Jackson, but at least my nephew would still be alive, and my sister wouldn't be heartbroken with grief."

"I understand. But don't worry, Bill. I promise you we'll figure out a way to get Hershberger eventually. My gut tells me he's got to be behind this."

"I trust your gut, Jackson, which means you're probably right," McCleary said. "Let's take this one step at a time. You got the video up on our site. Now we wait for it to go viral, which I'm certain it will. Then we go after Hershberger."

"Got it," Jackson agreed. "Talk to you later, Bill."

Jackson disconnected the call and turned to Sean saying, "Our work here is done for the time being, Double I. Now let's go tell the girls what happened today. They'll probably be mad as hell at first, but once they hear the whole story, hopefully we'll be off the hook; at least for a little while."

"I hope so as well," Sean agreed. "The only thing more frightening than a hungry mutant is Jyleen when she's mad. I know we've only been dating a little while, but I have seen her lose her temper already, and it's a scary sight."

They both laughed as Jackson picked up the special CU which now held both the raw and edited versions of the video. He was planning on showing the girls the edited version only after dinner.

As Jackson and Sean walked into the living room, they saw Jyleen, Andrea and Kyla sitting in a line on the sofa with looks of terror on their faces. Sitting on a chair directly across from them was Sean's former boss Wilbur Hershberger with a large gun in his hand, resting across his legs.

"Gentlemen. Please come in and sit down. I've been waiting patiently for your arrival,."

CHAPTER 41

"Wha . . . what's going on here?" Jackson demanded. "Who do you think you are barging into my home . . . scaring my family . . . and with a gun? What's this all about?"

Hershberger was dressed in a casual sports coat and matching pants with a bright white shirt with an open collar, sans tie. Sean realized suddenly he had never seen his former boss outside of work, where Hershberger would never been seen without his signature red bowtie. This new look of relaxed casualness combined with the calm expression on Hershberger's face made the fact that he was holding a gun seem even more terrifying.

"I think you both know exactly what this is about." He nodded at both men and acknowledged, "Jackson, Sean, I believe you have something I want, and I'm here to get it."

Sean said, "Jackson . . . it's Wilbur Hershberger . . . my boss . . . ex-boss."

"Yes, I know who he is."

Jackson took a step closer, and Hershberger picked up his gun from his lap. "Ah, ah, ah, Jackson. That will be quite far enough for now."

"What is it you want?" Jackson asked. "If I have it, I'll give it to you, no problem. Just be careful with that gun in my house."

Hershberger picked up the gun and waved it about casually. "You're absolutely right, Jackson. I had better be very careful lest this weapon accidently discharge and hit some innocent bystander. Or should I say by-sitter?"

Then his serious demeanor returned, and Hershberger said, "What I want, Jackson, is all of your copies of the Nathan Brody video. You know the one I'm referring to; the one he gave to your editor, McCleary and he in turn forwarded to you."

"The Brody . . . ?" Jackson started to say then stopped himself with a realization. He resisted the urge to turn and look over at Sean. He suddenly understood that Hershberger had absolutely no knowledge of the video he and Sean had just posted. He was way behind the curve, still looking for remnants of the Brody video.

"Mommy, I'm scared," Kyla said to Andrea.

"Sshhh!" Andrea shushed. She didn't want to bring any unnecessary attention to Kyla. She had already decided if that lunatic across the room tried to harm her daughter, she would throw herself into the line of fire. Death was preferable to seeing her daughter harmed. She had a vague memory of a dream from several nights earlier, which had faded but still left her with the feeling of dread and apprehension. Perhaps this was all somehow tied to her dream. She held Kyla even closer to her.

"Shut that kid up, or I'll do it for you," Hershberger snarled gritting his teeth, "I have no patients for winey little runts."

"Don't you dare threaten my family!" Jackson shouted angrily, but his voice suddenly caught in his throat as Hershberger pointed his gun directly at Kyla.

"Easy there, Jackson, my friend. Unless you don't want to have that family for very much longer."

Jackson tensed, "I swear if you so much as touch them . . ."

"Hershberger waved his other hand in the air dismissively, "Yeah, I know . . . If I hurt anyone, you'll kill me . . . blah, blah, blah. Now I suggest you stay where you are and shut your mouth."

"D . . . do what he says, Jackson," Andrea pleaded from her place on the sofa.

Sean looked across the room at Jyleen and did his best to give her a consoling look as if telepathically sending her a message to stay calm; that everything would be all right. But the look Jyleen returned was anything but relaxed, nor was it fearful. She looked furious. She looked like a wild panther waiting to strike at the first opportunity. This could prove to be either very helpful or tragic depending upon how things played out. He hoped Hershberger didn't notice for Jyleen's sake.

Jackson now addressed Hershberger in a much calmer voice, with both of his empty hands extended out in an unthreatening gesture, "Look, Wilbur. I don't have the video. You know that. I did have it once, but now it's gone. The NCDVC hacked my computer and destroyed every single copy I had. You should know that too."

"So you say . . . but here's the problem Jackson. I don't think I believe you. Before he died, Nathan Brody told me you were a very thorough professional. Surely a professional would have made back-up copies of such an important video."

"Who's Nathan Brody?" Andrea wondered to herself. "And what does all this have to do with Jackson or with us."

Jackson suddenly realized he was never going to convince the madman he no longer had the video. He assumed Hershberger would begin systematically slaughtering everyone in the room until Jackson eventually told him what he wanted to hear. So Jackson decided to try a different approach, the truth.

"Apparently Nathan gave me more credit than I deserve," Jackson admitted. "I know you may not believe me, but the truth is I never got around to backing up the video file. When the NCDVD hacked my computer, they got my only copy."

Jackson could see Hershberger's face begin to redden. It was clear he not only didn't believe Jackson, but it was very possible he was about to become angry enough to shoot someone in the room.

"Even if I did have the video, it would be irrelevant!" Jackson shouted in a last ditch effort to stop Hershberger.

Hershberger relaxed slightly, seeming suddenly interested and asked, "What do you mean, irrelevant?"

Jackson took a deep breath and said, "Nathan's video was of poor quality and one the NCDVC could have easily discredited as being nothing but a hoax. It was not worth Nathan being tortured and killed for, believe me. Did you even see it?"

"No . . . no, I didn't," Hershberger admitted, "but I did what I had to do to stop its publication, just like I'm doing right now."

"But here is what you don't know, Wilbur. After the NCDVC destroyed my only copy of the video and after you fired Sean, he came to me and asked for my help. And do you know what we did, Wilbur?"

Hershberger said with a sly smile, "No, but by all means enlighten me. But you had better do it quickly, or I'm going to start killing those you love one at a time."

"Ok. Ok . . . just listen," Jackson said once again holding out his palms in a please stop gesture. "Since the only copy of the Brody video I had was destroyed, Sean and I drove down to Cressota today. We went into the woods near the abandoned mall where Brody shot his original video and we got a video of our own; one that was a hundred times more detailed than Brody's."

"What?" Hershberger exclaimed. "Are you saying you have another video?"

"Yes, we do," Jackson said.

Andrea was looking at Jackson like he was crazy. Obviously if this madman was willing to kill for one questionable video, he wouldn't hesitate to kill for a much better one. She had no idea what Jackson was trying to do.

Hershberger said, "All right then. In that case you can provide me with all the copies of that video file, if you would be so kind."

Sean intervened, "That won't be a problem, Wilbur." He was holding up a high density thumb drive, "We only have two copies of the video file. One is on Jackson's CU, and the other is right here on this thumb drive. You want them, you can have them. Just leave the girls go, and keep Jackson and myself as hostages if you want."

"Do you think I'm an idiot?" Hershberger shouted. "Jackson probably already backed up the files on his computer. Nobody leaves here alive until I get all the copies. Is that understood?"

Sean smiled and let out a chuckle, "You . . . you are such an idiot Wilbur."

"What? What did you say? How dare you!" Hershberger shouted indignantly.

"Don't you see? It doesn't matter one iota if we give you every copy of the video, you moron!" Sean shouted. "Jackson and I already loaded a video presentation with audio narrative onto *The Schuylkill Daily News's* international web page though a secure secret portal. By now the video has gone viral and has spread all over the web and has been seen by millions of people all around the world. Don't you get it? The video has already been released. It's over, Wilbur. Everyone will soon know that mutants really do exist."

"What?" Hershberger repeated again. "This can't be!"

Jackson joined in shouting, "But it is, Wilbur. And now thanks to your confession we know for sure you were responsible for the murder of Nathan Brody."

Hershberger's expression took on a sinister, knowing look, "Maybe so, Jackson. But since no one in this room is going to leave alive, there'll be nobody to point any fingers at me."

Jackson carefully started to reach into his pocket. Hershberger raised the gun and shouted, "Stop. Stop right there."

"I only want to get my CU out of my pocket to show you something. Is that ok?" he asked.

"Two fingers, Jackson." Hershberger warned. "Only use two fingers."

When Jackson removed the CU, he said to Hershberger. "This isn't my personal CU. It's a special CU provided to me by the Yuengsville police department. As soon as we came in the room and I saw you here, I pressed a special record button on the outside of the CU. The really cool feature about this CU is that once I start recording, not only does it go onto the CU, but it also goes onto a secure computer hard drive at the Yuengsville police station. Also, once activated it sends out a signal and is instantly monitored by the officer on duty who is listening right now to everything we're saying. So, Wilbur Hershberger, Chief Medical examiner and coroner for Schuylkill County I've recorded everything you said. The police know you are here in my home and that you are pointing a gun at us, threatening my wife, family and friends. More importantly, they heard you admit to killing and torturing Nathan Brody. You're done for, Wilbur. So you might as will give it up now."

"I don't believe you. It's all a ploy meant to deceive me."

"It doesn't matter what you believe or choose not to believe, Hershberger," Jackson argued, "because by now the Yuengsville police have contacted the Ashton police, and very soon, they'll be here very shortly to take you down."

"If that's true, then I suppose I've got nothing to lose, do I? Six murders offer no more punishment than one. They can only execute me once."

In the distance sirens could be heard coming ever closer.

"That's the cops, Wilbur." Sean warned. "It's time to give it up."

Hershberger tensed at the sound of the approaching police cars. "If I'm going down then I'm taking all of you right along with me."

Sean took a step toward Hershberger and said, "No, Wilbur . . . you have to—"

Before Sean could finish his sentence, Hershberger turned the gun on him and fired. The incredible roar of the gun's report was deafening in the small space echoing from wall to wall. Kyla began to bellow as Andrea screamed and pulled the child to her chest, turning to shield her daughter with her own body. Then as if in slow motion, Sean fell backward, and Jackson charged toward Hershberger with his hand holding the CU extended reaching for the Taser button. But with surprising quickness, Hershberger had already turned the gun on Jackson and was about to pull the trigger.

However, at the same moment Hershberger was starting to point the gun at Jackson, something was happening off to the man's right which he would never have expected and which was not yet visible in his peripheral vision. The second after he had shot Sean, even before Jackson had started his charge, Jyleen had already begun her attack. Sean had been right in his assessment of the look in Jyleen's eyes; she had only been waiting for the right moment, and this was it.

As Hershberger attempted to squeeze the trigger Jyleen's right fist came down hard on the hand holding the gun. The sickening crack from her blow shattering the bones in his hand was audible throughout the room. When the gun exploded for the second time, the bullet sunk into the floor about a foot in front of Jackson. He looked across the room in disbelief as Jyleen's left fist smashed into Hershberger's nose crushing cartilage and spraying a gush of crimson down the front of his crisp white shirt.

Hershberger staggered back a few steps and somehow started to regain his footing. He was stunned badly, in obvious pain, but he was not yet down for the count. He gingerly began to transfer his gun from his injured right hand to his left. That was when Jyleen shot a lightning fast kick to his groin, doubling him over in agony, followed by a flying back kick to this throat, which sent his head snapping backward and had him wheezing, gasping for breath. He stumbled a few steps then bumped into an end table which sent him crashing to the foyer floor where his head hit the tile with a thud leaving Hershberger in an unconscious heap.

Jyleen turned and raced to Sean who was lying on his back with his arms spread moaning in pain. Jackson was on his CU calling 911. The old emergency number that had been put in use back in the previous century, somewhere around 1968, was still used almost a hundred years later.

Jyleen saw there was blood pouring from a wound high on Sean's upper-left arm. She tore off his shirt to examine the wound and was happy to see the bullet had passed through muscle and had not hit any bone. It was not a fatal wound but was obviously painful, and Sean had lost a good deal of blood.

"You're gonna be all right, baby. Don't worry," Jyleen assured as she tore off her own shirt, balled it up and pressed it against the wound to stem the bleeding.

Sean appeared to be going into shock and his speech was rambling and sometimes incoherent. "Jy . . . Jy . . ." Sean said. "You're . . . you're an angel."

Jyleen smiled then bent down and kissed him on the lips, "Sugar, you're angel was kickin' ass like a little she-devil a few minutes ago."

"That's my girl," Sean whispered in a fading voice; then he passed out.

Jackson was now kneeling by the sofa with his wife and daughter in his arms. "It's ok . . . it's ok," he kept repeating. "It's all over now."

CHAPTER 42

Suddenly they heard loud banging on the front door followed by a deep bass voice shouting, "Jackson Ridge, open up the door immediately. This is the Ashton Cooperative police department."

Jackson raced to the front door and threw the door open it to find a team of five local police, most of whom he recognized and two he knew personally.

One of the officers, Jim Arnold the chief of police said, "Mr. Ridge, is everyone in your home ok? We got an emergency call from the Yuengsville police telling us they received some sort of audio transmission suggesting there might be a possible home invasion or some other sort of trouble at this location. May we come in, sir?"

"Yes, absolutely. Please do come in. And call me Jackson, Chief, ok?" Jackson put out his hand to shake the chief's hand, "We've never met, but I know who you are."

The officer ignored Jackson's outstretched hand and instead pushed past him into the foyer. Jackson looked at the two officers, who he did know and greeted them with a tremulous voice, "Hi, Bob . . . John. Please . . . come in. I'm so glad you're got the message."

The rest of the police cautiously entered the home and saw one man down at the end of the foyer and another lying on the carpet across the room. A young woman was apparently tending that man who appeared to be wounded.

"Mr. Ridge," the chief said, as he hand reached for the butt of his still holstered weapon, "would you mind telling me exactly what the hell is going on here?"

Jackson realized the potential danger in the chief's not knowing the situation, so he did his best to summarize in a quick clipped voice fueled by the stress of the situation, "Here's what went down, Chief . . . A man with a gun came into my house, attacked us and held us for a time at gunpoint. We did manage to overpower him, but my friend,

Sean Patel, was shot in the process. He's over there. I've already called for an ambulance."

Chief Arnold instructed one of the officers who Jackson didn't know, to go check on Sean's status.

"That was very good thinking . . . I mean calling for an ambulance." the Chief replied. "Although I have to tell you that trying to overpower an armed man isn't something I would have ever recommended. But I suppose what's done is done. So tell me, is that the perpetrator?" He pointed to the apparently unconscious man lying in the foyer.

"Yes," Jackson replied. Then Chief Arnold signaled to another officer to go check on Hershberger.

"Please, Mr. Rid . . . I mean, Jackson, can you take a deep breath now and calm down as much as possible and tell me more about what happened?"

"Yes . . . sorry . . . Um . . . my friend . . . Sean and I were in my office at the back of the house, working on a story for *The Schuylkill Daily News* . . . You see . . . I'm a writer for the newspaper."

Chief Arnold smiled slightly and said, "Um . . . yes . . . I know you're a writer, Jackson. To be honest, anyone who hasn't been living under a rock somewhere for the past year probably knows you're a writer. You've become quite famous." He gave a small laugh.

"Oh . . . yeah . . . Sorry, Chief . . . I'm still a bit shook up, I guess," Jackson admitted, holding out his hands. Then he noticed the chief looking at the scars in his palms. He pulled his hands back reflexively.

"Um . . . sorry about staring, Jackson." Arnold said, "I read about . . . I mean . . . I assume those are from . . . well, you know."

"Yes . . . yes, they are," Jackson replied, embarrassed for some reason he couldn't explain, "They're getting a little better every day."

Then Jackson realized suddenly that the reason he might have involuntarily gotten embarrassed was because of how he had ended up with the scars. It had been a different chief of police from Yuengsville, Brent Holden, who had been responsible for his capture by the criminal Deimos, who had almost killed him.

Apparently as uncomfortable as Jackson was with the conversation, Arnold shouted over to the first officer, bringing Jackson back from his thoughts. He could hear the ambulance sirens outside getting closer.

"How is he?" Arnold asked regarding Sean.

"He's going to be fine," The officer replied. "Looks like the bullet passed through him. This lady is a nurse, and she's taken good care of him."

"What about the other guy?" Arnold shouted to the second officer.

"I think he's a goner sir. It appears his throat was injured . . . possibly his windpipe was shattered."

"Well, you'd better cuff him just in case . . . you know . . . in case he comes back."

"Can't I just pop him in the head now Chief?" the officer asked.

Jim Arnold shouted back, "No you can't just pop him in the head, Carl. He hasn't been officially pronounced dead. He might just be in some sort of coma. The coroner has to pronounce him dead first. That is unless he turns and comes back as a zombie. Then we'll know for sure he was really dead, and we can deal with him accordingly, so I'd suggest you'd better get him secured and pronto and don't forget to bind his feet too."

"Forgive the interruption, Jackson. Go on with your story."

"As I was saying, Sean and I were coming out of my office after finishing uploading a story for the Skook. When we came into the living room, we found that man holding my wife, my daughter and her friend Jyleen at gunpoint. And . . . oh wow! I just realized something. . . . You mentioned the coroner . . . you won't be hearing from him any time soon, since that's him over there dead on the floor."

"You mean to tell me Wilbur Hershberger . . . THE Wilbur Hershberger . . . the Schuylkill County Coroner was the man holding your family hostage at gun point?" Arnold asked unbelievingly. "Forgive me, Jackson, but that doesn't make a whole lot of sense to me at all. Why in the world would a renowned doctor like Wilbur Hershberger do such a thing?"

Then the officer snapped his fingers as if in sudden recognition and said, "Did you say Sean Patel earlier? Sean Patel? That name is familiar too. Isn't he the assistant coroner?"

"Yeah," Jackson said. "All of this a bit complicated."

"So we have a maybe dead coroner over there and a wounded assistant coroner over there. And you're telling me Dr. Wilbur Hershberger invaded your home for some 'complicated' reason and held your family at gunpoint?" He made air quotes when he said the word "complicated." "And now he's likely dead?"

"Yes," Jackson confirmed realizing just how strange the whole situation must sound to him, "I'm sorry, Chief . . . I don't think I'm doing a very good job of explaining this . . . I write a lot better than I speak."

"Did Hershberger and Patel have some sort of conflict? Is that what this was about?" Arnold asked.

"No," Jackson said quickly then he corrected himself and said, "Well, maybe. It's a bit more involved than that . . . See, Hershberger fired him yesterday."

"Now wait a minute," Arnold said as he placed his hand back on the butt of his gun, "What's really going on around here? How do I even know that things went down like you said? Just because you told me? Am I supposed to just take your word for everything? Maybe Dr. Hershberger came here to talk to Patel and things got out of hand. Maybe Patel attacked Hershberger and the man had to shoot him in self-defense. Maybe Patel killed Hershberger."

Jackson realized he had probably just messed everything up with his haphazard explanation. Then suddenly he realized he had a way to be certain the officer believed his story, "Look Chief . . . I have proof . . . I recorded the entire incident on this special CU that I received from the former Yuengsville Chief of Police. Not only is it recorded here but it's simultaneously monitored and recorded by the police command center in Yuengsville as well. That's how they knew what was happening here and knew to call you. The proof is all there Chief I swear."

Arnold recalled reading the various accounts of Jackson's near-fatal adventure in the newspaper over the past several months. He remembered reading about the CU which was given to Ridge. Apparently this was the same Communications Unit and was still in Ridge's possession. This seemed to relax him a bit.

"Ok Jackson. Look, it's not that I didn't believe you . . . but you have to know how this looks . . . I just can't be too careful."

"Understood. And it's not a problem whatsoever. You're only doing your job." Jackson assured, "Like I said, it's a bit messy; and you don't even know the whole screwed up story yet . . . it only gets weirder and a lot messier."

Chief Arnold smiled at Jackson then shook his head, "You apparently seem to have a knack for getting yourself into really bizarre situations if you don't mind my saying so."

"Unfortunately, you're absolutely right about that." Jackson admitted.

Andrea was on the couch holding tightly to Kyla who was sobbing uncontrollably. Jackson excused himself for the moment saying, "Look, Chief. I'll tell you everything I swear, I just have to go to my family, ok?" Then without waiting for a reply, Jackson turned and raced to Andrea and Kyla.

He wrapped his arms around them both and unabashedly broke down in tears along with them, "Oh, sweetie, I was so scared for you and Kyla. I thought the maniac was going to hurt you both."

"I did too," Andrea cried. "I was terrified." Then she looked over at Sean and Jyleen. "I heard that cop say Sean was going to be ok."

"Yes, thank goodness. And thanks for Jyleen. I had no idea she could be so . . . so . . . terrifying."

"Me either," Andrea admitted. Then she let her voice go quieter and whispered, "Did you see how she attacked that maniac? She was like a wild animal or something. She was almost more frightening than he was."

"That's for sure. And we can be thankful she was or else we might all be dead by now."

Andrea looked over and the still body in the foyer, "Do you think she . . . she killed him?"

"Pretty sure," Jackson admitted. "I suppose we'll know shortly.

"Wow," was all Andrea managed to say. Then she added, "What did you say that guy's name was?"

"He is . . . or I should say was Dr. Wilbur Hershberger, Sean's old boss. He was responsible for the death of a man at the Skook named Nathan Brody . . . It's a very long complicated story. I'll tell you all about it later as soon as things settle down a bit."

Andrea held him tightly and said, "Knowing my husband, I'm sure it's not only complicated but a dangerous story as well. Jesus, Jackson, how is it that you always end up in danger? This assignment was supposed to be an uneventful desk research thing. How did it end up being such a fiasco?"

"Later, I promise," Jackson assured. "I'll tell you everything. For now, let's just be thankful we're all safe. Ok?"

"I suppose that'll have to do for now," Andrea reluctantly agreed.

Suddenly everyone in the room heard a familiar low guttural growl coming from the secured body of Wilbur Hershberger. It had happened; he had died, and he had turned. There would be no need for an official death declaration now. The police officer looked over at his chief who nodded his approval. A moment later the house once again reverberated with the roar of a gun blast as the officer blew off the top of Hershberger's head.

Jackson held his wife and daughter tightly thankful that the crisis was over, as a team of emergency medical technicians came running in through the open front door and raced over to Sean's aid.

CHAPTER 43

Jackson Ridge stared absently at the computer monitor on his desk wondering just what else he could have possibly said differently in what seemed like his thousandth interview that month. Many of those interviews like the last one consisted of questions emailed to him for which he provided typed responses. He liked these interviews the best because he didn't have to think on his feet. In fact, every time he did one he kept a log of questions and his answers knowing most of the questions would be asked again by other interviewers. When that occurred, he could simply copy and paste his answer, and then tweak it slightly to read a bit differently which allowed the process to go much quicker. The problem he had was trying to say the same thing a hundred times and make it sound fresh and interesting each time.

After completing his final interview of the day, Jackson once again reflected back on the events, which occurred following the incident at his home with Wilbur Hershberger. So much had happened over the past three months, more than even Jackson could have imagined. Immediately following the incident he, Andrea, Kyla and Jyleen were taken to the Ashton Police Headquarters for questioning. They were each interviewed separately, except for Kyla, of course, because of her young age. Then the police placed them into a waiting area together where they were given snacks and soft drinks while they waited for the Schuylkill County District Attorney to review both their testimonies as well as the recording from Jackson's CU.

During the long wait, Jackson was able to tell Andrea and Jyleen the whole story, or at least his slightly modified version of the story Jackson was glad he and Sean had previously agreed not to tell Jyleen about how Sean had manipulated her into using Andrea to ask Jackson to investigate the mutant sightings. After having seen Jyleen in action, he figured the last thing Sean needed was to have that wildcat angry with him.

"With both you and McCleary asking me to look into the mutant one request coming on the heels of the other, I figured the story must be something worth investigating," Jackson had told her, being careful to not draw attention the chronology of those two events.

Watching his wife's doubtful expression, he wasn't sure she was buying everything he was trying to sell, but to her credit, she had chosen not to question his account, at least for the time being. He then went on to explain about the Brody video and next covered how he suspected the NCDVC had hacked his and McCleary's computers and destroyed their only copies of the video. At that early stage of the investigation, Jackson was unsure if the NCDVC had gotten Brody's files as well or if Hershberger had destroyed them at the time he kidnapped, tortured and eventually murdered Brody.

Then came the tricky part of his story, the part he knew he was would result in his taking a lot of heat for from Andrea. He told of how Hershberger had confronted and fired Sean, and how Sean had come up to Ashton the next morning to tell Jackson the truth about the existence of mutants. He tried to distract her somewhat by telling her how Sean had admitted he had been the one who saved Jackson from Deimos in the barn near Reading so many months earlier.

"I knew it was him!" Andrea exclaimed. "Even when he denied being there, I believed you were right when you said you saw Sean. But because he consistently said it hadn't been him, I eventually started to believe that maybe you actually had been hallucinating the whole thing. I even helped to convince you that you might have been imagining things. God, Jackson, I'm so sorry."

"That's not a problem, babe," Jackson assured. "I was in such bad shape I wasn't sure what I actually saw and what I imagined myself."

Jackson then continued his story by telling them how he tried to show Sean his copy of the Brody video and discovered it was missing. He said he called McCleary moments later and learned of the death of Brody. Then he carefully explained that he and Sean had decided to go to the site of the abandoned Cressota Mall to try to get their own video. He could see the anger beginning to rise in Andrea's troubled expression. Jackson was becoming very concerned about how this discussion might end.

She believed she had been the one to encourage him to take on this assignment because she had thought he would be safe at home in his office just speaking with people over the phone. Had she ever imagined he would have traveled south of Yuengsville to try to film actual mutants in the wild, she never would have agreed. Jackson tensed for a moment when Andrea asked him what she was going to see on the video when they were finally finished with the DA and back home from the police station.

"Look, honey," Jackson said trying to keep her as calm as possible, "I'm going to tell you all about this, but I want you to promise to do your best to remain cool. I know you're not going to like what I have to tell you, but I swear I honestly never expected in a million years to encounter what we encountered."

"You never do," she said sardonically, "yet somehow you always manage to find yourself in trouble every time, don't you?"

"Please Andrea." Jackson pleaded, "You can yell at me later all you want. How about I just tell you the story and get it over with. . Ok?"

So he told the story.

When he was finished, Andrea and Jyleen both looked at him in complete astonishment. As terrifying as their being held captive at gunpoint had been, it didn't begin to compare with the horror Sean and Jackson had experienced that day.

"I . . . I . . . I don't know what to say," Andrea stammered. "You . . . you mean to tell me you have all of that on video?"

"Yeah," Jackson acknowledged. "Unfortunately, I do. It's very graphic to say the least. The video we uploaded onto the web is edited and focuses on the mutants and not at all on what happened to Delbert Jones."

Jyleen said, "That Death Bringer guy saved both of your lives, and he died doing it."

"Yes, he did," Jackson admitted. "He died doing what he wanted to do and more importantly being who he wanted to be. I promise I'll show you both the entire unedited video if you want to see it, but I plan on eventually deleting the part where he died. I can't in good conscience allow that to go public, not after he sacrificed his life to save us."

"I agree," Andrea said, "but his motivation was not really to save you. He apparently followed you with the hopes of your leading him to a mutant. He wanted to kill one to reestablish his credibility as Death Bringer Jones. It was just lucky that he saved you both in the process."

Jackson offered, "Still, whether it was part of his plan or not, he did save us. And as such, I'll return the favor by respecting his death and not making it into a public spectacle. I also plan on doing a series of stories and maybe a book about the life and times of Delbert Bertram Jones, alias Death Bringer Jones. He deserves to be remembered, and if there is anything I can do to make that happen, I will."

By the end of the day, the District Attorney had determined that Jyleen had acted in self-defense when she attacked Hershberger, which resulted in his accidental death. To Jackson's surprise and pleasure, Andrea hadn't remained angry with him and had actually become very sympathetic regarding this latest misadventure. Once home, she and Jackson had watched both the original video together as well as the edited version. She agreed the edited version was the only one the public should ever see. As such, they deleted all traces of the segment where Delbert Jones met his death. They kept the segment where he was standing over the slain mutant striking his Death Bringer pose. That was how Delbert wanted to be remembered, so Jackson made sure he did whatever he could to make sure he would be.

Then that night something incredible happened, which Jackson hadn't anticipated. For the first time since his returning home from his ordeal in Reading a half year earlier, his nightmares stopped. The following morning he awoke at eight-thirty shocked to see Andrea standing over him staring down at him.

"Are you ok?" she had asked.

"Huh? What . . . what do you mean?" Jackson asked sleepily.

Andrea said, "I came up to make sure you weren't dead. It's eight-thirty, Jackson, and you're still asleep. Didn't your nightmare wake you?"

"Holy crap!" Jackson exclaimed. "I didn't have one." Then he jumped out of bed and hugged his wife with disbelief repeating, "I didn't have the nightmare!"

After suffering with the haunting dreams for more than six months, they apparently were over; at least Jackson hoped they were. "I wonder why I didn't have one last night," Jackson pondered. "What changed?"

"I can't say for certain, but I think I might know," Andrea said. "I'm only guessing here, but I think the reason you were having that same horrible nightmare over and over was because of some unfinished business. You didn't know who had rescued you from that barn, so in your subconscious mind, you never were properly rescued. I think since you didn't know who your savior was, your subconscious was replaying through your dreams what would have happened had you not been rescued. But when Sean admitted he had been the one who saved you, your brain finally had closure. Your nightmare had a beginning, middle and a definite ending. Not only were you saved, but you knew who had saved you. I think with the dream was completed and your mind was free to let it go."

"Wow!" Jackson said. "That does make a lot of sense. If you don't mind, I'm going to run that by Dr. Wakeman and see what he says."

"Of course, I don't mind. Go right ahead, babe," Andrea agreed. "I'm sure he'll have some fancy shrink way of saying it but my guess is he'll essentially tell you the same thing."

"I always knew you were smart, but it never ceases to amaze me just how smart you are,"

"Well. Not everything I do is smart. After all, I did marry a man who seems to get himself in the weirdest sorts of danger imaginable on a regular basis."

Jackson replied, "So then I suppose brains and taste in men are two completely different animals."

"You're right about that," Andrea agreed.

CHAPTER 44

Over the course of the next month or so, the NCDVC mutant cover-up story became international news as the word about the existence of mutants spread like wildfire. *The Schuylkill Daily News* once again went from simply reporting the news to being thrust into the forefront of the news, since it was the Skook's website which broke the story.

Jackson Ridge immediately was back in the limelight as well. He began writing a series of articles about the events leading up to the discovery of the existence of mutants. Also, as might be expected, these articles would soon be followed by another book and another movie deal. In addition, he still planned on working on a combination book and graphic novel based on the real-life legend known as Death Bringer Jones. Delbert would finally get the recognition he deserved, albeit posthumously.

The NCDVC predictably denied any knowledge of the activities of their apparently rogue employee, one Dr. Wilbur Hershberger. Since all emails concerning the cover-up of the mutant issue had self-destructed, there was no proof whatsoever to implicate anyone at the NCDVC whatsoever. The NCDVC had achieved the very plausible deniability Jackson and Sean had predicted they would. For a week or so, it looked like the NCDVC would walk away from the entire affair unscathed. However, that was apparently not to be. In fact, no one could have ever anticipated the public anti-NCDVC outcry or what effect it would eventually have on the agency.

When Jackson's story broke about the alleged involvement of the NCDVC in the cover-up of the mutant problem, the public went ballistic. Local governments all around the country were pressured by their constituents to take some sort of action against the agency. This heat was felt all the way up to the highest office in the country: the Presidency. Within one week, the revolt went from a grass-roots campaign to almost revolutionary status. Most of the local authorities and even the medical community in general never liked the fact that the NCDVC had become such a powerful organization in the first place. And apparently the executive branch of the newly formed national government didn't either, but the government needed a good reason to go after the NCDVC, and suddenly they had one conveniently dropped into their lap. As a result, the President and Congress decided something needed to be done to squelch some of that power. They determined nothing short of a complete overhaul of the NCDVC would be acceptable.

One of the first reforms to take place was to remove of all health workers and medical professionals nationwide from the authority of the NCDVC and have them placed under the direct authority of their local governments. Most local governments formed their own specific agencies to oversee their health professionals. This meant that those former workers who reported to the NCDVC now reported to agencies within the counties where they worked.

This ended up being a good thing for some people such as Sean Patel who not only was reinstated into his old position but also was subsequently promoted to Coroner and Chief Medical Examiner of Schuylkill County. However, for those less than desirable health professionals who were essentially hangers on, doing as little as possible and who had been leaching off the government, the new system wasn't quite as rewarding. Major reforms in the medical community took place once the NCDVC was removed from the equation and many of these undesirables found themselves unemployed. In addition several high ranking officials ended up in prison.

The NCDVC didn't go away completely as it was still a necessary entity. It simply became more of what it originally was formed to be: a medical agency to monitor the Z43 virus as well as other viruses in the world. It essentially lost the all-encompassing power it had achieved over the previous decade. Most of the political/managerial types within the organization found themselves out of work very quickly. The pure scientists remained. This was a good thing because the scientists cared little or nothing about politics or what someone felt the public should or shouldn't know. All they wanted was find new discoveries and report them. They wanted to cure diseases and stop their spread.

Another change which occurred was local medical examiners and other personnel as well as the various news media were all connected to the NCDVC information lines, and as soon as a there was a new discovery it became public knowledge. Gone were the days of classified emails sent to a select few people. Now everything went to everyone; for better or worse, no secrets were permitted.

Then, as a final farewell to the old ways of the NCDVC, the organization went through a major name change to match its new and hopefully improved personality. Gone were the initials, the acronym, which was replaced with a single name Viro. It stood for nothing; it was just a name which officials felt would quickly gain recognition as the organization whose purpose was to fight viruses. The idea of the new name was to solidify the idea that the old NCDVC was completely gone, replaced by a newer more science-based organization with less political influence known simply as Viro.

There was another problem which as of yet hadn't been addressed. That was the issue of what humanity was supposed to do about the mutant problem. There were so many unanswered questions regarding these new and terrifying creatures. One such question was should mutants to be considered human, or were they to be thought of as animals, or perhaps something else? When the virus mutated did it create a new superior form of being or did it actually de-evolutionize the former human into some form of ancient pre-prehistoric ancestor? Did these creatures pose a threat to people in the fortified cities or only to those savages wandering about in the outlands? Why did the mutations seem to only occur in the outlands? Was it possible that any living human could experience a mutation of the Z43 virus, which resided dormant in everyone? Or was it something in the unpurified water of the outlands such as that in the Schuylkill River, which caused the mutations to occur? What would happen if someone hunted and killed a mutant; would that person be accused of murder?

The video Jackson Ridge had shot indicated that at least three mutants were killed down near the Cressota Mall ruins, yet when a small army of retrieval squad personnel stormed the area in search of remains none could be found, including the corpse of Death Bringer Jones. The area was awash with blood, but no bodies were ever located. This led some to believe that perhaps there actually might be tribes of mutants living in the wild lands and that these tribal members had retrieved the corpses from the forest. It was also possible that they had been dragged deeper into the woods by yet other types of mutants whose sole purpose was to consume the bodies for their own sustenance. The truth was no one would ever know.

Jackson suspected many of these questions would take years of back and forth discussion among the legal community before decisions could be reached. For now, the public knew the mutations existed in the outlands, which gave them one more reason to stay within the boundaries of the city. They also knew that mutants seemed to stay to themselves in the outlands and didn't seem to try to venture anywhere near civilization. As the previous limited sightings of mutants suggested, encountering a mutant, at least for the moment, was rare for the average person. More likely to see them might be workers on the Systematic Expansion projects or adventure seekers exploring in the outlands. The SE workers were protected by armed spotters. As far as those who went out on their own into the wild lands, mutants or not, they were already taking their lives in their own hands.

However people like Jackson and others who regularly had to move from one fortified city to another for business purposes could only hope the mutants remained timid, solitary creatures, which continued to hide deep in their forests. The Odo-like mutant and the squid-headed thing which Jackson and Sean encountered seemed to be natural enemies, eager to kill each other. Yet both of the creatures which resembled Odo seemed to be mates. So it was possible that like mutants stayed with other like mutants, and when they encountered anyone different than themselves, they attacked. People also wondered what would happen if two similar mutants mated in the outlands, would they produce a human child or a mutant offspring? Another question people asked was did similar mutants communicate? And if they did could they possibly form mutant groups? Was it possible that at some point in time these groups of mutants might get together and form mutant tribes or communities? Would these mutant communities eventually form armies and would they eventually organize sufficiently to attack the fortified cities?

These were all questions, which may have seemed off the wall for some but were all questions which needed to be asked and which hopefully would someday be answered long before any potential mutant uprising could occur. These beings were a new form of life, and for those people who formerly felt safe and secure in their fortified cities, it felt very much like a return to the days when the dead began to rise.

CHAPTER 45

Sean Patel sat in his newly redecorated office, the office formerly occupied by the now deceased Dr. Wilbur Hershberger. Sean was still basking in the glory of the fact that he had been named Coroner and Chief Medical Examiner for Schuylkill County. This was an even greater achievement given the fact that he hadn't yet finished medical school. But now he at least knew he would get the opportunity to do so. Given his years of experience on the job and the lack of qualified candidates, he was not only offered the position, but the nominating committee insisted he return part-time to medical school so that he could eventually gain the credentials required for the job. And for his role in bringing down the NCDVC, his tuition would be provided free by the federal government.

In his new capacity, Sean was to be less hands-on and more administrative. As such, he would for the first time in almost a decade, have time to concentrate on his studies. In fact, part of his agreement to return and accept the position was that one-third of each work day be reserved for his medical studies.

Sean was happy to see the NCDVC had been revamped and streamlined into a strictly medical research organization. Viro was free of the shackles of politics. He also liked how now as soon as he received an update from Viro, so did thousands of other people in the medical profession as well as those in the news media. Now everything was instantly available to everyone, and that was exactly how Sean felt things should be.

The email he had just finished reading was certain to get the media buzzing with excitement. Apparently a nine-year-old child in one of the Midwestern states had contracted pneumonia and sadly had passed away one night while sleeping. Her parents found her body the next morning. They were so devastated by the loss of their only daughter that at first they hadn't even noticed the fact that she hadn't come back from the dead. They had looked at each other in amazement upon the realization. This was a miraculous unpresented event for this brave new world.

The couple called the minister at their church claiming a miracle had taken place. Equally overjoyed, but understanding the law, the minister contacted his local medical examiner and coroner. He was quite certain the girl was dead, but because she hadn't turned, he began to wonder if perhaps she might be in a deep coma yet still technically alive. That was something for the proper authorities to decide, not a humble Methodist minister.

Eventually the coroner did pronounce the girl dead and then took a variety of blood samples from the body, as well as some from her parents. Then he promptly sent the samples to Viro for analysis. To their shock and disbelief they discovered there was no trace of the Z43 virus in the girl's body whatsoever. Her parents both tested positive however, as was to be expected. Somehow two infected parents managed to conceive and give birth to a daughter who was virus free, and they had no previous idea of her condition whatsoever.

This discovery immediately set into motion a nationwide call for research samples in an attempt to statistically determine just how many children were free of the virus and what age groups were included. The report suggested that it would be very likely that many if not all of the younger children might be virus free. Unknown to Sean at that time, eventually thousands of children between the ages of infancy to thirteen would be randomly tested with amazing results. Every single child nine years old or younger was virus free. Those over the nine year mark were infected.

This would lead Viro to speculate that the airborne Z43 virus as it originally existed must have only had an active life of a year or so. The plague had occurred more than a decade earlier and they would discover that every ten-year-old tested had been infected. The scientists at Viro concluded that at least as an airborne contamination, the Z43 virus stopped spreading a year after the initial outbreak.

The thing that would be too early to determine was why the virus, present in both parents didn't spread to the children. Considering the babies were a product of both parents and grew inside the infected mother while floating in her amniotic fluid, then breast fed once born, it seemed impossible the virus hadn't spread to the children. But according to every test report, that had been the case.

One report speculated that perhaps it was that inability to spread to the next generation of humans that was causing the virus to mutate. Because of its inability to spread from one body to another through any other means. It was true people died from being bitten by zombies then came back as zombies. And at first scientists believed the virus was spread through the bite from one of the undead, but later it was discovered that the people who died had done so because of normal infection, and the reason the came back as zombies was because they, like everyone else, were already infected. Once this was made public, the rumor of the virus spreading through zombie bites or exposure to their blood all but died out. Now apparently Viro had discovered that the initial virus couldn't be spread through infected living human contact though a person's bodily fluid such as blood, breast milk or saliva.

Sean thought about the ramifications of this incredible discovery. It meant that when the last infected human eventually died and was subsequently terminated as a zombie, the Z43 virus would cease to exist. Generations down the road when these young children cremated their parents and grandparents it would be all over and mankind would be free to start again.

But then Sean wondered about the mutations. The version of the Z43 virus present in the untold numbers of mutants roaming in the outlands was no longer the same Z43 virus the NCDVC and now Viro had been studying for the past decade. It was different, something new. It was then Sean realized humanity really was living on the ridge of change and what effect that change would have on these virus free children was still a great unknown.

Just then his office phone rang. He reached down and spoke into the receiver, "Schuylkill County Medical Examiner's office, Director Sean Patel speaking."

"Wow! That certainly was an impressive mouthful," Jackson Ridge replied.

"Hey, Jackson. What's up?" Sean said ignoring his comment.

"So . . . where's your secretary or maybe even a receptionist? Do they have you answering phones now? I thought you got this big promotion, buddy. It doesn't seem that way to me. Do they have you cleaning the toilets now too?"

"Well . . . I'll have you know . . ."

"I don't think I wanna know . . ." Jackson broke in laughing, " . . . at least not about the toilets."

"Ha ha. Once again, that patented Jackson Ridge sarcastic wit we've all come to know and not necessarily love . . . but tolerate. Anyway, what can I do for you?"

"Your shoulder . . . how's it doing? You healing ok?"

"Oh, yes. It wasn't as much of a big deal as we originally feared. It's healing quite nicely . . . a little stiff from time to time . . . but all in all, not too shabby."

Jackson said, "Wonderful, that's great news, buddy." Then he got to the real reason for his call, "Hey, Sean, did you see the latest email from Viro about the virus and the little kids?"

"Yes. In fact, I just finished reading the message. May I assume you and Andrea will be planning on having Kyla tested?"

"Well . . . eventually, I suppose. From what I can tell there's no real hurry. We put in a call to Dr. Spencer this morning. He, of course, received the same email. His nurses have been fielding tons of calls from concerned parents already. From what they told us, there's no need for us to rush in for testing. They said when we come in for Kyla's annual checkup, the doctor can test her then. From what we both just read and from what the nurse has told me by that time, the test might be unnecessary. He said he seriously doubts they'll find the virus present in any of the younger kids. Although we still don't have all the data, he's fairly confident someone as young as Kyla might be clear of any infection."

"So, I assume this report brings you a bit of relief, my friend."

"Actually, Sean, I have mixed emotions about it. On one hand it's amazing to know that Kyla's generation could all be virus free and hopefully will remain that way, and in theory, once the last infected human is gone, the world should be free of Z43 forever."

Jackson hesitated and Sean prompted him, "I was thinking the same thing. However, do I sense a 'but' here?"

"Yes," Jackson said. "The 'but' is what about those infected with the mutated strain of the virus? I mean there are so many unanswered questions to think about. Will the mutating virus be able to spread to our uninfected kids? Will our own viruses begin to mutate within us and turn us into those horrible monsters? Or will our Z43 virus mutate just enough so it can find a way to spread to our children? So many questions . . . so few answers. I swear, Sean, if I think too much about it, it makes me crazy."

"Well, if it's any consolation, Jackson, you're right to worry, and it's prudent to ask these sorts of questions as well. They're questions we all should be asking. And as a world-renowned investigative journalist, I suspect you should be one of those leading the charge to ask the tough questions and get the right answers."

"So now what, my friend?" Jackson asked.

Sean said, "Now we go back to doing what we've been doing for the past eleven years. We live, we survive and we rebuild."

"And what about the mutations?"

"The mutations will be a problem for another day. Until someone captures or kills a few of these creatures and we have time to gather more data, we'll have to be content to know they exist somewhere out there in the wilds."

Then Jackson said, "And I suppose as long as they stay hidden and remain a non-threatening species for those of us in the fortified cities, investigating them and learning about them could take a very long time."

Sean said, "I believe you're right about that, my friend. I believe you're right."

THE END

ABOUT THE AUTHOR

Thomas M. Malafarina (www.ThomasMMalafarina.com) is an author of horror fiction from Berks County, Pennsylvania. To date he has published four horror novels *Ninety-Nine Souls, Burn Phone, Eye Contact, Fallen Stones*, and *Dead Kill Book 1: The Ridge Of Death* as well as several collections of horror short stories; *Thirteen Nasty Endings, Gallery Of Horror, Malafarina Maleficarum Volume 1, Malafarina Maleficarum Volume 2, Ghost Shadows, Undead Living* and most recently *Malaformed Realities Volume 1*. He has also published a book of often strange single panel cartoons called *Yes I Smelled It Too; Cartoons For The Slightly Off Center*. All of his books have been published through Sunbury Press.

In addition, many of Thomas's works have appeared in dozens of short story anthologies and e-magazines. Some have also been produced and presented for internet podcasts as well. Thomas is best known for the twists and surprises in his stories and his descriptive often gory passages have given him the reputation of being one who paints with words. Thomas is also an artist, musician, singer and songwriter.